Kiwi on a Cloud

A Murder Mystery Novel

Norm Aspen

Library of Congress Control Number:		2007900475
ISBN:	Hardcover	978-1-4257-5445-7
	Softcover	978-1-4257-5443-3

To order additional copies of this book, contact:
Xlibris Corporation
1-888-795-4274
www.Xlibris.com
Orders@Xlibris.com
35480

CONTENTS

For my wife, Natalie, and daughters, Karen Milchus and Sharon White, who are my heroines

ACKNOWLEDGMENTS

I thank the fine people I met in Croatia, Slovenia, and New Zealand for their hospitality and insights into their countries and histories. These are spectacular places with wonderful people that my readers should visit and know.

My gratitude goes to the helpful Xlibris Corporation people: Gian Duterte, Karla Miro, Catherine L. Domingo, Liz Calledo, Monique Garcia, Jonica Genovea, Sherwin Soy, Pierre Pobre, Daisy Paler, Floramie Tuastomban and the rest of the Xlibris Corporation professional team. Any flaws should be credited to the author.

—Norm Aspen

CHAPTER 1

The Meaning of Fear

General Ratac Bymarovitch caught the attention of the man in the wheelchair and laughed at him through the bandages on his face. "I find this most amusing. We old comrades and blood enemies meet again, Sadad. While the whole world searches for us, we sit alone, powerless, in our surgeon's garden smelling half-dead flowers and drinking vodka."

The man in the wheelchair spun around. "That voice! The Butcher! You murdering bastard!"

Bymarovitch shrugged. "I'm working on changing the voice, but I was afraid you wouldn't recognize your old army comrade with my mummylike bandages. You didn't change yourself nearly enough. You should have had Dr. Zbab make you look young and handsome."

Sadad seethed. "You killed four thousand innocent civilians—my people!"

Bymarovitch broke off a frostbit rose, sniffed for a fragrance that had long since dissipated, placed a lit cigarette in the slit between his bandages, and sighed with mock innocence. "Plus or minus a thousand. I only meant to depopulate a few villages—just enough to get you, and others like you, to retaliate. You did, and that secured my power."

"I swore I'd tear your heart out," Sadad shouted, staggering out of his chair.

"Now now, my old friend. I'm not a lad anymore, but I can still break a neck with one stroke of my hand. I do it now and then to impress my staff. They're always more alert and eager to please after they see me kill someone."

Sadad sagged back into his wheelchair.

Bymarovitch's cold staccato laugh made Sadad shudder. Bymarovitch leaned forward. "I miss power, General. I truly miss it. Genius like mine needs a target—a grand target. So I am going to be reborn. My few, but loyal, followers await the phoenix. I'll run for election, and this time . . . . I'll be prime minister, then dictator."

"You fool! The UN has a bounty on both our heads. We must run, hide, and never return to our homelands."

"You have no imagination, Sadad. Cower in a cave if you like. I will return more powerful than ever. I'll save our people from our enemies. If no enemies, I'll create some. I'll use ethnic hatred to enlist allies. Your feeble imagination can't comprehend the extent of my vision and what I can do with power. Our neighboring countries will quake with fear. I will *act* while the UN debates. Then it will be too late to stop me."

Sadad snapped back, "You can change your looks, but your voice will give you away."

"Ah, but what if it was the voice of *my brother*, Klav? You forgot about my brother. He's been in hiding from the KGB for twenty-six years. If Klav were to reappear, there would be no war crimes trials, no UN harassment—only supporters who remember their great defender, the great Bymarovitch name."

"You'd pass yourself off as your brother?"

"Precisely."

"No one would know you," Sadad scoffed. "Who ever heard of Klav Bymarovitch?"

Bymarovitch aimed a stream of cigarette smoke at his adversary. "If I—if Klav—captures one of the most wanted of our enemy's war criminals and promises to share the reward with unpaid solders, Klav becomes famous overnight. I'd be the most popular hero in Croatia again."

Sadad had backed his wheelchair against a wall. Ratac, "the Butcher," was no longer a fellow fugitive. *The Butcher intends to capture me and turn me in*, Sadad realized. He lurched from his wheelchair and grabbed a rake.

Bymarovitch waited until Sadad started to swing the rake at his head before he pulled the trigger. The bullet erupted from the thin blanket covering Bymarovitch's legs and entered Sadad's thigh. The shot dropped Sadad to the flagstone walk, where he gasped in agony.

Bymarovitch rang his silver bell as if the gunshot hadn't drawn the attention of his bodyguards.

One of Dr. Zbab's burly attendants was the first to arrive. Bymarovitch addressed him as soon as he heard the running footsteps. "Boy! My friend is in excruciating pain, and you must keep him from bleeding to death because I'll need him later. But first, bring me another vodka."

* * *

SARAJEVO, CAPITAL OF BOSNIA AND HERZEGOVINA

Frank Ferret didn't know the shadows who were following him through the bomb-scarred streets of Sarajevo, but since they hadn't shot him or arrested him yet, Frank wouldn't worry about it. He could evade them with ease, but that would arouse more suspicions. After all, he hadn't broken any laws—yet. And if the tails were from the CIA, CID, or MI6, it meant the big boys didn't have a clue where Bymarovitch was hiding out. If they were Bymarovitch's boys, that would mean he was close. Closeness had deadly implications for Frank's longevity, but as Frank said, he would cross that creek when he fell into it.

Frank put a cap over his black hair. With his new growth of beard, he could hardly recognize himself, but that didn't slow the men following him. Frank swung a clipboard in a handled paper bag. Unlike most investigative reporters, Frank seldom took notes. The quotes that he invented always sounded better than the real ones. The clipboard wasn't for note taking anyway. Frank walked a straight kilometer from his centrally located hotel on Zmaja Od Bosne Street to the aging hospital near Grbavica. He repeated the name of the street softly because he liked the way it rolled on his tongue. *Wonder what rhymes with it?*

He had visited the psychiatric facility twice before, without anything to show for his efforts. Frank slipped into a medical green jacket, complete with a good-for-anywhere nametag before entering the hospital. The hospital's cleanliness reminded Frank of an interstate rest stop on a bad day, unusual for people with a Germanic cleanliness, but the hospital was understaffed, and patients were lucky to be here instead of abandoned on the street. Frank studied his clipboard as he confidently strode past the security guard and nursing station. *A clipboard is an imposter's best disguise*, Frank thought. *Another visit and they'll probably put me on the payroll.* The nurses were too busy to confront him, even though a male in a psych ward that included a few Muslim women could be considered highly indelicate.

Frank's entrance caused an elderly woman patient near the door to scream loudly. Then she reverted to chanting an unintelligible mantra while rocking severely. Frank tried not to look at her. A radio played loud rap music, not to soothe sick minds but to drown out the moans. Frank took a deep breath of unsmelly air before entering the day ward.

Frank spotted his target and moved quickly. "Hiya, darlin'. I brought ya some Viennese chocolates today."

The emaciated woman sat propped up on a chair with peeling white paint, the color of her pallid skin. Her dark eyes vacant, she looked straight ahead. Her uncombed curly hair reminded Frank of paintings of Medusa, but the serpents weren't in her hair—they were in her tortured brain. The semicatatonic woman wasn't Frank's first choice as a source, but she was reported to know English. *If only she would speak.* She ignored the chocolate until Frank unwrapped it and put it in her hand. She wolfed it down. Food was scarce among the poor in postwar Yugoslavia—or what once was Yugoslavia.

"Great, Sophia!" Frank said. "We're makin' progress. The first time we met, you tried to stab me, you naughty girl. I was wonderin' if you'd help me find the monster who did this to you. I found this photograph of him. The only one there is. It's blurry 'cause it's old and a copy of the UN's copy, but you can make him out."

A red-faced patient in the next chair shouted, "Leave her alone! I know who you are. I heard you on the radio. You say there's a reward for Bymarovitch, but you also praised the reward for our leaders."

"Hey, I don't take sides, lady. A murdering bastard is a murdering bastard. If I can finger anyone of them, I'll have earned a good day's pay."

"You'd bring Bymarovitch in for what? To house and feed him? To make him a martyr? No one will testify against him. They'd be too afraid. He'll be acquitted. No! You must find him and kill him!"

"Lady, revenge isn't what it's cracked up to be, and I don't have time for it. *Killin' him* would make him a martyr. If I was the killin' type, I'd be no better than Bymarovitch, and—"

"No better than Bymarovitch!" the red-faced woman screamed. "Let me open Sophia's gown so you can see what that animal did to her."

"That won't be necessary," Frank said quickly and nervously. He didn't regard himself the squeamish type. On the war beat and crime beat, Frank had seen every kind of bloody atrocity, and it was a matter of professional pride never to show how much it bothered him. Rookie correspondents marveled at his icy demeanor, but Frank didn't look for more grizzly images to haunt his sleep. Those pictures found him all too often enough. "I've heard." He swallowed.

"But if I could help trot that monster in front of a court, in front of the TV lights, maybe the next monster might think twice before he kills, rapes, and mutilates. Maybe, maybe not. Maybe the bastard gets off, but maybe not," Frank growled. "Either way, I need that reward money to give me the freedom to go were I want and to write about the things that matter to me."

The red-faced woman cradled her friend with the explosive hair, as if to protect her from Frank's prying. "So does everyone need money. Do you think you're the first one here, American soldier? Spy!"

Ferret sighed. "Sorry I bothered you ladies. I'm sorry for a lot of things. By the way, I don't play soldier. I don't believe in it. And I don't have much use for the CIA, and they have less use for me. I want to believe in the UN, but sometimes it's hard."

Frank took his Wanted picture back. "Keep some chocolates."

Ferret started toward the door when the woman with the dark hallow eyes and wild hair whispered, "That's not Bymarovitch."

"What?"

"That's not him," Sophia said in a raspy voice that she had long discarded as unneeded in her safe private world. "That's someone else."

"I'll be damned! My picture's a plant? Misinformation to throw everyone off?" Frank explained. *No wonder no one can find him.*

"But if Bymarovitch doesn't look like this, what *does* he look like?"

"Average height. Average weight."

"Eye color?"

"He always wore mirrored glasses, even when he was raping me and my children."

Ferret tried to swallow, but his mouth was dry. *I need a more upbeat line of work—maybe as an embalmer.*

"Any scars or birthmarks?"

"No. Yes! A small round mole on his chest."

"That's good, that's good! What about his hair?"

"I don't know."

"How's that?" *The woman is supposed to say black—jet black. Maybe she doesn't know anything after all. I should know better to interview crazy people and politicians when I need straight answers. But there are so few witnesses still alive.*

"His hair was dyed. I could smell it. And cigarette smoke." The woman began to shake.

"Thank you, darlin'." Frank sighed with resignation. "You've helped a lot. Now I know I don't have anything to work with. I won't be collectin' that reward, but at least I won't be wastin' my time."

"Take the picture," she stammered.

"I have my picture," he reminded. "It's a fake, remember?"

"Take *my* picture," she whispered insistently. "It's in the back of my book."

Frank spotted the pocket-sized book next to Sophia and leafed through it. On the last page, Frank found the drawing, perforated with stab holes. The face was clear except for the eyes, covered with dark glasses. The body couldn't be seen because the woman had drawn it surrounded with flames.

*   *   *

Time to lose my tails, Frank decided. He pulled into a narrow alley, went into a cross alley, and waited. *The tails should split up, one to the alley on the left, and one to the right. Easier to handle one. Probably a rookie PFC who doesn't know what he's doing. I'll have him so embarrassed that he'll go sulking back to his commanding officer.*

When the unwanted follower turned the corner, Frank growled, "Enough is enough! I bet General Bream that he didn't have a grunt who could follow me without getting caught. Now go back and report that the general owes me dinner."

The man lunged at Frank with a broad-bladed knife.

Frank sidestepped. "Oops, mistaken identity. Can we talk this over?"

Another lunge.

Frank met it full force with a garbage can lid. The knife dropped, and when the tail stooped to pick it up, Frank swung the garbage can lid, hitting the attacker in the face. The man dropped to the ground, stunned, but still groping for the knife. Frank smacked him again with the lid and drove the heel of his boot down on the man's fingers.

"Fight's over? Fight's over," Frank reassured himself nervously. Frank exited the alley carefully, lest a lookout was guarding the passageway. *Someone at the hospital must've sounded the alarm.* An adrenalin rush pushed away his fear. *That means I'm warm. This drawing isn't a fake. Back to work!*

* * *

The major's feminine voice growled in the sergeant's earplug, "What did Frank Ferret do next?"

"He knocked out the thug with a garbage can lid."

"Ferret? Frank Ferret, fight? Are we talking about the same man?"

"I'm sure, ma'am, and I'm keeping my distance."

"Just don't lose him. He's on to something. He can smell reward money. Tabloid exclusives. Lecture tours. Weekend book launchings. Another Pulitzer. Ferret's scum."

"But he's good," the corporal observed.

"More than you'll ever know. What did he do next?"

"He went to Bymarovitch's old apartment on the north side. There are new tenants in there, but Ferret passed himself off as an Italian plumber. They let him in."

"Plumber?" The major tingled with excitement, and then fear. "Damn, Ferret's looking for hair in the pipes—the DNA sample we don't have. He knows something we don't, and Bymarovitch will know he knows. The next thug Frank meets will shove an AK-47 up his butt.

"Corporal, stick to Frank Ferret like yesterday's underwear!"

*　　*　　*

SPLIT, CROATIA

Frank found the teacher in a drab socialist-era apartment with a partial view of the Adriatic coast from the open stairway. Frank thought the graffiti-covered building suggested a losing entry in a Lego contest. The elderly man opened his pockmarked door a crack, saw Frank, heard him ask, "Dr. Slovitch?" and slammed the door.

Slipping a fifty-dollar bill under the door, Frank stood back and waited. The door reopened.

"English?" the man asked.

"Yes, please. I'm from the U.S. My name is Frank Ferret."

The man nodded solemnly. He had long thinning hair and a gray caterpillar mustache.

"I've heard of you, Mr. Ferret. I've seen you. I used to read newspapers from the West. It was a privilege accorded to those of us who taught diplomats and spies. I used to have a television. I had to sell it." He stared intently at Frank. "But I wouldn't have recognized you with your beard."

"Cold water and electrical blackouts aren't conducive to shaving."

"Would you like some tea? I must give you something for your money."

"No thank you, sir."

The man motioned Frank to sit down. "I've answered all these questions before."

Slovitch's clothes fit loosely—a man who had lost weight. The man seemed tired, like many others who had lost their spirit. "I have answered these questions before," he repeated. "No one's been willing to pay for them before. It must be the reward."

"That's part of it. Not all of it."

"I know nothing. If I did, I'd have been killed months ago."

"What was the color of his hair?"

"No one asked that before. His hair was black."

"Always?"

Slovitch chuckled softly. "The older students would tease him—say that he looked like a Nazi storm trooper with his yellow hair. He started dying his hair, but he still acted like a storm trooper."

"A blond, huh? That helps." Frank smiled.

"But hair color naturally changes with age," Slovitch cautioned.

Frank held up the blurry wanted poster the UN was using, "Is this Bymarovitch?"

"It could be," Slovitch said with a shrug. "Again, the last time I saw him, he was twenty years old. People change."

Frank unfolded the psychiatric patient's drawing of Bymarovitch. "Maybe this is closer."

Slovitch's mouth twitched. He didn't answer. "Be careful, young man. The closer you get, the shorter your life. I taught Klav and Ratac English. Klav was smart and well liked. But Ratac was *brilliant*. He had the highest intelligence of any student I ever taught, but he used it to humiliate his classmates. Once he stole the exam records and altered higher the scores of a student he particularly disliked. Our director blamed the student and expelled him. But I am certain that Ratac was the only one skillful enough to break into the records room."

"Sounds like a prick in progress," Frank quipped.

Slovitch nodded. "The other students hated him. So did his teachers. Ratac was devious. He delighted in tricking the others. As I said before, the other students picked on him. He soon found that he could fight them—that he could hurt them. But as clever and manipulative as Ratac was, he had no control over his temper. When a classmate boasted that he had sex with a girl who had turned Ratac down, Ratac exploded. Nearly beat the braggart to death. Not to protect the girl's reputation, but his own. No one teased Ratac after that. He could make them fear him."

"Your ex-student has made a career out of fear."

"Young man, give up your search. Until you meet up with Bymarovitch, you don't know the meaning of fear."

*   *   *

Ferret jumped to his feet at the first rap on his hotel door. He wrapped his flashlight in a towel so that it would look like a gun. A heavy-duty flashlight was as good as a blackjack. He positioned himself at the side of the door in case someone intended to shoot through it. "Who's there?" he asked in Croatian.

A business card slipped through the bottom of the door. The card was one of a hundred that Frank had strategically placed with soldiers, government workers, victims, and bartenders. This card was wrapped with the Croatian kuna equivalent of five dollars—the type that Frank had freely distributed with his requests for information.

Ferret opened the door, with his other hand on the flashlight behind his back.

The man on the other side was in his midfifties and didn't look threatening, so Frank opened the door wider.

"Lower your gun, Mr. Ferret. I won't hurt you."

Frank put his finger to his lips, slipped on a nylon raincoat that doubled as a bathrobe, and ushered the old man down the cold, unlit hall. Frank had found and neutralized two listening devices in his room. *But those bugs were too obvious—designed to make me think I'm so clever in disabling bugs that I'd let down my guard.*

Frank stopped at the dead-end of the hallway and waited for the man to speak.

Unlike the teacher, the man had a smart-fitting, Western-style trench coat and a neat appearance to his hair. He stood straight. The war and its aftermath weren't going to beat him. "You speak Italian?" the old man asked.

"Better than Hrvatski," Frank stated, using the local word for the Croatian language.

The old man nodded. "I am the father of Ratac Bymarovitch's wife. Late wife. The monster killed her decades ago. He suspected adultery, but my daughter would do no such thing."

"Do you have any idea where he is? What he looks like?"

The man shook his head. "No. He could be anywhere."

"What does he look like?" Ferret asked again.

"It wouldn't help. He must have changed his appearance by now."

"Plastic surgery?"

"Yes, there is a doctor—Dr. Zbab. The generals used him for face-lifts. I suspect Ratac should be totally different by now."

"Where would I find this plastic surgeon?"

"Zbab has a clinic in Lake Bled, the resort area in Slovenia. But don't expect cooperation. Zbab is a hard-line zealot from Tito's reign. He would turn in other doctors who expressed opinions different from the lunatic government."

Frank suspected a trick. *Better to go along with it.* "Well, I guess I've got nuttin' to go on. Might as well give up."

"Please don't give up, Mr. Ferret. If I was young and wealthy, I would hunt him down, myself."

"And how do *I* do that, sir?"

"I don't know. But I have something that may help. I have a granddaughter. Bymarovitch abandoned his baby after the murder. I had lost my wife the same year, and I was too ill and too depressed at the time to look after the baby. Bymarovitch's brother's wife took the baby."

Frank leaned forward. "Bymarovitch has a brother?" Frank baited.

"Yes, his name is Klav. He is a good man."

"Compared to whom," Frank muttered. "All this is interesting. Where can I find Klav?"

"Not here. Klav stole some gold from the KGB. Gold taken from the Nazis, who had stolen it from those killed in the resistance—a lot of gold. It must have been one of history's largest thefts from thieves. But I think it was the embarrassment that made the KGB so very angry with him. Klav had to flee the country with his wife and my granddaughter. I'm sure the KGB chased after him, and I never heard of them again."

Ferret sagged.

"Until recently," the man added. "A short letter from Klav. He must feel safer, but he put no return address on the envelope."

"I see it has a Christchurch, New Zealand postmark. May I have it?"

"You may look at it, but I cannot give it to you. If you are killed, and they find it on your body, Bymarovitch's men will come after me."

"Okay, eyes only," Frank said, "except I can't read Croatian that well."

The old man translated from memory the letter he had read a hundred times. "Klav says he lives comfortably with his books and says my granddaughter is a fine, lovely young lady of twenty-nine years, who guides adventure tours in New Zealand. I checked. The *only* lady who fits that description guides adventure tours for a Wellington travel company called Kiwi on a Cloud. I would give anything to see her. Unfortunately, the Slovenian travel agent quoted a fare that was far too great for my meager income. But the agent told me something very strange." The vengeful father stopped to look down the hall toward a noise. "The travel agent said I was the *second* person today to ask about New Zealand adventure travel conducted by a young woman."

Ferret clucked, "I'll bet Ratac Bymarovitch received a letter from his long-lost brother the same time you did. There's a good chance he's going to hide out with his brother and claim his daughter."

The man scowled. "Or kill her. Don't try to predict what Bymarovitch will do. No offense, Mr. Ferret, but Ratac will take as much pleasure in outsmarting you—as in killing you."

Ferret patted the man on his shoulders. "Thank you, my friend. I'll bring him back to face trial. And if I can collect the reward, I'll send you the money to see your lovely young granddaughter."

The grandfather smiled. "I was hoping you might."

CHAPTER 2

The Tale of Three Tails

Losing tails in Lake Bled would be difficult for Frank. Most of the streets were wide, with few places to duck into. The breakaway war in Slovenia started in 1991, after an 83 percent vote of the citizens agreed to declare independence from Yugoslavia. After a ten-day war and a few casualties later, Slovenia was on its way as a functioning democracy. Despite its peaceful status, the neighboring wars in Croatia and Bosnia frightened tourists into selecting other destinations. Frank was not surprised that the late autumn streets of once-popular Lake Bled looked like a ghost town—but it provided no crowds for him to merge into.

Frank took his rented Citroën out of Bled at 8:00 a.m. He drove past Hansel and Gretel-type homes with empty flower boxes and settled in the large but empty parking lot of the Vintgar Gorge. He paid his admission and waited until he was sure a tail was following him. Cameras dangled for Frank's neck, and he carried a long tripod. The props conveyed to anyone that Frank was planning a photo shoot, and Frank promised himself to shoot the Gorge when his search ended, and when the spring wildflowers returned.

Frank spotted the tail and moved quickly. Frank's long legs almost ran across the slim catwalk that hugged the Gorge. A swift, narrow river roared nosily through the narrow passage between two sheer overhanging rock faces, opposing sharply chiseled cliffs that almost touched.

Frank crossed sides on a wooden bridge. The Gorge widened. Forested hillsides dwarfed the ravine on both sides. The river hesitated in greenish pools, studded with dark boulders, only to rush, rapidslike to the controlled waterfall that Frank remembered at the end of the Gorge.

Frank had no intention of making the two-hour round-trip in the Gorge. The river meandered, as rivers do, and the catwalk rose and descended, so the line of sight between Frank and the tail was short. As soon as the cliffs gave way to a steep slope of leafless shrubs, Frank used the tripod as a walking stick to scale the slope and crouch behind a boulder.

Frank listened for the tail's footsteps on the pebble-covered path to trail off before sliding back to the path. Cleaning the mud off his tripod, Frank strode back to the entrance. He felt fairly sure that the tail would continue to a few feet from the waterfall before realizing he wasn't following anyone. Frank had almost two hours before the tail would be free to sniff him out.

Four cars shared the parking lot. One was Frank's, and one was most probably the property of the ticket taker. Frank assumed the empty car belonged to the Gorge walker. The occupant of the fourth car was the person of interest and probably unrelated to the first tail. A dark-haired, local man waited in the driver's seat, blowing smoke through a half-open window. He spotted Frank, then looked away. He wasn't calling to the Gorge walker on a cell phone, so they were probably not working together.

Frank retraced his drive to the tiny city, pulling up to the Panorama Restaurant on the edge of Lake Bled. Tail number two followed.

Entering and sitting on the restaurant's large patio, despite a windy chill, Frank ordered a cappuccino, a blueberry brandy, and the local favorite: *kremna rezina*—cream cake. He quipped that he would need a permission note from his cardiologist to eat the napoleonlike, custardy cake, but the waiter didn't smile. As soon as the order was delivered, Frank slipped a bill under his plate. He made a hand-washing motion so Tail Two would notice, and asked the direction of the restroom. He need not have bothered for directions because he had the restaurant scouted. Frank entered the near empty restaurant and asked the sole waiter the direction of the picturesque drying racks—a uniquely local construction. The waiter pointed west, as Frank knew he would.

Frank exited from the restaurant and stooped, as if to tie his shoe, next to Tail Two's car. The swish of tire air was instantaneous.

Frank approached a black Fiat that he had rented. Its driver nodded, and Frank traded him the keys to the Citroën. "Take a couple laps around the lake, then take it back to the rental company, like we discussed," Frank reminded the driver.

The driver nodded and smiled when Frank presented him a hefty tip.

Frank put on a short-billed black cap and aimed his Fiat south. Tail Two would eventually ask the sole restaurant waiter which way the American was headed. The man would answer south, so the follower would head north, assuming that Frank was trying to throw him off.

Frank drove past the last of the luxury hotels then began circling the lake. He passed the lone hotel that had once been Marshall Tito's summer residence until his death ended his rule in 1980. On the opposite side of the lake from where Frank started, he came to a clear view of the chapel perched on a hundred-yard-high, thimble-shaped island in the lake. Frank itched to take a picture, but drove on. He finally turned off toward the clinic. *Tail Two should be starting to change his flattened tire by now.* Frank smirked.

The clinic rose to a tall two-story putty-colored building with an unusual, pointed gothic façade over the front door. A tightly trimmed evergreen hedge almost hid the high metal fence. Espaliered pear trees hugged the walls and bracketed the entrance. The area behind the clinic showed the edge of a rose garden. *Landscapers. No shortage of money here*, Frank surmised.

Frank knocked on the heavy wooden door for the third time. An attractive woman in a nurse's uniform opened the door a crack. She scowled. "Sorry. Dr. Zbab is not taking any new patients."

Frank had rehearsed his lines in Slovenian. "Zdravo," he greeted. "I'm not a patient. I'm a doctor from Canada. I've come to Dr. Zbab for his consultative advice. I'm willing to pay." He held a wad of tolars, with the large bills showing on the outside, reinforcing his willingness.

"Wait," she said in English, closing the door.

She came back, smiled at her handsome visitor, and held the door wide for Frank to enter.

Frank gave the nurse his friendliest grin. "In case I forget to ask Dr. Zbab, who does the doctor collaborate with for dental work?"

The nurse reached into her desk drawer, handed him a business card, and smiled back flirtatiously as she led Frank down a long, hall carpeted with an expensive Turkish runner.

Frank pocketed the dentist's card. *Blackjack!* Frank thought. He was on a roll.

Zbab was a little man with a perpetual scowl that would benefit from cosmetic surgery. His office was lined by floor to ceiling book shelves, carved panels, and fine oil paintings. Large oriental porcelains sat importantly on pedestals. His window overlooked a carefully tended garden where dormant or dead plants fought the wind. *The plushest pad in the Balkans*, Frank thought.

"Sit down, my Canadian colleague. What can I do for you?"

"You already have. You've let me in the door. Talk to me about Ratac Bymarovitch, and what he looks like after availing himself of your services."

"Who are you?" Zbab shouted angrily.

"My name is Frank Ferret. I'm a freelance reporter from the United States. I'll pay well."

Zbab stood and circled nervously. "There is not enough money . . . you bastard! You've sentenced me to death! Just by coming here, I am now a dead man."

"I wasn't followed."

"But *I* am watched."

"Then you better give me some information so I can get him before he gets you."

"Never!" Zbab shouted, but to Frank's mind, he already had confirmed what the Butcher's teacher has suspected. Bymarovitch *did* have an altered appearance. Zbab rose his voice even louder, but it was directed to someone else. A large man in a white jacket rushed into the office. He looked like he had never smiled in years.

Frank picked up a large porcelain vase that he guessed was Ming Dynasty. "I'm going. Don't get rough. I wouldn't want to drop this nice vase."

The grim man seemed to understand, and he followed Frank to the door. Frank tossed the vase to the man, who juggled it, while Frank escaped to his car, grinning.

Frank didn't worry about Dr. Zbab's life because he knew that the doctor was also informing on Frank in hopes of buying favor with Bymarovitch. He thought of following Zbab's pretty nurse. *Maybe she would carry the message to Bymarovitch, but why endanger her too?*

Time to set out for a city with an international airport; but first, the dentist.

*   *   *

Frank was especially careful about not being followed to the dentist, Dr. Berg. Frank might not lose all the tails, but at least some of them. The dentist was a middle-aged woman only slightly more cooperative than Dr. Zbab. She claimed not to speak English, which Frank doubted, so he tried German, pointing to her diploma from a Berlin university.

She scowled, resigned to speaking with the American intruder. "Someone broke into my office and stole my records," Dr. Berg announced dryly in German, a language in which Frank felt comfortable.

"All your records?"

"*Nein*, just the one everyone's asking about."

Frank dismissed her story, but assumed the records were destroyed.

"Do you happen to recall if Bymarovitch had any crowns or extractions?"

"The lady major asked the same thing. I don't remember."

"Thanks anyway." Frank smiled. "Could I give you something for your time?"

"That won't be necessary," Dr. Berg replied. "But thank you for asking. The other questioners gave me orders and threats as if I was a collaborator with that murderer.

"We Slovenians are a humane and compassionate people, Mr. Ferret. So are the Croats. When rumors surfaced about General Bymarovitch's atrocities, one of their ministers of justice launched a secret investigation." She slanted the word *secret* like it was headline news. "The next day the minister's daughter and two grandchildren were missing. Little fingers appeared in a box on the man's doorstep. Then two little ears.

"The minister cancelled his investigation, resigned his post, and committed suicide in hopes that the mutilations would stop."

"Did they," Frank said with a dry throat.

"The hacked-up bodies of the mother and grandchildren were dumped on the minister's grave.

"Bymarovitch blamed the Serbs, gaining more support, but everyone who ever met the general knew better.

"And your American and British investigators waltz in here and expect us to risk our lives and the lives of our loved ones to catch a man who is already on the run."

"Please forgive my countrymen, Dr. Berg," Frank apologized. "They're under a lot of pressure to bring the Butcher in. Unless General Bymarovitch, and General Ante Gotovina are behind bars, the Serbs will never give up Ratko Mladic and Radovan Karadzic. Until *all* the 'alleged' war criminals share a cell, the countries in this part of the world will never completely heal. They'll never try to find mutual interests and become the great nations they could be."

Dr. Berg stared at Frank for a moment before nodding agreement. *Maybe the chase wasn't always about reward and revenge.* "You'd better go."

As Frank reached the door, Dr. Berg called out, "I'm surprised that you didn't ask if his fillings were silver or gold. The others did."

Frank shrugged. "What difference would it make. If I was on the lamb, I'd have a few molars removed and change my fillings from silver to gold, or from gold to silver, or that new stuff."

Dr. Berg smiled and, in perfect English, said, "I only use gold."

*   *   *

SPLIT, CROATIA

Frank strolled along the waterfront marina that once berthed luxury cruise liners before ducking into an alley to change clothes. Frank needed a disguise to lose his tails. It was a construction worker's uniform he had saved for special occasions. Visiting the arm's dealership known as Your Friend Pip was such a special occasion. Pip wasn't the Albanian's real name. He was Pip to the English, and had a half-dozen other names for the other nationalities who bought his weapons.

Pip's showroom looked nearly bare. A rocket launcher dangled from wires against the wall, as if it was a piece of sculpture placed by an interior decorator. Pip's conservative attire reminded Frank of a funeral director. The elderly rotund arms broker loosened his tie for Frank. Pip couldn't think of a worst sales prospect, but Frank was always good for laugh. "You were followed?" Pip asked.

"No," Frank stated firmly. "Well, yes. But when I want to lose 'em, I lose 'em. Frank wasn't sure that he hadn't been followed, but he didn't fret about endangering Pip's life. Pip never rationalized that his sale of arms saved lives, and that was the only honest thing about Pip that Frank could appreciate.

"Ferret, you besmirch my profession, and yet now, I find you as a customer."

"I haven't hurt your business, have I?" Frank replied with a shrug of innocence.

"Not really. Mine is the business of war. War is immune to reasoned logic, such as yours. I am not a bad person, Ferret. I don't take sides, and I buy from everyone: Czechs, Russians, Chinese, and of course, your people. And I'll tell you a secret. I sell to the underdogs at a discount."

"To make the wars last longer," Frank muttered.

Pip grinned.

"The war here's over, Pip. Maybe you should retire?"

"The war's over?" Pip exclaimed with mock incredulousness. "Only temporarily, my friend. This Kosovo cease-fire will never hold. The KLA Albanians won't go away quietly, so Kosovo is only taking a breather. And your General Short's threat to bomb Belgrade won't guarantee compliance.

"It's all in leadership. A demigod here and an ethnic hate monger there, and who knows? Croatia, Bosnia, and my beloved customers in Serbia could start the fun all over again."

Pip opened a large book. "This is my fall catalog. Pictures in color. I'm thinking of hiring sexy models and setting up a Web site."

"Sexy models could change your business," Frank quipped. "Make love, not war."

"What can I sell my favorite pacifist?" Pip asked. "Bulletproof vests, perhaps? Russian makes. I have your size in three colors."

"I'll put that on my Christmas wish list. What I need now is something to bring an unwilling person from here to there."

"Handcuffs?" Pip sounded disappointed.

"I was thinking drugs," Frank said hopefully.

"Aha! I have just the thing for you. A bargain at this time of the year. You could call it my fall down special." Pip laughed. "It's named *Long Sleep* in Korean. No lasting effects, but a sure cure for insomnia." Pip pulled a can of hairspray from a desk drawer. "Just don't get any spray on yourself, and it works fine."

"You're sure there's no adverse side effects?"

Pip smiled and squinted. "Only one. Your target remembers who sprayed him."

Pip cocked his round head as Frank examined the hair spray wrapper. "Ferret, is it true that you're looking for the Butcher?"

"Know where he is?"

"If I did, I wouldn't tell you. I like you too much. You're aware that the Butcher likes to torture his victims before he kills them." Pip snorted as he waddled out of his leather chair. "You'll need this." Pip produced a small gun from one of many drawers.

Frank sniffed, "I don't do guns. If I did, I might kill someone, and I don't kill."

Pip handed the Glock to Frank. "On the house, my friend. Don't expect to kill the Butcher with it, but if you find the Butcher . . . . and he finds out you found him, you can use the gun to kill yourself. Avoid much pain and suffering." The gift of a Glock pistol was an expensive suicide pill, but one that would protect Pip from any torturous interrogation the Butcher might perform on Frank. Confessions under torture could implicate Pip. Such a confession would be believed despite the arms dealer swearing he gave no assistance to Frank's quest.

"You're gonna tell him I was here, aren't ya?"

Pip shrugged. "I don't turn in my friends for money. It's just that I enjoy living. But I like you, Ferret, so I'll give you an hour's head start."

*　　*　　*

Rod Brickle held his glass toward the old wooden beams of the Dubrovnik pub. "Pencils, shutter-buggers, and you camera-ready smiles with the unlimited expense accounts—you know who you are—I propose a toast. To the late Frank, 'the Spider,' Ferret!"

"Amen!" the party of journalists chorused.

"Spider?" a rookie reporter asked.

Rod explained, "Black hair, long legs, always moving—a nickname from his New Orleans days.

"Oh Frank, wherever you are, we'll miss your sending us east when the story is west."

Rod burped. "Stop laughing! This is a serious wake."

"Frank we'll miss your fake phone calls just before the waiter brings the check. We'll miss your loony alliterations and infamous impersonations. We'll miss your showing us how unfaithful our girlfriends and mistresses are—a true humanitarian gesture on your part."

Rod put his hand on a television cameraman's shoulder. "Your wife will really miss the way he impersonated you one night." The group roared at the cameraman's expense.

A woman rose to challenge Brickle. With her glowing blonde hair and near perfect features, Ingrid "Ing" Carlsen stood like a bright blossom in a field of drab weeds. Ing growled, "I don't find this amusing."

A female reporter from Germany, who stuck by Ing because that was where the men gathered, said, "Frank's put another bull's-eye on his chest. You heard about the reward for the Butcher?"

"Two million? Yes."

"Ferret's working night and day to find him. He's running from country to country to collect that reward."

"If anyone can do it, Frank can," Ingrid remarked. "He has contacts in board rooms and brothels and everywhere in between."

"You're missing the point, Ing. Or you don't want to admit it. What happens when Frank finds the Butcher? He's like a frisky puppy following a viper into his hole. The puppy's going to get bit. Bit bad!"

Ingrid stiffened at the truth of her friend's logic. "Why doesn't he ask for help? Why isn't he here?"

Ingrid's friend shrugged. "Frank doesn't want to share the bounty. But to his credit, I think he knows that anyone around him could be killed."

*   *   *

LJUBLJANA, SLOVENIA

Dumb, dumb, dumb! I know better than to be sandwiched on an unlit bridge after dark, Frank scolded himself, knowing his luck had finally run out. *Helluva a way to die.*

The evening had started out calmly enough. He found a pleasant hotel after his long drive along the coast from Split. Ljubljana had an international airport that was closer to Split than Zagreb's in Croatia. He found a familiar restaurant in the Old Town, where he indulged a late supper of trout floating in tasty garlic oil. Frank felt the need to talk to someone. Some called him a loner, but that wasn't how Frank viewed himself. He needed other people to reflect back and amplify his energy. Yet this project was too dangerous to be shared.

Frank wandered into three pubs before settling on one near the university part of Old Town. He overheard political science graduate students arguing politics and bought his way to their table with the first of ten pitchers of frothy Laško Pivo, the local beer.

"Help me with my Slovenian," he asked of the students, all of whom spoke better English than Frank. The language lesson quickly switched to politics and political jokes. Frank liked political jokes. They identified hot button perceptions and misperceptions better than focus groups.

"Our small farms can't compete," a thin student complained.

"We have mercury and coal," another offered.

Frank winced. "The Greens could put both of those out of business. Tourism is your best bet if the fighting doesn't return."

"We're at peace!" the group collectively scoffed the notion of war.

"But the rest of the world still thinks of one Yugoslavia. The cease-fire in Croatia ceases every now and then. Trouble in Kosovo seems like trouble here," Frank explained. "And you're not out of the forest yet, 'cause any crazy military-type on any side could stir up enough angry and fearful folks to start stuff happening all over again. What if the Butcher Bymarovitch showed up, do you think the Serbs would sit still? And if they ever retrieved Croatia, you'd be next, while the UN was debating what to do about it."

The group stared at their beers. They knew Frank was right.

A student coughed. "Guri thinks we should form a federation with Croatia." The group laughed derisively. "Not in our lifetimes."

"Guri is half Croatian," a pretty young lady explained.

Frank singled out the most articulate and eldest of the students, a man already interning for government service. "Slovenia can't go it alone," Frank observed. "If you need a thesis topic, you could create your country's application to the EU."

The student, named Gregory, gave Frank a mocking laugh. A European Union application was way beyond his background.

Frank persisted, writing on the back of his business card. "Here's some folks to call that know how it's done, Greg. You can mention my name."

Gregory politely pocketed Frank's card, but wouldn't realize for a couple of weeks the lofty doors that Frank had just opened for him.

Safety in numbers, Frank thought. "Time to call it a night. I'm a little tired and a little drunk so could some of you help me find my hotel?" Frank *was* tired, but he prided himself that his passion for good food and drink never dulled his passion to stay alert. Confidences and state secrets revealed during a night flowing with spirits needed to be accurately quoted, or intentionally misquoted, the following morning.

The two women in the group bracketed Frank's arm and pulled him down the deserted street. Both women looked prettier to Frank than they did at the beginning of the night. *Maybe I am drunk*, he thought. They came to the Dragon Bridge, aptly named for the large, gargoyle-like dragons on each of the four corners of the bridge.

The prettiest of the two women said, "Legend has it that the dragons wag their tails if a virgin walks across the bridge. Their tails haven't moved yet."

Frank peered at a large dragon statue. "I think I saw his tail twitch."

"Then it must be you." The young woman giggled.

The male students excused themselves, but the women remained.

"Suppose we come up to your room and help you with your language lesson?" the quieter woman suggested.

Frank hesitated. The women looked even prettier under the lights from the bridge. Franks groaned to himself: *Too horny. But too eager. Too late. Too young. Oh my god, two!*

"Sorry darlins, I have to split back to Split for an early meeting tomorrow. Let me have your numbers, and we'll make a full scholarly night of it someday soon.

The quiet one wrote her number on a torn paper scrap, and Frank politely inserted it in his wallet as if caring for the Dead Sea Scrolls.

"We're roommates," she announced. She stood on her toes to kiss Frank, but with the tentative restraint of someone who had been rejected.

"Call you both," Frank lied. "Promise."

The prettier one snorted and stalked away. The quiet one followed. Frank was alone.

He strode past the confusing three-way bridge of which surrealistic painter Escher would have been proud, and past the narrow wooden bridge toward the Cobbler's Bridge. The Cobbler's Bridge was the widest of the bridges, and it led directly toward Frank's hotel. The pedestrian bridge had hosted craft stalls earlier in the day, but they had picked up without a scrap to hint of their bustling presence. Frank liked the width of the bridge. He fancied himself a broken field runner if chased. He stepped too far onto the bridge before noticing that the lights were out.

Dumb, dumb. A dumb way to die. Frank glanced at the icy water below. *If I start to jump, they'll shoot.* Frank held his arms out straight—crosslike. Even if Frank had had his new gun and gas spray on him, there were too many of them. "Hi guys! Anyone speak English? I was expectin' you'd drop by. We need to chat."

A large man moved quickly behind him. He raised his arm to hit Frank on the head with an object that Frank could only guess to be a pipe or a gun barrel. Frank put one hand on the waist-high rail. *I'll leapfrog the rail. The closer they come, the less likely they can shoot me without hitting each other. The darkness would help my escape, down in the water.*

A man in a long coat raised his hand, and the attacker lowered his weapon and stepped back.

"You think that your loquaciousness will delay your death, Mr. Ferret?"

"Let me tell you what I'm thinkin', pal. Either you're Bymarovitch, or you're not. Since you're older than Bymarovitch, you're not the Butcher. So you're either a friend of his . . . or you're not. If you're his friend, I'd be dead already, so I'm bettin' you're not. So assumin' you're *not* his buddy, then you're after his scent, and since I've got him treed, your sniffer's outta joint."

"Go on. I'll give you twenty seconds to expound your theories before I kill you."

Frank's mouth turned dry. "If you knew where Bymarovitch was, you wouldn't have the time to bother with me. So you *don't* know where he is, and *I do*." Frank closed his eyes. He knew jumping off the bridge had little chance of success, and he braced for the slam of a bullet.

"You're bluffing, Mr. Ferret. Simply stalling for seconds."

"Look in my jacket, I have airline tickets to the Butcher's new hometown. I tell ya, I'm hot on his hind end."

"You say that like I'm supposed to save your life." The man in the long coat laughed. He removed a pistol from his pocket and attached the silencer.

"Right as raindrops, you're gonna be glad you saved my life. Bymarovitch isn't your playmate, and you don't have a cussin' clue as to where he's split. *I* do. You need me."

"Really?" the man mocked.

"Damn betcha, if you chase after him, you'll be caught for sure. Your accent will give ya away. The police will ask, 'Were there any Yugos round here when Bymarovitch took a hit?' They'll look straight at you. Now me—I just sorta blend in. There's a reward of two million U.S. dollars when I bring the son of a bitch in. I'll split it with you if you'd be so kind as to cooperate."

"Mr. Ferret, you are so wrong that it is pitiable. Bymarovitch is *not* my enemy. In fact he is, or once was, my friend. I have no malice toward him. A million dollars to betray an old colleague—wouldn't be right. There are ethics involved. You see, Mr. Ferret, it's his brother, Klav, I want. Bymarovitch's brother stole what was mine to care for, and nearly destroyed my career, decades ago. When Bymarovitch reunites with his brother, I want to be there. I want to take back what was mine—about twelve million dollars in gold coins. I want to see the look on his face when I kill him. He'll look much like you. Your stalking of Bymarovitch has made it impossible for us to keep track of him. With your death, he will relax."

"But *I* know where he is."

"And so do I—*now*. I'll just take the tickets off your dead body."

Frank grabbed an envelope from the outside pocket of his thin leather jacket, and held it over the side of the bridge. "This isn't fun anymore. Why don't you scoot over to the other side of the bridge? And I'll leave these tickets on the curb for you. I usually expect half the reward, but I'll be happy with whatever you give me."

"Your argument has merit," the man in the shadows said with a hint of nervousness in his voice. "But we'll reverse the order. I'll take the tickets now."

"Suit yourself," Frank said, still holding the envelope over the river, thirty feet below. Frank was pretty sure he could make the dive. He had written many an article on his dangerous hobby of underwater cave exploration. *But is the river deep enough? What good to make the dive, only to break my neck?*

The man walked slowly toward Frank. From his gait, Frank judged he wasn't young. Frank waited until the man was within reach of the envelope before he tossed it high into the air. The wind blew it back toward the bridge. As the man lunged for the falling letter, Frank grabbed him by his belt, pulled and pushed him against the bridge rail. Both men rolled over the rail and hurtled to the water below. Frank couldn't completely straighten out, and he hit the water with a painful smack. Luckily, the man with the gun absorbed most of the impact, a hit that should have knocked him unconscious but didn't. Frank kept one hand on the man's coat belt, and pulled him deep under the water until Frank couldn't hold him anymore. *The snake's heavy coat will sub for cement overshoes.* Frank's own leather jacket and sturdy walking shoes made swimming difficult. *To the surface! The others won't shoot 'cause they'll be afraid of hitting their leader.*

Frank surfaced under the bridge. He was thankful the lights were out. He looked and listened for the man he'd pulled off the bridge. *No ripples. One less water moccasin, but a bridge full of gators—probably fightin' to read my envelope of hotel receipts.*

The whooping sound of a police car reverberated from the bridge. *Someone's lookin' out for me.* Frank swam along the shore. *Damn it's freezing! Be my luck to dodge another bullet, only to die of a chest cold. Hope it's warmer in New Zealand.*

CHAPTER 3

Grave Reservations

Chip Schumaker bicycled straight from his high school over newly fallen leaves to the post office. The post office was devoid of customers, so Chip dropped the package, wrapped in brown butcher paper, on the postal clerk's counter and walked away. He had to rush home and finish some Internet chess games before the World Series started.

"Don't you want to know how much postage?" the clerk asked.

"I've gotta 'nough stamps," Chip said. "Looked it up."

"Insurance?" the clerk pressed.

"Chip chuckled. "How do ya insure software worth a zillion dollars?"

* * *

32

BOSTON RED SOX CLUBHOUSE, A WEEK LATER

Clutch Cooper jokingly twisted the champagne from his soaked baseball cap. The surrounding reporters probed him with their microphones. "Besides going to Disney World, what's on your schedule?" asked the closest reporter.

Clutch opened a boyish, wide white-toothed grin. "Well now, if you promise not to tell anyone—"

The reporters snickered. Clutch's down-home Texas humor resonated well with New England's—indeed, with the nation's, readers, and viewers.

"I'm figurin' on gettin' married."

"Who's the lucky person?" asked a woman reporter, hiding her disappointment, as the media pack buzzed.

"I'd better not say. She hasn't said yes, yet. But I can tell you this. She's as beautiful as a grand slam in the bottom of the ninth—a wonderful girl. And right now, she's on the other side of the world.

"So, hon, if this reaches you, I'm comin' for ya."

* * *

SAN JOSE, CALIFORNIA

Willie Dern put away his stopwatch, popped the Breakneck Download disk from his computer, and scowled at the television screen, almost lost among a gleaming hedge of oversized computer screens. He rose and paced angrily around an oval teakwood desk, conspicuous for its lack of paper and the dominating, original Rodin sculpture of a Roman soldier topped with Willie's baseball cap. Willie settled back in his leather chair in front of the television. He finished his twenty seconds of thinking. Now he was prepared to act.

Virginia Slater peaked over his shoulder and slid her smooth cheek across his. Virginia's business uniform of a well-filled, white silk blouse and a trim, tailored blue knit suit contrasted with Willie's intentionally rumpled look. If it weren't for Virginia, headwaiters who didn't recognize Willie from the financial magazine covers would have "no tables."

Virginia peered at the celebrating ballplayers and looked at her watch. Working to 9:00 p.m. wasn't unusual, but staying late to watch a baseball game puzzled Virginia. Tonight would be another time she wouldn't see her son before bedtime. "I thought you didn't like baseball," she growled sexily.

"It's this pompous athlete that's my concern."

Virginia mocking patted her chest. "Clutch Cooper? Be still my heart! He's too cute for words—dimples and all. Do you want him to endorse our products?"

"Hardly," Willie answered curtly. "My products are user-friendly, not *idiot*-friendly."

He removed his glasses and rubbed his forehead. "Ginnie, I advised you at the start of our relationship that I had a significant interest in a New Zealand girl."

Virginia forced a smile. "The quirky tour guide you met on your one and only vacation?"

"Yes. I don't know where you got *quirky*. She's really quite remarkable. I'm a different man around her. She soaks up everything I say—like a flower needing to be watered with intellectual stimulation. Yet she's not reticent to take issue with me. When I'm with her, I'm more relaxed. I'm friendlier. I feel prouder of my successes without even discussing them. She does that for me. She has no idea of how much money I'm worth or how much influence I wield. She likes me for myself."

Virginia bit hard then said, "*I* like you for yourself."

Willie kissed her on the cheek. "You've been exceptional, Ginnie. You need a vacation. You can fly with me to New Zealand and handle business while I secure this acquisition."

"You're going to *marry* her?" Virginia blurted incredulously.

"I'm afraid I must. If I don't, the fool baseball player will."

Virginia fought to keep her voice from breaking. "Are you sure she'll want you, after ignoring her for five months?"

"As long as I arrive at her bus stop five minutes before that dolt ballplayer."

Willie clicked off the television. "At this busy time of the year, I don't need this distraction," he chuckled at his legendary work ethic. "But somehow I allowed myself to fall in love," he grinned. "So I must go, but not any sooner than I need to. I'll take the Breakneck disk with me. I have to figure out how this unorthodox primate of a programmer makes it work so fast.

"And—oh, have some researchers track Cooper's travel plans."

"By *researchers* you mean a detective agency," Virginia interpreted. "They would have to tap his cell phone! That's illegal!"

Willie gave Virginia a disapproving look. "How they do it is *their* business. When Cooper books his flight, put us on the same plane. I want to see the jock's face when he finds out he's too late. And buy me the largest, most vulgarly ostentatious engagement ring you can find."

Virginia turned her back to Willie on the pretense of punching up the "researcher's" phone number on one of six open computer screens. Willie would never be allowed to see her tears. "If she's as special as you say, there may be more than just one sexy ballplayer to worry about."

*   *   *

CHERRY CREEK, COLORADO

Gil Rocklin looked around his converted garage office for anything he might have forgotten. The sides of his garage, stacked to the ceiling with boxes of brightly colored merchandise, represented Gil's total net worth and then some. A tripod leaned against the wall, absent its video camera. Against the back wall, a slanted drawing table competed for space with two desks and a table full of office equipment. Over Gil's desk, a child's bright painting filled a slightly chipped, silver frame.

A large German shepherd put his paws on Gil's chest and whimpered. Gil stroked the dog's head. "Eiffel knows that something's about to happen. Sorry, Eiffel, you can't come along."

Gil turned to Margarita, his ever-smiling, round-faced assistant. "I feel terrible leaving before the big order goes out."

Margarita gave him a playful shove. "Go! Have a good time. I'll take care of everything. As soon as the PO confirmation comes in, I'll start shipping. When you return from Down Under, you'll be on the cover of *INC*. I can see it now. *Gil Rocklin, small businessman of the year* . . . working out of his garage."

"I'll settle for paying off my debts and making payroll on time," Gil grinned.

Margarita continued to shove Gil out the door.

"Could you water my plants?" Gil asked. "Careful not to water too much."

"Of course. I'll feed the hound, water the weeds, and pay the bills. I don't have to tell *you* to be careful. So go! Go! Amy's been cartwheeling around the van for fifteen minutes. And while you're in Kiwi land, try to meet some nice ladies for God's sake."

"When the nice ladies learn about me, they run terrified to the nearest exit."

"Then *don't tell them*. I'm serious. Don't tell them. My husband was afraid to have me work for you. But I'm glad I did. Neighbors were scared to send their kids here to play with Amy. But now she's the social magnet for every kid in the subdivision. Why? Because you spend all your time watching her. They know their kids are safe with the notorious Gil Rocklin. So listen to Aunt Margarita. Find yourself a mother for that little girl."

Gil chuckled. "Knowing Amy, she'll find one for me."

*　　*　　*

Kiwi on a Cloud

LOS ANGELES, CALIFORNIA

Dr. Eve King slammed the tour itinerary on the brass-legged, glass coffee table and gave her husband a disgusted frown. Their library was the warmest room in the large home. Other rooms, with their off-white and antique furniture, were for display and not for sitting, according to George King. The library was also a place where their son couldn't hear them arguing.

"George, I know you think it's a bad idea taking Martin out of school, but it's the only time I can get away from the hospital."

From his leather chair, George grumbled, "Martin won't fail. He's way ahead of his classmates. And he can bring his assignments and his clarinet. But it seems a crime to pay all that money for a fancy private school, and then flush away three weeks for a trip to New Zealand, of all places."

Eve stiffened. "To a policeman, everything's a crime. I pay for the tuition. I'm not complaining."

"Yeah, you pay for damned near everything, but I still think that Martin could wait till summer."

"It's almost summer in New Zealand," Eve snapped then she softened. "Martin could have waited. But can *we?*"

George made a nondescript gesture with his powerful arms.

Eve put her hand on his. "You won't go to counseling with me. Maybe a vacation will help. No country club activities that you seem to hate. No more of those dreadful crime stories and that disgusting street language that you come home with."

George stood up to hug Eve. "It's worth a try. Damn it, Eve, I love you so much. Something's gotta happen."

She kissed his ear. "This trip is gonna be great. I ordered a suite wherever I could. Second honeymoon."

"We couldn't afford a first honeymoon," George reminded. "But we were *happy*."

Eve nodded. "We'll be happy in New Zealand. It's a beautiful country. Did you know our tour guide was voted *Guide of the Year*? She's fluent in five languages."

"Right," George mocked. "I can only understand one language at a time, and if this New Zealander is anything like some Aussies I know, I'm not sure I can understand that."

"Any Aussies you would know are lowlifes. Our guide's probably very well-trained, very well-organized in the classic English tradition."

George smirked. "Probably a prissy, old bag with a tardy bell, a clipboard, and a mouthful of statistics on her country's agricultural tonnage. Give me someone who can show us some fun."

CHAPTER 4

The Kiwi on a Cloud

Debbie McWard tiptoed into her dark hotel room. The green glow of an open laptop computer's screensaver lit the room like a night light.

Debbie's roommate, Elizabeth Stevens, opened one reluctant eye, heavy with unwashed mascara. "Why so late, eh?" Elizabeth asked in her heavy North Island, New Zealand accent.

"The band's singer didn't show, so I filled-in. We had a splendid time!" Debbie bubbled.

"Ugh, multiple talents!" Elizabeth groused. "I wish I had just *one*."

Elizabeth rolled into an upright position, stretched her sturdy arms, and scratched her maroon streaked hair. "Bludge up any guys worth taking home for a shag?"

Debbie grinned. "None even worth window-shopping, actually. Maybe our next tour group will have better pickings."

"Hope so," Elizabeth snorted then pointed to the desk. "You have good news and bad news."

"Only *good* news," Debbie pleaded, as she pulled her dress over her tall, slender body.

"The good news is a letter from the yummy Yank, Clutch Cooper."

Debbie found the letter, picked it up gingerly, and bounced it in the palm of her hand. "Hotel stationary. That's the only way I could ever tell where he was. But if Clutch is the good news, I'd hate to hear the bad."

"Aren't you going to open it?"

Debbie flicked the letter into the wastebasket like someone trying to remove sticky tape from her fingers.

"Why?" Elizabeth exclaimed.

"Because I'm tired of crying myself to sleep," she said, forcing a smile.

"I thought you lightened your luggage of him months ago," Elizabeth commented.

"I did. What's the bad news?"

"You have an e-mail on your computer—which you refuse to learn how to use—from your brainy boyfriend, Mis-ter Wil-lie Dern."

Debbie sighed. "Did you read it?"

"No, 'cause I'm only a lowly bus driver, not expected to carry a dictionary round to translate the tour director's 'lectronic love letters."

Debbie bent over the computer screen. "How do you delete this, again?"

"Hit the delete icon. But geez, Debbie! Just 'cause Willie's too stuffy for me, doesn't make him a shabby catch. He's downright human the way he dotes on you. He sent you this nice laptop. You should at least read what he has to say."

"If he hasn't proposed by now, I don't want him. I don't want anything to do with these Yanks. From now on, Debbie McWard is going to be the most careful, conventional, and celibate gal on the island. No more taking chances."

*　　*　　*

WELLINGTON, NEW ZEALAND

Debbie peered out the open door of the biplane. "We're right on time—only two hours late," she shouted with a grin. She blew a kiss at the pilot and threw her body into the cloudless sky.

She arched her back and reveled in the press of the air and the landscape below as she hurtled to the ground. The hill directly below her was entirely golden with wild bushes. *Don't want to land on the prickly broom bushes.* Debbie waited until the last moment to deploy her hot pink parachute. She steered herself toward the large open field next to a cinder block motel that held their regional office and where her trampers would be waiting for their tour guide in a near empty parking lot. *Almost a full bus*, she noted, counting the tiny ground figures watching her descend.

From an inconspicuous spot in the back of the crowd, Frank Ferret peered at Debbie through miniature military binoculars. *She has a smile that lights up a meadow from a hundred yards up. Sun-bleached blonde hair. Black shorts and long tanned legs. Yummy! Under different circumstances . . . . Damn, I need a more gentile line of work, like public executioner.*

Debbie landed on the grassy part of the field in a fast walk—the kind of walk that you dare not stop too quickly.

She reeled in the chute while her tourists half circled around her. She did a quick study of the tour group while she put on a baseball cap to shield her porcelain complexion from the ozone-hole sunlight. *Half a dozen British. An Ozzie. An Italian couple. Nine Americans. A French couple? An African—East African? Ah, one Chinese couple!*

"Hello, g'day. Ciao, bon jour, ni-how, and kia ora—that last greeting is Maori, the original native Kiwis. Welcome to *Aotearoa*, trampers," she shouted. *Aotearoa* is Maori for *Land of the Cloud*—hence, Kiwi on a Cloud. Of course, a kiwi is a flightless bird.

"And tramping—is what we Kiwis call hiking and trekking and backpacking. Please forgive me for being late, but the last group lifted off from Auckland to Oz—that's Australia—three hours late, and I had to wave 'em a last g'day."

As Debbie continued her friendly welcome, Gil noted how her entire body energized when she talked. *Probably a dancer like Jean,* Gil thought of his late wife.

Debbie started shaking hands. "As soon as I pick up the travel vouchers, we'll board the bus—in about fifteen minutes. If you haven't signed in yet, see my boss, Mr. Carp Simpson, and then bring your bags to Liz, our driver, to load up." Debbie looked into the sky. "Let's hope *my* luggage doesn't land on the roof," she chuckled, as the duffel bag slowly drifted to the ground.

Carp Simpson briskly trotted toward her. Carp had a leathery face and beer belly that made him look older than he was. He held an open briefcase stuffed with papers. "Can't leave yet," Carp growled. "Three more passengers are on their way. They decided to share a rent-a-car instead of taking our van from the airport. Got lost."

Debbie laughed—a musical laugh. "Brilliant! An adventure travel trip whose trampers are lost before they even got started."

"We have to talk," Carp said. "The owner had doubts about your combining family-oriented sightseeing with adventure travel, but with this full boat at full fares, he's ecstatic. He thinks you're a genius, and he wants to take you off Australia, and give you the Fiji run."

"Fiji! I'd like that. Would sure beat leading those camel caravans into the Outback."

Carp wrinkled his nose, remembering his first and last camel ride. "You have another feather in the hat, Deb. You know how hard it is to crack the

Japanese tourist market? They always want to use their own tour companies and stay in Japanese-owned hotels."

"They feel more comfortable. Wouldn't you?"

"Well, we have two boat loads from Osaka on the condition that the beautiful young lady who sings happy songs and speaks fluent Japanese leads the tour. You're on a roll, Deb. I might have to give you a raise."

"Take your time thinking about it." Debbie smiled.

"Now the flip side. Did you see that little girl over there?"

"I see who you mean," Debbie squinted into the sun, spying the youngster with a straw-colored ponytail and wide smile, tiptoeing across the top of a short brick wall. "She's adorable."

"She's *seven*. None of us thought that family adventure meant *seven*. And there's a black lad who's only nine. His mother's a doctor. You'd think these smart parents would know better."

"It should work," Debbie clucked. "These trips are more scary than dangerous. As long as the kids don't panic, they'll be fine. We're more likely to have trouble with their parents."

"Maybe, but what if something happens to one of those kids. It would be your arse and mine too. We could lose our insurance and find ourselves as fourth-class shovelers on a sheep ranch."

"I've been there, but thanks for thinking about the safety of the little ones."

"What I'm telling you . . . is to stay close to that little girl."

"E-kay. No problem," Debbie consented.

Carp wasn't done. "You have a certified complainer: Mrs. Venus Klaus, a real wowser, who doesn't believe in children on a tour and doesn't think much of our bus."

"Only one complainer every other tour is a good average," Debbie noted. "You have to realize that complainers are enjoying themselves when they complain."

Carp snorted. His effervescent tour guide saw earthquakes as an opportunity to shimmy.

"Anything else?" Debbie asked, knowing that Carp always held the worst for last.

"Yeah, two of the three missing tourists are your old alumni. They refused the bus we had 'em scheduled on and insisted they had to travel with you. In fact, there were several requests for you."

Debbie brightened. "When you're good, you're good!"

Crap wondered whether to tell Debbie the names of the missing travelers. *She'll find out soon enough.*

Gil Rocklin folded up the chute from Debbie's duffel bag. He picked up Debbie's padded guitar case and duffel before heading toward the bus. *First, I'll have to retrieve Amy. The little imp is wandering again.*

Amy stood talking in her usual animated way to the attractive tour director, who was laughing with the little girl. They had traded baseball caps. Debbie had the Denver Broncos cap, and Amy swam under a black cap with an embroidered kiwi bird leaving embroidered gold tracks on the bill. Amy had gotten the best of the trade. As Gil approached, Amy's expression-filled face turned sheepish.

"Hi, I'm Gil Rocklin."

"Debbie McWard," she said with an outstretched hand. She pointed to the neat folds of the chute. "You know what you're doing."

"Yes—I stay on the ground," he grinned.

Gil dropped the luggage and chute, and he picked up his daughter, swinging her in a gentle arc and setting her down. "I see you've met my Amy."

He lowered his tall frame to Amy's level. "Have you been up to mischief again?"

Amy giggled.

Debbie laughed—a soft warm laugh. "Amy's quite informative. I know that Daddy's a widower who draws children's stories from his home in Cherry Creek, Colorado; gives Amy daily piano lessons; and cooks delicious crepes."

Amy beamed. Her bell-like voice had the seriousness of a trial lawyer. "Isn't Debbie pretty? She's not married and doesn't have a boy friend."

"Amy," Gil said sternly, "remember Ms. Fish?"

Amy mugged a hound-dog look and looked to Debbie for pity. "I had to a-pol-o-gize to Ms. Fish."

"Lot of good it did," Gil chuckled.

Gil handed Amy a New Zealand five-dollar bill with an engraving of Sir Edmund Hillary on it. "Amy, why don't you introduce yourself to that young man over there? Treat him to a lemonade if his folks say it's okay."

Debbie smiled as she watched Amy skip away. "Pretty, personable, and precocious—what a combination." Debbie cocked her head. "Ms. Fish?"

Gil snickered. "Ms. Fish is Amy's second-grade teacher. Now how would *you* like to get this call from school? 'Mr. Rocklin, your daughter insists on inviting me to your home for dinner. She's trying to fix us up.' Now Ms. Fish is pert, patient, and very pleasant, and I'd date her in a minute, except Ms. Fish is *Mrs.* Fish with a husband and twin boys."

Debbie laughed. "Ah, but sooner or later, Amy's persistence will find her handsome daddy a mate."

Gil grinned as he focused on Debbie's smile. "At least the little matchmaker has great taste."

"Are you pecky?" Debbie asked, then noting Gil's quizzical look she clarified, "Hungry? Lemonade and crisps?" she offered, gesturing to the motel coffee shop. "We're waiting for some stragglers."

Hearing of the delay, the rest of the trampers followed them to the coffee shop, the loud voice of Mrs. Klaus spewing displeasure at the delay. Debbie and Gil found a booth in the corner, next to a window. Gil sat facing the other travelers, so he could watch Amy entertaining a table of laughing adults with her effusive Disneyland travelogue.

Gil declined Debbie's offer of a half croissant.

"My lunch," she explained with a guilty shrug. "I model swimwear in the off-season, so I *have to* run about and climb mountains in the summer—or give up pastry."

Gil grinned thinking Debbie burned more calories sitting still and gesturing than others did running.

"What else did my precocious daughter tell you?"

"Amy said that she reads with the fifth graders and leaving school in the middle of the term was to give her teachers a rest."

"Partly true. She's seven going on thirty. My fault. I suppose you're wondering why I brought someone so young on an adventure travel trip."

"Amy told me that her 'Aunt Phyllis is a ped-i-atric psych-i-a-trist who thinks Daddy's over-pro-tec-tive.'"

Gil laughed at Debbie's imitation and said, "So maybe I'm ov-er-comp-en-sating for my over-pro-tect-ive nature. I can't win, can I? Actually, I've taken Amy on long hikes and floats. She swims like a fish and skis down the bunny hill like a runaway rocket. Obviously, she can't go rappelling or rock climbing, so we'll sit out those activities for a few years."

"No problem. You might want to reconsider rappelling. With harnesses, it's quite safe, actually."

Gil nodded. This woman knows what she's doing. He would consider it.

From the center of the room, Frank Ferret, adorned in a persimmon orange sweater, stood on a wooden chair. He rapped on an empty coffee cup. "Attention fellow trampers. I'm Dr. Frank Whistle, painless dentist from N'awleans. I don't like payin' this exorbitant single supplement that they're stickin' to us. Is there any other single who'd like to share a room?" Frank scanned the crowd. *If the Butcher is traveling alone, I might pick him up as a roommate.*

No one answered, so Frank sighed and began to sit down.

A woman's voice replied, "I'm for saving money. I'm Rose O'Hara, painless attorney from St. Louis." The voice came from a woman with short red hair. She sat alone in the corner and faced the other way.

She's not even looking at him! Debbie noticed.

Another nicely shaped woman, Gil thought. *Smartly dressed, European style. A professional woman in her midthirties,* he noted. *St. Louis isn't that far. Ah, forget it, the pushy dentist is grinning through his beard. I'm too slow, too out of practice.*

Frank laughed raucously at his good fortune. "I *like* this trip! Can Miss O'Hara and I get refunds on our single supplements, darlin' Deb?"

"Not a problem, Frank and Rose," Debbie answered. Debbie felt her family tours should have at least the appearance of morality, but the loudmouthed dentist and the sexy redhead had just openly destroyed it. What they did in the privacy of their hotel room was their business, but these Yanks were flaunting it. Debbie hoped they didn't offend the other trampers.

Mrs. Klaus coughed conspicuously and shared disapproving eye rolls with her husband then switched to complaining about the beets on her hamburger.

A bustling at the door to the coffee shop caught everyone's attention. Clutch Cooper and Willie Dern pushed in with their battered suitcases, each trying to be first. Virginia Slater followed in a two-piece, knit, business suit. Clutch stood five inches over Willie and had a deep tan. Willie had a permanent pink blush, but next to anyone other than Clutch, he was fairly handsome. Clutch showed the biceps of an athlete under his short-sleeved designer sport shirt. Willie wore a faded tee shirt with a magnified computer chip on it. Clutch looked anxious, compared to the confident air of Willie. Both men searched the room with their eyes, while Virginia stood by attentively, hoping the Kiwi competition wouldn't be found.

Debbie slouched behind the padded seat. "I'm gonna die. I'm going to quit this job effective immediately."

"You're avoiding one of those two men?"

"Both of them. Old boyfriends. Former lovers."

Gil blew a silent whistle. "Willie Dern and Clutch Cooper?"

Debbie stiffened in surprise. "You know them?"

"I know *of* them."

Debbie hid her face in her hands. "Months ago, I had this thing with Clutch. I expected that he'd send for me. Instead, he wrote boring letters. 'I hit four for four. I got six RBIs.' Whatever *RBIs* are. Clutch still writes, but six months ago I stopped answering. Then five months ago, I met Willie. Willie is brilliant. He knows everything about everything—except me. Did he propose? Did he even bring up the subject? No. He sent me a computer so that he could send me e-mails now and then. I don't want anything to do with either of those dags."

Gil raised a dubious brow. "Here they come."

"You don't suppose you could pretend to—no, forget I said anything."

"Deb honey," Clutch announced, "I've come back for ya."

Willie followed a pace behind. "I have a trinket for you, Debra." He placed a thin gift-wrapped package in front of her. The long package was the kind that typically held necklaces or bracelets.

Debbie pushed the package away. "I don't want anything from you, and I'm giving your computer back."

Clutch slapped a square ring box on the table.

Willie frowned and slapped a similarly shaped box between Clutch's box and Debbie.

"I'm going to scream," Debbie groaned, as her eyes welled with tears.

Gil stood up and stepped between the two suitors. He spoke softly so that the curious onlookers couldn't hear. "Gentlemen, this isn't a game of checkers. You're embarrassing Debbie and annoying me. Debbie and I have agreed to get to know each other. You've had your chance, and you blew it. Now it's my turn."

"Are you sleepin' with this guy?" Clutch demanded.

"If I am, it's not your affair," Debbie snapped.

"Gentlemen," Gil whispered, "I'm traveling with my daughter, who is never out of my sight. So sleeping with Debbie is the least of your concerns.

"Because if all works out between Debbie and me, you'll never have another turn at bat, Mr. Cooper. On second thought, I wouldn't want to marry this fine lady and have her sitting in the rocking chair forty years from now saying, 'I should've married Willie Dern or Clutch Cooper.' So it might be in her best interests, and mine too, for her to tell you how much the two of you hurt her with your neglect. In turn, maybe you can explain how your work interferes with basic human relationships, then again, maybe not. *But* when Debbie talks to you, it will be when *she's* ready—not before, and not after. So in the mean time, *back off!*"

Debbie planted a hard kiss on a surprised Gil. "See why I love this guy? It's called *consideration*. You two should take lessons."

Frank placed money in the jukebox to drown out the conversation, and the lively music blared. Maybe Frank could induce Debbie to dance, but with three guys arguing over her—it didn't matter because this time Frank was too slow.

Gil felt the need to end the encounter with the suitors. "So if you'll excuse us, Debbie and I are going to dance while you tardy trampers check in."

Gil pulled Debbie to a small open space where they began a lively two-step. The Chinese couple joined them on the makeshift dance floor.

Debbie felt breathless. "Mr. Rocklin, you are incredible! Absolutely incredible. Those two jerks are scraping their jaws off the floor. A moment ago, I was having the most humiliating, miserable day of my life, and you turned it around. Now *I'm* in control."

Gil nodded. "This will give you time to forgive and forget, and pick who the lucky guy will be."

"Or I can tell them both to jump in the bay."

"Even dags have feelings—whatever a dag is. I think you'll be more sensitive than that."

"Dags are characters, and you really *are* a nice guy? You better be careful, or I'll stow away in *your* suitcase." She looked up at him. Debbie was tall, but Gil was taller. "I'm not kidding, Gil. I'd like to have a fair go at getting to know you."

Gil smiled. "Back there . . . when you kissed me, I said to myself, 'This is the highlight of my vacation. Forget Milford Sound and Mount Cook. It won't get any better than this. Here is an appealing, personable young lady who would be very easy to fall in love with.'"

Debbie blushed. "Those are soothing words for my bruised ego."

"But it won't happen."

"Oh? Well, I can't blame you. I've been a little too free with my affections in the last year."

"That's not it, Debbie. You're romantically involved with two jerks or dags, who play by different rules. There are two reasons why nothing will happen between us. One, there's not enough time to do it right. A trip like this is too ideal. Too perfect. And three weeks is too short a time to get to know one another. As my psychiatrist sister says, for two people to get to know each other, they have to experience bad times as well as good. They have to plan together, work together—"

"Suffer together," Debbie inserted. "I get the idea. If I had followed it, I wouldn't have expected so much from my previous relationships, and I wouldn't have gotten hurt."

Gil forced a laugh. "It's a damn shame we can't get together because you're an exceptionally appealing woman. But I can't afford to rush into a mistake. Amy's lost one mother. I won't let it happen again."

Debbie felt stunned. "I met you minutes ago, and we're talking more seriously than I ever talked with my two . . . jerks. There's a lesson in that, but I'm not sure what it is."

Frank Ferret, now known as Dr. Frank Whistle, played a Latin number on the jukebox. A samba could force Gil to sit down and give Frank a chance to show off. *Damn, Gil Rocklin dances like he was born in Brazil. They look great together.*

Rose suddenly grabbed Frank's arms to dance. She didn't say a word and neither did he.

As the dancers picked up the Latin tempo, Debbie regained her composure. "Oh, you said there were *two* reasons we'll never get together."

"Two or three. Willie and Clutch. I get the feeling you don't know just how important your suitors are."

"Sure I do. Clutch plays professional baseball. Willie has a good job at a software company."

Gil chuckled. "Clutch was the MVP—Most Valuable Player—in our World Series that recently ended."

"Baseball's not big down here," Debbie said apologetically.

"Uh-huh. Well, Clutch doesn't have as many endorsements, kids' camps, and card signings as Michael Jordan, but he's on his way. It's a wonder he has time for a three-week vacation.

"Willie Dern is the chief operating officer, heir apparent, to one of the world's bigger software giants. He's not quite as accomplished or nearly as rich as Bill Gates, but with stock options, Willie is—according to the *Wall Street Journal* and *PC Magazine*—one very rich and powerful geek."

"Oh, I didn't know," Debbie said.

"Really? You're the envy of every single woman in North America, and you don't even know it?"

"I knew they were both well-off," Debbie sniffed. "These trips aren't exactly cheap. But Willie, in particular, doesn't dress very fancy."

"*Dress fancy?* The man's a premeditated slob. It's his eccentric trademark. But see how you're choosing your words since you found out." Gil snickered.

Debbie sulked. "I get it. You're saying the rich blokes always get the girl even if the blokes are insensitive jerks. I find that insulting."

"I didn't mean for it to come out that way. Let's just say that a suitor with only a modest income is at a severe disadvantage when it comes to competing with a fair maiden's affections. I'm a realistic fellow, Debbie. I've learned to pick my competitions carefully and win. I generally win."

"Sure you do, mate. You give up on the hard ones—like me."

"Ouch, I think we're even."

"Does this mean we've survived our first fight?" Debbie grinned flirtatiously. "Look out, Gil. If we live through a catastrophe or two, we could be stuck with each other."

"I'll never look forward to a catastrophe with more anticipation."

CHAPTER 5

Penguins

CHRISTCHURCH, NEW ZEALAND

After a couple of hours punting the Avon River in the Christchurch Botanic Gardens, the jet-lagged trampers boarded their bus to the hotel. Venus moaned that her husband strained his back poling their boat, but the other trampers were too tired to offer sympathy. Amy's head bobbed. Even Willie, who never had more than five hours of sleep a night, appeared ready to doze off.

Debbie wanted to start her trampers off slow, but tempering her exuberance was impossible. She pulled Eve aside and whispered, "There's a splendid Antarctic attraction near the airport. It's open up to nine. And it doesn't get dark around here till nine thirty. I don't think the group is in the mood, but if you'd like to give it a go, I'll take you there."

"Why?" George grumbled, leaning forward to hear.

Debbie shrugged with arched brows, and still whispering, replied, "Well, actually, there's an exhibit of blue penguins."

From ten feet away, Amy's head snapped up, and she yelled. *"Penguins? Martin! Penguins!"*

* * *

Gil carried Amy over his shoulder. The dead weight of the seven-year-old and the furry penguin doll tucked under his arm didn't alter his erect posture. Martin leaned against his father and shielded his eyes from a street light. The kids had lobbied for some kiwifruit ice cream cones, and the adults had yearned for coffee. The kids had sleepily left their ice cream cones unfinished, and the adults had to wait for coffee.

The Cathedral Square area of Christchurch had few pedestrians on this weekday night. Closed shops lined the street leading to the hotel. The two families and Debbie took a diversion through a small park area, with George and Eve trailing behind. George skipped the park and kept his wife and son on the sidewalk. They would catch up on the other side of the brick wall that edged the park. The separation seemed a way of giving Gil and Debbie a chance to be semi-alone. *They seem to be enjoying each other's company*, George thought.

Gil and Debbie had the same thought.

"You're obviously at the top of your game," Gil began. "Do you expect to—"

"To be a tour guide forever?" Debbie finished the question with a laugh. "Everyone asks me that. So I ask you, would you, or any other man, want his wife traveling away from home seven months of the year? Or let me rephrase that. What loving wife would want to be away from her family seven months of the year?"

"Travel and marriage aren't a good mix—at least your kind of travel," Gil agreed.

"And don't think I didn't, or don't, consider that when it comes to Clutch hopping from city to city. He says that when he's home, he's home—full time. But will I be home? I expect to work. I don't want companionship that I have to turn on and off?"

Debbie held her head ashamedly, "Oh my, I'm rambling. But you're so easy to talk to."

"Will you miss it?" Gil asked.

"Running tours? A little. It's been fun, but I'm ready for something else. My degree was in music education and modern languages. I substitute teach during the winter, and I love it, but I can't find a full-time position close to where I want to live."

"Sounds like Willie has the advantage," Gil noted.

"I don't know. Liz thinks there's something going on between Willie and Virginia, but if there was, he'd never take her with him on a courtship trip. Would he?"

Gil shrugged.

"Willie's awfully self-centered, but he doesn't pull that nonsense with me."

Gil heard the angry shouts from the other side of a brick wall. He peered over the top of the wall and saw six skinheads surrounding the King family.

The thugs ranged from their late teens to early twenties. All wore black sleeveless tee shirts as a uniform. Their chrome chains glinted under the streetlight. Two held beer cans. One threw a can in the Kings' direction. "Yankee Maoris!" one snarled, as the beer can ricocheted menacingly against the wall.

Other persons, walking the sidewalks, gave the racial confrontation a wide berth.

Debbie heard the taunt and looked at Gil. "Do something."

Gil's eyes narrowed. His reaction was not emotional, but studied. "They may declare victory and leave. If I go over the wall, it's all-out war."

On the other side of the wall, George's anger began to build. As a desk sergeant, George often had to settle down the prisoners brought before him. He knew what actions dowsed fires and what caused them to flare up. But with his boy fearfully clutching his leg, he wanted to kick butt—even if there were six of them. "That's enough, guys," George snapped authoritatively. "You've had your fun, now go sleep it off."

The group walked single file past the King family without saying a word. The last skinhead pretended to walk away, then turned and lurched toward Eve, grabbing her buttocks with one hand. *"Nice ass!"* he crowed.

Eve slapped the mauler hard enough to raise a welt. If the battle had stopped there, the thugs might have had a good laugh and moved on to torment someone else.

George knew that, but some things just couldn't be ignored. George's left uppercut landed in the punk's stomach and dropped him into a painful, breathless ball. The punk rolled painfully on the sidewalk, gasping for air.

The five remaining skinheads gaped in disbelief. The attack on their drinking mate by a man of color must be avenged. They circled ominously. Each punk wanted a turn at beating on George, but given the force of his uppercut, they knew they would have to attack all at once.

Gil handed Amy to Debbie. "This is getting out of hand." He leaped over the five-foot wall with ease, startling the thugs and halting their attack.

"Get the family out a here," Gil murmured to George. I'll take care of it."

"They'll kill you, man," George fretted. "I'll be back."

"No!" Gil ordered. "You're fuel on the fire. I want to incapacitate one punk—at most—not five."

Gil held up his palms in a nonthreatening gesture. Suddenly, the well-built American switched to the focus of their hostile attention. The attackers knew that as harassers, they couldn't allow even one person to stand up for their victims. If one do-gooder got away with it, everyone could end up interfering with the persecutors.

Smiling, Gil said, "Whoa there. We're just guests in your great country, and we don't want any trouble. Why don't you let me buy you all a drink, and you can tell me what's gotten you so pissed off at the world."

The punk on the ground rolled and groaned.

"About your mate, here," Gil pointed. "If anyone pinched *your* women, I'm sure you'd do the same thing my mate did. Maybe worse. And I know I'd never want a buddy of mine get creamed without wanting to do something about it. But your grabby mate is a dag. Help him learn from this experience. If you take his side, he'll go through life thinking he can maul ladies and get away with it. The next lady could be one of yours."

Gil's calm patter broke the momentum of the gang. Who was this guy who fearlessly stood before them? He was an American, and *all Americans carry guns.*

The largest of the gang swaggered forward. Being the leader of the pack required him to act. His bulging biceps looked pythonlike with blue green tattoos. His lower lip curled defiantly under a twisted, untrimmed mustache. Six feet from the stationary American, he stopped and smirked, hearing the metallic click of his switchblade. The click alone was usually enough to send an adversary running or begging for mercy.

"Aw naw, you don't want to do that," Gil said, making a distasteful face. "If you come after me, I'll have to break your arm. I don't have the time to play around. You leave me no other choice. I'll have to disable you so I can chase your mates into the bay."

"Oh my, I'm scared, Yank," the thug mocked, taking a half step backward. He lunged toward Gil, thrusting the knife at his chest.

Gil swiveled and mule kicked the skin head in the crotch as he pulled the trusting arm forward. Gil's arm grab blurred to the gathering crowd, but they all heard the breaking of the knife wielder's elbow.

The attacker screamed with pain. "The son of a bitch broke my arm," he cried, as Gil scooped up the knife and placed his foot on the thug's neck.

Gil gripped the man's hand as the five, standing gang members crouched for an attack. Each waited for the rush. No one wanted to be the first.

"Back off buddies or I'll have to break his fingers. All of them. When your friend gets out of his casts, I suspect he'll repay the first man that caused his pinkies to be turned into sausage links."

One man, his bravery fortified with beer, shuffled forward to challenge the American.

Gil began to squeeze on the leader's hand.

From under Gil's shoe, the leader of the gang whimpered, "Please don't break my fingers. Please, please, please don't hurt me." The leader would never command the respect of his followers again, but whoever had the guts to lead the attack on Gil would be the new leader.

Debbie charged from the circle of spectators like a runaway rocket, whacking the punks unmercifully with her hot pink umbrella. "Go home! Go home!"

Spectators, who had stayed embarrassingly neutral, now followed Debbie's lead and started to goad the punks. The "Go home" shout soon filled the street.

Gil picked Debbie up with his arm around her waist to turn her around. "The skirmish is over, Tiger. Let's scoot before the constables arrive."

Debbie and Gil broke into a slow run to where Eve was huddling over the children. In front of the hotel, they broke out in laughter.

"Talk about a tiger cat!" Gil chuckled. "They were more frightened of your umbrella than they were of my t'ai chi."

"For a minute, I thought you'd wimped out," Debbie said.

Eve gave Gil and Debbie hugs, and George shook Gil's hand vigorously.

Amy did a rapid karate, one-two punch, showing that she had watched her father in martial arts tournaments. "Never hurt anyone unless you have to pro-tect yourself," Amy parroted an earlier lesson. "Does that mean you pro-tect your friends too?"

"We'll talk about that later," Gil stated.

George hugged Debbie. "You're quite a gal, Kiwi."

Then George turned back to Gil and shook his head in disbelief. "I've seen expert karate before, but I've never seen such a cool confrontation—unbelievably *cool*."

Gil nodded a thank-you. If the policeman only knew how long and hard Gil had worked to control his rage. Without *cool*, Gil could have easily killed the six punks.

Martin requested, "Can you teach me karate, Mr. Rocklin? I've been asking for lessons." The boy didn't mention that his dad approved of lessons, but his mother didn't.

Gil patted the boy on the head. "First move. Are you listening?"

"Yeah!"

"Run like heck! Got it?"

"Yeah." The boy laughed, temporarily hiding his disappointment in not being told the secrets of breaking bones. But Mr. Rocklin liked to kid around. Maybe he'd share his expertise later.

Gil put his hand on George's shoulder. "Your dad knows how to deliver a punch, and more importantly, *when* to deliver a punch and when not. Listen to *him*."

Eve wasn't going to let this violence go unchecked. "I agree that we all should have 'ran like hell,' but what if one of those creeps had a gun?"

Gil nodded and juggled the switchblade knife. With a single sidearm motion, he slammed the knife into the low-hanging branch of a nearby tree.

"Wow!" Martin exclaimed.

Eve snipped, "And what if there was *more* than one gun?"

Gil nodded. "I had scanned their clothing for bulges. The only danger back there was *to* the six punks—not *from* the punks. But your point is well-taken. Talk first. If that doesn't work, running is still the best move."

"You're a hero," Debbie said, not wanting to hear "run away."

"So are you, Deb."

Feeling that she had acted ungratefully, Eve murmured, "You're *all* heroes."

Gil said, "I'm sorry that you had to experience that. I'm very sorry the kids were frightened."

"I wasn't scared," Amy protested. She had seen her father winning martial arts competitions.

"Good," Gil said. "Let's not make a big deal out of this."

Debbie scowled, examining her bent umbrella. "Big deal? Darn right it's a big deal. I busted my new brolly."

*   *   *

Frank had spent two weeks in Antarctica hiding from a drug cartel's hit man and never wanted to see another penguin—fascinating as they might be. He chose to watch his fellow travelers chat in the lobby of the hotel. None of them wanted to go into town either. *The Vatican has more spirited nightlife*, Frank grumbled to himself. *Who's retiring early besides the two families with kids?*

The parents and their limp bundles of children had slid in minutes before. Debbie and Gil Rocklin were arm and arm—looking like they had a secret they weren't going to tell. *Too bad*, Frank thought. *Neat couple. Too bad for both of them. Rocklin can't possibly know about her ill-fated future, and Debbie probably doesn't know about his homicidal past.*

Debbie's definitely tasty, but with one slight defect—a genocidal murderer for a father. I should do her and her three boy friends a favor and tell them—at least her. The boy friends will drop her like a leper.

Damn, Debbie's hot—nice hot. But if I say anything to her, I blow my cover. She may already know. Probably not. She's too cheerful. What do I say? "Debbie, one of your trampers murdered your mother for sleeping around. He's your real father, and he enjoys killin' folks—lots of folks. The parents who raised you are thieves who took you here as an infant. They're on the lamb from KGB thugs, who want to kill them.

And, Debbie, did I tell you that your daddy is an indicted war criminal who destroys whole villages—women and children?" Wonder how she'll react when she finds out? Will she believe the Butcher's inevitable line of smoke and keep his secret, or will she turn him in? Who, other than me, would turn in their own father?

Frank caught himself thinking about Debbie's firm figure and scolded himself. *That's not why you're here, stud. Find the Butcher! What to look for? Who may be overeager in establishing his false identity? Who's telling more about themselves than people want to know. Hell, that's me!*

Frank counted the prospects. *Ten middle-aged men. Only the Chinese and Ethiopian men can be ruled out, leaving eight middle-aged men. Doubt if the Butcher would pose as an American. But he could impersonate a Brit, easily. The Brits—Paul Stanley, Marcus Turner, and Abe Goodman—meet the "average" criteria. But so do the Frenchman Jacques Lafate and Italian Antonio Borolo. Joseph Tinsley, the Australian bachelor, is a little too muscular to be average, and he has a shaved head.*

Do any have light roots that might indicate that their hair was dyed?

No, Frank answered his own question, *but watch the bald Aussie Tinsley for light stubble.*

Excessive makeup?

Not so you'd notice.

Frank had made a point of hearing Lafate speak in French and Borolo in Italian. *Lafate's French seems French enough and Borolo's Italian sounds better than mine, but then, what do I know? Both spoke English well, but with an accent. If the Butcher is the expert linguist they say he is, he should speak English without an accent—unless he's so good he can fake an accent.*

I need to concentrate on the Brits—Stanley, Turner, and Goodman. They blend in too well. None of them say much. Maybe the wives will give

him away. I could flirt with them, but they're older, only average in beauty,
except for Mrs. Turner, and any time spent with them would be obvious
and suspect.

Frank studied the larger women. If Bymarovitch was in drag or had a
sex change, there might be telltale signs: large hands, facial hair, voice
changes, or hip-to-shoulder ratios. Ferret ruled out all but the one uniquely
ugly and perpetually complaining woman, Venus Klaus, before deciding
she was too short, and left for his room frustrated.

When Frank cautiously opened the door of his hotel room, he had almost
forgotten about his roommate. Rose was at the door with an embrace and
a long open kiss. Frank gasped for air. "Rose, darlin', I better tell ya, I'm
kinda engaged. At least I think I am. I haven't called in for a few weeks,
and before that she wasn't pickin' up the phone."

"Engaged?" Rose said skeptically. "What's her name," she said, as she
ran her hand between his legs.

"I just forgot," Frank grumbled.

"You're scum, Frank Ferret," Rose snapped.

"Hey! You stalk me, and worm your way into my bedroom, just to tell
me that?"

"You know why we're here."

Frank sat on the bed and took off his shoes. "I guess you want to spend
a lot of money just to join me on my holiday. Otherwise, that general you
report to will be askin' why you're pissin' away taxpayers' money to make
up to an ol' boyfriend."

"Don't evade, Frank. It just wastes time. We can help each other. I'll
show you mine, and you show me yours."

"Darlin', I don't think you have anything I haven't seen."

"That sounds like you're short on information," Rose clucked.

"If I was short, you wouldn't have chased me round the world," Frank grinned.

"Ugh!" Rose grunted. "Do you know who Bymarovitch is, or not?"

"*Not*. Not yet. Got it narrowed down to six. But your people can't just barge in and scoop me out of my bounty."

"There is no *my people*. I'm alone on this, and if you've found him and I bring him in for you, you'll still get the bounty."

"But you'll want half," Frank stated.

"You know better than that," Rose growled. "I can't participate in the reward even if I received an instant discharge. No, the bounty is all yours, darling. The only way I could share your bounty is to marry you."

Frank pondered the subtle proposal. "I suppose we could try a trial . . . whatever."

Rose laughed raucously. "Frank, Frank, *Frank!* You can't even say the word, and yet you tell me you're *engaged*? Before I'd let you in my body again, I'd sooner be gored between the legs by a tsetse-fly-infested, dung-smeared rhinoceros with an attitude."

"A vivid description. Did you practice saying that?"

"I had plenty of time between your calls to practice," Rose said flatly while pulling her sweater over her head. Rose's solid body looked great, and she knew it. *Let Frank suffer*.

Frank blew a thin hard column of air. "We were pretty cozy back in Vienna, Captain Rose."

"I'm a major now, and it was Budapest, you louse."

"I get 'em mixed up."

Rose dropped her tight-fitting stretch pants. "Of course, you could try *taking me* with your masculine brute force."

"So you could paint the ceiling with me with your judo thing?" Frank groused.

"Well, that's the chance you'll have to take." Rose smirked. "True love never runs smooth."

"You've made your intentions or nonintentions perfectly clear, darlin'."

Rose tugged scornfully on Frank's beard. "Good! You know where you stand. *Strictly business*, so is there anything you want to tell me? I'll share what I know. Ask me anything, Frank."

"Wouldja like to take a shower together?"

"I thought you'd never ask."

*   *   *

George kissed Eve's breasts slowly. George was a patient master of foreplay, Eve thought. And she wasn't so shabby herself. They could drive each other crazy before the night was over.

"I love you so much," George murmured. "We're gonna make it, aren't we?" It was as more of a question than a statement.

"We have to," Eve answered.

"For Martin's sake," he said.

"For our sakes," she said. "I'd never want to be a single mother like Virginia, having to put up with a chauvinist pig like Willie."

"You'd have so many of those white doctors hitting on you—"

"They hit on me now. But I've always been faithful. George, the trouble between us is not me, it's you. I fell in love with a real man. A proud man. A proud black man. A man proud of who he was and what he did for a living."

"I can never be as successful as you."

"So I make more money than you," Eve snapped. "Get over it!"

George turned his back. Foreplay was over for this evening.

*   *   *

Rose stirred her breakfast coffee aimlessly. "Frank, honey, promise me that you'll never marry me?"

"Was I that bad?" Frank groused.

"That good! But you're not marriage material, dream boat. The way you travel and the risks you take."

"Well, you travel too, darlin'. Panama, the Gulf War, and how many peace-keepin' missions?"

"Ah, but in five years, I can retire. The Army's been good to me. They paid for a JD in international law and a PhD in criminal justice, so I can teach in almost any English-speaking law school in the world. How's that for roots? Good roots. Secure roots in a stimulating university environment."

"I wouldn't know about university environments," Frank snorted. "I dropped out."

"You were *kicked out,* a week before graduation," Rose corrected. She knew his file by heart.

"I had good recommendations," Frank recalled.

"Sure." She laughed. "Your lacrosse coach said you were the sneakiest and dirtiest player with a lacrosse stick of anyone he'd ever coached."

Frank feigned a hurt look. "I took it as a compliment. We won three straight championships."

Rose snickered. "And . . . you received an honorary degree from the same Ivy League school that gave you the boot. With your Pulitzers, you could teach journalism anywhere."

"Now you're saying that we should tangle roots on some campus?" Frank said suspiciously.

"Just the opposite, Frank. I just wanted you to see that there *is*, or rather *would've been*, a future for us. But you'd be unhappy. It wouldn't work. You'll never have a future with anyone, until you're too feeble to chase stories, and you run out of words to rub into the faces of the world's endless supply of bad guys."

"You don't pay a pretty picture of me, darlin'."

Rose switched to a whisper as a nearby table filled. "Do you have any idea how dangerous this . . . mission is? Our Balkan buddy would take us out in a minute. And you think you can make him turn himself in?"

"I'll figure that out after I find the ol' scorpion."

"Ugh, he probably has a body guard armed to the teeth, as if he needed one. And you know your fondness for weapons."

"Hey, I'm carryin' one of those porcelain pieces."

"Have you ever fired it?"

"You know I hate guns. I've seen what they can do to folks."

"Then maybe you're going to overpower him—an old scorpion—with his twenty years of martial arts expertise."

"Oh."

Rose smirked. "You're so used to bluffing yourself in and out of trouble, you think you can do it to anyone, anytime. You can't! And you'll never change. So please don't ever marry me. No matter how much I might beg. Slap me. Step on me. Forget where we met. Anything to keep me from making the mistake of my life."

Frank wondered why he didn't feel relieved. "Does that mean we can't?"

Rose dipped her head and looked innocently at Frank through her long eyelashes. "I didn't say that," she grinned.

*   *   *

Carp Simpson knew instantly that the flicker of flashlights in the reservation office meant trouble. A year before, three teenagers had broken into the office and scattered records looking for the petty cash box. After the break-in, Carp put on heavier lock. He moved into a closer room in the half-empty motel that had become his home when his wife threw him out. From his room, Carp could look across the courtyard and see the reservation office. Every night when he went to bed, Carp would take one last look at the office window—even when he was drunk, which was most every night. But tonight Carp was nearly sober, and the thought of cleaning up the office without anyone to help him made him as mad as hell.

Carp slipped back into his shoes without tying them. He plucked the older of two putting irons from his golf bag and rushed to the reception desk.

The young night receptionist looked up from his homework. He had never seen Carp move so fast.

"Call the police!" Carp yelled. "Those damn kids have broken into my office again."

Carp dashed along the side of the building. He would be all over the punks before they knew it. The dark windows gave Carp pause. *Did I imagine the lights? No! The door! Half open!*

Carp kicked the door open and jumped in the door frame. His large body could block the punks from escaping even without swinging his golf club.

Carp never felt the blow to the back of his neck. He was unconscious before he hit the floor.

*   *   *

The hospital was nearly deserted at 3:00 a.m., which added to Debbie's loneliness. Debbie fought tears as she spoke into the pay phone. "A fractured vertebra. Concussion. Paralysis—maybe temporary—and possible brain damage."

Mr. Armstrong, the owner of the travel company, groaned. "Sounds like Carp won't be back to work anytime soon—if ever. You're in charge, Deb. You're the new manager."

"I can't run the office and the trampers, both!" Debbie exclaimed with dismay. "As it is, I'll be lucky to make it back to the trampers before breakfast. What kind of guide will I be with two hours sleep?"

Armstrong sighed. "Debbie, I wanted to make this change long ago. Carp hasn't been the same man since he started drinking again. I'll send a temp down to cover the office and a part-timer to clean the buses. But you know the personnel. Hire and fire, Deb. Thirty percent raise. E-kay?"

"E-kay," Debbie agreed somberly. Debbie had always thought she could do a better job of running the office, but she didn't want the job this way, and she wasn't ready to give up the closer contact with trampers that she enjoyed as a guide. Still, she owed it to Carp to hold his job, in the event he recovered enough to return.

Armstrong said, "Rent a car and get back to your trampers. You're more wide awake with three hours sleep than the rest of us are with eight. I'm sure you can do it. G'night, Deb. G'luck."

Debbie would have to take a cab to the airport to find a car rental, and *would they be open?*

She spotted Willie half asleep on a hospital lobby couch. "What are you doing here?"

Willie popped up. "I followed you when the hotel manager told me you were hitching a ride back to Christchurch."

"You're having me watched! I don't like that, Willie. I don't like it at all."

"Be realistic, Debra. There's nothing you can do here. The man's in a coma. And you have a tour group to lead in a few hours. The driver will take us both back, and we can get some sleep in the backseat."

"A cab will cost you a fortune. It's a ninety—kilometer trek!"

"Well, Debra, I'm weary. I'm going back to our hotel. If you want to join me, and get some repose, do so. If you prefer to hitch another ride with a truck driver, go ahead. I'm trying to be obliging, Debra. I know you're irritated with me, and I know I must make it up to you. So if I dispense a million dollars on cab fare, it'll be worth it if you forgive me—for whatever I've done or haven't done."

Debbie sagged with submission. "Very well. I'm too tired to argue."

Willie smiled. He had won his first victory.

* * *

Ferret nearly pushed the other trampers out of his way so that he could hear Debbie's story.

Rose had beaten Frank to a closer position. "What did the thieves take?" she asked.

Debbie shook her head. "Someone set fire in the file cabinets, so it's hard to tell what they took. Fortunately, the police arrived with a fire extinguisher before the office was damaged too much. The only good thing to come out of this is that Carp's wife—they're separated—came to the hospital; otherwise, I'd still be there."

Rose pulled Frank aside as the crowd dispersed. "Looks like the Butcher pulled Debbie's records out of the file. The records would have a *Who to notify in case of accident* card. That would be her father. So Butcher has his brother's address. He should be leaving the tour at any minute."

Frank snickered. "The Butcher didn't get Deb's records. I borrowed all of Carp's personnel files the first day while she was floating to earth."

Rose joined Frank's snicker. "I knew I could trust you, partner."

* * *

Frank and Rose snuggled. Rose liked the way Frank continued to embrace her after they made love. Frank felt delighted with Rose, but he was particularly energized by the break-in. At least, he wasn't wasting his time. The Butcher was here! The single blow to Carp's head was characteristic Bymarovitch karate. The only surprise was that Bymarovitch didn't kill the interfering office manager. Maybe the Butcher purposely held back, not wanting the attention a murder would bring.

"What do we know about the Butcher so far?" Rose asked.

"That he's average-looking, extremely clever, and has an explosive temper. His hair is blond and his eyes are mirrored sunglasses. He's a chain smoker and may, or may not, have gold teeth."

Frank sat up. "Are you sure we can't get an up-to-date photo from the Brits? He did an embassy gig in London."

Rose shook her head. "The CIA ticked off MI6, so even if they have something, they're not sharing. I'm sure they want to make the collar themselves, and they pulled their team out of Croatia to scour Argentina for Gotovina and Bymarovitch."

"When?"

"Three or four weeks ago."

"Then who was the tail I lost in the Gorge."

"Corporal Smathers. He worked for me—past tense."

"Sorry about that," Frank said, but he wasn't sorry. He would prefer his adversaries from the United States to be more competent than those from other countries.

"Back to our suspects," Rose pressed. "Is there anyone we can rule out?"

"Not yet," Frank grudgingly admitted.

The Butcher could do a believable Italian, like Borolo 'cause there are lots of Italians in Croatia. Same with Lafate. Bymarovitch was a spy in the Paris embassy for a while. Whaddya think of Lafate's French?"

"A very slight German accent," Rose noted. She was fluent in French. "Aha!"

"But he says he's from Colmar, which is—"

"On the German border," Frank finished. "Bummer."

"The Englishmen are the best bet, although the Butcher spied long enough in Sydney to pick up the accent and local trivia."

"I'd like to see our Aussie tramper's hair color when his shaved head grows back," Frank said, holding Tinsley's photograph next to Sophie's flame-covered drawing.

"Let's get back to the Englishmen," Rose said. "All have muscles. The Butcher is supposed to be incredibly strong for his size. We have to trap one of them up without him knowing we're doing it."

"The last part is difficult. If he knows we know, we're dead. But chances are he's too smart to make a verbal gaff. We have a better chance gettin' his spouse to make a mistake. Whoever the spouse is, she's not the Butcher's wife. The Butcher had no present wife. So the wife he brought along for cover might not be as sharp."

"So you'd concentrate on the ol' chicks, would you?" Rose shook her head.

"Well, I can't very well concentrate on the ol' chicks. They all think I'm a letch for shacking up with you. But you, my dear partner, can do the subtle interrogations. Ask about their homes and kids—you know, that girl-to-girl stuff."

"If they'll have anything to do with me," Rose agreed, and added, "but only you would think home and kids are girl stuff."

Frank sighed. He had never known a real home and family for long, and Rose's comment hurt.

"Well, for one thing, we have the North Island post office box address for Debbie's father, who is really her uncle, Klav Bymarovitch. That's where Ratac, the Butcher, her real father, is headed, and that's in the direction that our tour is headed. My guess is that's when the Butcher will leave the tour. Then we'll know who he is."

"What will the Butcher do when he has his reunion with brother Klav?" Rose mused.

"Well, Klav has a fortune in gold that could fund Ratac's escape."

"Or return," Rose muttered. "With his plastic surgery . . . ."

Both remained silent. If Ratac did return to Croatia, it could only be for three reasons: fermenting hate, killing his enemies, and expanding the war zone. Rose shuddered at the thought. Ratac was not the type to permanently hide. Every horrendous thing the Butcher had done suggested a man obsessed with seeking power at any cost of life. He was still a danger to peace. "Klav might go along with him, but—," Frank was saying, before Rose interrupted him.

"But what?"

Frank bite his lip. "Debbie doesn't seem like someone raised by anyone remotely like Ratac. If Klav is halfway sane, he could sound the alarm and be a threat to the Butcher's comeback."

Rose finished the thought, "The Butcher will kill him."

Frank sat up, "Oh damn! If Klav is in the Butcher's gun sights, then—"

"Debbie will be next."

CHAPTER 6

Jostling for Position

Amy and Martin raced to the breakfast buffet. Dr. Eve King and Gil exchanged dismayed looks as the children threaded between the empty dining tables like broken field runners. Eve laughed. "If you'd like, I'll watch Amy so you can catch up."

"Catch up?"

"The Kiwi is leading an 8K, prebreakfast run, with your rivals in hot pursuit."

"They're not my rivals," Gil protested.

"Yeah, sure." Eve laughed. "They went thataway."

"You think I can head 'em off at the pass, Doc?"

"Why bother? You're obviously not interested in the Kiwi," Eve smirked.

Gil shrugged. "Well, can I help it if I need some exercise? Please don't think I'm trying to run fast or anything. I always sprint till I drop."

"Sure you do," Eve chuckled as she pushed Gil toward the door. "Run, you fool!"

Gil quickly caught up to George King. "Your wife is watching Amy. I didn't thank her enough."

George grunted. "Speaking of thanks, your daughter is a sweetie. Thanks for raising her that way. Without her, Martin could be bored to death."

"That's true for Amy too."

"But not as much. When Martin went to this all white, private school—my wife's idea—none of the little snots spoke to him for three days. He'd come home and bawl his eyes out."

"Did you pull him out?"

"No. We Kings don't run."

Gil nodded approvingly.

George smiled. "Martin's class president now. But enough of me. If you don't speed up, you'll never catch her."

"See ya," Gil murmured, and he streaked uphill where Willie was struggling.

Willie glared at Gil. "This terrain is bad for one's knees. A treadmill is superior. You can read while you run. Right?"

"Read the sunrise on the clouds," Gil replied in admiration of the scenery.

Willie snorted. "Cumulus nimbus. It'll probably rain."

"Then enjoy it while you can. Excuse me. I'm going to run ahead."

Willie increased his pace. "Enjoy *her* while you can. You're not going to get her, you know."

"I know that."

"Then don't prolong it."

"I'll prolong it as long as she wants," Gil answered good-naturedly. "Then we can both watch her run off with Clutch, which she seems to be doing now. See ya."

Gil pulled away from Willie. He passed Tinsley and Stanley, who seemed to run without effort. When out of sight on a curve, he turned on the jets then coasted casually next to Debbie who was laughing at Frank's jokes while Clutch looked miserable.

"Hi, folks!"

Debbie looked aside to Gil with her genuine smile. "G'day, mate! Frank was just interrogating me about my family."

"I want to hear this," Gil said.

"I'm really the lost granddaughter to the Russian throne. Or at least that's what I'd pretend when I was Amy's age. But the dull reality of it all is that I grew up on a farm out in the middle of nowhere. I mean nowhere! Just my parents, three stepbrothers, and trees. Trees instead of neighbors. Oh, we had plenty of books in three languages, and my mum was a teacher. But I didn't have a school to go to till I was ten. There were other kids! There were people! I was in heaven! I vowed never to be far from people."

Frank beamed. "Your mum taught, huh? What about your dud?"

"Dad is a great farmer. He's a smart man, but his accent is so strong, the town folk can barely understand him."

"He immigrated?"

"Yes. How about your family, Frank?" Debbie asked.

"Didn't know my dad. My stepfather's a televangelist who's sure to sizzle in Hades for prying pension checks from his parishioners."

Clutch inserted, "Where's your pretty roommate, Whistle?"

Ferret grinned. "Why Clutch, if I didn't know better, I'd think you brought that up because you're jealous of me monopolizing this jewel of the islands."

Clutch scowled. "I was thinking of your lonely roommate. A man should only play on one team at a time."

Ferret clucked. "Where have I heard that one before? Well, I'm sure you won't believe me, but Rose and I are just friends—nothin' more."

Debbie coughed her skepticism.

Frank continued his position between Debbie and Clutch. "If Ms. McWard doesn't like my attention and intentions, she'll tell me to bug off."

The runners came to a dead end where they stopped to view a scenic overlook of the shoreline. Debbie planted a kiss on Ferret's cheek and whispered in his ear. She playfully slapped Gil's hand. "My number one suitor is neglecting his duties. Race you back, mate."

Clutch and Frank followed three strides behind. Clutch glared at Frank who didn't seem the least out of breath. "You run pretty fast for a dentist."

Ferret grunted. He didn't want to talk to Clutch. *Clutch has never had to run for his life*, Frank thought.

Clutch persisted. "What did Debbie say to you when she kissed you?"

Frank wrinkled his nose. "She said, 'Bugger off!'"

* * *

Rose lightly bit Frank's ear while they waited for the bus to load. "Are you sure she's the long-lost daughter?"

"'Fraid so. It's a damn shame. Great gal like that. See how swift Clutch and Willie scoot out of here when they discover she's the daughter of a demon."

"That's one of the few things you're right about," Rose agreed. "Deb's real father would be a career breaker for persons in the public eye like Willie and Clutch." She paused. "That includes you too, sport, when you crawl out from under that beard. Then again, whenever did you care what people thought about you?"

"I care about what you think about me, Rose. I really do." He kissed her neck.

Rose looked at the sky thoughtfully and punched his hard stomach. "Scum, Frank. You're slimy, sour pond scum. I'd be in real trouble if I was in love with you."

*   *   *

QUEENSTOWN, NEW ZEALAND

The morning activity couldn't have been better to look for clues on the identity of the Butcher, as the trampers were introduced to skeet shooting from the end of a dock. "With Bymarovitch's ego, he won't be able to resist showing off," Frank surmised.

"Yeah, right, just like Robin Hood winning the archery contest?" Rose replied skeptically. "Except if he's as smart as you say, he'll purposely do poorly."

Most, but not all, of the women trampers stayed back with the children, holding their ears, while Debbie manned the thrower and instructed.

Stanley said, "I've shot a rifle before, but never at these bloody clay pigeons."

Turner claimed, "I've only tried trap shooting once before."

Given their limited experience in trap shooting, the two Englishmen shot moderately well, but not at the level of persons with a lifetime in the military. Goodman and Lafate hit a couple clay pigeons after a few tries—definitely nothing to brag about. Tinsley and Borolo looked awkward and laughingly missed all but one of their shots. Frank held the shotgun like a frozen snake, missed all the clays by a wide margin, and looked glum because his Robin Hoods weren't performing as expected.

Among the other trampers, Clutch and Rose led everyone with only one missed throw, followed by Gil with two misses. Willie hit two clays, an acknowledged accomplishment for a person with no previous experience.

"Is our instructor going to take a turn?" Gil asked Debbie.

Debbie shook her head and whispered with grin, "It's not polite to show up my guests. Although I'd love to show Clutch how it's done."

*   *   *

The afternoon free time found most of the wives dragging their husbands to the outdoor crafts show by the lake. Debbie led a dozen trampers to a lush golf course for a quick nine holes. Frank attached himself to the golfing Englishmen, hoping to spot telltale, aggressive behavior in the sand traps. Clutch, Willie, Gil, and Debbie made a foursome.

Willie twirled his driver. "Let's make it interesting. One thousand a hole—just for the men, of course." Willie's bet painfully pointed out the income disparity between himself and Gil. He also had enough confidence in his game to show up Clutch. Techies, as he preferred to be called, could be accomplished athletes too.

Gil laughed at the bet. "Outta my league, Willie. How about $5 a hole?"

Willie sniffed in disgust. "Better yet, winner gets to buy Debbie lunch."

"Sounds good to me," Clutch agreed confidently.

Gil quickly stated, "How Debbie spends her time and attention is up to her—not a bet."

Debbie bristled, "Damn right! Why don't you two dolts just fight a duel over me? I'll supply the bloody shotguns."

Clutch apologized and led off with the first of five, long, tape measure blasts from the tee.

Willie took the lead on the seventh hole with masterful putting. He studied each putt like an astronomer charting the arc and velocity of a planetary body.

Gil parred the eighth hole to pass Willie.

Debbie chipped her ball over a stand of eucalyptus trees to birdie the ninth and win by two strokes. Sometimes a hostess must show up her guests.

*   *   *

Gil bought curried samosas at a fast food, takeaway shop, and Debbie and Gil found a shady spot to sit in the well-manicured park.

Gil said, "I'm really enjoying your company, but—"

"It can't go anywhere," Debbie finished his sentence. "I enjoy your company too, Gil. And I appreciate your candor. The last thing I need is falling in love again, only to have my heart stomped on."

"Do Clutch and Willie get a reprieve?"

Debbie paused, "I try not to think about it. No, that's not true. Clutch can be adorable. He's a year or two younger than me, and sometimes acts sophomoric. But as, Elizabeth says, 'He's trainable.'"

"Willie, on the other hand, is Willie. There's no changing him. He's the smartest person I've ever met, but his people skills with Virginia and others are just plain stupid. Yet . . . he's usually as sweet as he can be with me."

"Liz says, 'Billionaires don't come around every day,' but that would be an awfully cheeky reason to marry someone."

"Well, good luck. Whichever one you choose will be a very lucky guy."

Debbie playfully planted a kiss on Gil's cheek. "But he might not be my first choice."

* * *

Martin imitated Amy's spinning kick. "Don't kick high," she instructed. Someone will grab your leg. Go for their foot or knee."

"I wish I could take lessons," he complained. "My mom thinks I'll get hurt or hurt someone. But my dad thinks I need it to protect myself."

Amy nodded. "So does my dad. He teaches me t'ai chi. It's fun. But you can use it if someone grabs you."

"No one's ever grabbed me," Martin grumbled.

"Me too," Amy said.

"You got a nice dad."

Amy smiled. "So do you. You're mom's nice too."

Martin looked as stone-faced as he could. "They didn't tell me, but they're gonna get a divorce. They took this trip to fall in love again, but all they do is argue."

Amy nodded sympathetically. "Lot's of my friends have parents who are divorced. They don't like it much. But it's not as bad as when your mom's dead."

"Your mom's dead? How'd she die?"

"Dad doesn't want to talk about it. But I heard at school. She was murdered."

* * *

As the bus swept by another dry riverbed bordered with the palettes of wild multicolored lupine, the trampers settled in for the long, slow two-lane-highway ride. Golden broom blanketed the rolling hills. Among the flowering hills and verdant pastures black-faced sheep and penned deer passed by. An unbroken line of pointed snow-streaked geologically young mountains stabbed into a crisp cerulean sky. After two hours on a bus, even the nonstop display of beautiful scenery begins to wear on a traveler. That's where a bubbly tour director comes to play.

Debbie had become a master of her craft her first year on the job. Now, six years later, Debbie had the assurance to spontaneously improvise almost anything she wanted; and she did.

The adults related to the children well, so Debbie played to the kids. She knew how her trampers' eyes glazed over with names and statistics and acted accordingly. "This mountain is Martin Mountain. It's higher than a beanstalk. And this lake is Amy Lake."

While the kids giggled, the trampers followed their highlighted maps, knowing that from now on, every river, dam, waterfall, and glacier would have one of the children's names attached to it.

"The glacial 'metal' floating in the water adds to the reflectivity of the lake. It used to be called Mirror Lake—a magic mirror."

Debbie bounded down the aisle and stroked her hand on Clutch's cheek. "Mirror, mirror in the lake, find me a husband for heaven's sake."

"And the mirror answers, 'Debbie, Debbie on the bus, can I help it if you've been dating a *wuss*?'"

Frank watched the trampers laughing at Clutch turn red. A Croatian might not know the Yiddish term for *wuss*. Yet *all* of the trampers laughed at Clutch's expense—except Clutch.

Debbie brought out her guitar to give a lesson on the devastating effect of rabbits on New Zealand's farmers and the unusual, but futile, biological means taken to stop them. She sang, "Two little bunnies went round and round / Now dozens of bunnies abound, abound / Dozens of bunnies abound."

Venus Klaus growled, "I didn't spend all this money for an infantile sing-along."

Undaunted, Debbie worked the chorus of trampers to "millions of bunnies" before slowing to a low minor key. Debbie rapped about the farmer's plight. "The brussels sprouts are all gone, all gone / The brussels sprouts are all gone." Debbie stopped to explain how the desperate farmers released a rabbit-specific "virus in the lettuce . . . to rid us of the critters."

The trampers leaned forward to watch the worried wide-eyed reaction of the children.

Debbie started again, slowly and sadly. "All of the bunnies ate and ate, all of the bunnies got sick / A million sick bunnies spun round and round / A million sick bunnies went round." Debbie twirled and sat down as if dizzy. Her sweet voice turned more somber. "When the farmers woke up, they looked up and down, the farmers looked all around / And guess what they saw!" Debbie brightened as she directed the trampers to join the chorus. "A billion new bunnies going round and round . . . / A billion new bunnies abound!"

Amy sat up in her seat in the front of the bus, leaned back to where Gil was sitting, and whispered to her father, "I love Debbie, Daddy."

Gil smiled at his daughter and stared at Debbie's curvy figure, which always seemed to be in motion. "So do all of us, Amy."

*   *   *

Clutch's frustration grew with every glimpse of Debbie laughing with Gil and Amy. *How do you compete with a cute seven-year-old?* When Gil and Amy and the rest of the trampers weren't monopolizing Debbie's attention, Willie was instructing Debbie in more than she needed to know about business software. And the damned dentist was never far away, asking questions and chattering like a prairie dog.

When Debbie headed for her hotel room with Elizabeth, Clutch waited outside her door. "Liz, will ya let me talk to Deb, alone?"

Elizabeth smirked and muttered something about rotating the tires on the bus.

Debbie opened her hotel room door. She didn't want to be seen talking to Clutch in the hall, so she left the door open for him to follow. "I apologize for embarrassing you in front of the other trampers."

"I'm glad you're sorry. Frank told me what a *wuss* was. Or at least, he tried to."

"I didn't say I was sorry. I said I apologize. You deserve worse, actually, but I lowered myself to embarrass you, and for that I'm ashamed of myself."

"I didn't come here for an apology. You're right. I deserve worse. I just want to talk."

"Say your piece," Debbie said flatly, looking at her watch.

"Debbie, I haven't had a chance. Everyone's talkin' to ya, but me. I love ya, Deb. I came halfway round the world to marry ya. I've been thinkin' 'bout ya ever since we met."

"I'm sure you had a few distractions to take your mind off me."

"Distractions?"

"Chicks, Clutch. That's what women are to you, Clutch. Just chicks to collect in a pen. We all look alike. We get to share the rooster. Then we have our heads chopped off."

Clutch looked pained. "Ah, Deb, you can't imagine how it is to be a pro ballplayer. The women are like a field of wheat in front of a combine. You're bound to run into some of 'em."

"And you bailed up your share while I waited for a ticket in the mail."

"Damn, I'm sorry, Deb. But there was spring trainin', and then the season started. I was fighting for my spot in the lineup. If I'd have ended up back in the minors, I could never afford a family. But I kept thinkin' of you, Deb. I never forgot what we did the last night of the tour. I worked hard. I took extra batting practice when the other guys were sleeping in. I kept saying to myself that at my age this is my last chance at the big time—my last chance to deserve Deb. I had a great season, all because of you." Clutch pulled Debbie into his arms, kissed her, and pressed his body against hers.

Debbie couldn't help but think of their night together. On that night, she thought it was the beginning of a new life with Clutch. She had been ecstatically happy, only to end up feeling used and stupid. The ecstatic part resurfaced, but she tried not to show Clutch. She kept her arms at her side while he held the kiss and caressed her breasts.

"Are you done mauling me, Clutch? And as for that last night together, you said, *what we did?* I'm sorry, Clutch. I must've forgotten. Was it anything important?"

"Deb, it's not like ya to be so grumpy. Ya know lovin' don't get any better than what we had that night."

"What a pity for you," Debbie said with mock sympathy.

Clutch shuffled like he did when hurrying back into the batter's box after being brushed back by a bean ball. "You can't look me in the eye and say that Willie is a better lover than I am."

"Willie doesn't have to be," Debbie snapped. "I'm good enough for the both of us."

Clutch mounted another argument, but Debbie cut him off. "You studs think that if you have physique and endurance, that's all that counts. Well, I have news for you! Foreplay starts long before petting. It starts with a smile, a conversation—a real honest conversation—*caring*, and maybe a pat on the back or a caress. It's *looking forward* to holding and being held. That's the biggest part of lovemaking, Clutch. I thought we had it. But we lost it."

Clutch scowled. This conversation had not gone well. "I suppose you're *lookin' forward* to teamin' up with Rocklin."

Debbie glared at Clutch. "I suppose I would. As a matter of fact, I wouldn't mind teaming up with Gil. But I'm not going to make the same mistake again.

"So goodnight, Clutch. If you want a refund on the rest of the trip, I'll arrange it."

"Don't bother, Deb. I run out grounders. I don't give up that easy. I still think you'll pick the best man for you."

"Maybe I already have, Clutch. Maybe I already have."

Debbie walked Clutch to the lobby. She'd have to tell Elizabeth that she wouldn't have to sleep on the bus. Gil was leaving the lobby gift shop with two boxes of orange-mango juice. He saw Clutch and Debbie together and smiled.

Oh God! He's gonna think I'm bonging Clutch, Debbie fretted to herself. Debbie swung into Gil's hallway.

"Wait up, Gil. There's something I've been wanting to thank you for." Debbie put her arms around Gil and gave him a tight squeeze and a kiss on the lips. She had no fear of Gil. *Gil would never hurt me.* His body felt like Clutch's, but not as tense. Gil was sure of his every move. Except now, he was hesitating.

Gil smelled Debbie's freshly washed hair and felt the firmness of her arms and the softness of her body. He politely returned her squeeze and backed away.

"Well, thank you back, Debbie! What did I do to deserve such appreciation? Tell me, so I can do it again."

Debbie couldn't think of anything to say. "Ah, thanks for not trying to hit on me."

Gil laughed. "Another thank-you kiss like that one and I might spoil my record as a gentleman. But I can see your dilemma. The beaus are coming at you from all sides, aren't they?"

Debbie felt she had to explain. "I'm *not* sleeping with Clutch." Then she blushed over having excused herself for something that wasn't Gil's concern.

"Pity the poor ballplayer," Gil said. "They have a saying about ballplayers when they're taken out of a game. They call it being sent to the showers."

Debbie tried to ignore the churning that was going on inside her body. "Yep, showers. Cold showers."

* * *

As the trampers waited to board the bus, Rose asked Frank, "Who are you looking at now?" She leaned next to him so as not to be heard. The women trampers considered her the other kind of tramp and seemed to avoid her, so Rose purposely flaunted her flirtation with Frank. She particularly enjoyed the disapproving looks of Venus Klaus.

Frank nodded toward the Englishmen gathered behind the bus at the rest stop. "Ratac was a chain smoker. I'm looking for one of the Englishmen who smokes."

"But none of them are smoking," Rose noted, pawing at Frank's neck. "In fact, there's hardly any smokers on the tour—only the Chinese couple and a few of the women. Anyway, if I was a known chain-smoker trying to hide my identity, I might try to quit."

"Easier said than done," Frank replied.

"I suppose you want me to kiss each one to sniff out which one snuck a cigarette."

Frank waited too long to shake his head.

"Go to hell." Rose laughed. "You can do the kissing."

* * *

Gil and Amy and the King family shared the supper table and talked about the day's parasailing adventure, in which half the adults had participated.

Frank table hopped and offered to share an older vintage Beaujolais with the Lafates. "Here, folks, taste this. Somethin' special. Twelve years old."

The Frenchman quickly corrected him. "Dr. Whistle, thank you for your gracious offer, but begging your pardon—Beaujolais must be drunk young."

Right answer. Frank sighed. He checked the tramper's cocktails for vodka and brandy, Ratac's favorite drinks, but tequila and gin drinks seemed to prevail among all his male suspects and their wives.

Frank thought of humming a Croatian tune to see if any of the Englishmen would join in, but that could give him away as well. In desperation, Frank turned the conversation to British football or soccer. Stanley took the bait and began a heated discussion with Goodman.

Borolo joined in from two tables away. "None of your teams could beat our national girls' team."

Debbie thought a fistfight might break out—another reason to dislike Dr. Whistle.

For the first time, Frank began to doubt that Ratac was among the trampers. *What if he's signed up for the next tour? What if he's not on any tour at all?*

Debbie bounded from table to table. Gil thought she danced as she moved and couldn't move his gaze away from her.

Debbie spun to his table last. "Trampers, if anyone needs me, I'll be at the motel across the street. Seems that a member of our rival tour group went into labor, and I've been called upon to midwife until the doctor arrives."

"Midwife?" the adults exclaimed together.

Debbie laughed. "One of the many things you learn when you live in the middle of nowhere. My mum is a midwife, and she taught me."

George stated, "As a policeman, I've been trained for such emergencies. I'll help. Eve's liability insurance won't—"

Eve interrupted, "I'll be right with you, Deb. George has training, but he's never had occasion to use it."

"Thanks to you both, but no need. The baby's almost full-term, and if the doc doesn't show, this will be my third delivery. I'm looking forward to it. It's quite a rush, actually."

Debbie scooted away, and trampers stared at one another. "What an amazing young lady!" Eve finally said.

Gil didn't know what to say. *Amazing* didn't do Debbie justice.

*　　*　　*

On the bus rides between attractions, on the horseback riding, and on the hot air balloon ride, Debbie never stopped talking. But she was a good listener too. Gil couldn't remember when he had such a lighthearted, interesting conversation. Debbie continued to grow on Gil, and he felt guilty for the way she positively responded. He imagined holding Debbie in his arms, and the tingle wouldn't go away.

Gil missed sex. It took a long time after his wife's death before he would even consider dating. The parents without partners group at his church provided his first venture at dating, and it was a disaster. The first lady he took out could only talk about what a louse her first husband was. One date and out.

Gil's second try at dating was an oncology nurse who insisted on knowing how his wife died. She was clearly uncomfortable with Gil's answers. Gil decided to put parts of his life in a locked box, but too many people had read about the events surrounding his wife's murder to keep it a secret.

Then there was Rhonda. Rhonda was glamorous. Rhonda owned a small chain of art galleries. It seemed like a good match: two single parents with the same artistic interests. Best of all, Rhonda liked sex. She liked it in the car, on the couch, and in her kitchen—and that was on the first date. If Rhonda hadn't come prepared, Gil could've found himself fathering a child with a woman he didn't love. Gil wanted to love her, but on the second date, Rhonda met Amy. Rhonda dripped with saccharine sweetness. Amy acted politely, but didn't respond in her usual way. *Kids know*, Gil told himself. Rhonda's relationship with her son put the final frosting on the fritter, as the fake dentist would phrase it. Rhonda's boy appeared sullen and distant—the mother-son relationship seemed formal.

Breaking off the two-date relationship proved painful for Gil. He didn't want to hurt Rhonda, but he did. Rhonda responded with a venomous temper that reaffirmed that their coupling wouldn't have been a wise choice. Gil vowed that his next relationship would go much slower. Debbie fell into the *go slow* category, yet the more Gil saw of Debbie, the more appealing she became. *It sure would be nice to hold Debbie in my arms again.*

*　　*　　*

At the lunch stop, Frank was the last one to leave the rest room and late to board the bus. "Sorry," he said to Debbie, whose perpetual smile hid mild disapproval.

"What took you so long?" Rose asked, hugging him like a long-lost lover.

"On the ground," Frank whispered, "where the nonsmoking men were gathered—" Frank opened a tissue with a still, warm, moist half of a cigarette butt.

"D-N-A," Rose mouthed slowly.

"But from whom?"

*　　*　　*

A New Zealand rainforest is an eerie world of deep emerald green. Huge tree ferns give the shadowy moss-covered paths a primeval look that seems to vibrate. A few russet skeletons of dead pines reach twiggy fingers trying to snag a visitor's clothing or scratch their arms, but they're passed unnoticed among the living flora. When sunlight spears through the towering conifers, the leaves of the lower plants glow like stained glass. Birds call in unfamiliar melodies, and trampers breathe humid air, alive with the smell of ozone and chlorophyll.

Every tramper froze when they heard the snorting.

The wild boars exploded from the underbrush and sped toward Debbie, who headed up the hikers' column. Debbie giggled as she put a tree between her and the pigs. She shouted, "Find a tree to climb, trampers. Boars have the right of way."

Not everyone sought a tree. Frank amplified the warning. He had seen Colombian villagers killed by animals just like these. "Pigs don't pose for pictures, people!"

Wild boars should have caused panic and fear among the trampers, but Debbie's laughing made climbing a pine tree in a temperate rainforest seem a lark. The lower branches of the pines, nearly bare from lack of sun, made a natural ladder on many of the trees. After helping some of the older trampers mount a tree, Gil joined Debbie and Amy in a moss-covered pine. "Not so high, Amy! You don't have a spotter," Gil warned as Amy showed off her monkey bar skills.

The six peccaries moved remarkably fast, moving in circles around the smaller tree ferns. They looked nothing like lethargic barnyard pigs. These beasts were fury on the hoof.

Willie hissed from a nearby tree where he and Virginia perched on the first high branch, "Shouldn't we endeavor to make noise and scare them away?"

"Try, Willie," Debbie advised.

Willie bellowed at the boar. "Depart from here, you ill-mannered pork chop!"

The large boar responded by ramming Willie and Virginia's tree. Virginia roared with laughter.

"Keep it up, Willie," Frank shouted. "Maybe he'll knock himself out."

"I do believe our tree is tilting, Virginia," Willie stated in a rare display of his dry sense of humor that Debbie had found so engaging on their first meeting.

The laughter stopped when Venus Klaus lost her grip on the slippery moss-covered branch. She fell and tried to scramble to her feet, but slipped on the spongy wet ground. The boar noticed the intrusion and snorted in Venus's direction.

Gil sailed off the tree as he might have dismounted from parallel bars. Clutch and Frank followed. George, the furthest away, also hit the ground and waved a stick. The large boar swung his huge head between Clutch and

Gil. Frank hollered, "Oink, oink!" causing the boar to hesitate, but only for a moment. The boar charged Gil, the closest. The trampers screamed. The animal's menacing tusks aimed at Gil like guided missiles. A half second from impact, Gil leaped for a branch and pulled himself over and around the branch in a gymnastic move. Amy watched her dad's move and duplicated it from her high perch. Clutch helped Mrs. Klaus to her feet, and her husband pulled her back into the tree with fear-inspired strength.

"People one. Pigs nothin'!" Frank announced the score from back in his tree. The trampers cheered. Their laughter resumed.

After several minutes, the boars lost interest in terrorizing the trampers and moved thirty yards away. Debbie announced, "We'll waive the surcharge for this vertical side trip. I do advise you to stay put for a few more minutes."

Debbie launched into observations on Maori myths regarding the sacredness of trees. "No myths on pigs, actually. Pigs were brought in by Europeans."

"Strange beliefs," Willie remarked.

"No stranger than many of ours, Dern," Frank chirped from his tree. "Just what *do* we believe, anyway? Not our religious poetry. Not the heaven and hell stuff. That's only the backdrop for our act. The stage directions are what we believe—how we improvise on the stage of life. We can all mouth the same lines, but our beliefs make all the difference."

"You're too deep for me," Clutch grumbled.

"No, I'm not," Frank countered. "You have a belief or set of values that govern your life. Your rule book, Clutch!"

"Ya mean like teammates and winning?"

"There ya go," Frank beamed. He was determined to get one of the suspects in an argument. Frank couldn't tell what slip would give Bymarovitch away, but he'd try anything to tease him out.

"I believe in *holding on!*" Mrs. Klaus laughed nervously.

George said, "I believe in a world of law—with justice."

Rose piped, "As a lawyer, I'll second that, and add *passion*."

The trampers hooted. "Lucky, Frank!"

Rose waited for the laughter to subside before amending, "Frank does too, but not with each other."

A chorus of sad *ahhs* echoed through the forest.

Virginia said, "I believe in security and power—power to do good."

"Friends and family," Debbie contributed.

"Hard work," Tinsley shouted, "and the rewards that come with it!"

"Freedom," the Ethiopian tourist inserted.

Willie sniffed, "I don't know what I believe, except I don't believe in anything I can't count."

"I believe in vintage years," Lafate stated holding an imaginary glass.

"So does my husband, Mrs. Stanley inserted. "I only wish he had a few more in him."

Willie threw a taunt at Gil. "You've been quiet, Rocklin. What do you believe in? A man with your history of violence must have *violence* as one of your guiding beliefs." The prosecutor's edge to Willie's voice conveyed more seriousness than his words.

The forest fell silent except for an angry bird and the distant squealing of the wild pigs. Gil waited a few seconds before answering. "What Mr. Dern is referring to, but is too polite to mention aloud, is that I was involved in a . . . ." Gil looked at Amy making monkey faces at Martin. "Involved in a homicide."

Willie smirked. "Well, your fellow travelers all hope that killing is not your number one belief."

All eyes turned back toward Gil, sitting with his arm around Debbie on a branch. Gil scratched his forehead. Gil started to feel a sense of relief. He hadn't wanted to keep secrets from Debbie. Her affection for Gil wasn't a sham. *Everything about Debbie is sincere. She likes me, and she could be hurt or afraid. Better that she knows now. When the trip ends, Debbie can look back and shudder.*

As for Willie's challenge, Gil would not be provoked. "Sorry to disappoint you, Willie, but I value control over violence. But if I change my mind, you'll be the first to know," he added with a grin.

Gil's soft, deep voice resonated slowly through the forest. "No, I'd go along with the beliefs that were mentioned, and add one more—*enduring love*. Love gives direction to freedom and purpose to hard work. It gives meaning to passion. Love keeps you holding on when your world falls out from under you, and grief makes you want to shoot your brains out. Love grows faster than you can count it."

The women in the forest took a collective deep breath, while the men fidgeted. Debbie rewarded Gil with a kiss, to Amy's delight.

"Aren't you concerned over my violent past?" he whispered.

"Whoever you killed either was the result of an accident, or he had it coming."

"Nobody has it coming. I don't believe in capital punishment."

"And you don't believe in talking about it. I'll respect that."

Gil kissed Debbie back.

Frank called to Willie. "Hey, Dern! Aren't ya glad you brought up the subject?"

CHAPTER 7

Smooth Talking

Venus Klaus leaned on her walking stick and scowled at the turquoise-streaked ice at the base of the Tasman Glacier and at the world in general. "Ms. McWard, why did you insist on us wearing shorts to scale a glacier? Do you want us all to catch pneumonia?"

Debbie tried not to focus on Mrs. Goodman's stubby, bare legs. "The glacier is melting, Mrs. Klaus. We're going to get wet. The water evaporates off our skin, but long slacks stay wet all day. And besides, I love the orange color of your Bermudas."

"Really? I thought they were too bright." Having had the last word, Venus wobbled away toward the rocky moraine leading to the base to the glacier.

Debbie scampered ahead to lead the trampers over a shallow stream of icy melt-off. Rose followed with a video camera, recording the fellow trampers stepping across the steam. She would add these photos to Frank's rogue gallery of tramper's photos. They just didn't know which one was the rogue.

Debbie stood with Rose, waiting for the last tramper to forge the wet spot. "Rose, is the shared room arrangement working out? If not, I can put you back into a single supplement."

"Don't do me any favors, Debbie." Rose laughed. "I'm very satisfied sleeping with Dr. Whistle."

"E-kay. Just thought I'd ask."

"Thanks anyway. You don't like Frank very much, do you?"

"I don't know why you'd think that. Frank livens things up."

"That's not what I mean, and I think you know what I mean," Rose said with a chuckle that seemed sad, not hostile.

"Ah, Frank's a little too hyper for my taste. I'm hyper enough."

Rose chuckled. "Just as well. I don't need the competition. Frank thinks you're the 'neatest thing since spoon bread.' He *does* come on strong. But it's an act. He's really very sweet, and I love him very much."

"If you say so," Debbie said. She hesitated, then grinned and asked, "Is something permanent developing here? If so, let me in on your secret."

Rose scowled. He voice turned soft and sober. "Frank and I have been friends and off-and-on lovers for years. He doesn't know it, but I'm going back to Germany to marry a very, very rich Frankfort industrialist. I'll give up my legal career to entertain his boring friends and find creative ways of spending his money. I'll be comfortable beyond my wildest dreams." Her voice broke. "And I'd chuck it all for six months married to Frank, before he leaves me or gets himself killed."

Rose's candor embarrassed Debbie. Debbie was accustomed to her friends and trampers dumping their troubles on her. Debbie was easy to talk to, but Rose had never sought her out before. *Is Rose telling me this so I'll stay away from Frank, or is this a woman who's losing it? And 'getting himself killed?'* Rose had always been outspoken, but now, why so overdramatic? *Rose is losing it, and it's all that bastard Whistle's fault.*

Debbie patted Rose's arm. "Well, Rose, it seems you know what you want. Go after it."

She gave a weak laugh. "After what? After who?"

* * *

After a morning pushing their bodies up the gentle, scenic slope of a glacier, nothing feels better than a hot tub or the warmed waters of an indoor swimming pool. Gil and Amy had joined Frank and the French and Italian couples in a helicopter trip near the top of Mount Cook for some spring skiing. The Englishmen had begged off saying they didn't know how to ski. Frank seemed more disappointed in their not skiing than they were. Yugoslavians skied.

Now Gil sat at the edge of the pool, his eyes never leaving Amy, in spite of some long-legged, bikini-clad ladies cavorting in the pool. Amy swam well, and it pleased Gil.

"Aren't you swimming?" Virginia asked as she sat next to him, and Gil momentarily lost his focus. Virginia' figure definitely demanded attention.

"Just being an overprotective father," Gil replied.

"Amy looks part dolphin to me. You're doing a great job with her."

"Thank you."

"I'm a single parent too," Virginia announced. "My mother helps, or I don't know how I would cope—certainly not working in a job that requires this much time and travel."

"That's why I chose to work at home," Gil said.

Virginia splashed water with her shapely legs, and Gil fought not to stare. "This is one of the few times I've seen you without the Kiwi," Virginia noted.

"She's making arrangements for the next stop."

"Are you going to turn the mighty Willie Dern into a loser?"

Gil laughed. "No, I'm just enjoying the company of a personable young lady. If Willie or Clutch loses the Kiwi, it's due to their bumbling, not anything I do. And it'll be because three-week romances aren't supposed to last. Debbie's a bit wiser now, so her suitors will have to polish up their acts before they regain their luster."

"So you and the Kiwi are doomed to lives exchanging Christmas cards?"

"You're spoiling my fun with a dose of reality," Gil chuckled.

"Do you know the way to San Jose?" Virginia sang softly. "I mean do you ever get to the San Francisco or San Jose area?"

"Only to pitch my software to your company, but you know that."

"Yes, and I think it's hilarious that Willie's company is financing his rival."

"I'm sure Willie knows?"

"No, he doesn't." Virginia chortled. "He seldom bothers with contracts under seven figures. And I certainly won't tell him. But he doesn't completely trust me. He's been doing his own research on you. Willie was upset when he found out you had a doctorate in computer science—an achievement he could never master.

"And I know you've been through the ringer, mister. To a lesser degree, so have I. We're survivors, you and I. I slid my card under your door. If you want to have dinner next time you're in San Jose, I won't be working for Willie by then. Three-week time constraints won't be a problem."

Gil gave Virginia a full appraisal: beautiful, sexy, pleasant, and competent—certainly a step up over his recent dates in Denver. "Ah, Debbie's such a wonderful gal, and she feels betrayed by her suitors, so if I were to suddenly switch my attention—"

"Don't worry, big guy. Have fun with your Kiwi. I wouldn't want to see her embarrassed, either. Your time spent with her is worth it, if it makes Willie suffer. Now, Clutch Cooper, I can see, but God help your Kiwi if she ends up with Willie Dern."

*   *   *

Frank had signed up for the optional helicopter ride to the top of the Tasman glacier, hoping his Serbo-Croatian general, having lived in a mountainous country where skiing was a way of life, couldn't resist such an impressive skiing opportunity. If the Brits included the Butcher, none of them was willing to display his skiing skills. None of them signed on. Frank ended up skiing with the Borolos, who didn't live far from the Alps, so that didn't prove anything. Frank knew he was focusing on minutia, but as least the skiing was spectacular.

Frank finally got his chance to see the quiet wives of his suspects in action on a long bus ride. Mme. Lafate heard Amy say *Merci*.

"Amy, *enfant cheri*, let me teach you a few words in French."

Not to be outdone, Maria Borolo switched seats to be next to Martin. "Ciao, Martin. Would you like to learn some Italian?"

By the time Mrs. Yung jumped in with Chinese lessons, the children suddenly found more pressing things to do.

Frank watched the women interacting with the children and decided to focus on the British wives. "Have any pictures of your kids?"

The three Brits, Mrs. Amelia Stanley, Mrs. Ruth Goodman, and Mrs. Paula Turner each took turns produced pictures, albeit without the gusto of most parents. Mrs. Turner didn't hide her suspiciousness of the pushy dentist. Frank wouldn't disappoint.

"Nice looking boy, but have you thought of an appliance—braces?" Frank beamed.

"My son is twenty," Paula Turner answered Frank coldly, as she replaced the years-old photograph to her wallet. "If he hasn't bloody had them by now, he never will," she snapped.

Frank noted that the children's photos of the Goodman and Turner children resembled their mothers more than their fathers in appearance, but a case *could* be made for a resemblance. Amelia Stanley clarified that "my two children are from my first marriage."

Rose cornered Frank at the edge of a photo stop, where he was feeding the scavenger Kea parrots. "Hi, honey," Frank said without looking up. He handed her some peanuts. "What color are these parrots? Gray, tan, some green? Like camouflage, don't you think? They kinda blend in. How do you tell them apart? The birds seem friendly, yet they're called feathered wolves. They can kill sheep."

Rose put her arm around Frank. She hadn't seen him depressed before. "Well, what did you learn?" she asked.

"What did I learn? I learned that finding the Butcher is gonna be a harder than a day ol' beignet. Can't rule anyone in, for sure, and can't rule anyone out. These people have done their homework. They've thought of everything to blend in. If one of these women is an actress, she's damn good."

"But sooner or later, one of these babes will slip," Rose stated confidently.

"And we'll be ready," Frank said, trying to mirror Rose's confidence.

"Will we?" Rose said.

*   *   *

Debbie had selected modest to plush hotels and dinner spots that had dance floors. One with a weekend band, several with jukeboxes, and short of that, she had a CD player. Small or nonexistent dance floors didn't faze her; she had the tables moved as soon as dessert dishes were cleared.

"Wallflowers are not an option," she declared with the authority of an Apollo Mission commander. Debbie coaxed the tired trampers into more activity on the dance floors, only resting for sing-alongs. For Latin moves and line dancing, she recruited Gil, now her steady partner, to help instruct the steps.

During a drink break, Frank produced a harmonica and played a polka. Folks from the Balkans can't resist polkas, he figured. The Stanleys and the Chinese couple took him up, although their dancing didn't qualify for any prizes.

At the break, Gil had to excuse himself to tuck Amy in bed. Clutch immediately came to Debbie's side. He'd help her instruct the others on polkas. The dancing instructor partnership with Debbie had been his prize months earlier, and this time she didn't push him away.

Virginia had danced with Willie, but Willie left to decipher his precious computer disk. Joseph Tinsley quickly seized the opportunity to put his arm around Virginia before she could retire as well. To leave now would be rude. The polkas went well, but when the slow dancing began, Tinsley was far too close for first time social dancing.

"We're both single," Tinsley noted. "It's a shame for a pretty sheila like you to waste this trip sleeping alone."

"It'll have to be a shame then," Virginia snapped, not sure if she could pull away from the strong man.

Clutch saw her plight and said, "Partner switch?"

Debbie caught on and snatched Tinsley away from Virginia. Her strong arms made sure Tinsley stayed three inches away until she could switch the CD player to a fast number that Tinsley had no hope of dancing. He left, scowling.

The next number was slow, and Virginia didn't mind Clutch's closeness. "That was nice of you to leave your true love to rescue me," she purred.

She expected Clutch to say, "Aw shucks," but he said, "Ginnie, a classy lady like you shouldn't have to put up with the likes of a Tinsley, or Willie either, for that matter."

Virginia felt a warm feeling for the first time on the trip and gave Clutch a quick kiss on the lips. "You're all right, Mr. Cooper."

* * *

On the following evening, the dancing ended early, but the night wasn't over for Debbie. The administrative work was as boring and as tedious as she had feared. Debbie entered the information in her red notebook and sighed. The paperwork wasn't hard, but it took time. *Reservations; payroll taxes; advertising approvals; bus maintenance schedules; customer satisfaction surveys; gas, hotel, and dinner bills to pay. Ugh!*

Willie saw his chance. "If you'll get your laptop, Debra, I'll show you how to cut out the duplication. Updates will take a fraction of the time."

Debbie hesitated. She had been purposely cool to Willie, but another offer of help didn't deserve a rude response. She nodded affirmatively, and Willie pulled his chair next to Debbie.

Debbie's claim of computer ignorance was quickly exposed as a postured rejection of everything Willie had given her. She knew more than she acknowledged, but still needed Willie's experienced nudge to efficiently handle the burdensome paperwork.

An hour later, Debbie finished another spreadsheet, and admitted, "This will work. Thank you, Willie."

"Can we talk?" Willie asked.

"Things that are unsaid have a perishable half-life, like cheese," Debbie muttered. "After a while, the words come out, but they just don't taste the same."

"Will you let me try?" Willie asked.

Debbie looked into the blank computer screen and nodded.

"I guess I am too late. Rocklin has taken my place."

"Gil and I will never hook up," Debbie said. "We like each other, but Gil's a realist and knows you can't make a life commitment after only a few days."

"I'm a realist too, Debra," Willie said softly. "I knew the odds were against us, and I didn't want either of us to jump into a mistake. But my mistake was not acting quickly to download you into my life. The longer I delay, the more I think of you and want to live out my life with you.

"People seem like frozen statues compared to the way you move. The most enthusiastic persons I know are pall bearers compared to you. I could listen to your laugh all day. To hell with Mozart and the sound of song birds, just to hear you laugh."

Debbie stroked Willie's hand. "Our time together was . . . nice, but I expected too much, and I didn't know what you expected. That was my mistake."

Willie squirmed. She was getting away. "Debra, I'm not the most popular person in the world. In business, I'm abrupt with people, and I have to be in order to win. But when I'm around you, I want to be kind, gentle, and generous—anything to make you happy. I like the way I act when I'm with you."

"You're saying all the right words, but the—"

"Debra, you said you loved me once, when you had no idea that I was a wealthy man."

"I don't judge people by how much—"

"I know you don't. And that's commendable. But in two years, I'll be the CEO of one of the world's top software companies. I'll be able to cash in my stock options and have more money than either of us can spend."

"So why have it?"

"Well, you have passionate feelings about the environment and the arts. You empathize with the poor. Think of the good you could do, of the good we could do together."

"I would have to love you, Willie."

"I know you would. All I ask is another chance."

Debbie sighed. She gave Willie a quick kiss on the cheek. "We'll see."

* * *

Debbie peeked into her room, not sure whether to call it a night or to make a room call. Debbie's roommate, Elizabeth, lay in bed watching an adult movie on television.

Elizabeth looked up and grinned. "Do you want me to leave so you can have the bloody room to yourself, or should I say *yourselves?*"

Debbie made a face. "I shall be perfectly chaste this trip and all other trips."

Elizabeth laughed. "You mean *chased* by the four best studs on the tour. Why don't you throw me some of your discards?"

Elizabeth combined plain features with the stocky build of a linebacker. Her spiky maroon-streaked hair was too punk for her age. Until a few months ago when Carp threatened to fire her, she had a fine gold ring through her nose. Carp even warned her against tattoos. "Too late, Mein Carpfer," she had screamed at him, "I already have a tulip on my breast. Want to see if it will meet with customer approval?"

Carp didn't like confronting angry women. They reminded him of his first wife, so he got off Elizabeth's back after that. Debbie had enough charm and femininity for the two of them.

Elizabeth knew that too. There was no way of competing with Debbie. But Elizabeth's lack of traditional glamour didn't stop her from having a tourist examine her tulip now and then.

Debbie made a grumbling sound. "How many times have I had to sleep on the bus so you could bong a tramper?"

"Not enough times, actually." Elizabeth snickered. "But *four* studs? *Really* Deb!"

"Where do you get four?"

"Dr. Toot-Your-Whistle, Clutch Me, Wise Willie, and Daddy Gil."

"You want one? Take one. Which one do you want?" Debbie smirked.

"I'll have to think about it. With Dr. Whistle, I'd get free dental care."

Debbie shook her head. "You don't need to bong him for that. Frank's looking into everyone's mouth for free. He's a walking, talking toothache, and while he's bonging Rose, he's trying to pump me for personal information and who knows what else."

"Well, then there's Mr. Good-in-the-Clutch," Elizabeth teased. "You said the sex with the handsome ballplayer was fantastic."

"I did? Maybe I did."

Elizabeth leaned forward, wide-eyed. "I wouldn't mind two hours a day being clutched by Clutch."

"Try four hours, but you have to come up for air sometime, then what? What do you talk about during the twelve hours that you're catching your breath? Baseball? I have nothing against American baseball, but that's all Clutch knows."

"And that's why you fell for Wise Willie? He talks?"

"Yes, Willie knows about everything, has an opinion on everything. He's definitely the smartest man I ever met. And now he's lathering up smooth talk to get back into my good graces."

"And tell me again why you dumped him?"

Debbie waited before answering. She thought of Willie's revelation of wealth and how unhappy Rose felt choosing her Frankfort billionaire over her love for Frank.

"I didn't dump Willie. He dumped me. He didn't sense how I felt about him, and where I thought the relationship should go."

Elizabeth nodded dolefully, "I get it! Willie's such a great talker, he doesn't bother listening."

"Remind me to set you up with Tinsley," Debbie groused.

Elizabeth's energy began to build. "That leaves Daddy Gil. What's his problem again?"

"No problem, actually. Gil's wise enough to know that these brief affairs can't develop into a relationship. He made that clear ten minutes after we met."

"Really? After ten minutes, Gil knew where you were coming from and was so bloody stupid as to tell you not to waste your time getting bonged. What a dumb, unmacho thing to do. Gil's not very smart. Probably not man enough for you. What does he do for a living? Draw children's stories?" Elizabeth pretended to draw in the air with her little finger extended. "And what lousy father takes his kid on his vacation, when the little tyke could've been left home to play with matches?"

"We spend time together, but it's all a pretense," Debbie said sourly.

Elizabeth looked for a reaction that didn't come. "Sure, I hear you three talking all day long. You . . . pretending to laugh at his jokes. Him . . . . pretending to hang on every word you say. Amy . . . pretending you're her fairy godmother. And all the time, the big guy's a wimp that doesn't know a good thing when he sees it."

"You're right, Liz," Debbie snapped. "Gil is a stupid wimp. Bad father. Lousy conversationalist. So you wouldn't want him either."

"I didn't say that." Elizabeth grinned.

"Yes, you did!" Debbie commanded. "I'll see you later."

Debbie left her room and checked her watch. *Amy should be asleep by now.* She knocked gingerly on Gil's door.

Gil answered the door quickly. To Debby's relief, Gil was still dressed.

"Hi, mate," Debbie bubbled. "Do you like your suite?"

"It's great! Thank you. Amy can sleep in peace, while I read or work on my laptop."

Debbie waved five photo envelopes. "Well, I'm here because you retired early and missed the grand showing of Dr. Whistle's photographs. He snaps everyone and everything."

They sat at the edge of the bed and thumbed through hundreds of snap shots. Gil laughed. "Frank has a knack for catching people off-guard. Very candid."

Debbie chuckled, "Of course, Mrs. Klaus complained he made her look fat."

"But the scenic shots are well composed," Gil noted. "Quite professional—even with that old camera he uses—because he *is* a professional." Gil stopped short of exposing the reporter he recognized.

On the dresser, Debbie spotted a bright felt pen drawing in an open notebook. "What's that?"

"Amy's journal. We never take a trip without Amy drawing her impressions. Plus it's in lieu of missing schoolwork. She knows how to scan it and upload it to her very own Web site. Take a look."

"They're charming! These drawings are sensational! Pink parachutes. Penguins. Mount Cook. Is this me?" Debbie blushed.

"'Fraid so. She thinks you're the greatest, and who's to argue with that. Amy's even imitating your accent."

Debbie flipped pages. Debbie didn't think she had much of an accent. *But why argue.* "More drawings of me. You and me holding hands. When Amy embarks on a campaign, she never lets up, does she?"

"I'm sorry. If Amy's getting to be a pest, I'll have another talk with her."

"Please don't. I mean . . . do what you want. I can't tell you how to raise your child. But she's such an angel. I won't want her to think that I wouldn't *want* to be her mommy. In fact, who wouldn't want to be her mommy?"

"All those who realize that I'm part of the package," Gil chuckled.

"You're a pretty nice package, Gil," Debbie said.

Gil stood up and squinted. "Did you come here to show me pictures or to get away from your suitors?"

Debbie tugged his arm to sit down. "My suitors are trying their best, and I'm not running from them anymore. I came here because I wanted to see you. You're an attractive man, Gil. Way up there on the nice guy charts. It's a damn shame we'll never really get to know each other."

"A damn shame."

Debbie put her arm around him. "How did you put it, Gil? People need to know each other in bad times as well as good. And you can't do that in a three-week vacation."

"Can't be done," Gil said hesitated before revealing his plan. "I've thought of coming back here to see you in your off-season, when there are fewer folks around, but you'd probably be working then too."

"I'm always working at something or another," she admitted.

Gil sighed. "And about the time I could afford to get back to the islands, you'd probably be an ol' married lady, saying, 'Gil who?'"

"That could happen, *or* I could wait—like I did for Clutch and Willie."

"A great gal like you should never have to wait . . . should never be hurt and disappointed."

Debbie stroked his muscular forearm. "We could make love, but knowing me, I'd expect promises."

"And I'd probably make 'em and keep 'em, Deb."

She squeezed him lightly. "It would be a relationship based solely on sex. Raw animal lust. Adolescent fascination from people who should be old enough to know better. But . . . it would never amount to anything. Never last."

Gil moved his face inches from Debbie's. "Never last."

They kissed each other gently, with a soft, savored embrace that wasn't meant to end anytime soon.

"Dad-dy," Amy's bell-like voice called. "I had a bad dream."

The kissers laughed.

Debbie leaped up. "Let me show off my maternal skills. I am the oldest of four."

Debbie tiptoed into Amy's room and gave the girl a hug. "Hi, punkin. What's the problem?"

"Bad dream," Amy whimpered.

"Well, then you have to have a *good* dream. What would make you happy?"

"Having a baby sister to take care of. But first, Daddy has to have a mommy. A mommy like the other kids. A mommy like you."

This family doesn't play fair, Debbie thought.

Debbie stroked Amy's hair. "I'd like to be your mommy, Amy. But I'd have to marry and live with your daddy forever. And your daddy and I don't know each other well enough for a *forever*."

"How do you get to know him?"

"Good question. Well . . . . we would have to talk. Talk a lot. For a long time. Alone. Without being interrupted."

"I won't in-ter-rupt."

Debbie kissed Amy and pulled her covers over her. "Dream about little sisters. Only good dreams come true."

Debbie tiptoed back to Gil and kissed him.

"Well, how did your maternal debut go?"

Debbie kissed him again. "We have to talk."

"Talk?"

Debbie started to unbutton Gil's shirt. "Hush up and talk."

*　*　*

A shaft of sunshine slipped through the sides of Gil's window. Debbie pulled the covers to her lower lip, looked at the ceiling, and swallowed hard. "This is the awkward part."

"It doesn't have to be," Gil murmured.

"Normally, my many escapades—really, Gil, only two—began on the last night of the tour. I say bon voyage, and think *call me, write me, send for me*. And I wait . . . wondering why did I do what I did? In your case, there's lots of tour days left."

"Are you wondering if you made a mistake?"

"Not last night. That was no mistake. It's the next two weeks I'm worried about."

Gil sat up. "*You're* worried. I'm afraid. Afraid to death."

"I can't imagine you being afraid of anything."

"I'm afraid of losing you, Deb. I'm afraid you might not fit into my suitcase."

Debbie paused thoughtfully before wrapping her arms around Gil. "Does that mean what it sounds like?"

"It means Amy and I want you to come back to the States with us. You can see our house. It's a four bedroom ranch with my office attached— very comfortable. We have a Steinway baby grand, a small swimming pool, and a workout room. I have to warn you that I'm a workaholic, but I'm also a halfway, decent cook. I'll give you a week to get used to my cooking then you have to marry me or swim back to New Zealand. Are you game?"

"I'm very game."

They kissed.

Amy crawled onto their bed and bounced trampoline-fashion. "Are you done talking yet?"

*   *   *

The cashier at the hotel checkout window said, "One minute, Mr. Rocklin. I believe we have an 'urgent' message for you to call your office."

Gil checked his watch and figured the time difference. Margarita would be making supper about now. Gil found the hotel pay phone and waited for the connection. His face paled then reddened as he heard the message.

He found Debbie supervising the loading of the luggage into the bus. He pulled her back into the hotel lobby.

"We have to talk."

"Here?" She giggled.

"Don't say anything to Amy."

"Why, Gil?"

"Debbie, something's happened. I think we'd better put the marriage thing on hold."

"Oh?"

"Just for a year. Maybe less."

Debbie fought tears. "I keep reliving the same bad dream."

"Bad news," Gil explained. "My business just lost our biggest contract. I'm stuck with a fortune in inventory. I borrowed on the house in anticipation of receivables, and now . . . I'll probably lose it. If I'm not bankrupt, I'm close to it."

"You'll start over? Maybe in something else?"

"It's what I do best. I can build the business up again. But this buyer is telling everyone that my software has viruses. It's not so, but the damage is done. I can change my business name and redo everything I'm selling, but it'll take time, and a lot of hundred-hour workweeks. I'd go home, right now, if I could afford the extra air fare."

Debbie swallowed. "I can help. I don't have much in savings, but I've always worked. I have a university degree. I don't have to be an underpaid tour director. There's lots of things I can do."

"I can't ask you to do that. I won't let you do that. But when I get back on my feet, and if you're still interested, we'll start over again."

"No, no, no, *I* just lost interest," Debbie said in a breaking voice. "Not because you've hit bottom, but because you won't let me help you back up again. How did you put it? Bad times as well as good? Well, we were lucky to sneak in a bad time. Now we won't make a mistake." Debbie ran from Gil in tears.

Frank slid up to Gil. "Have you checked your office?"

"Yeah."

"Sounds like you were somewhat screwed," Frank chuckled, holding a fax of a press release."

"You know a lot about my business, Dr. Whistle."

"I look for investments." Frank laughed. "Doesn't look like Rocklin Software will be listed on the NASDAQ anytime soon."

"I'm glad someone thinks its funny," Gil said bitterly.

"I was just thinking about how you're going to get even." Frank smirked. "Not that I believe in revenge. Revenge is overrated. But to have that weasel Willie blackball his rival is definitely a low ball."

Gil stiffened. He didn't want to believe it, but who else but Willie had the power to torpedo his business?

Frank read Gil's enlightened grimace. "Do you want me to tell Kiwi that her fiendish friend fouled you up?"

"The damn damage is done," Gil muttered. "I just lost the woman I love."

"I'll bet the Kiwi would break Willie's kneecaps if she knew," Frank said gleefully.

"She won't know. Am I supposed to tell her that Willie hits below the belt? And do I know that for a fact? What if I'm wrong? Then who's playing the dirty trick? And will telling Debbie change anything?"

Frank gave Gil a sympathetic punch to his shoulder that didn't quite land on the bigger man. "Been there. I can help you if you will help me."

Gil sighed. "Let me guess. You don't want me to tell anyone that you're Frank Ferret, investigative paparazzo."

Frank smiled. "The beard doesn't help?"

"Oh, it helps. But how often does an amateur take pictures that should be on magazine covers? You fall into your distinctive, alliterative prose now and then. And what dentist gives children Viennese chocolates and has a Glock pistol strapped to his leg?"

"Good, you have observation powers and a good ear. You keep my secret, and I'll keep yours."

Gil stiffened. "You know about me?"

Frank nodded. "I reported on the murders. The police said you broke the man's neck with one punch. That's the sort of resourcefulness that I require."

Gil turned. "Our conversation is over, Dr. Whistle."

"I need brawn to help me bring in a buzzard—a fugitive. You know firearms, I don't, and I don't want to. I could reach for this Glock and shoot myself in the foot."

"Could it be that you're in over your head?" Gil cautioned curtly.

"I'm always in over my head. But this time, there's a reward. I'll tender for twenty thousand dollars for only twenty, maybe thirty hours, of work."

"You want me to capture someone?"

"More like compassionate kidnapping. We drug him, put the buzzard on a Boeing and hand him over in The Hague."

Gil felt the effects of his bad morning, and he didn't try to hide his sarcasm. "If your buzzard is drugged, why do you need me?"

"Even buzzards have friends."

Gil shook his head. "You're even wilder than they say. Ferret, there is no way in hell that I'd help you with anything that could endanger me and my daughter. I put in my time as saving the nation from evil-doers, and my wife paid the price. Amy lost her mother, and she *won't* lose her father. I have too many responsibilities. Good luck on bringing in your fugitive."

Frank shrugged. "Thought I'd ask. I suppose policeman King will give me the same brush off."

Gil nodded affirmatively then hesitated. "Assuming your fugitive is on this tour . . . does he pose any danger to the rest of us?"

Frank wrinkled his nose. Debbie could be in danger, but maybe not. "I don't think so. First of all, I don't know which one of our travelin' companions is the buzzard. But when I figure it out and confront him, I promise not to stir things up when you or your cub are around."

"Thank you," Gil muttered. He boarded the bus and vowed not to speak with Frank Ferret, a.k.a. Dr. Frank Whistle, for the remainder of the trip. It was a promise that events would not allow him to keep.

CHAPTER 8

Motive for Murder

Amy sensed the coolness between her daddy and Debbie, so when the group gathered for dinner in the outdoor patio of the hotel, she pulled Gil to the long table where Debbie sat with Willie and Clutch. Frank Whistle had burrowed into the party and dominated the conversation to the annoyance of Willie and Clutch. Amy liked all three of the Debbie's suitors, especially Frank who always had a knock-knock joke for Martin and her. If she knew they were her dad's rivals, she might not have been so friendly.

Frank made a point of sitting across from Debbie. He reasoned, *Debbie has information and access to the trampers that might ID her father. Or her father might reveal himself to her. Would she tell me? What if I told her?*

I think it would really scramble her life. She's lost Rocklin, and I can't see Clutch or Dern marrying into a family with a mass murderer for a father-in-law. Deb's on the verge of goin' nuts, and how will she take it when I kidnap her real dad to face trial?

Why don't I hook up with nice, normal girls like Deb? Hell, Rose is as nice and normal as they come. Rose is smart and sexy, and she can even be pleasant when she wants to. Rose is definitely growin' on me.

Frank's white light jacket hung on a chair to hold a place for Rose.

* * *

Rose finished putting on her makeup as if she were a Flemish painter detailing a masterpiece. She didn't have opportunities to fuss with makeup on the job. It wasn't military. But for Frank, she'd call in the Airborne. Then there was Gil Rocklin. Gil had caught Rose's eye. He wasn't doting over Debbie today, so Gil might be in play. Rose made a face at herself in the mirror. *What's the matter with you, girl? Don't give up on Frank. If Frank could bring in the Butcher, how could he possibly follow his scoop of a lifetime? Maybe he'd settle down long enough to have kids. Then his priorities would change. But would he be happy? Would I?*

Wait till my brave reporter hears my theory about the Butcher, she thought. *Maybe then he'll leave chasing killers to the police.*

She headed toward the closet where her sexiest blouse hung. The knock on the door was Frank's shave-and-a-haircut rap. *The idiot forgot his key.*

* * *

Frank looked at his watch. He had ordered a small rack of lamb for Rose, but she still hadn't arrived. "Excuse me folks, I think Rose has a stuck zipper. Don't blame me if I don't come back." Frank hurried to his room. Maybe a new file had come in on Rose's computer. She said she had a theory on who the Butcher was, but needed confirmation.

Frank opened the door gingerly, as he always did. The sound from the television blared louder than usual. Frank saw no sign of Rose in the room.

Maybe the bathroom? The hum of the vent fan could be heard coming from the bathroom. Frank saw the blood-diluted water on the floor and instantly knew what had happened. His neck hairs tingled with fear, and his ears burned hot with anger. He reached under his pant leg and drew his gun. Frank crouched. *No one behind the drapes.* No one inside the open closet. *Maybe hiding on the other side of the bed?*

No. Frank followed the wall to the bathroom door, looked inside, and saw Rose's red hair floating on the surface of the overflowing bathtub. Frank's head reeled.

*   *   *

The waiters cleared the main courses, and the trampers waited for the pavlova meringue that Debbie called *pav* for dessert.

Frank returned. He whispered in Gil's ear and then in Debbie's. Both reluctantly followed him into the garden.

"What's wrong?" Debbie asked, noting Frank's red eyes.

"I need your help," Frank choked.

"We've been through that," Gil said curtly.

"Hear me out. Don't say anything. Don't react. The Englishmen, the Aussie, the Frenchman, the Italian. Were they at dinner?"

"For most of the dinner, yes," Debbie said. "I always make note of who doesn't show up, but I came in late."

"She's right," Gil confirmed, "but Amy and I arrived late too."

"And I came early before anyone else." Frank scowled.

"What's going on, Frank?" Gil asked apprehensively.

Frank thrust his laptop carrying case into Gil's hands. "Take this. Read this. I'll give you are a hundred thousand dollars each if you'll finish what I started. What's wrong with me? Make it a half million each."

"For what?" Debbie asked, taking a step back.

"You have access, Debbie. You can ask questions without arousing suspicion. Eventually, a certain person's going to tell you something about himself."

"What's going on, Frank?" Gil repeated sternly.

"Rose is dead."

"Are you sure?" Debbie gasped.

"I know dead—in the bathtub with slit wrists."

"Oh my god," Debbie cried. "She killed herself over you."

"No."

Debbie put her hands over her face. "Rose was in love with you, and it wasn't going anywhere."

Frank shook his head. He didn't want to hear that Rose was in love with him.

"Murder?" Gil asked.

Frank nodded.

Gil took a deep breath. "Minimum blood?"

"Yes."

"Drowned before the wrists were slit," Gil stated. "When someone slashes one of their wrists, they usually don't have the strength to slash the other."

"So I've been told," Frank agreed. "The tub was overflowing. The murder had to take place right after I left. So anyone could have done it."

Gil frowned. "The police will say the tub was full when you left. And you shouldn't have taken so long when you went back to the room."

"I got sick. I think there was some kind of gas used. Smelled a little like chloroform, but it wasn't chloroform. Maybe nerve gas?"

Gil shook his head. "Nerve gas is odorless, but I've read the specs on other secret weapon aerosols that can anesthetize you for days."

"Who *are* you two?" Debbie wailed, but neither man answered.

Frank held his head in his hands. "I'll bet that's what the killer used. Gas! Rose didn't know what hit her. She didn't have a fighting chance. She was a woman who fought hard for everything she earned." Frank started to choke and cleared his nose. "The vent fan was on, but the autopsy will ID the gas."

Gil shook his head. "Not necessarily. Not unless the examiner is specifically testing for it. Did you find any other clues?"

"You're both crazy!" Debbie exclaimed. "You probably smelled nail polish. You Americans are so used to crime, you see it everywhere. This is New Zealand! We don't have murders in New Zealand!"

Gil placed a comforting hand on Frank's shoulder. "The murder weapon?"

"My pocket knife. I used it to carve into the fruit basket. It was placed on the edge of the bathtub so as not to smear my prints."

"Was the sharp side of the blade facing right or left?"

"Right. Does that mean the killer was left-handed?"

"You're left-handed," Debbie noted, not liking the continuing direction of the discussion.

"Good point," Gil said. "You think the killer is trying to frame you?"

"Damn right he is. It's a murder made to look like a suicide, but on closer look the police will do an autopsy and conclude murder. Who would want to make it look like a suicide except the primary suspect? That's me!"

"This is incredible!" Debbie snapped. "Call the police."

"I believe you, Frank," Gil said. "But as I said before, I can't help you."

"Goddamnit, Gil, if anyone should know what I'm feelin' now, it should be you! Help me, for Christ's sake! It's not a matter of money anymore; it's pure, simple raw revenge."

"Revenge doesn't help," Gil said solemnly, pushing the laptop back at Frank. "A fine woman is dead. Now the safety of everyone else is the issue. Let the police handle it."

"No, Gil. Give me a chance. Look at Rose's laptop. The killer didn't get it, 'cause it was locked in a suitcase. The password is Hunter2. Look at it—please! Look at the faxes. If you think for one minute that I murdered Rose, give the computer to the police, but if you don't, then there's only one thing you can do. You have to help me."

Debbie turned away. "I'm going to call the police."

Gil watched her go. "She's one reason I can't help you, Frank. Amy's the other. There was nothing I can do for you anyway. I'm just a computer geek who writes software for children."

"Don't give me that! You've been trained." Frank handed Gil his Glock, a handover he didn't want Debbie to see. "You're smart and tough, and you know what it's like to have gone through hell." Frank started after Debbie before Gil could return the computer and the gun. He turned to Gil with a warning. "In case I'm in jail and don't see you again, you should know that Rose was a judo expert. Rose didn't have a chance to defend herself. You won't have a chance either."

Gil dropped the computer in his room before retrieving Amy and hid the gun in his binocular case. He hurried back to the dining room. He hugged his daughter and worried about the murderer among his traveling companions. There was only one safe thing to do. Go home.

*   *   *

Inspector Harper handled homicides and suspicious deaths, but since these seldom happened in New Zealand, he also investigated vice and missing persons. To have a dead tourist was bad enough, but to have a suicide that could be a possible murder made it the case of a lifetime. Harper had no intention of making a mistake. His dapper appearance, so unlike his American counterparts, suggested his ordered attention to detail. Harper would treat the tourists with his usual Kiwi good manners, but no one—absolutely no one—would get away with anything.

Frank Ferret, a.k.a. Dr. Whistle, sat before Harper looking agitated, but silent. Frank's strategies for coping with the law were to either talk so much that the police would get rid of him as a crank, or to play dumb and frustrate them. Seldom did either technique work as intended, but Frank was still testing the results. Harper didn't look like a person with a sense of humor, and Frank didn't feel up to his usual game playing. Harper waited for Frank to speak, trying to increase the stress in a situation that had long passed Frank's tolerance for stress. *Bastard!* Frank thought. *When all else fails, tell the truth, but not all of it, not yet.*

"What do you want to know?" Frank asked, breaking the war of silence.

Harper shuffled two documents under the table. "What's your name?"

"Frank Ferret."

"Who is Dr. Frank Whistle?" Harper asked.

"Whistle's my nom de guerre, which means—"

"I can speak French, Mr. Ferret," Harper stated dryly.

"As a celebrity, I find that using a false name keeps me from autograph seekers. My rivals in the news business would track me thinking I'm on to a big story, when I only want an undisturbed holiday. It's not uncommon in my line of business."

"The news business?"

"Yes, I'm a fairly famous journalist in North American and Europe."

"I'm sorry, I never heard of you, Dr. Whistle."

Frank deflated. "It's Ferret."

"Is that a nom de guerre also?"

"No, I legally changed my name when I became a reporter."

Harper produced a photocopy of Frank's phony passport. "Do all American journalists use fake passports?"

"If I broke some rule, deport me," Frank snapped. "My good friend is dead, and you're screwing around with me."

"Deportation may come; then again, it may not be possible. What was your relationship with Rose O'Hara?"

"She was Major Rose O'Hara, from the Criminal Investigation Division of the U.S. Army. We were collaborating on a book together."

"Only a business relationship?"

"Do I look like a eunuch?"

"You didn't answer my question."

Frank ground his teeth. "We were lovers. We went back together several years. We only pretended to be strangers."

"Why is she dead?" Harper asked.

Harper hadn't asked, "Why did she kill herself?" Frank pondered. *He knows. Here goes the two million dollars.*

"Why? Because one of the trampers killed her," Frank blurted.

"Really. And how did they do that?" Harper wasn't sure of the cause of death.

"Gas had something to do with it," Frank offered. "When I found Rose, there was a medicinal smell in the room."

"Really?" Harper said. "I didn't smell anything."

"The fan was on."

"You think she was gassed. Just what kind of gas would that be? Something a dentist might use?"

Frank bit hard to control his anger. "It doesn't have a name. In Yugoslavia, it translates to 'long sleep.'"

"How would you know that?"

"Spent time in that part of the world."

"How was it administered? A rag? An aerosol?"

"An aerosol," Frank said, sorry that he had brought up the subject of the gas.

Harper took Frank's two aerosol canisters made to look like hair spray and set them on the table. The writing was in Serbian. Frank had dropped them in the hotel dumpster after wiping off his fingerprints. "Like these?" Harper asked.

"Looks like hair spray to me," Frank said.

"My deputy wondered why a full can of hairspray would be thrown out. He squirted it and damned near passed out. You can be sure we'll test it."

Harper scrutinized the odd lettering on the can. "Your plane originated from Croatia, didn't it?"

Frank ignored the question. He had screwed up on disposing the cans, but hopefully Harper could find out who else had arrived from the Yugoslavia area, obtaining records that the airlines wouldn't release to Frank. "Find out who else flew in from the Yugoslavian countries, and you'll have the killer."

"You're the only one, Mr. Ferret. And *killer?*"

Of course, the Butcher would go to a neutral country before booking to New Zealand, Frank realized.

Frank leaned his aching head against his fist. "Yeah, I meant *killer*. Like I said, someone gassed Rose and tried to make her murder look like a suicide."

"The last part of that we know, don't we? But who do you think would do such a regrettable thing?" he said, holding a plastic bag containing Frank's still-open, army knife.

"Look at the British tourists. Check their passports for fakes."

"You can be sure, I will, Mr. Ferret." Harper said with a slight rise in his even-toned voice. "And I'll know *why* I'm checking them. Do *you?*"

"Rose may have recognized one of the Brits as being *wanted.*"

Harper ignored Ferret's closest statement to the truth. He leaned forward, "Was Rose having an affair with one of the Brits?"

"Of course not," Frank spat.

"Your relationship with Rose O'Hara was a good one? A romantic one? You were planning to marry, maybe?"

"Yes, yes, and maybe." Frank's voice tightened. "We had never gotten along as well as we did in the last three days. Things were startin' to heat up."

"Passionate?"

"Why don't you back off a bit, Inspector. I just lost a person I was in love with."

"'Passion, but not for each other,' perhaps?" Harper quoted from the information volunteered by Venus Klaus.

"Rose was teasing when she said that," Frank hissed. "Now if you have nothing better to do than to grind a grieving guy, I'd like to find an open bar and numb my nerves."

"Why did you kill her, Mr. Ferret?"

"I loved her. You can't prove I didn't love her. Without a motive, I'm the least likely person to have wanted to hurt her. So go after the damned Brits. But if there's a reward for one of 'em—aw, to hell with it!"

* * *

Inspector Harper summoned Debbie to the interrogation room. "Ms. McWard, I'll have to detain your entire party. Can you put them up in the hotel until we're through with the investigation?"

"How long? Our lodgings are paid for—all the way up to Auckland—but not in our present hotel. My tourists will go volcanic if they're stuck here and have to pay for lodgings."

"It's only a week or so. We need the results of the autopsy. Then your folks will be free to go."

"You don't really expect foul play?" Debbie asked, as she mentally prepared an argument to defend the reputation of the nation's tourist industry.

"Can't say at this time," Harper clucked.

123

"It was a *suicide*," Debbie insisted. "Rose told me she was madly in love with Dr. Whistle, but she was going back to Germany to marry a man she wasn't all that crazy about."

Harper smiled broadly. "Thank you, Miss. Thank you very much."

The inspector whispered to a colleague who also smiled. Debbie heard the word *motive*.

Harper's demeanor warmed. "We'll need you to testify at the trial. Your tourists are free to continue on the trip, but I don't want any of them to leave the trip. If anyone does, call me immediately, and I'll have them arrested."

"Then we're all free to continue," Debbie said with relief.

"Not everyone. We're holding Dr. Frank Whistle, also known as, Frank Ferret for having a forged passport. Now that we have a motive, he'll probably be charged with premeditated murder."

"That can't be!"

"I'm afraid so. The murdered woman had a bump on the base of her skull. She was gassed, hit in the head, and drowned, and then her wrists were slashed to make it look like a suicide." Harper's icy demeanor became emotional. "That murdering bastard Frank Ferret will never harm another woman. The last woman he'll ever see in his lifetime will be the judge."

*   *   *

Debbie knocked on Gil's door softly. "Is Amy asleep?"

Gil nodded and opened the door widely to invite her into his room.

Debbie dropped her forehead on Gil's shoulder and said, "This has been a horrible night with the police and everything. And I did a terrible thing. I gave the police a motive. I told them that Rose was going back to Germany to marry someone else, so they arrested Frank. They think he found out, got mad, and killed her, but I don't think he did. He just doesn't seem the type."

"There is no type. You're too trusting, Debbie. Any type can be a killer. There's a murderer on our bus, and he or she, could be any type, any one."

"Don't trust anyone. You're so right. Who are you, Gil? Why did Frank pick you to help him out?"

Gil began grimly. "I used to work as an undercover agent for the FBI. It's not what it sounds like. I am, or was, a computer security expert—one of the best in law enforcement. I put a Trojan Horse in the encrypted files of a major hospital chain."

"Pardon?"

"I hacked into secret files and documented an intentional policy of massive Medicare billing fraud—one of the biggest busts of the decade. Had to hospitalize the chain's CFO and three of his security guard thugs who tried to stop me from leaving the building with the *smoking-gun* evidence." Gil closed his eyes thinking of how important those things seemed at the time and how trivial they seemed now. "Two hundred million dollars had to be returned to the taxpayers, except the citizens saw little of it. The hospital declared bankruptcy and reopened under another name, but just as corrupt. Of course, I didn't know that at the time. At the time, I received commendations and a promotion. I was called law enforcement's poster boy."

"But not anymore?"

"No. Not anymore." Gil swallowed hard. "I managed to get indictments on the entire executive staff and board of directors. The CEO of the company was out on bail. He got drunk, bought an AK-47 at a gun show, and shot up my house. My wife was hit. She took two weeks to die."

"Oh my god! How horrible!

"What happened to the killer?"

"He started to enter my house to finish us off. I jumped him. I made the mistake of hitting him—killing him. *Not very professional,* my boss told me before I threw him across the room."

125

"Now it's clear," Debbie muttered. "Frank knew about you. That's why he wanted you to help. You were a policeman."

Gil nodded. "I had all the tough-guy training, but it's been a long time."

"Is there anything on Rose's computer that would implicate Frank?"

"No. But Frank seems to think there's an indicted war criminal on our trip—Ratac Bymarovitch, one of the butchers of the Balkans. Here's his picture—his only picture—a drawing."

Debbie frowned. "That's ridiculous. We don't have anyone here from that part of the world, and that strange drawing . . . . is not really any of the men. But it doesn't rule out most of the men either."

"According to Frank, Bymarovitch speaks five languages fluently. He lived all over the world as a diplomatic courier—another word for spy. He could pass himself as being from several nationalities."

"But no disguise—"

"Plastic surgery."

"That's why Frank was trying to look into everyone's mouths. He was comparing dental records."

"And?"

"Frank concluded that Bymarovitch must have added some fillings. Frank couldn't tell. But then . . . most of the trampers didn't avail themselves of his free dental appraisals."

"The man's delusional," Debbie concluded, remembering how Dr. Whistle's "open wide" routine had, at first, amused, then annoyed the trampers.

Gil tapped the computer. "I don't think so. Rose was a major in the U.S. Army's Criminal Investigation Division, assigned to the UN peacekeeping command in Croatia. It all makes sense. Bymarovitch suspected the two of them, so he kills Rose and blames it on Frank. Subtly, cunningly, gets rid of them both."

Debbie sandwiched her face between her hands. "Then Rose didn't commit suicide. Frank didn't kill her. There is a genocidal, murdering maniac hiding amongst my trampers."

"That sums it up. But you left out psychotic genius. Bymarovitch is a true sociopath genius. Any other nut would've killed Frank and Rose and tried to make it look like an accident. But the Butcher doesn't do things the easy way. He has to outsmart the rest of us, morons."

"What are we going to do?"

"Nothing."

"We can't just let Frank rot in jail."

"From what I've heard about Frank Ferret, it's not the first time. Frank is a survivor. When he goes to trial, I doubt if there will be a conviction."

Debbie shook her head. "Our Kiwi courts aren't as lenient as yours. Frank could hang, or I guess not. We abolished capital punishment here about ten years ago, but still . . . Frank won't go free, and the Butcher goes on his merry way. Aren't you going to do something about it?"

"What can I do? Maybe I should go up to each of our fellow trampers and ask, 'Are you the vicious animal who killed that fine lady? Are you one of the worst mass murderers since Hitler? Is that nose sewn on your face the same one you were born with?'"

"And the Butcher answers, 'Of course not. But by the way . . . what's your room number? How many relatives do you have, and where do they live? And do you want your daughter to see her next birthday?'"

"No, Debbie, I've done my duty for law enforcement. I felt pretty good about my work back then. I was going to save the nation from bad guys. And my wife paid the price for my folly. I can't let that happen again. I'm not going to leave Amy an orphan.

"Sooner or later, Bymarovitch will get his comeuppance, but someone else will have to deliver it."

Debbie bit her lip. "I understand. I really do. Amy comes first. Someone else will have to get the son of a bitch."

Gil kissed Debbie on the forehead. "Thanks for understanding. I don't feel good about it. I'd love to bust this bastard, but I have no choice."

Debbie pulled away. "I still hate you, but not because of this. No, I don't hate you. I'll never hate you. I'm very sorry it didn't work out. You're realistic and sensible. I'm impulsive and impracticable. I have to go."

Debbie rushed back to her room thinking that each door she passed might contain a murderer who could reach out and drag her into his bathtub. *Just let 'em try. Gil can't undo what I did to Frank. He really can't.*

But I can!

Chapter 9

Falls and Fundamentals

As the trampers settled in their bus seats, Debbie effused on their next destination. "You're going to love Milford Sound. The fjords and waterfalls are a wonder of the world. And I hope you brought plenty of film."

Two hours later the camera bags stayed tightly closed under the ponchos as rain plummeted on the trampers. They looked down to an ocean inlet bracketed by tall forested cliffs. Waterfalls spouted from a hundred spots that normally didn't have waterfalls, but the trampers could barely make them out. Debbie shouted over the torrent to be heard. "Normally, we'd see the fjord by Zodiacs, small rubber boats, but it's too dangerous. The surf's the nastiest I've ever seen. So we'll wait up here on the cliff till the rain blows over. Maybe the sun will come out, and we'll see a rainbow."

The trampers didn't buy Debbie's upbeat attempts. Grumbles and moans echoed throughout the group. "It's cold, and this poncho you gave me is too small!" growled Venus.

Debbie tried again. "At least the rain keeps the mozzies and sandflies from biting." The trampers didn't buy it. They would rather put up with mosquitoes and sandflies than this driving rain.

Amy started to sing, "*I'm sing-ing in the rain.*"

Martin and Gil joined in. Within a minute the whole group began to laugh and sing.

Debbie gave Amy and Martin hugs. "I'm going to keep you two as official assistants in charge of happiness."

The singing continued with "Oh, what a beau-ti-ful morn-ing," but the rain only fell harder. The midmorning light turned nightlike with visibility down to a few feet. The trampers didn't look forward to the long muddy walk down to where the bus had dropped them, but it would be better than the feeling of standing under a fire hose.

Debbie looked pained. "Let's see if the catwalk along the mountain is clear. Sometimes we get little waterfalls right on the ledge. But if they're not too heavy, we can do a steep shortcut down to the bus." Debbie groped down the steps along the narrow ledge that circled the mountain. Much of the rocky path had rails, but several of the flat sections did not. The poncho-covered trampers followed. "Careful!" Debbie called, "these rocks can be slippery when wet."

Gil waited with Amy until all the faster moving trampers followed Debbie. Gil caught up to the group huddled under a rock ledge. The waterfall about which Debbie had warned spouted over the edge. "Where's Debbie?" Gil asked. Debbie had a hot pink slicker. Everyone else's poncho was black.

No one answered. Finally, one said, "She and a few others went exploring."

Gil placed Amy's wrist in Eve King's hand. "Something's not right. If the path is clear, Debbie should be back by now." Gil sidestepped around the pouring column of water and peered ahead. No visibility.

"Debbie!" he called. He slipped on the wet stones and found himself dangerously close to the edge with no rail. The sheer side of the cliff had a plumb line's vertical drop to the ocean, but the path was wide enough for safe passage. Gil looked down as a lightning bolt lit the surface of the water below. *A hot pink poncho!*

Gil saw George close behind. "Debbie's down there! Get to the boats, or I'll never get her out!"

George turned to trace the long path back to the boat launch. He saw Gil shedding his poncho and yanking off his boots. "You can't jump, you'll be killed."

In one motion, Gil emptied his camera bag of its lens, refastened the cover, and tightened its strap around his body. "If I don't come back, Amy knows my sister's phone number."

Gil looked into the dark below him. "Tell Amy I love her." Gil pushed off the edge of the cliff, held his position, and dove into the water with a nearly splashless plunge. With a dive of such height, even the clean entry felt like dropping through a plate glass window. As Gil pierced the waves, he could feel the force of the current. It seemed an eternity before Gil sensed upward motion. He stroked slowly, knowing it would conserve more air. The waterproof camera bag acted as a buoy, but even its pocket of air couldn't match the force of the waves. Just when Gil's lungs felt they could no longer prevent a fatal breath, his head broke the surface. He gasped for air, but a second later his mouth filled with brackish water. The waves tossed him against the vertical rock surface before he could cough and take another full gasp of air.

The frothy swell rose against the rock, giving Gil a high view of the surrounding water. *The pink poncho! The air pockets are holding her up.* Gil struggled to reach Debbie. She looked lifeless—floating with her head back. *Unconscious! God, let her live!* A flurry of strokes brought him within a yard of Debbie, only to be swept away. Debbie floated closer to rocks that could smash any remaining life from her. Another flurry of strokes, timed between the crashing waves, pulled Gil next to her. Gil cradled Debbie's limp head in one arm, and thanked himself for a long-forgotten life-guarding job.

We can't just float here. We'll get smashed against the rocks or swept out to sea. Oh Lord! Debbie's not breathing.

Another lightning flash showed waves plummeting over a small ledge. Gil swam into position. As the wave crested, it carried the two bodies toward the ledge. Gil wrapped his legs around a short pinnacle of rock, rounded smooth by a millennium of wave action. He pulled Debbie. *Dead weight.* He could make it to the ledge, but not with Debbie. He thought of holding his lifeless wife. The same despair, fear, and anger he felt then swelled within him. With an adrenal surge, he pulled harder on Debbie's limp body. Another wave gave him the needed push to mount the ledge. Gil dragged her away from the edge and immediately started CPR. The cold spray drenched his back, but wasn't strong enough to sweep him off.

Gil held her nose and put his mouth to Debbie's cold lips. *Count! Unfasten the slicker. Count. Press on her chest. Get the rhythm.*

A long minute later, Debbie coughed.

Gil stopped the CPR and began to sob. Laugh and sob. "Damn you, Debbie, don't you ever take chances like that again. You *said* the rocks were slippery."

Between gasps for air, Debbie said. "Didn't slip. Wasn't . . . even close to the edge."

"What are you saying?"

"I was pushed."

* * *

Thirty minutes passed, and the water continued to rise. The rain subsided to drizzle, but the tide made each wave a little higher. Gil calculated how far the water had risen and estimated that the waves would be licking over their bodies in five minutes.

"Can you stand up, Debbie? We may have to."

"I'll give it a fair go, but my head's spinning like a Frisbee."

Gil pulled her up, and she clutched him. Obviously in pain and discomfort, she said, "I want to sleep."

"You can't Deb. I think you have a concussion. You can't sleep."

"There's a goose egg on the back of my head. Whoever pushed me, hit me on the head when I tried to grab him."

"Who?"

"How in the hell should I know? I think I remember a black poncho sleeve. I think. Maybe I didn't grab him. I'm not sure of anything right now. Maybe it didn't happen."

"Then don't say anything, Deb. If you're not sure, say you were hit by a falling rock. But you *are* sure, aren't you? Damn it, Ferret was right! You must have been nosing around, weren't you?"

"I nosed, but I didn't smell anything."

"You must have been close to Rose's killer. Who? Who were you questioning?"

"I was close to everyone, questioning everyone."

Cold spray drenched their bodies.

"The tide is going to cover this ledge, Gil," Debbie warned.

Gil looked about to see if they could swim up to a higher ledge. He only saw sheer cliff. He could climb *maybe ten feet*, he thought, but how could he pull up Debbie?

*   *   *

Elizabeth led the way to the marina. Clutch and George sprinted ahead of her once the marina came in view. If George had trouble keeping up with Clutch in earlier runs, it didn't show in the race to save Debbie and Gil.

The Closed sign on the marina's shedlike office added to the chill.

"Whadda we do now?" Clutch wailed.

The boats aren't locked," Elizabeth gasped, staggering, and collapsing in the mud.

"Not locked?" George yelled through the rain. "Are you sure?"

"This is New Zealand, yank," Elizabeth spat.

Borolo and Stanley caught up with them. The others trudged far behind.

Borolo surveyed the situation. "It won't do us any good. The waves are worse. Taking the Zodiac out would be suicide."

Elizabeth gave a half smile, "That's about the size of it."

*　　*　　*

"There!" Debbie said weakly between the crashing of waves. She grasped Gil's arm in a futile effort to raise her head higher. "Is that the sound of a boat, or is that a rugby match in my head?"

"A Zodiac! It's King." Gil began to shout and wave Debbie's pink slicker.

George King and Clutch Cooper and Elizabeth bounced among the ten-foot waves with a small motorized rubber boat. Elizabeth, the navigator, pointed to Debbie's pink poncho. As the cresting waves pushed the small outboard motor out of the water, it floundered like a cork. Then between swells, the boat made it to the ledge where Gil grabbed a thrown rope and wrapped it around the pinnacle-shaped rock.

"Take Debbie," Gil said as he threaded a life jacket over her head. "Leave me a life jacket and get your tails back here as soon as you can."

King shook his head. "The way the tide's rising, you won't be here when we get back. *If* we can make it back."

Clutch caught Debbie and held her in his arms. "Get on board, Rocklin. There's room for five—almost. 'Cause *I'm* not coming back for you. I'll risk my life for Debbie, but there's a limit."

"Thanks, sport," Gil said and half jumped, half rolled into the inflatable boat.

George snorted at Clutch. "Remind me to have Martin burn your baseball cards."

*   *   *

The tour group waited anxiously at the small marina that rented rafts and ocean kayaks. They were oblivious of the squall. "I see them!" Willie shouted.

The crowd waited silently. They had watched Gil's rescue, but couldn't see the CPR that had taken place directly below them. The unspoken question was *Is Debbie alive?* Her pink poncho lay flat on the rubber boat. When she moved, the crowd cheered.

The raft bobbed and filled with water as it approached the narrow beach with its large breakers. A dozen men and women waded into the surf, pulling the boat onto the wet sand.

Clutch carried Debbie ashore in his arms.

Amy rushed to Debbie's side. "You scared me, Debbie. Don't ever go close to the edge again."

Clutch strode forward toward the bus, which stood one hundred yards from the landing spot. A weary and ignored Elizabeth followed. Someone had to drive the bus.

Eve and Martin embraced George. George kissed them both and turned toward Amy who was holding her exhausted father's hand. "Little girl, your father is the bravest man I have ever met."

Amy hugged her father. "I was worried about Debbie, but not my Dad. He's a good swimmer. He taught me to dive and swim. He never takes chances that he can't do."

*   *   *

Fortunately for Debbie and the soaking wet trampers, the bus took only fifteen minutes to reach the hotel.

Again Clutch carried Debbie to her room, despite protestations that she could walk.

Eve took over and pushed everyone from Debbie's room. Mrs. Yong insisted on helping, and they propped Debbie under a warm shower while they took off her clothes.

Dried, naked, and prone under a mountain of blankets, Debbie's teeth chattered when she tried to lift her head from the bed.

Hush!" Eve ordered. She bent over Debbie's bed and flashed the pen light into her eyes. "Pupils look normal, but to be on the safe side, I don't want you to sleep. And I'd feel better if we could take a few head-to-toe pictures."

Debbie murmured, "No X-rays. I don't have any broken bones. I'm just sore all over. And my head aches like hell, and I don't think I'll ever be warm again."

"Hypothermia," Eve explained. "It won't last."

Eve opened the door to order some hot tea. Gil stood at the door, a tray of hot pitchers in hand. Gil and the others pushed into the room, catching Eve off guard. Eve turned to the crowd and shouted, "Out, out! She's gonna live. She'll be fine."

Debbie smiled at the onlookers. "I can't thank George, Clutch, and Elizabeth enough for coming after us. I love you all."

Clutch bent over her, "Then maybe we start again where we left off?"

136

"Out!" Eve growled. "It's not fair to hit on a woman who's been through what's she's been through." Eve herded her fellow travelers from the room. She turned to see Gil sitting in a corner chair and huddled under a blanket. "You too, hero. I'd better look you over for abrasions."

Gil shook his head. "Not necessary. Mostly bruises, and I have aspirin, antiseptic, and antibiotic cream back at the room."

"A traveling dispensary, are you?"

"When I travel with Amy—"

"We almost had two fatherless children, today," Eve sniffed.

Gil nodded gravely, "Go to *your* hero, Eve. He saved two lives today."

"Can't. I have to keep our Kiwi awake."

"I have more to talk to Deb about than you do. Go to your hero."

Gil walked her to the door.

Eve stopped. "Things weren't going well between you two."

"Did it show?"

"I'm sensitive to that type of thing. You almost lost her; you saved her life and almost lost your own. That's an enormous emotional experience that can overwhelm one with feelings of passion and love. But when the rush of emotion subsides, nothing fundamental changes. Are your fundamentals in order?"

"No. Our fundamentals stink. How about yours?"

Eve closed her eyes. "Does it show? My fundamentals stink too. This morning I would have gladly have traded George for you, or even Willie. But now I'm overwhelmed with passion and love. I'm going to my husband to kick his ass for almost making me a widow, then I'll cuddle him to death. I'll worry about the fundamentals later."

When Eve left, Gil turned to Debbie. "Can you walk?"

"No. And I don't have any clothes on under these blankets."

"Then I'll carry you."

"The hell you will!" she said in a weak voice.

Gil's stern voice said, "Debbie, someone tried to kill you. He probably won't try again because he'll figure you got the message. But he doesn't know you. You won't give up. So your life's in danger, and I'm not letting you out of my sight."

Gil scooped her up, blankets and all. Ferret's gun was in Gil's room, and unlike Frank, Gil knew how to use it.

"Put me down," Debbie groaned.

"This is not negotiable. You're coming with me."

"Where are you taking me?"

"My room. Our fundamentals haven't changed. I have chaos at home, and I can't even afford to leave this damn trip to do anything about it. You sleep with Amy for the rest of the trip."

*   *   *

When Amy left the bedroom to brush her teeth, Debbie sat up in bed and faced Gil. "I feel better. A new head and a good sleep and I'll be perfect. I have only one complaint—the way you acted yesterday."

"Huh?" Gil grunted.

Debbie growled, "'Not negotiable,' he says. What a bully! I never suspected you were one of those power and control freaks."

"I'm doing what I must, Debbie."

"Sure you are! Gil, the do-gooder. Do your duty, mate. Save the poor girl's life, then put her in your pumpkin for protection."

"You're starting to sound like Frank."

"Do you realize that by forcing me to sleep in your room that I lose any chance of getting back together with Clutch or Willie?"

Gil sighed. "I'll tell them how it is."

"Don't bother," Debbie snapped. "I'm taking a different tack. I'm going to become a bully like you. What I have to say is *not negotiable.* Hear that, Rocklin? Not negotiable."

"Maybe I should call Dr. King."

"Oh, so now I'm a crazy lady who's talking nonsense. You haven't even heard my nonnegotiable demands."

"Fire away," said Gil, hiding his annoyance.

"Now hear this! One, I'll take you back to your home in the States. When the bank bastards take your house away, I'll show you how to pitch a tent. When Amy outgrows her clothes, I'll sew. When we run out of food, I'll have my dad send us kiwifruit. And if you have to work hundred-hour weeks, I'll be there . . . to help Amy with her calculus homework, her hair curling, and how not to make mistakes with boyfriends, like I did. I might be able to convert my teaching credentials, start a travel agency, or go into modeling. There'll be enough in the cookie jar to send Amy"—Debbie's energy began to wane—"and two, all I expect from you . . . is to help me make little brothers and sisters for Amy. Preferably after we're married."

Gil stood looking at the wall.

Debbie bit her lip. "Not negotiable," she said weakly.

Amy bounded into the room. "What are you two arguing about?"

Gil picked up Amy and gave her a twirl in midair. "*Fundamentals.* Debbie loves us as much as we love her. So if I do say so, you're a pretty decent matchmaker, Amy."

"Fun-da-medals." Amy laughed—a delightful laugh.

Gil kissed his daughter. "Little pumpkin, meet your new mommy."

CHAPTER 10

Get Out of Jail Dead

Ferret groused over the phone from his cell in the prison. "Rocklin, you can't marry the Kiwi. First of all, I didn't get a chance to make love to her. Second, there's something you don't know. I'm pretty sure Debbie doesn't know either. I should have told you both before."

"Spit it out, Frank," Gil said, "but whatever it is, it won't change our minds."

"Do you want the half-million dollars I promised you?"

"Want it? I need it. It's my only quick way out of the hole I've been put into."

"The man who killed Rose and tried to kill Debbie is . . . her father."

"Whose father?"

"Debbie's father," Frank replied soberly.

"Her father is the *Butcher of the Balkans*? That can't be."

Gil motioned for Debbie to put her ear to the phone. "You have to hear this," he whispered.

"It seems to be the cussed case," Frank insisted. "Twenty-eight years ago, the Butcher abandoned his infant daughter to his brother, Klav and his wife—a teacher. Bro was a university professor and part-time crook working for the KGB. His employers trusted him with the key to the cookie jar. Big mistake! Uncle Klav fled to New Zealand with a boatload of stolen bouillon and the Butcher's baby. The gold wasn't the whole Mint, but it was big enough for some ol' KGB alumni to carry a grudge for twenty-eight years. The Yugos want the gold back with a blood chaser.

"Bro Klav and his wife bought a sheep ranch far out in the country—reclusive relatives of one of the worst mass murderers since Po Pot."

"Hold on," Gil said. "This country is wall-to-wall sheep ranches."

"Ah, but the latest screw in the sarcophagus is a letter from Klav saying that the Butcher's daughter is a lovely twenty-eight-year-old adventure travel tour guide. That's probably all the information the Butcher had to go on. Butcher flies to Christchurch—the postmark on the letter. He finds his daughter, the tour guide. The daughter leads Butch to his reclusive brother and whatever's left of the KGB loot.

"That's why I went on this trip. Find the daughter and the Butcher can't be far behind."

"You're not making sense, Frank," Gil said.

"Listen, damn you! Debbie is twenty-eight and blonde. The Butcher is blond. And Debbie's own words: 'My father and mother immigrated to New Zealand. Living in the middle of nowhere'—a recluse. Yet several languages spoken in the home. A literary home, full of books. *Stepbrothers!* 'My mum was a teacher. My dad has an accent that makes him hard to understand.'"

Debbie stood stone-faced as she spoke into the phone. "Then the man I've called father all my life is really my uncle? My mum isn't my mother? And you think my true father pushed his long-lost daughter off a cliff?"

"Any other father, no. But the Butcher—"

"And my fake father will take in the would-be murderer of his cherished adopted daughter? He will welcome his brother—my true dad—with open arms and give him a basketful of bouillon to escape?"

"Something like that," Frank admitted.

"And all the time I thought you were after another sexual conquest; you were only after my address." Debbie began to laugh.

"It's not funny," Frank protested.

"Oh yes it is," Debbie said.

"What do you think about Frank's theories, Gil?" she asked.

"I think prison food has damaged Frank's brain. No single gene pool could produce you, your family, and the Butcher. You were obviously brought up in an open, loving home—not a home where people were hiding from KGB assassins."

Debbie looked wild-eyed. "Ah, but my loving home folks will have to honor their butchering brother and help him escape. Gil and I must have Grandpa Butcher over for Amy's birthday parties. He'll come disguised as a clown, of course. He'll bring hand grenades wrapped in ribbons for party favors, and a machine gun for a noise maker."

"I get the feeling you don't believe me," Frank said.

"*Believe you?* You're a bloomin' idiot!" Debbie broke into raucous laughter.

Frank grumbled, "Why am I an idiot?"

"First of all, I just turned twenty-eight, not twenty-nine. I skipped a year in school, so when I graduated college, I lied about my age to get this job. Second, my surname is McWard, hardly a Croatian name. My father didn't immigrate after I was born, but three years *before* I was born. He came from bonnie ol' Scotlan', mon. He has an accent as thick as your head, Frank. He only raises enough sheep to keep us in lamb chops. He's one of the island's largest producers of kiwifruit and mandarin oranges, and he's a citizen advisor to the New Zealand Board of Agriculture—hardly a recluse. Do you want to hear about my mum too? She's a music teacher, but also the pianist for the Auckland Symphony."

"Then all of this was a mistake?" Frank exclaimed. "No, it can't be! Who killed Rose if not the Butcher? I know for a fact that the Butcher booked an adventure travel trip in New Zealand. We could've been on the same plane for all I know. If he were lookin' for his brother or daughter, he'd ask every travel agency to book him with the adventure tour guide whose name he'd 'forgotten,' but who was a 'beautiful twenty-nine-year-old.' That's what *I* did. That guy Carp said there was only one tour guide on the island that met that description. Maybe the Butcher made the same mistake I did. He *has to be* one of the tourists."

"You're sounding desperate," Gil noted.

"Oh my god!" Debbie exclaimed.

"What?" Gil asked.

"I know who the daughter is!" Debbie cried.

"Who?" Frank urged. "My time is almost up."

"I could be wrong, but—"

"Who?" Frank begged.

"Elizabeth! She's about my age, maybe a year older."

"Lovely?" Frank scoffed.

"In the eyes of a father," Gil offered. "But a tour bus driver is hardly a 'tour guide.'"

"Liz took the guide license test twice and failed. She's clever, but her test-taking skills aren't that sharp. Her family lives on the North Island, but Liz could mail a letter from almost anywhere. I know they're farmers, but Liz has never invited me to her home. I've had her visit my folks. Oh my god, she's one of my best friends."

Ferret yelled, "They're gonna cut me off. I didn't want to use this, but they're gonna formally indict me for murder tomorrow. They're askin' me to post a million-dollar bond to see daylight."

Gil sighed. "If someone wants you out of the way, you might be safer in jail."

"No, no," Frank pleaded, "I've gotta get out. So call the phone number on the red card. *Please!"*

"And congratulations on your engagement. I'm glad Debbie's dad is not a killer. You don't know how happy that makes me. Now Amy can run for president."

The voice of a policeman could be heard in the background and the line went dead.

Debbie's eyes misted. "I'm sure Elizabeth doesn't know. I hate to be the one to tell her. She probably won't believe me. I know she won't believe Frank. Then what?"

Gil tapped his finger on the side of Ferret's computer case. "There's another way. Liz doesn't have to know. It's only important that the Butcher knows you're not his daughter."

"How do we do that?"

"Take your trampers to visit a real, working kiwi orchard. The pretense is that Amy and I have to meet your folks—which we do—and that they'll see an authentic Kiwi farm."

"Brilliant! That's a great idea. And my folks will be happy to host an authentic Kiwi barbie. At our home, Butcher will see that I'm not his daughter when he gets a look at my dad. And with any luck, he'll give up and terrorize some other tour group."

"We'll watch to see who leaves the tour. That'll be the Butcher."

Debbie poked his chest accusingly. "I think you're still interested in sharing Frank's reward."

Gil sighed. "It would make things a lot simpler. Living in a tent gets cold when the Colorado snow starts to fly."

Debbie said, "Maybe we should settle on shaking Mr. Butcher off our chops and getting Frank out of jail."

Gil didn't reply. He pulled a red business card from a side pocket of Frank's computer case. "He has to be kidding. It's a business card for a Lisbon casino."

"There's a phone number on the back." Debbie observed. "Probably a Portuguese brothel that Frank is depending on for a character reference."

Gil puzzled over the number. "When I worked for the FBI, I memorized almost every area code in the States and Canada, but I don't remember seeing this one." He punched the number. The connection took a few seconds. "If this is his lawyer, he or she is probably not in."

Debbie smirked. "I'll make you a bet of a brew that his lawyer's a woman."

"No bet! No answer. I'll try again later. But I think Frank is off base using an American lawyer."

Before Gil could hang up, a female voice answered, "Hello."

Debbie pushed her ear next to the phone and whispered, "I win."

"Hello? This is Mary Beth. Are you there?"

"Yes, my name is Gil Rocklin. I'm calling on behalf of Frank Ferret."

Mary Beth laughed. "What trouble has that no-good, sneaky rascal gotten into now?"

"He's in a New Zealand jail held on a million-dollar bond."

"I knew I never should've given him my direct number. I suppose he's charged with a capital offense, no doubt—like murder or high treason."

"The murder of Major Rose O'Hara, but he didn't do it."

"Of course not. Get him out."

"I beg your pardon," Gil asked. He vaguely recalled hearing Mary Beth's voice before, but couldn't place it in this bizarre context.

"Get him out of jail!" Mary Beth said sternly. "Never mind. It'll be a bit embarrassing, but it's the least I can do. Tell him I'll bake him a cake with a file in it. That's why you called, isn't it?"

"You'll need to know where he's being held."

"Don't bother. I don't have a pencil anyway. It may take some time. You said New Zealand, right?"

"That's correct," Gil replied. "Thank you, but Mary Beth, just who are you anyway?"

The woman laughed. "He didn't tell you? He's too much of a smart ass to ask for help, unless he's *really* desperate. Oh, and I'm Mary Beth Palmer. I think you've heard of my husband—the president of the United States."

Chapter 11

Welcome to the Family

Eve King shuddered. "You're scaring the hell out me, Gil."

"Me too," said George King, looking back at the locked hotel room door and clutching his frightened wife. "I don't doubt what you say is true. I thought I recognized Frank Whistle or Frank Ferret, but I couldn't place him until now. Never thought he was a killer. And Debbie isn't the kind who would slip off a cliff."

"But a *genocidal murderer* on our tour group!" Eve muttered.

Gil's calm demeanor made the tale seem unreal. "Look folks, I need your assistance. The smartest thing to do is to leave the tour, but the police will be back for more questions. The prosecutors will want depositions. If we're not here, we could be rounded up and jailed as material witnesses. Plus, we'll get Debbie in big trouble for not reporting us gone."

Debbie gestured helplessly. "I can't leave. I'm responsible for the trampers."

147

George patted Debbie's hand. "You're too good for your own good. I'd like to stay and help you, but I have to think about Martin's safety."

Eve nodded, "Even if we're arrested, it's a small price to pay for Martin's safety."

George shook his head. "If we cut out, Inspector Harper will blow a fuse, but I don't think he wants us in jail. The tourist lobby will be on his ass. And Eve said it all: we have to leave the tour because of Martin. Any bastard who would kill Rose and try to kill Debbie wouldn't hesitate killing any of us, including our kids, if he was cornered."

Gil smiled. "Deb and I have the same fear, but we've solved that problem. Once the Butcher decides that Debbie and her family are not his targets, it becomes a safe house. So we're going to board Amy—and Martin too, if you'd like—with Debbie's parents. We'll say, they want to play Kiwi farmers for a couple of days."

"Thank you, Debbie," Eve said. "I'll feel a lot better when Martin's far away from this animal."

"We need to figure out who the Butcher is," George growled.

"We've started," Gil said. "We have it narrowed down to six trampers, based on the man's age and build. Here's a chart."

The Kings eyed Gil's chart in alphabetical order:

Antonio Borolo	Italian	Accountant
Abe Goodman	British	Government Manager
Jacques Lafate	French	Shopkeeper
Paul Stanley	British	Retired Builder
Joseph Tinsley	Australian	Real Estate
Marcus Turner	British	Restaurant Owner

Gil added, "All are married, except Tinsley.

George scratched his forehead. "Why all the Brits?"

Debbie explained. "Bymarovitch is supposed to be some kind of genius. He speaks six languages fluently, and he was a spy at the Yugoslavian embassy in London. So it'll be hard to trip him up on British trivia. He'd know more about being British than we would."

"We need Frank back," Gil stated. "He worked for a London tabloid."

Debbie sniffed. "It figures. A scummy stalker."

Gil gave a half smile. "If memory serves me, Frank wrote a book exposing their slimy tactics before they caught on to what he was up to."

Eve pointed at Tinsley's name. "Single."

Gil shrugged. "Bymarovitch had money. He could rent a wife—an actress, a hooker, who knows? If so, she could be dangerous too."

George frowned. "What if we asked the same question of the wife and the husband? Whoever gives us different answers is our man, or couple."

Gil nodded. "We've already started with the wives. Innocent questions that anyone would answer. 'Do you have any grandchildren? Have any pictures? Where was your last trip?' We need someone else to talk to the men."

"I don't like Turner," Eve said. "For a man who's supposed to be running a restaurant, do you see what he does with ketchup?"

"He's an owner, not a chef," George cautioned, "plus he's English."

Debbie sniffed, as if personally insulted, and offered, "Stanley retired early due to disability. Maybe Eve could ask him about his injury and see if it makes sense. Then there's the hair. Bymarovitch was light-haired like Turner, Lafate, and Borolo, but Bymarovitch could be dying his hair. Try to find a follicle on the back of a chair. A light root from one of the dark-haired men like Goodman or a blond stubble on Tinsley's shaved head would be a smoking gun."

George grimaced. "Warm, but not smokin'. Ya can't arrest a person for being blond. I'm afraid we won't be able to finger the Butcher until he tries something else."

*   *   *

THE McWARD FARMHOUSE

From his multicolored stone farmhouse, Ian McWard suspiciously eyed the trampers unloading from the bus. Debbie had never brought a whole busload before. She had never brought a young man before. Well, that wasn't exactly true. Many a young man had visited the farm, but Debbie had always shrugged them off as good friends. But when Ian asked about this Gil fellow, Debbie evaded him. Debbie was obviously saving up for an announcement, and it worried Ian. Now she bounded off the bus holding the hand of a pretty little girl with a handsome tall man walking closely behind.

The dogs greeted Debbie first—jumping and furiously wagging their tails. Mary McWard hugged her next. Debbie's three stepbrothers each gave her a peck, while disappointingly scanning the women tourists for anyone young and single.

Ian waited for Mary and his sons to show off their English perennial garden and start their guided tour of the orchard before approaching Debbie. The little girl left in search of fruit, but Debbie's young man remained. *Worse than I thought.*

Ian strode to the garden and embraced his daughter.

Debbie almost danced in place. "Dad I'd like you to meet"—

Ian gave her a gentle push. "Aye'd like ta talk ta yar youn' mon—alone."

Debbie forced a smile. "Good luck, boys." She ran to catch up with her mother.

Ian started walking in a fast gait, and Gil followed. Ian pointed to the tall hedges with staked kiwi vines in between. "Str-rangers think the kiwi is a tree. The kiwi is really the Chinese gooseberry. It's a vine—a fr-ragile

150

vine. The tops o' those windbreaks create a dr-raft that keeps bees from flying off. The bees stay put an' fertilize the kiwi blossoms."

"Very interesting," Gil commented, thinking how much Ian's rolled *r*'s resembled growls.

"Yer intentions, mon?"

"We plan to be married in three weeks."

"O' course," Ian grumbled. "Ye've known Debbie for a week?"

"A little longer."

Ian snorted, and the accent, which he used as a wall to strangers, melted in the direction of Standard English. *The young man must understand.* "When I saw ye with Debbie, I wanted ta take the shotgun to ye."

"Welcome to the family," Gil muttered with a roll of his eyes.

"Do you know why I want ta shoot ye?"

"Yes. I think I do, Ian."

Ian stopped his brisk walk and looked at Gil with surprise.

Gil resumed the walk. "If I were you, I'd want to shoot me too. I'm an American. For me to immigrate to New Zealand, I'd have to post a third of a million-dollar bond, which I don't have. My work is in the States. So I have to take Debbie away from you."

Ian grunted.

Gil continued, while he still had the stage. "Naturally, Debbie will miss her family, and we'll have to visit every Christmas, Easter, and your winter when my daughter's not in school. Maybe after your harvest, you and the wife can drop in on us. In any case, I promise to keep your family together as much as I can."

"Ye have a little lassie?"

"Yes, her name is Amy. I'm a widower."

Ian put his large hand on Gil's shoulder. "It's a good thing ye're a father. Ye understand.

"Ye'll protect Debbie from your American criminals?"

Gil thought about lecturing Ian about taking Hollywood crime flicks too seriously, but crime was too real to Gil both in the States and New Zealand. He only nodded.

"Ye're built strong like a farmer," Ian noted.

"I grow three rows of vegetables for the neighborhood rabbits. I write and draw educational computer software for children. I was doing fine until a few days ago. Now my business is floundering, at best."

Ian pointed to a steep hill doted with a pattern of conifer saplings. "See those *Pinus rigatus?* An eight-thousand-dollar investment per hill. Fast growin'. In twenty-five years, each hill will be worth more than a million dollars. Debbie is entitled to a chunk o' the profit. We're a wealthy family, but all our riches are still in the ground. I can't help ye much. I still have two more lads in college. Maybe sixty thousand as a wedding present."

Gil mentally converted the gift to thirty-nine thousand American dollars—not enough to help. "Thank you. We'll put it to good use."

"Too bad ye business is busted. Ye can make enough money ta travel?"

"Right now, no. But I'll see that it gets better. I promised you, didn't I?"

"We McWards keep promises," Ian warned.

"So do Rocklins," Gil replied with full eye contact.

Ian brushed his eyes. "I'm worried about Debbie. She loves everyone. She trusts everyone. I was afraid she'd make a mistake. 'Twas stupid of me. Debbie is a smart lassie; she picked a good mon."

Gil smiled. "And her parents raised a wonderful woman."

"We should ha' ne'er sent her to Japan. Wait'll she serves ye raw fish."

Gil looked shocked. "I didn't know!" He laughed. "I love good sushi now and then. And Amy likes dashi."

Ian shuddered. "Ye odd people deserve each other," he growled.

"Then there's Scottish haggis," Gil teased back with a grimace.

"I'll send ye some, mon. Ye don't know what yer missing. Let's ha' a drink 'fore her trampers return," Ian offered. "I haven't gotten smashed in years."

"Sounds like an area of agreement. But forgive me if I don't get smashed, Ian. I have to keep an eye out for one of the tourists who tried to kill your daughter."

"Ye ha' a strange sense o' humor, mon."

*   *   *

With the meal still cooking Maori-style in a pit in the ground, the McWard family brought out the musical instruments, including a piano lifted and carried down to a large patio by the three stepbrothers. While the brothers set up their ensemble, Ian brought out his bagpipes, and his piping filled the valley. For even those who didn't like bagpipe music, which was almost the entire group, the piping seemed appropriate.

Debbie, her mother, and the McWard brothers took over playing blue grass and spirited chamber music to the delight of the trampers. Debbie played cello and switched to her guitar to lead the singing and sing-alongs. As the sky started to darken, she placed a pillow on the piano bench and dropped Amy on it. Debbie grinned at her mother. "Wait'll you hear this."

Martin assembled his clarinet, and the two children started a simple Mozart duet that they had been practicing together in hotel lobbies. Then Amy launched into a solo Chopin etude with all the gusto of a concert pianist. The trampers, their hands already sore from applauding the McWards' entertainment, bravoed with sincerity. Gil quickly gave Amy the hook, lest she become too swellheaded.

Mary McWard waited to take her turn at Gil. Dinner had been eaten, and Gil began to help with the clean up without asking permission. *Thinks he's already a member of the family*, Mary sniffed to herself.

In the kitchen, Mary put a finger in Gil's shoulder. "You're neglecting your daughter," Mary stated curtly.

Gil puzzled. "Amy has plenty of company. Your sons are tossing her around like a beach ball."

"I mean *neglecting!*"

Gil stood with his mouth slightly agape. Of all the things he'd ever been accused of, neglect was never one of them.

"Who teaches your daughter piano?"

"I do."

"Amy's a prodigy."

"I don't think so. I give her a lesson every day—that's all. Give kids time to do something worthwhile that they think is fun, and they'd all look like geniuses."

"Are you a professional musician?"

"No, but I've had years of lessons, including music theory, and I can still play better than average classical and passable jazz. I've seen Debbie giving Amy a few pointers."

"That's not good enough. I *am* a professional pianist and the most sought after music teacher on the North Island—no small accomplishment considering how far we are from the city. I know prodigy when I see it. Stringing notes together is one thing; *feeling* the music is another. Amy is already interpreting feeling. Some musicians never reach that point. So get her the best teacher in Colorado. I'll pay for it, until your business gets on its feet again. And I'd like three or four days with her before she gets into any more bad habits."

Gil tightened his lips but managed a "Thank you." The devastation to his business was sinking in. Swallowing pride was an unfamiliar skill for Gil. *I need a share of Ferret's reward money*, he reminded himself.

Mary wasn't through working Gil over. She put an arm around Gil. "I knew Debbie would find a good-looking one—a smart one too. Tell me about your late wife, Gil."

"If you don't mind, I make it a practice never to talk about her."

Mary hesitated. Her baby, Debbie, was about to leave her, and Mary had no time to be patient or tactful, but she would start slow. "Who decorated your house, Gil?"

"I see what you're driving at, Mary. If Debbie wants to change the wallpaper that Jean picked out, will I get upset? Well, that's not a problem. After I lost Jean, we moved. I decorated the new house. I have a picture of Jean on my bed stand. I'll move it to Amy's room."

"I think it's time you started to talk about your first wife," Mary said, not as advice, but as an order.

Gil took a deep breath. "Jean was Phi Beta Kappa senior at the University of Montreal when we met. She was a dancer and figure skater—Olympic caliber before she threw out a knee. We met at a gymnastic competition in Montreal. She saw me compete against her brother on parallel bars. Jean and I had two dates, then I had to return with my team to Wisconsin. There were many phone calls during the next week. French was Jean's first language. I crammed more French textbooks in one week than most French majors see in a year. Ten days after we met, I scrapped up all the money I had and flew back to Montreal. We had our third date and set the wedding date."

Gil stopped to swallow. "Am I comparing Debbie to Jean? That's what you want to know, isn't it?"

"I want to know if Debbie is competing with a ghost who never grows old. Your Jean will only get more beautiful, more intelligent, and loving with time. Debbie's similar, isn't she? Athletic, talented—full of energy?"

Gil nodded. "And loving, which only gets better with age. The only comparison that counts is that Jean and I were wonderfully happy together. I'm wonderfully happy when I'm with Debbie. And I think she is with me."

Mary gave Gil a squeeze. "Make sure you visit us often, or I'll poison your kiwi juice."

Gil kissed the cheek of his would-be mother-in-law. "Now I know where Debbie gets her spunk."

*   *   *

George frowned. "I'm not sure we'll be able to get Martin to stay with Debbie's parents. Martin's never been away from home." He gave an accusing glance at Eve. "He'll get lonely."

Debbie's arms waved away the problem. "Let me try. Whatever Amy does, Martin wants to do, and vice versa. The two of them have a synergistic bravery when it comes to trying new things."

Debbie snatched a textbook from her library and corralled the youngsters petting the McWard tricolor border collie on the porch. "You have a choice, little trampers. One, you can come to the East Dodo Island with us. The trip over will be on a rough bouncy ocean." Debbie moved her arm up and down to simulate rolling waves. "But you can hunt for the tuatara beak-headed lizard. It has three eyes. And if you cut off its tail, it grows back." She showed them a picture from the book. Indeed, the iguana-like reptile had an eye on its forehead.

"The tuatara is really a small dinosaur, no different from the ones two hundred million years ago. The only ones left. New Zealand's the only place where you can find them."

"Cool!" Martin beamed. "I'm gonna stalk a dinosaur."

"I thought we'd be snorkeling with the dolphins," Amy reminded. She had memorized the itinerary.

Debbie furrowed her brow. "The sharks scared the dolphins away." Her hand made a dorsal fin cutting through the sea.

"But"—Debbie grinned—"you two will be perfect for hunting the tuatara. You're small enough to corner them in their caves. Bring a flashlight."

"Caves? Can these dinosaurs bite?" Martin asked.

Debbie pondered the question. "They're not real big—only sixty centimeters. Sharp teeth though. Sharp claws."

Amy knew when adults were being evasive. "Do they bite?"

"No worry," Debbie said. "I've seen the two of you run. You both run pretty fast. But split up. That confuses the tuataras. They don't know whom to chase—'less there's a herd of them. But whatever you do, don't trip. Another trick is to leave a hat or jacket for them to tear up while you climb a tree, and the shredded clothing pieces will help us find you. You're both good tree climbers, and the tuataras are lousy climbers. They just chew on the tree until it topples. But that takes 'em forever, so by that time, we'll have sent out a search party to chase them away."

"What's the other choice," Amy asked.

"Other choice? Oh yes. My mom. Your new grandmother wants to teach you piano—Martin too. Grandma McWard"—Debbie stopped to chuckle at the thought of her youngish-looking mother as a grandmother—"is one of the best concert pianists in New Zealand. But to pay for your lessons, someone has to help Grandpa McWard feed the lambs and kids, watch over the puppies, and taste the Mandarin oranges in case they get too sweet. Then there's the chicks and—"

Martin tugged on Debbie's sweater. "Can you get my toothbrush off the bus?"

"Okay," Debbie sniffed, "Guess you can always chase the tuatara next time."

"Yeah, next time," Amy said.

CHAPTER 12

Breakneck

Impatience is the greatest gift a teenager has. Impatience propels them from a sheltered, nurtured life with minimum responsibilities to the uncertain joys of adulthood. Impatience caused Chip Schumaker to do poorly in school. His assignments bored him. He treated obvious test exams as trick questions, as he looked for exceptions to the rules. He finished homework in a hurry so he could get on with more exciting things. As a result, Chip's counselor, Mr. Sand, called him in for his annual guilt session.

"Chip, I don't know how you're going to make it into college," Mr. Sand announced gravely. The community college will take you, but you could've gone to the University of Illinois or even Cal Tech."

"Couldn't afford it, anyway." Chip shrugged.

Mr. Sand sighed. "I can't figure this out. You have the highest IQ that ever passed through this office but, your teachers say, you're just going through the motions. Your junior year grades were awful."

Chip had dreaded this lecture. "I won't lose my eligibility to the chess club, will I?"

Mr. Sand shook his head. By rights, the underachieving boy should be banned from extracurricular activities, but Sand knew the tragically high dropout rate among gifted youth, and that nonclassroom activities and relationships were the glue that kept kids in school. "Maybe you should add some other activities."

"I like chess. I'm state champion."

"Sure. Stick with chess. But add something else. You'll enjoy school more."

"I've always wanted to try out for the baseball team."

Mr. Sand shrugged. "Why not? Not everyone makes it, though. The coach may not want to invest time on a senior. How about the computer club?"

"They're too elementary. I help 'em out sometimes, but"—Chip paused—"I won't be able to get into a four year college, will I? What if I finish my senior year with all As. I can do it. Maybe there's a scholarship—"

"I suspect you can. But you should have decided to buckle down a year ago. You're a senior. Scholarship decisions are made at the end of the junior year."

Chip left the meeting feeling mildly depressed. He had resigned himself to getting a job. A year ago, he started a business that printed address labels for a dozen small businesses whose owners had never met him or had the foggiest idea that they were doing business with a fifteen-year-old. Chip gave half his earnings to his mother and poured the other half into buying components for his build-it-yourself computers.

Chip said hello to all the people he passed in the crowded halls of the school. He called them by name. Memorizing names was easy. Chip thought of himself as friendly, but classmates were standoffish. If they got too close to a nerd, it might rub off.

He approached a circle of seniors, smiling cordially. "Hi!"

"Hi, Chip. How's the chess champion?" Rick Taylor asked. Rick was running for class president. He had to make a political pretense at being friendly. A vote was a vote. Rick also captained the football and baseball teams, which gave him first pick of the pretty cheerleaders.

"Okay, I guess," Chip grinned. Chip had his name in the school paper, but he never received a varsity letter like he thought he should. None of these jocks would be state champion at anything.

"What kind of jobs do chess champions get?" Rick asked, hiding a smirk.

"Some turn professional. For most of us, it's just for fun. Like anything else, how many high school athletes turn pro? The statistics are dreary. So you do it for fun."

Rick bristled. "I *expect* to turn pro."

"You're fighting the odds," Chip said, "but you're having fun, so what do you care."

"I care," Rick said seriously. He could think of no other options in life.

Chip said, "I'm thinking of trying out for the baseball team."

Another senior said, "You need muscles for baseball, Chip. I bet you have great wrist muscles from watching all that Internet porn."

The circle roared with laughter. Chip joined in laughing at his expense then excused himself.

Chip bicycled home, alone. His future wasn't going the way he had hoped. His ACT test results weren't in, yet, but he was sure he had a perfect score, although he mulled whether to formally contest one physics question that was obviously written before the latest findings were published. Maybe he could get into a challenging university with his scores, but could he afford to stay there? But the more pressing problem was the prom. Chip let his troubles evaporate as he concentrated on his computer program.

In his room, Chip logged on to the Internet and downloaded his *Stopwatch* program, along with a huge benchmark file. He activated his Breakneck plug-in and repeated the benchmark download using Breakneck. *One point three seconds.* He smiled. He did the division in his head. Faster by 11.02 percent. The results always came back 11.02 percent faster, and each of the five hundred times he had gone through the exercise gave him a warm glow.

His mother stuck her head in to his untidy room, made untouchable for cleaning by a maze of wires, stacks of disks, and an unruly scattering of programming texts. "Supper gonna be late. And don't waste any more money on those damn toys. My car needs new tires. If you want to go to the prom, you need tires."

Mom didn't understand that today's proms meant out-of-the-question limousines, tuxedos, pricey flowers, group dinners, and hotel rooms.

Chip turned to his mother. She didn't want to understand anything about computers despite his frequent attempts to interest her, and she resented the time and money he spent on "his toys."

"Hey, Mom, someday we're gonna have a lot of money. I mailed my Breakneck Download to one of the top geeks in the country, Willie Dern. If his company buys it, we could make a giga million."

"Yeah? I'll have to see your gigas, to believe it. Did you get an answer back?"

"Not exactly," Chip admitted. He had expected at least a rejection letter by now and had hoped for a letter that Dern had received the software and was reviewing it.

"I thought so. Don't waste your time, Chip. And for God's sake, turn off your toys and rake the leaves."

*   *   *

ROTORUA, NEW ZELAND

Willie didn't like the smell of the sulfur springs, so he sequestered himself in his hotel room, while the other trampers headed toward the spas. He wanted to invite Virginia to his room, but that would mean giving up on Debbie. Willie didn't give up easily.

161

Willie hit the enter button on his computer and checked the speed against the benchmark, and swore at the unconventional programming. "Damnit, 11.02 percent faster!"

Willie rubbed his head. Given another week or two, Willie could figure out the hybrid programming logic, or so he kept telling himself. Breakneck had only a half-life of two years at most with the inevitability of broadband, but it would position him to launch his own company and give him the momentum to become one of the richest men in the world. He wondered if his golden future could have made a difference in courting Debbie. *No, and that's not a bad thing.*

There were rumors of an engagement, but Debbie and Rocklin were playing it coy with no public announcement. But the signs were there. Losing Debbie should have dampened his love of the vivacious young woman. Instead, it just amplified his love and stabbed his every thought with the pain of loss. It was especially insulting to lose Debbie to a nobody like Rocklin.

But when Debbie finds herself trying to support a bankrupt husband and living with a blackballed failure, the fireworks in her romance will fizzle, Wille predicted. *Then maybe she might reconsider.*

And I'll take her back in a heartbeat.

CHAPTER 13

We Know Who You Are

East Dodo Island, the gem tourist stop of the Kiwi on a Cloud travel company, sat like a yellow ribbon twenty miles from the North Island. The two-square-mile island of coral sand lay far enough from the usual tourist islands to insure privacy for the trampers. A sparse strand of coconut palms leaned toward the sun. The coral reef provided unspoiled and uncrowded snorkeling for the travel agency's tourists—including an area staked out for those adventurous enough to swim in the buff.

Accommodations were another matter. A long wooden hut supplied fifteen small rooms with comfortable beds, but little else, and two community bathrooms. Three full-sized tents on cement slabs gave additional sleeping places for larger families, like the Kings. Cooking took place on a large outdoor barbecue pit, rain or shine.

Elizabeth set frozen Cervena venison tenderloins on a bench to thaw and started the fire while the trampers changed clothes for a day of snorkeling and surfboarding.

Gil instructed his core group to watch the suspects for moles, scars, dyed hair, and any lapses in language.

The trampers were still buzzing over Mrs. Turner. She had taken ill in Rotorua, and Debbie had her put up in a hotel with the promise of sending Elizabeth to sail back to pick her up a day later. The owner would have a tirade over the extra cost of fuel, but what else could Debbie do?

"What husband leaves his sick wife in a hotel while he goes snorkeling? George asked. "I think Mr. Turner is our fugitive."

Gil nodded. "Turner said he was complying with Harper's order to not leave the trip, but I agree. Turner is our number one suspect."

Mr. Goodman approached the group with a bloody foot. "I cut my toe on a clam shell." He swore in an unintelligible tongue.

"Let me to look at it," Eve said.

"My wife can take care of it," he growled, limping toward the community hut and still swearing.

"Does anyone know what language that was?" Willie asked. None did. "I've written in phonetically. When we get back to electricity, I'll have the computers back home work on it."

"I believe it's Yiddish," Debbie guessed.

An hour later, Eve, attracting more-than-usual male attention in her bathing suit, inspected the men inspecting her. Eve caught Gil long enough to whisper. "Lafate's wet hair. Look at the hairline. Is that a face-lift line or a hair transplant?"

"You know the most about those things."

Eve scowled. "I'm an ob-gyn and geneticist for God's sake. I don't know from wrinkles about plastic surgery."

Debbie checked in. "I caught the Stanley family in an inconsistency. He says he's an architect. His wife says he builds houses, or *did* build houses.

"That's just the usual marriage gap," George explained. "I talk about being a three-letter man in college; Eve talks about my screwing around with sports."

Gil nodded. "We'll ask Stanley's advice on a hut repair."

"No signs of the mole that Frank talked about, or a scar that would show where it had been removed," Virginia said, "except on Mrs. Klaus. She has more moles than the Wicked Witch of the West."

Clutch had been ordered to ask no questions because of his lack of subtlety, but he watched the suspects' wives, and they watched him. "Gil!" Clutch confided, "Mrs. Stanley came on to me, and I think Mrs. Borolo is interested. Do you think the Butcher rented a wife?"

"Of course," Gil answered, "what better cover? A rent-a-wife for a job like this is probably being paid a bundle. She's not likely to blow it to have an affair with you, unless ordered to do it. So go for it, Clutch. But if I observe Mr. Stanley drowning you in the surf, I won't come to your rescue."

"Mrs. Stanley is too *crumpets and tea* for me, anyway," Clutch grumbled. "She talks funny."

After Clutch romped away, Gil thought, *What if the Butcher sent his phony spouse to Clutch to extract information?*

* * *

The McWards couldn't have been more pleased to have young children in their home. Mary McWard made the children homemade croissants for breakfast.

"Crois-sants," Amy exclaimed. "Daddy doesn't make them very often. Too much cho-les-ter-ol."

"You pronounce croissants like a Frenchie," Brian noticed.

"My mother was French Canadian. I don't remember her."

"Ye think ye were born speaking French?" Ian chuckled.

"My dad has a new computer CD to teach French to kids. He draws neat pictures."

"And writes cool programs too, I bet," Brian inserted.

Amy nodded as if programming didn't deserve the same status as a neat drawing. "He tests them on me. He does it over until it's fun. My picture's on the cover and inside too."

Martin dribbled the strong tasting New Zealand honey on his croissant. "Mrs. Lafate was teaching us some French."

"And Mme. Lafate isn't even French," Amy added.

"Why do you say that, Amy?" Mary quizzed.

"Daddy says most French people speak softly. Mme. Lafate is loud."

* * *

No more information flowed until after the evening's marshmallow roast and sing-along. The trusted detectives gathered in Debbie and Gil's tent.

"We figured it out," George exclaimed, as he and Eve were the last to enter Debbie's tent. Clutch and Willie, looking sullen, sat on a cot. Virginia, still playing the role of Willie's loyal assistant, stood behind them with her arms folded, as if cold, in the night air.

"Have you noticed how many of the men could pass for brothers?" Eve whispered with a mixture of elation and fear in her voice.

"We know who the bad guys are," George announced smugly.

"So do we," Debbie said grimly. She leaned against Gil.

"There's more than one villain," Eve said.

"Unfortunately," Gil confirmed. "Look behind you, folks."

George and Eve turned to see Lafate, Stanley, and Tinsley standing against the tent flaps. Pistols dangled at their sides.

Ratac "the Butcher" Bymarovitch laughed, his French accent discarded as he blew a column of smoke to the top of the tent, "So you know who we are, and we know who you are: small people who would interfere with world changes that you could not begin to understand."

"I understand you're a fraud and a murderer," Eve snapped.

"Fraud? Yes. Murderer? *Of course!* I made a pretty convincing Frenchman, didn't I? It took you a long time to find me. You were looking for me among your trampers, among my soldiers. All in all, I have six high priced soldiers. Turner is guarding the outside of this tent. His wife, if I can call her that, is on a mission. All are English speaking mercenaries to be sure, but the men were selected for intelligence and similar physical characteristics meant to divert attention from me. Assuredly, three are women, but each is adept with weapons and explosives, and all have killed before."

"Are ya gonna to kill us?" Clutch asked.

Lafate answered, "Maybe. Maybe not. I had hoped that killing the redheaded army spy would put the meddlesome Mr. Ferret in jail, and I wouldn't have to trouble myself with any of you. But sadly, you persisted, so you needed a warning.

"I must admit that after I pushed Debbie off the cliff, I had regrets." Bymarovitch stretched his gun-free hand affectionately toward Debbie's head. "You showed me a fine holiday, Debbie. Even your feeble attempts at being a detective were more amusing than annoying. You were like what we call a *cmrlj,* a bumblebee, a pest, yet easy to swat. I should thank you by showing you the joys of the flesh as only a real man can deliver them."

Debbie dodged his touch, and Gil stepped between Bymarovitch and her.

Bymarovitch pointed his gun at Gil's chest.

"You'll have to kill me first," Debbie snapped in an effort to distract the Butcher.

"It wouldn't be the first time, my love." Bymarovitch smirked with side glances at Eve and Virginia. "But I don't have the time to do any of you justice, dead or alive, because I have to get back to my people. So let me tell you what *you* will be doing. You will call in on your shortwave radio tomorrow, as you did today, to tell Inspector Harper that *all is well.* You will entertain your trampers the same as usual. You will spend a week snorkeling. Each day you will call your whereabouts to Inspector Harper.

What? You think General Bymarovitch has lost his mind? You're thinking the crazy general will let you use your radio and phones to alert the Kiwi authorities to block my flight?"

The Butcher laughed as he gestured for Debbie's cell phone. She handed it to him. He dropped it to the ground and smashed it with a powerful stomp of his hiking boot. "You say the cell phones are out of range, but just in case—"

"Yes, Debra McWard *will* radio the policeman." Ratac was enjoying himself. "Except it will be one of my actresses, Mrs. Stanley, who will be calling in for you from the mainland. She's been practicing a surprisingly accurate imitation.

"So why should I keep you alive, at all? Huh? That's a scary thought, isn't it? There's only one scenario in which you'll be needed. That's if Inspector Harper decides to pay you a visit in the next two days. We wouldn't want him to find no one home. You can tell him what an evil man Frank Ferret was and send him on his way."

Clutch countered, "Eventually, someone will believe Frank's story and come a lookin' for ya."

Ratac's cheek twitched nervously before he laughed. He had a cruel laugh that captured the hate in his thoughts. "Mr. Ferret will never come to trial. His jail is small enough to accommodate about three well-placed explosives by Mrs. Turner who should be close to her target by now. Ferret's absurd rants will never be heard, nor will there be anyone left alive who remembers them. So you are my only remaining concern.

"At the end of the week, instead of traveling back to the mainland, you will stay here, until someone finds you. What would you say? A week? A month? How did you put it, Debbie? *This island and reef are off the beaten path. We have it all to ourselves.* You see, I'll have your boat. It'll be found swamped along the coast after we disembark. People will assume the entire party drowned. They'll look for bodies, but in the wrong place.

"So thank me. You'll have an extended holiday. Eating the fish you catch—just like a band of Robinson Crusoes. Maybe you'll choose to dine on the giant weta insects that Debbie told us about. Eventually, your tour company will buy another boat, and a new group of trampers will interrupt your holiday or find your bleached bones, depending on how resourceful you are. Remember how the Donner Party survived? At least some of them. Now *they* were a resourceful bunch." Bymarovitch laughed.

"You're disgusting," Willie snarled.

"I've been called worse." Ratac put his pistol to Willie's forehead, and Willie's burst of bravado withered. "Tell me, my rich friend, how much is it worth to spare your life?"

Willie trembled. "I'll have a million dollars wired. Half now and half when I'm freed."

"Really?" Bymarovitch clucked. "Such a small portion of your net worth. Surely, you discount your worth."

"Two million, then." Willie choked. "True, I'm worth more, but it's all in stock options. I'm required to work five years for my company before I'm permitted to exercise them."

Bymarovitch waved away the explanation. "Two million sounds fair," he said seriously. "How much for your friends?"

Willie squirmed. "A quarter million for Debbie's life. The same for Virginia, and fifty thousand for the others."

"Each?"

"For all of them."

Bymarovitch laughed. "You drive a hard bargain, Willie. Too hard for me. And forgive me for saying this, but you have a less than sterling reputation for honesty. In fact, on the Internet your competitors say you would screw your mother. I'm sorry, Willie, but I'm an honest barbarian. If I promise to impregnate all the women in your village, fry your testicles

169

with electrodes before I kill you, and burn your houses with your children inside, I keep my word. But you, sir, cannot be trusted. I cannot do business with you."

"I *can* be trusted!" Willie protested with panic in his voice. "Look, I'll give you this disk I'm reviewing. It's new software to speed up Internet transactions. It's not copyrighted. It's worth at the very least twenty or thirty million. Have someone who knows Internet software run it! You'll see! I'm not making this up."

The Butcher took the disk and squeezed it into his jacket pocket. "As I said before, Mr. Dern, you can't be trusted."

"*I* can be trusted," Clutch blurted. "I can give ya—"

"Save it, Clutch," Gil snapped. "The Butcher intends to kill us, no matter what we do."

Bymarovitch laughed. "Dr. Rocklin, Dr. Rocklin. The fallen FBI agent—a man who doesn't parade his intellect like Mr. Dern. I'm sorry to contradict you, young man, but I'm going to let you live. As I said, I'm concerned that Inspector Harper will take a chopper over here to gather more depositions. Debbie will explain my absence in a believable way. I'm sure she'll think of something. Skinny-dipping on the other side of the island? Collecting seashells? Something."

Debbie blurted, "I'll be glad to. Just so we part company."

"You will?" Bymarovitch responded with mock shock. "You'll do that for me? You'll see that Inspector Harper goes away happy and doesn't put out an islandwide search for me? Such consideration! Well then, I must do something for you. I'll let your bus-driving friend, Elizabeth Stevens, live. She'll be with me, you see. In fact, she's on the boat waiting for me, as we speak. She sends her regrets to Debbie for not saying a proper good-bye in person—which, of course, I wouldn't allow."

Gil bristled. "She's your daughter for God's sake!"

Bymarovitch's taunting voice turned stern. His face turned red, and his hand tightened on his pistol and began to shake. "Maybe she is, maybe she isn't. If a father has to question it, she is not worth keeping alive. But Elizabeth doesn't have to know my true feelings. As far as she knows, I'm her long-lost father returning to be reunited with my beloved daughter and my faithful brother. Elizabeth will take me to him—take me to his hideaway in the hills. Then we will all leave your country—never to bother you again."

Ratac laughed. "Oh yes, for good measure, we'll have two delightful children along for the trip."

Clutch and Debbie grabbed Gil so that he wouldn't rush the Butcher. George looked ready to pounce.

"Aha! Suddenly, I sense a degree of compliance that didn't exist before." Ratac laughed.

Bymarovitch laughed raucously as he guided Debbie to the shortwave radio. "You say that cell phones are out of range on the oceanic debris, so here, Debbie, call your home. I saw their radio. Tell your lovely mother to give Mme. Lafate the children when she comes. Don't use any tricks, warning names, or code words. I can have an actress do it, but I'm sure *you* can be a more convincing you. If you do that, we won't have to kill your parents."

Debbie looked at Gil for guidance. He swallowed hard and nodded. She placed the call.

"Excellent, Debbie," Bymarovitch crooned. "Short and sweet. No funny business. That's the cooperation we need."

Bymarovitch turned to Willie and Clutch. "Naturally, you two don't have the vested interest in the children that the others do. But if either of you endanger Dr. Rocklin's daughter, I'm sure he can be most unpleasant."

Bymarovitch poked Gil with his pistol. "So you killed the murderer of your wife with one punch? We're two of a kind, Doctor. I'm sad that I don't have time to give you a lesson on lethal punches. You'd be a worthy student. Maybe some other time—some other life."

"I can hardly wait," Gil muttered.

Bymarovitch glanced at Virginia. There was no leverage over her. "I can shoot you now as an example to the others, or I can take you with me for fun."

Virginia grabbed Willie, as if to say she was with him.

Ratac screwed a silencer on his pistol.

Willie sensed that the Butcher was about to shoot Virginia and said, "I control her."

As much as Virginia hated the meaning of Willie's words, she found herself grateful for Willie's chauvinism. Control was something Bymarovitch understood, and Willie's statement seemed to satisfy him.

Ratac smiled to himself. Ratac needed twenty-four to forty-eight hours, then he would take what was left of the gold, kill his brother and his wife, and fly back to Croatia in the plane he had chartered. Mrs. Stanley, a former bomber pilot, would fly the plane. After that, the trampers were of no use, except for Elizabeth. He had plans for Elizabeth.

Elizabeth must not see the death of her friend Debbie and the trampers. Ratac needed his daughter's cooperation. Threats would most likely work, but Elizabeth was tough and unpredictable. She risked her life taking the Zodiac after Debbie at Milford Sound. Elizabeth could get herself killed helping her friends or protecting her stepparents.

The children were added insurance in case something went wrong, and they could also guarantee Elizabeth's cooperation upon returning to Croatia.

Ratac's story to the trampers of needing to keep them alive until he departed New Zealand was conjured up to avoid a general panic. What if the cell phones could reach the shore? And he didn't want to have to chase down frightened trampers scattering all over the island. True it would be amusing, but the need for a quick return to his homeland pressed on him more than he was willing to admit. Harper's edict not to leave the tour group had wrecked Ratac's timeline.

But as for killing all the trampers at once, *no problem*. The well-hidden plastic explosive under the propane tanks heating the hut would simultaneously explode as the trampers slept. Separate charges would level those sleeping in the tents.

*   *   *

The trampers watched as Ratac and his party sailed into the night with their boat. Gil gathered the group. "Kids are in danger, and Frank may already be dead. The bastard had an army with him."

"But he was the one who killed Rose O'Hara," Virginia said.

"And attacked Carp," Debbie added.

Willie growled, "There goes your best friend, Debra, waving to us. Little miss maroon hair has run off with her crazy father and left us here to die of starvation."

"She may not have had a choice," Debbie replied, but Elizabeth's willing desertion added to her depression.

Eve said. Let's not tell the others right away, or they might start acting like I'm feeling."

"They'll find out soon enough," Debbie said. "There's no food."

Willie nodded. "We have to take stock."

Virginia observed, "Ratac's destroyed our generator, dumped our food and water, smashed our shortwave radio and cellular phones, and took our flares."

"No way of communicating," Willie clucked grimly. "My computer is out of range."

Debbie said, "We won't starve. There are plenty of shellfish. Water won't be a problem if we get a little rain."

Clutch said, "So we eat oysters for a couple of days. It'll do us good. Sooner or later someone will come looking for us."

Debbie shook her head. "It'll be *later*. Normally, it's the office manager who would know when a group doesn't show up and find out why. But *I'm* doubling as office manager. It could be four to six days before anyone wonders what happened to us."

George pointed helplessly in the direction of the mainland. "Maybe Inspector Harper will come for more depositions."

Debbie kicked the sand. "Unlikely. I convinced Harper that we'd meet him in Auckland at the end of the trip. Fortunately for us, Lafate didn't know that. We're stuck here for a while."

Gil shook his head. "We can't wait that long. Ratac will take Amy and Martin as hostages. So we have to tear apart the hut and make a raft. We make a sail from the tent and get back to shore."

"I can navigate," Willie offered. "I need my disk back."

"And maybe we can save Frank and his jailors," Virginia added, but no one acknowledged that possibility.

Eve looked at the hut. "How do we take the hut apart? We have no tools."

Debbie put her forehead on Gil's shoulder. "Even if we had a raft, we'd be going against the current and the westerlies. It could take more than a day. The kids will be gone, and Frank will be bombed."

The group fell silent. There was no easy solution.

"At least this Lafate or Ratac critter didn't kill us," Clutch offered.

Gil grimaced. "I don't think Ratac intended us to live very long—just long enough for him to board a plane or a boat. After that, he doesn't need us to slow down Harper. After that, he doesn't want us alive and doesn't need hostages. He'll kill the kids."

Eve began to sob.

Gil took a breath. He knew that his boiling emotions could only interfere with his protecting Amy. "I don't buy his story of keeping us alive. This Ratac animal intends for us to die. What we have to determine is *how?*"

CHAPTER 14

Bad Things Happen

Mrs. Paula Turner prided herself in her bomb-making abilities. The plastic explosives she'd sent to the island would blow all the witnesses to shreds. She only regretted that she couldn't see the explosions. She had enjoyed being Mrs. Turner and sharing the bed of her mercenary lover. Paula's ability as a bomb maker, honed with the IRA, had brought Marcus and her together. A successful bombing of Frank Ferret's jail would surely elevate her in Bymarovitch's eyes. She entertained the thought of replacing Mme. Lafate as first lady when Ratac gained control of his country.

The short flight to the South Island and the rental of a car got her to her destination earlier than she planned. Daylight was not the best time to plant bombs. She would wait until nightfall, and when Harper and his cohorts arrived in the morning, they would join Frank Ferret as shards of flesh in a large hole in the ground.

*   *   *

Mary McWard received Debbie's call and sat back, perplexed. The following morning she shared the message. "Pack your bags kids." The murky and misty sky had relegated the children to the indoors. They were tiring of the intensive music lessons, and didn't protest as much as they would have a day earlier. They waited until evening before Mme. Lafate pulled up in a rented car. Joseph Tinsley drove, and he held the umbrella for Mme. Lafate as she scurried up the porch.

"Oh good! I see the children are ready," the French woman gushed loudly. "Can I talk to you alone, Mary?"

Mme. Lafate's tone exuded sweetness and sympathy. "Your future son-in-law broke his leg on a hike. Debbie didn't want to mention it over the phone. And of course, she can't leave the campers."

"That's more reason to leave Amy here with me," Mary argued.

Mme. Lafate shrugged. "That's what Debbie said, but Gil wanted her back." Lafate looked at Tinsley fidgeting in the rain. Tinsley wanted to kill them all, but with a farm this large, he might miss a farmhand who could set off an alarm—or so Ratac judged.

Mary scowled. "Why didn't the King family come?"

"Oh, Dr. King is looking after Gil's leg, and George King doesn't want to drive on the left side of the road. I adore the youngsters, and I don't snorkel, so I volunteered to accompany Mr. Tinsley."

Mary forced a smile.

Amy gave hugs and sloppy kisses to all the McWard family. Mary McWard's eyes watered at losing her new step granddaughter. Martin shook hands with everyone and promised to come back someday.

As Mme. Lafate, Tinsley, and the children drove out of sight, Mary said, "Ian, Brian, follow them! All the way to East Dodo Island, if necessary. I don't feel comfortable with this. Not comfortable at all."

"My thoughts, precisely." Ian loaded his .22 caliber rifle as he and Brian bounded into the pickup truck and started after Tinsley and the kids. The rain turned to a torrent, which helped the followers. Ian knew the gravel road as well as his own driveway and needed no lights. Tinsley's tail lights would provide the beacon to follow.

About three miles from the McWard farm, Tinsley sat between the children while Mme. Lafate drove. He crowed, "I thought they'd give us a tougher time."

"Our leader forced the Kiwi to call." Mme. Lafate smirked. "What choice did they have."

Martin picked up on the meaning of the words. This was not right. His father had briefed him on all the tricky ways that bad guys used to get children in their cars. This wasn't one of them, but this was not right. "I'm going to throw up," he announced. The panic in his voice sounded real because it was.

Tinsley swore, and Mme. Lafate pulled the car to the left side of the road. Martin opened the back door and bolted out clutching his stomach. He looked back at Tinsley, who grasped Amy's arm while his other hand curled around the top of the door opening. With two arms, Martin slammed the door as hard as he could on Tinsley's fingers. Tinsley screamed as his fingers snapped.

"Run, Amy! Run!" Martin hollered. Martin attacked the thick brush with frantic strides.

Amy opened the door on the roadside and began to follow Martin into the brush.

"Split up, Amy! Like being chased by the dinosaur."

Amy threw her cap on the road and veered left as she struggled deeper into the yellow broom. She squeezed between two shrubs that would be too tight for Mme. Lafate and Tinsley to follow through. Amy's bright yellow clothing, purchased to provide safety when crossing streets, provided camouflage among the flowers, but not for long.

"I-see-you, Amy," Mme. Lafate cooed as her flashlight played over her crouched form. As a soldier reporting to Bymarovitch, Mme. Lafate had run a small prison camp until the Butcher cleansed its population. No one escaped from her prison camp, and a seven-year-old would not be the first.

Amy bolted. Lafate couldn't have planned it better. Amy almost ran into Tinsley's arms then she reversed her path. Lafate met her. The French imposter sprayed Amy's face. Amy took several steps, staggered, and fell.

Mme. Lafate walked over to the unconscious girl and picked Amy up over her head like a weight lifter. "Martin, dear! I have your little friend. Come out, dear. If I have to look for you, I'm afraid I might drop Amy and hurt her. Your father will be very angry with me if I don't bring you both back safe and sound. Come back to the dry car. And don't worry about Mr. Tinsley. He was just teasing."

Martin peeked out from the underbrush. "We want to go back to Mrs. McWard's."

"Very well, Martin. Have it your way."

Martin wormed his way back from a position high on the hill. He had made good headway. Catching him in the dim light would be difficult. Now he stood three yards from Mr. Tinsley and Amy. Lafate's canister flashed. The spray hit Martin in the face. Spinning twice, Martin crumpled.

"I'm going to kill the little bugger!" Tinsley roared. Tinsley gripped an Uzi in his good hand as if he was going to hit Martin with the butt.

Mme. Lafate barked, "You won't do a damned thing, until I tell you that you can! Understand?" She didn't wait for an answer. "Pick him up and put him in the car. I'll look at your fingers later."

Tinsley dumped the children like potato sacks in the backseat of the car. Tinsley looked up to see a rifle barrel pointed at his nose. Brian McWard held the small-caliber weapon. "Drop your gun," Brian said angrily.

Ian rounded the car. With Tinsley between Mme. Lafate and Ian, Lafate couldn't use her gas spray.

Ian spotted the canister. "Dr-rop the can, witch," Ian ordered.

"Brian! If the witch doesn't drop the can, shoot her in the leg."

Mme. Lafate dropped the gas canister. "The children are fine. They're just asleep."

Brian felt Amy's pulse. "They better be e-kay or . . ." He patted Amy's cheeks to wake her up. His rifle sagged, clamped loosely under his arm.

Ian picked Tinsley up by his chin and pressed him against the car. "Ye 'ave some explainin' to do, mon."

"You have no idea who you're up against, you bloody fool," Tinsley snarled.

Ian hit him in the stomach hard enough to cause internal injuries. "That's not an explanation, mon."

Tinsley gasped and vomited. The second punch in the stomach caused Tinsley to pass out.

Ian turned to Mme. Lafate. "I'd never hurt a lady. But ye're not a lady. Ye're some kind o' monster!"

Mme. Lafate put her hands to her eyes as if crying. "You're so right!" Her roundhouse kick surprised Ian, but even if he had been prepared for it, he couldn't have blocked it. Her second kick sent Ian sprawling in the mud. Lafate picked up the canister and emptied it toward Brian. Two more steps and she had scooped up the Uzi.

"Good try, big man." She laughed. "Now pick up your son and drag him into the brush. One twitch and I'll shoot you both and throw in the kids for good measure."

It would be so easy to just shoot them, Mme. Lafate reasoned. *But if I shoot them, General Bymarovitch will say I disobeyed orders.* She reached into her traveler's pouch for two pairs of handcuffs that she had brought for the children. *The cuffs would probably be too large for the kids anyway,* she rationalized, and she would have an excuse not to endure the sadistic bondage that Ratac enjoyed at her expense.

Mme. Lafate spotted a metal fence post in the ditch. The post pointed straight up in the center of the deep ditch. She tugged on it to see if it was hard into the ground, and it was. She fastened both sets of handcuffs to the bottom holes. Forcing the men to kneel at the bottom of the drainage ditch would hide them from any passing cars. Tinsley could drive the McWard truck away, and it would be days, if ever, before their bodies were found.

"Try them on for size, big man," Mme. Lafate ordered. "First your son, then you."

"Don't do this," Ian pleaded. "These ditches fill with water after a rain."

Mme. Lafate saw the rising stream of water and pictured the men under five feet of water. She laughed. "You should have thought of that before you followed us. I could shoot you now, so you don't have to wait for the water to rise over your gasping mouths. Would you like that?" She laughed again. "I promised our leader that I wouldn't shoot anyone, unless absolutely necessary. He has a fear of ballistic tests ever since the police proved that his gun killed his wife. Unfortunately for you, he didn't say anything about drowning."

Mme. Lafate motioned for the woozy Tinsley to take the McWard truck. "Dump it a couple of kilometers up the road. I'll follow you in the car." The children were in her car, and she didn't trust Tinsley with the children.

"Good-bye, Mr. McWard. I'm afraid you're, as they say, in over your head."

*　　*　　*

Ferret pocketed the playing cards and patted his jailer on the back. "Sorry about that royal flush. I usually don't leave jail richer than when I came in."

"Sorry to see you leave, Ferret," the jailer said. "It's seldom we ever get a genuine lady killer in here. And it's seldom the judge comes in the middle of the night with a release. Just who in the hell do you know?"

181

"A nice ol' lady I ran into in Lisbon. I helped save her life."

The policeman glared as he handed Frank his belongings, less passports and the murder weapon. "You know you can't leave our country, and you're to check in every day as to your whereabouts."

"I'll be with the tour group. I'll leave you their itinerary."

"No, you won't. Mr. Armstrong, the owner, doesn't want you back on the tour. It makes the paying customers nervous to have a murderer in their midst."

Frank clucked, "If they only knew—"

After his release from jail, Frank Ferret called for a taxi and headed to a nearby *document expeditor* as he called her. People in her profession were so easy to find. Frank thought they should have a directory on the Internet: *Counterfeit_passports_dot_com*. He needed a passport to leave the country.

The forger introduced herself as Matilda and looked suspiciously at Frank. "You the bloke that murdered the tourist?"

"I didn't know it was in the papers," Frank groused.

"This is a small country. Helping a murderer adds to my risk. You'll pay a premium."

Matilda had the look of a retired hooker with a hint of earlier beauty. She had seen and done it all, but her hard eyes were penetrating and intelligent. Her cover business was rare books. Matilda had to be smart to do what she did without being caught.

"You'd think murderers should get a professional discount," Frank said with a wink.

Matilda chuckled. "I like you." She shuffled through the passport-sized photos that Frank removed from the heel of a shoe. "And you take great passport photos. I'd give you a job if you weren't a killer." She studied Frank's list, and her eyebrows raised. "Quantity discount: only one thousand U.S. dollars each. I'll take cash or traveler's checks, no credit cards."

"No credit cards?" Frank grumbled in mock indignation. "All I have is five thousand in traveler's checks."

"I'll take it, and since you're such a good customer, I'll throw in a credit card for you. Pick a name."

Matilda soon gave Frank passports and, using Frank's template, copied visas to be used for entering Croatia. Another set of documents were made for each of the male suspects whom Frank had photographed. He knew his idea of drugging Bymarovitch and flying him to The Hague for trial wasn't the greatest game plan in the world. Rose had made that disturbingly clear. Undermining his original plan was the loss of Frank's gas canisters. Maybe sleeping pills in the Butcher's coffee would suffice. *Not much of a plan, but it will have to do until I can think of something better.*

Frank didn't linger in Matilda's office. He left with what he thought was the most expensive edition of an early Geoffrey Chaucer ever sold—stuffed with phony passports. He was glad Matilda hadn't added sex to her package price. Frank was short of time for such decadent luxuries. He was also short on cash and down to a thousand dollars in traveler's checks after paying her. Frank took a bus to the car rental office, getting off sooner to use an ATM. He walked the rest of the way to the car rental. He picked out a clean Toyota sedan with higher mileage than he would have liked. He could afford no breakdowns. The car rental manager explained, "We Kiwis have a contract to buy used cars from Japan, so *all* our cars have high mileage." Frank paid with cash, using the false name on the credit card as backup.

During the walk to the dealer, Frank confirmed that someone was following him, and his best guess was that the Kiwi police had assigned a tail. *Story of my life lately*, he thought.

When the tail came closer, he recognized the driver and felt a brief surge of elation. Even with her black wig, he recognized Paula Turner. Frank hit Debbie's cell phone number. He had to warn the trampers that

Marcus Turner was the killer. *No answer. Not even a ring. Out of range? Not good.*

Paula is either here to watch me or kill me. Frank did what he usually did when confronted with a distant enemy. He'd get closer and talk her to death. Frank ignored opening his rental car and flagged her down.

Paula Turner was upset at the change of plans. Frank's early release changed everything. Paula doubted the Butcher's claim that Frank was a CIA spy, but she knew he was a journalist and dangerous to the operation. She wasn't given a gun, only three bombs.

She had watched Ferret dawdling over forms in the car rental office while the manager pulled up the car he was renting. She'd have to plant a bomb in Frank's car before he got in. She pulled up beside the empty car. Paula reached into the backseat and set one of the bombs to explode in a half hour.

Suddenly her car door opened and Frank surprised Turner with a kiss. "What a wonderful surprise. Of all the trampers, you're the only one who cared. Now I don't need to rent a car. Move over, we're going to go up to East Dodo together." He tossed his duffel bag in the backseat. "I'll drive. Unless you'd like to fool round along the way. Oops, sorry if I offended you."

Paula took the bait. "No offence. That's why I'm here. Things haven't been going too well with Marcus and me. Maybe we *could* park somewhere." Paula had a pretty face with Irish blue eyes. In her early forties, she was reasonably sexy for a tall woman forty pounds overweight.

Frank drove Paula's car to the back of the rental car lot. He spotted a narrow space between two aging vans, and squeezed between them. "No one will see us sandwiched in here."

"Frank, I'll have to do my duty in the bushes before I can do you. But you parked so close, I can't open my door. And I have to go. Now!"

"Really?" said Frank coldly. "It wouldn't have anything to do with that ticktock in the backseat?" Frank pulled the blanket off the bomb, wiped his fingerprints off the steering wheel, and laid the blanket across his open window. "You might try being disarming."

"I can't," she screamed. "It's booby-trapped. If the lid's opened, it'll blow."

"And if the lid's not opened?"

"It's set to go off in thirty minutes—*less than thirty minutes!*"

Frank snickered.

"And you thought *I* was a boob. Do you know any yoga, Paula? I dated a yoga instructor once. She taught me how to turn myself into a pretzel—helluva position for making love though." Frank twisted his body to reach for his duffel bag and threw it out the window. He contorted his thin frame through the open window of the car, squeezing between the cars, and pulling himself to the roof the van where his duffel precariously sat. "You ought to try this."

Frank dangled the car keys out of the reach of the now hysterical bomber. "Rose O'Hara used to tease me. She'd call me a pussy because I hate to fight. I really hate to hurt people. But hon, in your case, I'll make an exception. Rose would've been proud."

"You bloody bastard!" she screamed. "You know I can't get out."

"Oh, that's dreadful. But to show you that I can forgive and frickin' forget, I'll give you my cell phone, and you can confess all to the police. I'm sure they'll figure a way to pry you out, and you can explain what you're doing with all those explosives. I'll bet you have even more bundled in your boot."

Frank dialed the station house number and tossed his phone to her. "Make sure you mention my name 'cause there's a reward involved."

She spit at him. "I can't confess. The Butcher never forgives failure. He won't be caught. He's too smart for you. He'll arrange my bail, just so he can torture me."

"Paula, Paula, your boss is goin' down, and you're never gonna see bail."

"He'll find me—even in prison. You have no idea of what he's capable of. I've seen what he did to women recruits that turned him down. I'd rather die."

"Suit yourself. You can think about bombs and all the other bad choices you've made in your life, but don't take too long. The police are only twenty minutes away. *If* they come. They could be on doughnut break. I left the car in neutral, so they can push you out. Of course, you'll have to explain why you left the tour with all those explosives."

The fake Mrs. Turner screamed unintelligible obscenities at Frank. She contorted herself and began to kick unsuccessfully at the windshield. Tossing the bomb out the car window wouldn't help. Even if the bomb didn't go off, she wouldn't be able to throw it far enough to make a difference.

Frank walked back to his rental car and drove slowly, inconspicuously away. Police might look for the last person seen on the dealer's lot, the one who looked tall, thin, and dark like Frank Ferret but who had an Italian accent and used the name James Cook, RN, on his credit card. Frank wondered how long before the police realized the name was the same as Captain Cook, Royal Navy, the father of their county.

He played the Kiwi version of country music on his radio and barely heard the explosion.

*   *   *

Frank's car started to stall sixty miles later. *Try harder, car. Try harder!* Frank didn't want to stop in the country. *What if Marcus Turner is floating around?* he thought. *Damnit, don't stall!* Frank coaxed, but the car barely coasted and coughed into the next small town. A simple adjustment of the idle fixed the problem, but Frank lost time. He decided to drive through the night, but finally had to pull over for a twenty-minute catnap on a scenic overlook.

Frank decided it was too late to join the trampers on the island. Apparently, Debbie's phone was out of range. With no way to reach Debbie, even if he bought a new phone, he'd have to rent a boat. *With my luck, I'd get lost at sea.* If Frank did get there in time, he could warn them about Turner, but now it didn't seem like a good idea. Alerting the trampers might tip the Butcher that he'd been found out, and that could be dangerous. *Turner probably wouldn't try anything until he's off the island, so the trampers are safe. I hope. But what excuse did Paula Turner have to leave the tour?*

His alternative plan meant going directly to Klav Bymarovitch, Elizabeth's adoptive father. Klav could ID his butchering brother, if he would. But all Frank had was a post office box number that he had stolen from Elizabeth's personnel records—records that he had taken so as not to focus the theft on Debbie's file alone. Frank needed help from locals, and the only locals who might be able to help him were Debbie's family. Would they know who he was? Would they help him? At this stage, Frank didn't know, but he would settle for a shower and a beer.

* * *

In the drainage ditch, the water flow from the foothills soon reached to chest level on Ian. He held his unconscious son's head out of the water. Even Ian's muscular free arm ached from the cold water and his son's dead weight. The rising water slowed as the level reached the wider part of the ditch. But it didn't stop.

Ian realized that Mary would not come looking for him. She expected Brian and him to go to East Dodo. Ian and his son would drown, and there was nothing he could do about it.

* * *

Frank's headlights provided the only light in the inky night by the time he found the gravel road to the valley where he hoped to find the McWard's farm. The road seemed longer than it looked on the map, and with the heavy rain, Frank became increasingly impatient with the slow pace. *At least there's no traffic. I spoke too soon.* Frank slowed to a creep when he saw a white truck on the side of the road. The side of the truck had *McWard's Kiwis* stenciled on the side. *This can't be it,* Frank told himself. *It's too soon.* Frank drove on for another mile. An object caught Frank's eye, but he drove past it. He stopped and backed up fifty yards until he saw it again. *Damn! A baseball cap, just like the one that Debbie gave Amy. What if it's Amy's? What if she lost it.* For most anyone else, Frank wouldn't bother getting wet to retrieve a baseball cap, but he had a genuine affection for the youngster. As soon as Frank stepped into the rain, he heard the call.

"Help us, mon. Help us!"

The voice came from the drainage ditch. Frank's key-ring flashlight barely made out the two heads struggling to stay above the frothy torrent in the ditch. Brian had regained consciousness from the shock of the cold water. He joined the call for help.

Frank asked, "You guys fishing for smelt or somethin'? Need a hand?"

Brian said, "We're handcuffed to the bottom. Can't move. Water's getting higher."

Frank whistled. His mind raced for tubing the men could use as snorkels. *It won't work. The current is too strong. After a while the tubing will fill with more water than can be cleared.*

"Is there somewhere I can go to get help?"

"Not enough time, mon. Go to the truck. There's a long metal cable in the back."

"Your truck's a couple of kilometers from here. Hang on."

Frank turned his car around and gunned it. Several times the car threatened to go into a slide on the gravel. Frank reached the truck. It was locked, but

Frank could see the outline of the key in the ignition. *Hell, I thought Kiwis didn't lock their doors. Must have been driven by a non-Kiwi.* Frank found a boulder to smash the side window. He quickly found the cable and a pair of small metal snips. He gunned his car back to the baseball cap marker. Frank snipped the rusted wires connecting the posts. But the tempered steel of the handcuffs resisted all the pressure he could put on the chains. Frank threaded the cable through the open back windows of the car.

Brian was standing on his father's feet to elevate another inch.

Hurry, mon!" Ian urged.

Frank waded into the ditch and tried to thread the other end of the cable into one of the higher holes in the metal fence post.

"The hole's too small for the cable. There's nothing to grab on to." Frank knew that the cable could be wrapped around the handcuffs. If he used the handcuffs to catch the cable, both men could have broken wrists or worse. He also knew that the wheels of his small car would spin on the loose gravel. He might not have the traction to pull the post out of the ground. Frank put a loose hitch on the post. He moved the car. The post tilted, and the hitch flew off the post, smacking the car.

"Damn it, mon, the post is lower!" Ian hollered.

"Let's try yankin' it from the ground."

Ian said, "We've tried, mon. This post is anchored in twenty kilograms of cement with the suction holding it in."

"Sorry," Frank said, "but at least it moved. Let's rock it, pal. It should be embedded in mud soup by now."

The three men put their heads under water and rocked the cement block holding the post. They repeated the action two more times.

"The water's up ta Brian's neck," Ian said. "It's now or never, mon. We hav' to drag it."

Frank waded back into the trench. They pushed the post, and it tilted lower.

Ian said, "Do you have a knife, mon?"

The implications of the question made Frank shudder. The police still held his pocketknife as evidence. "No," Frank answered, "but I can get broken glass from the car window. Let's try again."

They pulled and began to drag the block to a higher level on the ditch. The slippery footing of small pieces of shale made it difficult, until Ian lifted the entire piece of cement from the water. They carried the cement to the high edge of the ditch, breathing heavily. Prone on the gravel road in the headlights of the car, they started to laugh hysterically then cry.

Frank pulled a custom-made key from his boot heel and tried to pick the handcuff locks.

"Couldn't have done it without ye," Ian stated. "And why didn't ye use that pick in the first place?"

"Ah, last time I used it, it took me an hour to get loose from some corrupt Nigerian police."

"Who in the hell are ye?"

"Frank Ferret's the name. You must be Ian McWard."

"Aye, Ian McWard. This is my son, Brian." Ian cocked his head. "How is it ye know our name?"

"The sign on your truck. I was comin' to see ya."

"Why?"

"'Cause I love your delightful daughter."

"She already has a good mon."

"True. Nothin' to worry 'bout. I'm not the marryin' kind. And Debbie hates my act. But that doesn't stop me for wantin' to help Debbie and Gil share my reward."

"What reward?" Brian asked.

"For the bastard who pushed Debbie off a cliff. He's a murderin' war criminal who killed a friend of mine. He has to be stopped."

"Gil wasn't joking then," Ian reflected soberly. "We've got some serious talkin' ta do. My new granddaughter and her young friend have been kidnapped."

*　　*　　*

After a long walk up a path strewn with volcanic, black cinders, Elizabeth came to an area of boiling mud. Steam vents hissed like underground exhaust pipes, and the sulfur smell made Ratac Bymarovitch gag. Brother Klav had picked the most unfriendly spot he could find to hide his stolen treasure. Elizabeth pointed to a shed nearly hidden behind a leafless tree. The shed looked no larger than a double-sized duck blind, and it leaned forward from years of being shaken by the North Island's frequent earthquakes. "It's sturdier than it looks, Papa. Is it all right for me to call you Papa? You look just like the man who raised me."

Ratac nodded. "It warms my heart, Elizabeth. After all these years, I have so much to make up to you, my child."

Elizabeth put her arm around Ratac. "Before my father—my uncle—died, he told me about you. He felt miserable for what he did to you and said he wanted you to have the stuff he stole from you. He never said what it was."

"It's all in there?" Ratac asked.

"So he said. At least most of it. He claimed he sold only enough to buy the sheep farm. What's in there anyway?"

"You'll see, my child."

Using a tire jack rod, Ratac knocked a rusted padlock off the door with one swing.

He opened the door. The shed was empty with wood floors and no windows. Nothing. Not even a piece of paper or a rag.

Elizabeth could see the rage building in Ratac's face. "Below, Papa. Under the floorboards."

191

Using the same rod as a crowbar, Ratac began ripping up the floorboards. Within minutes, he held a heavy bag with two hands. "Kugerrands! They're worth over 400 of your U.S. dollars each. And this hole is full of bags. I am rich, Elizabeth. We are rich. I am so lucky to have a loyal daughter like you."

"I don't want any of the gold," Elizabeth muttered. "Take it. It belongs to you. My other father was sorry he ever touched it. Take it with you. But I'm sad, Papa. I'll never see you again."

"Nonsense, my dear, you're coming with me. I insist. My political advisors tell me that the voters will rally to a man with a family."

"You have Mme. Lafate."

Ratac shook his head. "We tried to be together, but she wouldn't have worked out as a first lady. A gifted linguist, to be sure, but she's too rough around the edges. I want to run a gentle campaign based on peace and living together in cooperation. The campaign has already begun."

"Sounds good. Sounds important."

Ratac nodded. "My election could prevent a third world war. You must help me get elected, my dear."

"How can I refuse," Elizabeth answered.

*   *   *

The horizon line hid behind the clouds and mist that had quickly descended on East Dodo Island. The faint glow of light where the sun had plunged into the seas quickly dimmed. Soon blackness would cover the island like a shroud.

On the bottom of the propane tank, at the back of the tramper's wooden sleeping quarters, the timer on the explosive device ticked to zero. The explosion rocked East Dodo Island. The roof flew thirty feet in the air, and the walls collapsed in three directions. The interior turned into a ball of fire, and sleeping water birds erupted into the night sky in panic. No person could have survived the bomb.

The stunned trampers watched the destruction of their living quarters from a natural trench two hundred yards away. Venus murmured something about wanting her money back, but the trampers had stopped listening to her complaints long ago. The reality of their plight started to sink in.

"Will anyone on the mainland see the explosion?" Willie asked.

Debbie shook her head. "Probably not—at least no one who can or wants to help us. The flash will get lost among the lightning strikes. Or they might mistake it for fireworks."

Venus rushed up to Debbie. "Why did you let them blow up our shelter?" Even a crummy shelter is better than sleeping outdoors."

George answered. "First of all, the bombs were probably booby-trapped. Would *you* have liked to cut the wires?

"Second, we suspect the bad guys who took our boat left a spotter to see if the explosions went off. If the bad guy doesn't see a flash, gunmen come back to finish us off."

Venus moved her mouth but not even a cry could come out.

Gil waded through acrid fumes and burning debris to a windowless wall. Moving up the timer on the bombs had done its job. A light rain sputtered on the wreckage. "The plastic explosive made a lot of toothpicks! But it left us one intact wall. George! Clutch! Give me a hand. This is our raft!"

Borolo, Goodman, and the other men and their wives began to pitch in. The Ethiopian was particularly talented in securing buoyant surfboards to the raft.

Eve clutched Debbie, who held a canvas tent piece laboriously cut for a sail. The sense of accomplishment in cutting the sail disappeared. This was *not* a good idea. Their men would try the impossible. Talking them out of rafting would also be impossible. They could drown crossing over to the mainland. Everyone knew it.

* * *

Frank arrived at the marina as the patrol boat pulled out.

"Lots of excitement, this morning," the marina manager rasped. "The *Kiwi on a Cloud* boat was found on the coast, burned with no one on board. The passengers must've jumped overboard rather than get barbied."

"Have they found any survivors?"

The marina manager touched the brim of his hat as if in a salute to the departed. He knew Debbie and Elizabeth and liked them both. "No, a boat just went out to look for bodies. I don't give 'em much hope. The swells are getting higher, and a squall just came up."

Frank's mouth went dry. "Where can I rent a helicopter?"

* * *

When the squall peaked, the rafters couldn't see their mainland target. Gil and George's makeshift, weather-beaten raft, started to dip low in the water after it had sailed a third of the way to the mainland. Willie had surprisingly volunteered to navigate, but he had no stars in the sky from which to navigate—just a totally dark, wet cocoon of a storm. The raft barely floated above the water's surface with the weight of the heavy men. Gil and George tied themselves to the raft as waves washed over the surface. Their sail, which had worked well for the first three hours, was too heavy with salt water to function. They hoped the width of the raft would stop it from flipping over. Their voyage would fail, but what other choice did they have.

They had to stop the Butcher from taking the children out of the country. At the very least, the Butcher had to know they were alive and pursuing him. Ratac would keep the children alive as long as he thought they were needed to keep their parents from revealing his secret. But if Gil and George died in the storm, Ratac would assume the trampers all died in the explosion. There would be no need to keep the children hostages alive. If they knew what Frank knew about Ratac mutilating hostages, they might have second-guessed their strategy.

The storm eased, and a faint glow of light appeared in the east. The men struggled to see the mainland, but only knew it was opposite the glow. Then another squall began.

The raging squall broke as quickly as it began, replaced with an even noisier roar. A few minutes later, Frank dropped the rescue rope ladder.

*   *   *

Gil quickly explained what the Butcher had done.

Frank shouted something to the helicopter pilot about sending a rescue boat to the island then gave him another destination for the crowded helicopter.

"We have to warn the family at the McWard Station to protect the kids," George yelled over the roar of the chopper's engines.

Frank didn't like this part. "M. Lafate or Ratac Bymarovitch already has your kids. We're on the way to the airport to stop 'im."

"Auckland?" Gil asked.

"No," Frank replied. "I'm guessing that Ratac Bymarovitch won't try a large international airport." Frank purposely avoided using the Butcher nickname. The fathers were ready to explode. "Ian told me about another airport that just does cargos and charters. If the Butcher tried a commercial flight, he'd have to pay excess baggage and excess questions on a ton of gold he intends to swipe from his brother, Klav."

"A ton? Of gold?" Willie asked incredulously.

"More or less." Frank shrugged. "Don't know how much, but enough to finance a lot of charter planes, bribes for everybody, and seed money for a private army and a new war."

"How did Klav—" Willie started

"Tell ya later," Frank interrupted.

Frank continued, "Ian alerted the police at both airports to delay anyone traveling with kids that met the description of Amy and Martin. He told 'em the kids were involved in a custody dispute, so the airport security wouldn't overreact. But . . . if Bymarovitch takes a boat, we're screwed."

George said, "The Butcher said something about not blocking his flight."

Frank nodded, "Hum, could be misdirection, but since he thought he would be killin' ya all in one blast, I don't think so."

The helicopter landed, and the men ran to the security office. The airport was a far cry from Auckland's modern international airport. Cargo and mid-sized charter planes loitered inside and outside of semicircular Quonset hangers. The office consisted of a blocked-off section of a hanger. Four desks crowded back to back in the small room. At one desk, a youngish-looking security guard in a starched Bermuda shorts uniform sat reading a newspaper.

"Did you get my message about two children?" Frank asked.

"Who are you, mate?"

"James Cook," Frank said in case James Cook needed to charge more on his newly minted credit card.

"Oh yes." The guard scowled. "Couldn't very well miss two kids, one black boy, one white girl."

"Where did they go?"

"Hanger Four. The kids looked like they were asleep. Two of our officers went out to check out your claim."

"How long ago?"

"'Bout an hour ago."

"Can you stop the plane from taking off?"

"I can, but I can't."

"Why," Gil asked.

"The plane lifted about fifteen minutes ago."

"Who was on it?" Frank pressed.

"I'm not sure. About six passengers, not counting the two kids, of course, and I guess they checked out, or my boss would have stopped 'em. Oh, one was a woman pilot with a flight plan to Jakarta."

"Anyone with maroon hair?" Willie asked.

"Not that I remember. No."

The guard was glad to see the visitors rush from his office and take up the problem with his boss. A contested custody suit was the last thing in which the guard wanted to get involved.

The pursuers gathered outside the office. "Sounds like Liz was killed," Gil murmured.

"Let's check out Hanger Four," George said in a swift walk, fearful of what they might find there.

The cramped hanger held two planes and room for one more—the one that had left. "Split up," Gil ordered.

The men stalked the sides of the hanger, looking for anything or anyone that may have been left behind. Halfway across the hanger wall, Willie began to wave frantically. He said nothing. From the bottom of a lidded container, a trickle of fresh blood stained the floor.

Frank took a deep breath. He didn't want the fathers to see the contents of the container. He lifted the lid before the fathers could move closer.

Frank coughed at the sight and quickly put the lid down. "Not the kids," he said to the panicked fathers. He swallowed with difficulty. "Two security guards . . . shot at least five times each—probably with a silencer. I'll bet Ratac started shooting at their feet and worked up to their foreheads."

"So they'd feel the pain," Gil concluded.

"Yeah," Frank agreed. "Well, two good things: We didn't catch up with him. If we had, we'd be in that dumpster with the guards and the kids. The other good thing is that he knows someone tried to stop him. So in his eyes, that makes the kids more useful.

"But I feel responsible for these two poor souls in the tub. If I had asked Ian to give a stronger warning, they might not have been taken by surprise."

George said, "It wouldn't have made a difference. You heard the other guard. Ratac has a small army with him."

Frank sighed. "Another bad thing is that my James Cook name is associated as the bloke looking for these murdered guards, and the baby-faced guard in the office knows what Cook looks like. Inspector Harper has had his pecker perplexed ever since I was released." Frank would skip telling about his encounter with Mrs. Turner. "Harper'd love to have an excuse to get me behind bars again."

"There's nothing we can do for these guards," George said, "so let's get to Auckland, get a plane, and go after the kids. If we report it, we'll be delayed with questioning."

Gil shuffled. "I have to go after him too, but my credit card is maxed out. Can you help me, Frank?"

"*I* can," Willie said grimly. "I'll charter a plane for all of us."

"Thank you," Gil, said appreciatively.

"You're sure this bastard is going to Yugoslavia and not Argentina?" Willie asked.

"Yep," Frank quipped, "Argentina is already too crowded with aging war criminals."

Willie didn't like the flip answer, so Frank restated, "Bymarovitch isn't done causing trouble in his home country. It's not in his nature to retire."

CHAPTER 15

The Brother

Bymarovitch settled into his swivel chair and smiled as he reviewed the success of his plan. Ratac's former villa, partially looted at the end of the war, had been refurnished in his absence. Posters and commercials touting his presidential candidacy started running shortly after Ratac left for New Zealand, and the foolish American spies were totally unaware of his bid for power after the police confiscated Major Rose O'Hara's computer link to Croatia. Now, with public curiosity at its peak, he would cement his popularity with personal appearances.

Ratac's personal wealth, swelled by two decades of extortion and bribes, would easily finance his political comeback. His plane full of gold coins would restart a military build-up of his private army—until the nation's army became his. This time he would win. This time he wouldn't stop at Serbia and Bosnia. Once momentum was gained, he'd go after Montenegro and Albania, then he'd turn north to bring Slovenia back to the federation.

200

Ratac told himself that Austria was defenseless, not belonging to NATO, but that was a dream he didn't dare yet share with his followers.

Under a parliamentary system, direct elections for president didn't apply, but with a small country, the election was still a popularity contest. The men in his party, there were no women, had served under him or were those easily manipulated with bribes. Many of his supporters were old holdovers from their power days as communists under Tito, but were now running under the new *Justice Party* label that Bymarovitch provided.

Ratac no longer needed Mme. Lafate. She would take care of the unfinished work in New Zealand then disappear. As his former prison camp commander with a command of French, Mme. Lafate had served him well as his make-believe wife, but he needed a younger, more beautiful woman, or maybe a dozen younger women. Bymarovitch paid her and ordered her to avoid all further contact. Eventually, he would have to send someone to New Zealand to kill her, but for now, he had more pressing concerns.

His daughter, Elizabeth, had followed him like a lamb and accepted the required makeover. She would be useful during the election, but not after.

Elizabeth had lied to him. Elizabeth told him that Klav was dead, but he did not believe her. His soldiers confirmed the lie with simple research. Ratac's estranged brother had written him the letter recently, and there were no recent obituaries that could have been Klav's in the local newspapers in the area in which he was hiding. None of the area's funeral parlors had hosted anyone remotely resembling Klav. Elizabeth's loyalty to Klav was admirable, but she would still have to die for it.

The island trampers must be charred food for the seagulls and crabs after their sleeping quarters blew up. He was only sorry that his rush to fly back and campaign prevented him from seeing the carnage and the murder of his brother, if he was not already dead.

Then there were the children. They seemed to calm Elizabeth, so he kept them alive even after their parents were killed. The incident at the airport startled him. *Was there anyone left who could expose him?* The guards were focused on the children, but they also wanted to search the plane. He had to kill them. *Are the children more of a liability than they're worth?* Now he wished he had thrown them both from the plane. They could be a source of danger, the same as Elizabeth.

"Commandant Tinsley," he barked, "the two brats must go."

Tinsley made two cutting motions across his neck and grinned.

The Butcher nodded approval.

"Your daughter will be upset," he cautioned.

"I'll tell her we sent them away for their safety," Ratac said and added, "as if it matters."

"What about those guards in New Zealand? Someone must have alerted them."

"Yes, someone did," Ratac acknowledged. "Our Mrs. Turner has failed to call in. She knows the price of failure. Apparently, Mr. Ferret was released before she could do her job. Ferret must have called the airport to stop me, so he is as much a suspect for the dead guards as we are, and they don't know who we are. The next time, the meddlesome American won't be played with. He will die a slow painful death."

The phone rang, and Ratac picked it up. "Bymarovitch, here."

The caller waited to speak because the Bymarovitch voice that answered was not familiar. When the arms dealer from Split finally spoke, Ratac frowned then asked, "They're coming when?

"Sell them whatever they want. They're less likely to seek help from the UN. Plus, it'll make for a more interesting confrontation."

Bymarovitch dropped the phone in its receiver and smirked with anticipation.

"I rescind my order about the children—at least for the next few days. A rather challenging event has occurred. My enemies will see what a true genius I am. But for them, it will be too late.

*   *   *

AUCKLAND, NEW ZEALAND

Willie ground his teeth before signing the service agreement. "I've chartered the airplane, you're welcome to come along. Rocklin and the Kings want their kids. Ferret wants his revenge and reward. I want my software CD back. If we find Bymarovitch, we find my CD. I'm also going to hire a dozen private detectives from London and send them to Yugoslavia."

"Croatia," Frank corrected, "the old Yugoslavia is cut up like a relish tray—one tray for every nationality. And as for your private detectives, unless they speak Croat, they'll just drive Bymarovitch further into hiding, if he doesn't eat them for lunch first."

"Then how do we find him, smart ass?" Willie snapped.

Frank stretched a clenched fist in Willie's direction. "Your check book will only get you only so far among folks who've forgotten how to trust. I have sources—sources that hate him and trust me. These people won't telegraph an alarm."

Willie backed off, sulking, while Frank thought of his phone call to Split and what he had said about telegraphing their arrival to the Butcher. *Hell, the Butcher is probably already waiting for us.*

*   *   *

Clutch and the women caught up with the other men at the Auckland Airport.

Gil hugged Debbie then approached Clutch, who was pacing around the edges of the group. "Clutch, I want you to come too."

"Why me?"

"Because you love Debbie. You risked your life for her at Milford Sound. I think you'd risk it again, which is something we can't say about Willie's private detectives. I can't force Debbie to stay home without losing her, so I want you to watch her back . . . Virginia's and Eve's too."

Clutch pouted. "What if Deb falls in love with me again?"

Gil nodded an acknowledgment of the possibility. "That's a chance I have to take."

Debbie glued herself to a new cell phone, feverously arranging for a new tour director and hotel accommodations for the island trampers. "The boat was insured, but the sleeping quarters on the island were not. The unexpected hotel stay is costing a bundle. And when the bad publicity hits, *Kiwi on a Cloud* will be in free fall. It's a good thing I'm marrying you, Gil, because I'm sure to be out of a job, even if the company survives."

Debbie wasn't all that sure there would be a marriage. Gil could rush into the nest of killers and never come out. If Amy was killed, Gil could be depressed to the point of illness or suicide. If Amy was killed, would he be fit for a relationship? Would *she?* Would Gil's gentle sense of humor remain? His relaxed manner? Gil would need her more than ever, but would he accept her?

Debbie knew her future paled in comparison to Amy and Martin's plight. She tried to keep her focus and tried to help. But how? Gil had turned into an unemotional gladiator, armed only with his martial arts skills against the Butcher's AK-47s and explosives. Yet Gil was totally focused—his mind mulling an endless list of possibilities and solutions.

Frank knew this new Balkan territory, but he gave Debbie the impression he was flying by the seat of his pants.

Willie was computing logistics for which he had no solid information.

George and Eve were doing their best to comfort each other.

Clutch looked like a lost soul, but Debbie had to admire that he'd risk his life to help—if he only knew how. Debbie didn't regret or feel guilty anymore for having loved him. Clutch was a good man.

Only Virginia appeared calm, but she was a consummate actress. She had to have a facade to put up with Willie. Any risks Virginia took were risks to the future of her son. That risk had to weigh on her, but despite her fears, Virginia's organizational skills handled the minute, yet essential, travel details the other rescuers were too distracted to attend to.

Debbie wondered what chance their collective fear, anger, and love could have over the Butcher's resources. *Will we be able to save the children? It seems doubtful.*

She cuddled next to Gil, a frozen soldier on a mission, and knew that because of him there was a chance. She prayed there was a chance.

The flight on Willie's chartered jet seemed to last forever. First, a fuel stop in Jakarta and bumpy ride to the Indira Gandhi International Airport in New Delhi left them further exhausted. The messages that Gil and George exchanged between their eyes were anything but Gandhi-like. If their only children were dead or hurt in any way, the fathers were prepared to become assassins. Frank didn't say much, unusual for him, but there was little doubt that he too was on a mission to avenge Rose's murder.

The three women mutually decided they needed sleep and fresh heads if they were ever to confront the Butcher and retrieve the children. The sleep didn't come easily, however.

Clutch said what everyone was thinking, "What if he's already killed 'em?"

"He'll keep 'em alive," Frank assured. "He knows *we're* alive and comin' for him. He also knows we won't turn him in, as long as he has the children as leverage over us."

"How does *he* know we're coming after him?" Willie asked.

"Because I indirectly told him so," Frank answered. "I telephoned a gossipy arms dealer in Split that I need some hardware waiting for me and my friends for the sole purpose of killin' the Butcher."

Willie rocked anxiously, "Hardware?"

"Not your kinda hardware, I mean weapons and protective stuff."

"Then the Butcher will be waiting for us," Willie exclaimed. "It seems the biggest mistake you've made is underestimating this fiend's innovative genius, and you've done it again."

Frank didn't want to hear "mistake," but Willie was right.

"If he gives me my program back, I won't tell his secret," Willie promised. "Perhaps when Bymarovitch regains power, he won't fear us anymore, and he'll give up the children."

When Willie moved away, Gil snapped, "I'm tired of hearing how Willie lost his million-dollar piece of uncopyrighted software. Why doesn't he ask the programmer to supply another CD to copyright before Bymarovitch does?"

Frank chuckled, "Because, my naïve friend, Weasel Willie doesn't intend to give the original programmer a piece of the action."

"Willie would take all the credit?"

"You bet your bandits, he would," Frank replied.

Clutch held his neck, wondering why he had gotten sucked into this journey. "Could Willie be right about the Butcher regaining power and—"

Frank suppressed his laugh and said, "Oh, there's a better than good chance he could regain power, all right, but for us, there is only one possible ending. *We kill the Butcher before he kills us.*"

*   *   *

PLESO AIRPORT, ZAGREB, CROATIA

After Gil's search team passed through an intrusive customs inspection, Frank noted the nervousness of the team was attracting attention, so he quipped that the inspectors thought they were smuggling in vowels. Frank's attempt at humor failed to invoke a smile on the tense faces.

A stocky man approached them at the terminal's exit. He looked to be a local. His manner was serious, but relaxed. "Dr. Rocklin? Mr. Ferret?"

the man called. "Professor Bymarovitch would like to talk to you. Not Ratac. His *brother*, Klav."

Frank cocked his head. "We'd love to meet with the . . . brother? How about at the UN High Command Headquarters in one hour."

The man smiled. "Excuse me, gentleman, ladies, my name is Zirov. Professor Bymarovitch is my leader. Klav's returned from New Zealand to save our homeland. You must think this is a trick—that the Butcher wants to snare you into a trap. That is not the case. If the Butcher knew you were here, he'd have your airplane strafed or your hotel bombed. There is no defense."

"Then aren't you endangering yourself by talking to us," Virginia said sarcastically.

"Ah, you don't believe me. Our leader will explain. From a political standpoint, he cannot be seen consorting with the UN occupation force. He will meet you in the lobby of your hotel in ninety minutes. He has news of your children."

*   *   *

The caravan of Mercedes stopped in front of the hotel. As Professor Bymarovitch left the car, a crowd gathered. By the time he walked to the entrance to the hotel, the crowd began to chant and clap rhythmically.

Eve asked Frank, "What are they hollering about?"

Frank rubbed his head, "'Patriot, patriot! Justice, justice!' and something about 'next prime minister.'"

Gil said, "By the way, don't shake his hand. One prick from a poisoned ring, and it'll be the last thing you remember."

The eight trampers watched Professor Klav Bymarovitch, flanked by six bodyguards, stride into the hotel.

Clutch held Frank's gun under his jacket. He had argued that he was the best shot and the most appropriate to care for the gun. But now that he was responsible for covering his companions, he dripped with nervous perspiration.

Gil looked coldly at Klav and his guards. Even a suicide rush to kill the man claiming to be Klav might not succeed with six bodyguards. Anyway, he had to hear what he had to say about the kids.

Klav, if he was Klav, resembled his brother Ratac, except for darker eyes, less hair, and heavier hips. Klav's upper lip crawled with a thin handlebar mustache that Frank would have pulled at if he could have reached it. Unlike the Butcher, the professor sported a tanned and slightly more wrinkled face. He wore a black armband of mourning around his arm.

He went straight to Debbie. "You must be Debbie McWard. Elizabeth speaks well of you. A good friend. He appeared to be ready to embrace Debbie, but when she backed away, he stopped. "Don't be afraid."

Bymarovitch rubbed his chest as if to assuage a pain and sat down. "Forgive me. The shock of the last few days has been too much for me. Her body is being shipped here for burial."

"Whose body?" Gil asked.

"My wife." Dr. Bymarovitch put his hand over his eyes. His shoulders shook. "Ratac killed her."

The eight ex-trampers waited silently until the man stopped sobbing and stood up, looking taller. "Of course, you want your children back before this madman kills them too."

"What do you know?" Gil commanded.

"I think I know where he might be and where the children are. I would break down his doors and strangle him for what he did, but the memory of my mother prevents me from killing my own brother. There are political reasons as well. And I am not a killer."

"You want me to do it for you?" Gil accused. "If he's hurt my daughter, I'll guarantee it. If you're a fake, I'll throw you into a grave too."

"I see you don't trust me." Klav looked to the door. "We must have Elizabeth explain. She feels terrible that she led Ratac to our home, but at least it gave Elizabeth a chance to escape."

Elizabeth stepped into the lobby. Her hair was jet black and no longer spiked. She wore a full-length mink coat. She ran to Debbie and hugged her. "Lafate or Ratac killed my mother," Elizabeth cried, but my father drove him away. Now Ratac has followed us here." Elizabeth's tears seemed genuine.

Debbie accepted her embrace, and Elizabeth wiped her tears. "I see you met the father that I grew up with. He's come back to undo the damage that his awful brother did. I've come to help him. I'm sorry I didn't have time to leave you a message. When we found out that Ratac kidnapped your kids, we were sick. Dad has hired an army of men to hunt them down. We know that he returned to Croatia to come after us."

"Then you know where they are?" Gil asked.

"We've narrowed it down," Klav inserted. "Ratac is in hiding. He had intended to pass himself off as me. But my being here has foiled his plans. As soon as we know for sure, we'll mount an attack. Force is the only thing that my sick brother understands. Whoever has money can buy force. I have money."

"From the gold you stole from the KGB?" Frank speculated.

"Yes, I've never touched the gold until now. When Ratac followed Elizabeth to our farm, he already had the gold. I knew he would do evil things with it. I hoped for a reconciliation. I hoped to talk Ratac out of returning to Croatia. I hoped he would hide, like I hid, and would give up his evil ambitions. I realized his intention was to kill us all. I aimed my shotgun instead. I drove Ratac and his thugs off. He was furious—definitely a madman. We knew he would return for the gold and that we had to escape. Elizabeth and I eluded him, but my beloved wife was shot as we fled. We cashed in some of the gold and realized we would never be safe as long as my mad brother is alive. I also realized that I must undo the damage he did to my homeland. If I must use my infamous brother's name recognition, so be it."

Elizabeth blotted her eyes, again. "We have to rescue the children." She looked at Frank. "Maybe if you gave up trying to collect a reward on Ratac, he'd return the children."

"Okay. I'll promise not to go after Ratac if he releases the kids in the next hour," Frank promised.

"We have to locate him first," Klav said. "Maybe in a day or so."

"Sure," Frank said with a half smile. "Ratac wouldn't believe my promise anyway. Would he?"

"Probably not. But if you would leave Europe, Mr. Ferret, perhaps if you took a voyage to South America, it would convince Ratac that he could come out of hiding long enough to seek refuge in another country."

Willie didn't give Frank a chance to answer. "Your brother stole something that belongs to me. I want it back, and I have the money to hunt him down unless he coughs it up."

Klav looked at Willie with disapproval. "Young man, we are talking about the lives of two children. We are trying to salvage the future of my country. Whatever my brother has of yours is of little consequence."

*   *   *

As Bymarovitch removed his padded clothing, he smiled at Elizabeth. "You did fine, dear. Your friends will take their children and go far away from here. We have a duty to perform here. They believe the false rumors about me were spread by the Bosnians and Serbian war criminals. And as long as they believe that I killed the lady assassin, instead of that imposter Whistle they will try to expose me and prevent us from saving our homeland."

"You won't hurt my friends," Elizabeth advised and questioned.

"Of course not," Ratac said. "That's why I took the children. As long as Whistle and the others seek a reward for capturing me and sending me to prison for life, I need to bluff them into giving up that idea. When they agree to go back to America and mind their own business, it will be with the children."

"Thank you, Papa," Elizabeth said. She kissed his cheek and left the room.

Ratac laughed. "Elizabeth is enjoying the taste of power. She *is* like her father."

CHAPTER 16

Boxed In

George pounded frantically on Gil and Debbie's Zagreb hotel room door. Then he changed to the prearranged rhythmic knock.

Gil cracked the door.

"Come quick, you have to see this," George urged.

In the suite across the hall, Willie, Virginia, Frank, and Clutch huddled around the hotel room's television set.

The screen filled with a close up of Elizabeth, her wild hair pulled back in a simple, classic style in black. She still wore the fur coat she wore in the hotel lobby and looked more attractive than any of the rescue party could imagine. She spoke in unhesitating Croatian. Behind her was a poster of Bymarovitch. Suddenly, her image disappeared, and Bymarovitch appeared, placing roses on a military grave.

"It's over," George muttered. "A frickin' political commercial for Klav, if he is Klav. But if he's the Butcher, he's got us confused as a rookie cop shooting at rattles in the dark. Are we shooting at a rattlesnake or a baby?"

George sighed. "He *has* to be Klav. Klav's the only one who can find the kids. Remember the airport guard couldn't place Liz on the plane with the kids."

Willie elaborated, "I asked about maroon hair. The guard couldn't remember a woman with maroon hair."

"But what if she had her makeover before she got to the plane?" Debbie countered.

Virginia added, "With the politics involved, I'm sure Ratac would want Liz transformed *before* arriving in Croatia."

"But so might Klav."

"We're back where we started," Clutch concluded. "We just don't know."

Gil stared at the television. "What was Liz saying?" he asked, nudging Frank.

Frank scratched behind his ear. "As best as I can tell she said somethin' 'bout how Klav Bymarovitch is goin' to bring peace, prosperity, and justice to the land. Justice is a synonym for revenge for some folks round here."

"Lizzie's gone over to the dark side," Willie stated.

"Never!" Debbie protested angrily. "Liz doesn't know there are such things as sides. Her knowledge of politics comes from comic books."

Willie shrugged. "Consider it. A plain girl with no future is suddenly given the chance to be the first lady of this God-forsaken country. Still, it's a country. She must be drunk with power. From loser to first lady."

* * *

THE BYMAROVITCH VILLA

It's surprising how brave a person can be when resigned to death, Elizabeth told herself. Over a month ago, her father, Klav, had a heart attack. For the first time in over twenty years, Klav saw a doctor, and that was only because Elizabeth drove him to the hospital under his protestations to let him die. After being treated, he refused to go back for follow-up treatment and medication. Hospitals ask questions. Records are kept. Information on Klav could endanger his daughter.

Klav told Elizabeth the whole story. Learning that the woman who raised her, and whom she had called mother, wasn't her mother hit Elizabeth like a meteorite.

Klav Bymarovitch explained, "Your birth mother was a gentle woman who looked for the love that she couldn't find with Ratac. She found it in one man, but when he rejected her, she became depressed and took several lovers—as if her promiscuity would punish the husband who hurt her. She knew Ratac suspected her and feared what he would do. So she left him and hid. Ratac stalked her and found her in bed with another man. Ratac killed the man with his bare hands, and shot his wife in the head."

"Why wasn't he imprisoned?" Elizabeth cried.

"Ratac had influence. If he says he killed a man who was raping his wife, and that she committed suicide in shame, who is going to challenge a man with such powerful associates and the potential for retaliatory blackmail and murder? He spent only a few days in prison—just enough time for us to take you away. I was a professor, but also a high official with the Yugoslavian version of the KGB, a position I grew to hate. When I left, I took some of the riches they had stolen from others. I thought I'd need wealth to get us started here. Actually, what I stole was worth well beyond our needs. My theft must have added to Ratac's rage. No one goes to the top when their brother is a thief."

"But why did you take me?" Elizabeth puzzled.

"Who else would care for you? Your grandfather couldn't do it. And . . . from his prison, Ratac vowed to kill you too. He called you "part whore." It may have been his insanity of the moment, but I couldn't chance it. Ratac is vicious, even when he's normal. Mama and I loved your birth mother, and we thought we owed it to her to protect you. So we ran."

"If Ratac was executed for murder, we would return. But he wasn't. He was released and given an even more powerful position than before."

Klav coughed. "So we kept running and settled here in New Zealand, hiding from Ratac's agents and the KGB. And we loved you more than any parent could."

"I can't remember any parents other than you and Mama," Elizabeth sobbed.

"Mama couldn't have children of her own, but she loved you like you were her own."

Elizabeth nodded sadly. "I can see why you wouldn't tell me—couldn't tell me. It must have been hard on you, hiding all this time. I thought it strange how a man so warm and friendly could exist without any friends."

"I'm telling you this now, Elizabeth, because you must know some things before I die. It took twenty-six years and a heart attack before I could find the courage to write two letters—one to your grandfather on your birth mother's side, the other, an almost identical letter to Ratac. I hoped that maybe time healed the wounds. I tried to instill in Ratac some parental pride. Then when you took the envelope to be mailed from the South Island, I knew it was hopeless. Ratac could never derive pleasure from the accomplishments of others. I shouldn't have had you mail it. With my bad heart, my time on earth is short, but now I realize *you* could become his target."

"Do you think he would seek me out after all this time?" Elizabeth asked with a voice sore from crying.

"I was hoping the letter would fill him with shame for what he had done to your mother. He should be too full of guilt to ever show his face. That's what we want from him: never to seek us out."

"And if he does?"

"Maybe he'll be content with killing me and taking what I stole. But the safest thing for you to do would be to find a young man among your travelers. Get married. Go live in the United States or Canada or Chile. You can write to me, but never tell me where you live."

"I'll do no such thing. You've lived in fear for too long. Look what it's done to your heart."

As the days passed, Elizabeth's shock and sadness turned to fear. *I'm going to end up like my father—hiding like a fugitive, afraid of making friends. Afraid of venturing outside of the valley.* Elizabeth had to get far away from New Zealand—away from the postmark city on the letter sent to her killer father.

Any young man with a job and a different nationality was a possible way out of New Zealand. If any prospect asked her to follow him back to his country, Elizabeth would go in an instant, and Papa would come along.

Husbands didn't come easy to a woman with the femininity of a lumberjack. Elizabeth couldn't afford the luxury of playing hard to get while looking them over. The younger single men whom she had once expected to meet on the tours weren't to be found. They couldn't afford expensive travel. They could be found in the cheap bars straddling their backpacks and smelling bad. The few single men who did sign up for her tours went straight after Debbie.

Now Klav's warnings came true. When Elizabeth first spotted M. Lafate, she realized he looked like her father. She knew that doing anything unusual would attract Lafate's attention and confirm that she was his daughter. She couldn't even tell Debbie of her fears. Debbie would have seen the situation as a reason for a reunion party. Debbie would never accept the idea that a relative could hurt a relative. Neither could Elizabeth. She hoped that time had healed Ratac's hate. She hoped that a guilty and contrite father would beg forgiveness for taking away her mother and abandoning her.

At first, she tried to dismiss the break-in at the office as unrelated. Ratac could be after her address in the company's records, but he'd find nothing but a post office box in a remote area of the North Island. But if Ratac was responsible for the break-in, he was responsible for attacking Carp. That someone would nearly kill for an address seemed unbelievable.

Then Rose died. *Suicide or murder?* Elizabeth's hopes for a happy father and daughter reconciliation vanished, and her fears nearly exploded under her casual façade. No one believed Frank Whistle was capable of killing, no matter how noisy and annoying he was. Debbie's suspicious fall from the cliff filled Elizabeth's sleepless nights with guilt. *How could I have let my best friend be mistaken for me?* She had to risk her life on the rescue boat to help save Debbie from drowning. She had no choice.

Elizabeth wished she had disappeared upon first seeing M. Lafate. She should have left the trip and camped out in the mountains. By the time Ratac figured out who his daughter was, Elizabeth would be impossible to find. But she waited too long. Trying to escape now would accelerate any evil intentions that Ratac had for her. Ratac could afford a corps of eager mercenaries who would track her down.

When Ratac finally approached her, Elizabeth was prepared. *Ratac's here to kill me and my father. The most I can hope for is to save my father by telling Ratac that Papa's dead.*

Ratac approached Elizabeth with friendliness and humility. To temper the shock he said, "Of course, I had nothing to do with Debbie's fall."

Elizabeth resolved to go along with Ratac as best she could, escaping whenever a chance was presented. Elizabeth didn't count on Ratac kidnapping the children, however.

"Papa, why are you taking the children?"

"For our protection. Frank Whistle, also known as Frank Ferret, is the CIA's most notorious assassin. Ferret killed Rose O'Hara and tried to make it look like a suicide. Gil Rocklin is an undercover FBI agent. He doesn't just arrest people, he kills them. So you'll believe me, I'll show you copies of the newspaper clippings on Rocklin, written by Ferret. Those two pretended not to know each other, but they're working together with that policeman—plotting against me. But they dare not hurt us as long as the children are in my care. As soon as I become prime minister, they won't ever be able to touch me. I'll have an army at my disposal. Then I'll send the children home to their assassin fathers. I would never harm them, but they, with their sick minds, don't know that."

"I don't like the idea," Elizabeth protested, knowing she dare not protest too much. "Promise never to hurt them and try not to scare them."

"Of course, my dear," Ratac reassured.

*   *   *

Elizabeth waited at Amy's bedside, mopping her forehead with a warm wet towel until she awoke. Martin lay with his head rolling under his pillow on the other side of the spacious, rococo antique-filled room. Both had been awakened before and given doctored juice, but each time they quickly relapsed into a deep sleep. Faint and fading twilight came from a high window with bars.

"How do you feel, honey?" Elizabeth asked.

Amy clutched her head. "I have a headache."

"I have an aspirin and bottled water waiting for you," Elizabeth said. "Martin's already taken one."

Martin called from underneath his pillow, "I smell like a dentist's office."

Amy looked at the aspirin and put on her sad hound-dog expression. "Can't take medicine from strangers. Only Daddy or the doctor." Elizabeth poured the bottled water into a glass, and Amy quickly drained it.

Pouring more water for the children, Elizabeth said, "I'm not a stranger, Amy. I'm a friend. But that's a good rule about medicine. Your headache will go away in a couple of hours or so without any medicine."

"I'm pecky," Amy said.

"Me too," Martin grumbled.

"I brought you canned fruit, some cheese, and some crunchy rolls."

Amy sat up, threw off her fluffy quilt, and dug into the food. She went to her duffel bag for her winter coat. "Chilly in here."

"They don't believe in toasty warm houses," Elizabeth agreed.

"Where are we?" Martin asked.

"Mr. Lafate's house. You remember Mr. and Mrs. Lafate?"

"We know Madame, Lafate," Amy wailed. "She is a bad lady. She and Mr. Tinsley took us away from Debbie's house."

Martin finished his hard roll and added, "I knew something was wrong, so we ran. But they caught us and sprayed something in our faces. That's what smells."

Elizabeth nodded. "It put you to sleep for a long time." *They may have used something else, as well,* she thought but didn't voice.

Elizabeth looked at her watch. The guard generally changed after six o'clock. She suddenly felt rushed. The children had a better chance in the dark, and only the bushy-haired guard with garlicky breath had shown any interest in her.

"Kids, M. Lafate is a bad man too. A very bad man. He's going to hurt me, but he's *not* going to hurt you—because you're going to leave this house. There's another bad man at the foot of the stairs. His job is to stop you and me from leaving. I'm going to try to take him to another room. If he goes with me, you leave—on tiptoes. Don't slam the door when you leave. Don't even close the door all the way. There's another guard who circles the house."

Elizabeth put a chair on Amy's bed and turned to Martin. "Look through the high window. Amy will have to hold the chair steady for you. When you see the guard on this side of the house, start down the stairs. By the time you make it out the door, the guard will be in the back of the house."

"Is Daddy waiting?" Amy asked.

"Yes, I've seen him, and Mr. King too. They're looking for you, but they don't know where you are. Your daddy was an FBI agent, wasn't he?"

"No, I don't think so," Amy answered truthfully.

"Wow! That's cool," Martin said. "That's why he knows all those killer punches."

Elizabeth wished she knew some killer punches. "Your daddies may be with Dr. Whistle. His real name is Frank Ferret. He might be with the CIA, but probably not." Elizabeth thought, *Heaven help us if Frank's the best the CIA has.*

"What's CIA?" Amy puzzled.

"Double wow!" Martin exclaimed. "Dr. Whistle's a spy."

Elizabeth rose. "Go to the city. It's a long walk, but I've seen you both keep up on the hikes. Just follow the lights. Find a soldier with a blue helmet. Ask to be taken to their headquarters. Your families' hotel is close by."

"How about a policeman?" Martin asked.

Elizabeth thought about the house teeming with policemen, whom Ratac had entertained on the night of their arrival. "Maybe not. Some of them are working for M. Lafate."

Fishing under her blouse, Elizabeth removed a diskette and slipped it into Amy's carryon suitcase. "Take this. Lafate seems to think it's important."

Elizabeth paused at the door. "Children, you're too nice. These are bad people—evil people. You can pretend to go along with whatever they ask. But when the time is right, fight back! Amy, I'm going to give you my tube of pepper spray. I was saving this to protect myself, but in my case, it probably wouldn't help much. The bad people who sprayed you deserve to be sprayed too. Now count to four hundred before you peek out the window."

* * *

Tinsley finished his bottle of wine. His broken fingers throbbed. *Damn that boy!* He walked along the second floor and looked down the stairwell. Elizabeth was flirting with the Croatian guard at the front door. *Maybe I'll get a turn with her before the Butcher kills her.* Tinsley just assumed Bymarovitch would kill her. He didn't know how or when. He just knew.

Tinsley also knew that he had to pay Martin back for breaking his fingers, and now was as good a time as any. If the parents threatened Bymarovitch, he would send them body parts from the children until they backed off. Tinsley would be happy to assist. That was if Ratac didn't kill the parents first.

He tried the door of the children's room. It was open. Amy was in her winter coat and hat. Martin wore two sweaters and stood on a chair on his bed. Martin was looking out the high window. Both children looked startled to see Tinsley.

"Going somewhere?"

"It's cold in here," Martin said.

"I'll get to you later, brat. "First, I'm going to concentrate on the cutie pie."

He loosened his belt. "Take off your coat, cutie pie."

As he moved closer to Amy, she looked at the arrow on her pepper spray canister. *The safety lock,* she remembered. Martin had just showed it to her. His father had taught him about such things. Amy twisted the safety lock, turned toward Tinsley, and aimed at his face. She closed her eyes tightly and pushed the button.

Tinsley dropped to his knees and clutched his eyes as the pepper spray made a direct hit. He muffled what would have been his scream of pain. Tinsley didn't want to be caught in the off-limits room. But his anger swelled as much as his eyes. *To hell with Bymarovitch's order. I must kill the girl.*

Tinsley didn't get a chance to make a threatening gesture. Amy's tiny knuckles slammed hard left and right into Tinsley's Adam's apple and into his already burning left eye.

Martin lifted the lookout chair over his head; it wobbled, and its weight brought it crashing down above Tinsley's ear.

The hired henchman gasped and groaned in semiconsciousness.

Amy starred wide-eyed. She had never hurt anyone before.

Martin pulled her out the door. They crept down the hall. Martin peeked down the staircase. An empty guard's chair barred the side of the front door. The children could hear Elizabeth's loud laughing far away. "Now!" They scrambled down the stairs. Together, they struggled to open the metal front door, made even heavier with bulletproof armor. There was no time to check which side of the house the sentry patrolled. Martin peeked out. "No one there. Let's go!"

The late November wind and mist hit them hard, but it helped clear their heads and soothe their burning eyes from Mace pepper spray that had drifted. The darkening sky provided little reflected illumination, yet with the snow, they could still see.

"Lights!" Martin pointed down the valley, "That's the city."

"Looks far," Amy said. It was. Bymarovitch's prison mansion sat upon a foothill. Denuded of trees, the hill sloped too steeply for other dwellings and provided an open expanse to expose approaching enemies. The thin blanket of snow would make escapees stand out. Anyone who looked from the Bymarovitch villa would surely spot them running down the winding road.

A distant howl caused Amy to cringe. "That's a wolf call. I heard them when Daddy took me camping."

Martin scoured the forest edge. "Sounds far away," he said hopefully.

Martin spotted a large, flattened cardboard box. Bymarovitch had lost no time in refurnishing his mansion and putting a refrigerator-sized cardboard box next to the road was cheaper than burning it. Homeless refugees and less affluent passersby quickly grabbed up such cardboard plums for insulation or the few pieces of reinforcement wood that could be used in a fireplace. Martin stomped on the box to flatten it further. "I saw people on television decorate boxes and use them as sleds. I've never been on a sled."

Amy helped Martin pull the box across the road to the crest of the hill. She instructed, "It's just like skiing."

"Huh?" Martin said. "I don't ski. I've only seen snow once."

"If you want to go faster, you lean back. If you want to slow down, you lean forward. The front catches the snow and slows you down."

The push-off took two tries, but when the box started to move, it accelerated like a runaway toboggan. They didn't see the sentry turn the corner, and he was too busy lighting a cigarette to see the movement already past one hundred yards down the hill. The box lurched to the side and flew toward one of the few pine trees on the hill.

"Lean left," Amy ordered. The box hurtled to the right, past a near collision with the pine tree. The makeshift toboggan rotated, spinning three hundred sixty degrees before straightening out. The box slid for four hundred yards before coming to a rude, fish-tailing stop in front of a ditch by the road. The box could take them no further, but their shortcut had severed a mile from taking the mountain-hugging, switchback road.

They hurried down the deserted dirt road in the direction of the lights. Amy had clothes appropriate for Denver, but Martin didn't expect to have cold weather when he got off the plane in southern California. Amy saw him shivering and gave him her spare cap. "I have longer hair," she reasoned.

Their escape road carved through a rocky area. The sides of the road were walled with jagged rock.

An old truck with one headlight pulled alongside them and stopped. There was no place to hide—no place to run.

They dropped their bags and ran forward. "They got us," Martin cried.

The truck started up and pulled alongside them again. An elderly man and his young daughter peered out at them. He said something in a strange language. The old man smiled and laughed. Then he opened the door and gestured for the children to enter.

"They seem friendly," Martin concluded, retrieving their bags. "Let's go."

The truck left the dirt road as the city neared. The children never saw a city like this. The houses looked different, and the words on the storefronts made no sense, except for *cola* and *pizza*. Amy knew café meant restaurant, but they had no money. Near the center of the city, the truck stopped, and the children scrambled out while the driver uttered unintelligible advice.

"At least it's easier to walk on these sidewalks," Martin noted. The children couldn't have guessed the asphalt patches on the paved road and sidewalk were cosmetic repairs of mortar shell holes.

"But where are we?" Martin asked aloud.

"Must be France," Amy surmised. "Mme. Lafate was French."

"France is on the other side of my globe. Wow, we went halfway around the world. It's winter in France when it's summer in New Zealand."

"I know," Amy nodded. "They take turns."

After walking a couple of city blocks, they saw a man in uniform.

"A soldier? But no blue helmet," Amy noted.

"Yeah, better keep going," Martin agreed.

*   *   *

Ratac looked at Tinsley, gingerly sitting down and rubbing his head. His eye was black and swollen. "What's wrong with him?"

Zirov laughed. "He thought he could do whatever to the children. The children did it to him."

"Explain!"

"The little girl played punching bag with his vocal cords. While he was writhing in agony, the boy broke a chair on his head."

Ratac strode to the room where the children had been drugged and imprisoned. Elizabeth was there. The room felt colder than usual, as if a window had been opened. "So tell me, Elizabeth, did you sound the alarm as soon as you found them missing?"

"Not instantly," Elizabeth answered with sincere concern. "Remember how the kids used to play hide-'n'-seek on the trip?"

The Butcher nodded. "It matters little. The police will find them. But I'm afraid they'll be frightened. And you'll be surprised to know that we have a large number of brown bears in this part of the world—in these very woods." Ratac forced a worried face. *If the children are found, I can explain their death on the bears. If I choose to explain.*

Ratac stopped his nervous pacing and put his hands on Elizabeth's shoulders, close to her neck. "My election advisors claim that you're an important asset in my presidential campaign. A widower draws sympathy, but not enough to balance off the fact that I bring no woman to the presidential palace. You provide that balance. Your television commercials have had a positive response. However, I'm still low in the polls. I need more from you. We'll make a personal appearance together—the day after tomorrow—in the capitol square. There will be a half million adorning fans for the television cameras—on the eve of the election."

Elizabeth smiled. "I'll start writing my own speech. It'll sound more natural in my own words."

Ratac smirked. "A splendid idea. Why don't you surprise me?"

Ratac smelled the burning residue of pepper spray on his eyes and in his nostrils. The children's carry-on luggage had been searched. Elizabeth's wasn't. The children had some clothes, a clarinet, a couple of disposable cameras, and a colorful journal. *No pepper spray.*

Ratac smiled at Elizabeth. "Let's have dinner and wait for the police to bring back our little wanderers."

"It's our fault," Elizabeth ventured. "We frightened them. They could freeze to death in those woods. They should be back with their parents."

"Soon, my dear. Sooner than I originally anticipated," Ratac replied.

Ratac felt a rush, as thoughts of his next plan became clear—an ingenious plan. *Your murder will be sooner than originally planned, my dear.*

CHAPTER 17

Crepe du Chocolat?

The dank Zagreb hotel bar was as empty and dark as a funeral parlor waiting for a customer. The free-spending tourists and international business people wouldn't return for years. The refugees who filled most of the hotel stayed in their rooms. They had no frivolous money to spend as their homes were being rebuilt. The bar depended on the journalists to turn on the lights after supper. The journalists had to be there, at the capital of the interim, independent Croatian government. The print and television crews cursed with boredom when nothing was happening and were frantic with excitement when the neighboring Serbs initiated more military actions.

At night, the correspondents sought security and comfort by boasting and arguing with their colleagues and rivals. The hotel suffered no damage from the Serbian attacks, but if you believed the owner, the journalists caused more damage when they got drunk—which was almost every night.

"Say Ingrid, I've found more lost children for you," the mustached reporter called in Croatian from the end of the bar.

"Slink off, Sergei!" the shapely blonde snapped. "I learned my lesson the last time. I fed, washed, and clothed those gypsy kids for two weeks. When I found their parents, the damn parents didn't want them. And while I'm calling the police on their papa, my little friends are cleaning out my purse. So if you want to take care of lost munchkins, be my guest. I've done my good deed for the year."

Sergei shrugged. As a Bulgarian news correspondent, he didn't have the expense accounts that the Western reporters had. He couldn't afford to stay in this hotel or eat their overpriced meals. But Sergei liked to hang around and tried—not without success—to be a pest. The western reporters tolerated the weasel-like Bulgarian because he could speak Russian, German, and Serbo-Croatian. His translation skills were worth many a mug of beer, even though he couldn't speak English very well. In addition to the drinks, Sergei would get a reciprocal translation of the UN's latest directives from the English and French reporters.

Sergei also enjoyed ogling Ingrid even though she didn't live up to the quick-to-bed reputation he would like to believe about Scandinavian women. Ingrid made him smile without sex. She had dozens of funny stories that she would tell after a few beers. Sergei especially liked the story about her American reporter friend, Frank Ferret, who would crash diplomatic receptions posing as a world-renowned sex therapist. Ferret would dance with the women, and they would tell him the most intimate details of their love life, hoping for free advice or a demonstration—which he occasionally provided. The next day he would visit their husbands and lovers and extract news leads and confirmations that would leave his fellow reporters with blank pages and angry editors. Ingrid would retell the story over and over, getting madder and madder as she embellished the embellishment.

Sergei persisted. *If Ing wouldn't look into the kids, who would?* "Hear that piano?"

"Chopin? In this dump?"

"It's from a little girl. She couldn't be more than eight years old. The boy with her is a Negro—from America, judging from his tennis shoes. They speak English, maybe French. I can't understand them. The boy says his father is King George."

"Another generation of con artists," Ingrid sniffed at Sergei's gullibility.

"They mentioned some other name: Clutch Cooper. I've heard of Clutch Cooper."

"They're taking names from magazine covers."

"They mentioned a few other names. One was Dr. Whistle. I know the American word whistle. I thought it was a funny name."

Ingrid showed no reaction other than to study her cocktail napkin. She walked closer to Sergei.

"Sergei darlin', here's some kuna. Would you please buy a round for me and my fellow correspondents and a pint of vodka for yourself? I'd do it myself, but I need a trip to the bathroom."

Ingrid turned right from the bar area then turned around and headed for the hotel lobby. Indeed, the pianist was quite young, and her companion held an ashtray to collect tips. A night clerk watched the children from the reception desk, ready to take away their money, and throw them into the street. Their ashtray wasn't full enough, yet.

Ingrid waited until Amy finished her piece. Amy would soon run out of the solos that she knew from memory, so she didn't start another piece when the pretty blonde woman sat on the piano bench next to her.

Martin thrust the ashtray in front of Ingrid, and she responded with a large bill.

Amy said, "*Merci.*"

"*De rien,*" Ingrid replied.

At last, someone to talk to! Amy rejoiced.

Amy looked the pretty lady in the eye, handed her bill back, and tried desperately, "*Bonsoir, mademoiselle. Crepe du chocolat, s'll vous plait?*"

"*Bonsoir,* but I don't work here and I'm not French, dear. I'm Swedish. You're American or Canadian?"

"American. Can you help us?" Martin blurted ecstatically. "You're the only one who speaks English."

"Oh, there are others here, but I'm not sure you want to talk with them," Ing reflected.

"We lost our parents," Martin said with a breaking voice.

Ing hesitated. *Is this a practical joke from my fellow pencils? They should know they always get back worse than I get. You'd think they'd know better. But even these creeps wouldn't use children in a joke. And these children look red-eyed and frustrated. They smell funny.*

"Where did you lose your parents?"

"New Zealand," Ami and Martin chimed together.

"Your father is King George?"

"No, George King. He's a policeman, and when he catches the bad man we ran away from, Dad will arrest him and put him in jail."

Ing had heard many uncomplimentary adjectives applied to Frank, but seldom "bad man." Yet these children mentioned Dr. Whistle to Sergei, and Dr. Whistle was one of Frank's standard impersonations. "Really, and who is this bad man?"

Martin took Ingrid's hand and walked her around the corner of the lobby where a presidential election poster of Bymarovitch hung tacked to a bulletin board. Martin pointed to the poster and said, "M. Lafate took us away from New Zealand, and he's chasing us. If he finds us, he'll hurt us. That's what Elizabeth says."

Ing felt her knees go weak. Klav Bymarovitch was supposed to have returned from exile in New Zealand, even though he never mentioned it in his radio commercials. *If the Butcher is a monster, could his brother be any better—chasing children?*

"Maybe you should go to the police," Ingrid muttered, her head swimming with possibilities and fears.

"I don't think so," Martin replied. "Elizabeth says the police are friends with him."

"There may be some truth to that," Ingrid agreed. *Steady girl*, she told herself. *Don't let the children see you're afraid.*

Ingrid realized there was still much she didn't know. "Do you know a Frank Whistle?"

"Dr. Whistle is nice. He talks funny and gives us Vi-en-nese chocolates," Amy answered quickly.

"You must be hungry."

"And thirsty too," Martin added.

Ing caught the attention of a waitress and showed her the room number on her key. "Some chocolate crepes and milk for my little friends. And bring some *rozata*." *Rozata* was sweet, so the children should like it.

"Our cook doesn't make crepes, except at breakfast," the waitress grumbled until Ing dropped two large bills in the waitress's hand.

The waitress smiled. "I'll make them myself, if I must."

"*Hvala lijepa*." Ingrid smiled a thank-you.

"Tell me more about Mr. Whistle," Ing said as she gently eased the children out of the lobby to a hallway leading to the stairway to her room. She didn't want anyone else seeing her with the kids.

"*Dr.* Whistle," Amy corrected. "The police put him in jail for murdering Rose O'Hara, but my daddy said he's not the murdering kind."

"He's not the marrying kind either," Ing murmured.

"M. Lafate is afraid of Dr. Whistle. That's why he took us, so Dr. Whistle would stop chasing him."

"Did Dr. Whistle say anything about a two-million-dollar reward?"

Martin tried to hush Amy, but she said, "My Daddy needs to share some reward money with Dr. Whistle so he can save his business and marry Debbie. He needs it real bad."

"Don't we all," Ingrid clucked.

Martin said, "Our parents are here, in a hotel near the UN headquarters."

Amy added, "But they don't know where to find us. I have to call my dad, but I don't have his phone number and—" She pointed to the hotel phone on the far wall, and with annoyance in her voice said, "Someone put the phone too high."

Ingrid stifled a smile. "I'm a friend of Dr. Whistle. If he's in town, I know where he usually stays, and your parents should be with him." *Ferret hasn't shown himself, but if there's trouble, that's understandable.*

Ingrid used the backstairs to take the children to her room. She had to find another place to stay *and fast.* The children wolfed their crepes and insisted on washing themselves in the hotel's lukewarm water. They began to nod off.

Ingrid couldn't wait. She packed a change of clothes and hurried the children down the backstairs and back into the cold night. Ing didn't bother checking out.

On the street at the back entrance, a drunken German reporter, in need of fresh air, said, "Hey, Ing, the local police are here looking for those children. They even had guns drawn."

"Here?"

"Yah, just now. They're probably in your room by now."

"Don't say anything, and I'll get you a date with my sister," She said, relieved that she didn't have a sister.

"*Mein* lips are sealed," he belched.

Ing saw the rotating reflected light from a police car. The car parked at the hotel entrance off the main square, where nonessential auto traffic was banned. Ing and the children would stay on the narrow backstreets. She had a vague idea as to where to hide the children, but it was not without risk.

Need to call Frank. If he's a target and flying low on the radar, he won't stay in his usual hotel—more likely the place near the UN headquarters like the children indicated. His phone and room will be bugged. It often is.

But first, find a place to bed down where Bymarovitch's sympathetic police won't be searching with drawn guns for two young children.

*　*　*

Sergei held out his hand. Zirov, guarding the entrance to Bymarovitch's villa, provided a handful of money. Sergei left smiling. He had pulled off a good deal telling the Bymarovitch camp about the American children who were spreading rumors about him. *Well, at least a good deal for myself.*

"Where are they?" Bymarovitch snapped at Zirov from his out-of-sight position behind the door.

"A Swedish reporter took the children to a whorehouse hotel. I'm surprised our police didn't think to look there first," Zirov chuckled.

Bymarovitch wasn't amused. Zirov didn't appreciate the danger the children's parents poised. "The police had better start thinking if they want a role in my new empire," Bymarovitch growled.

Directing his anger at Tinsley, he said, "I've had enough of this game. Stake out the hotel. Find the Swede and follow her. Set a trap. Kill her and all the Americans, then the children."

"What about the Bulgarian reporter?"

Bymarovitch shook his head in disgust. "Must I make every decision? How do you expect to get ahead in my new empire? You are empowered! When in doubt, *kill!*"

*　*　*

George grabbed the phone on the first ring. "George King here." The travel alarm clock showed 1:00 a.m., but George couldn't sleep.

Ingrid altered her voice the best she could. "I'm a friend. I have some things that belong to you and your associates. The merchandise is in perfect condition, but fragile, and the road to your office is full of dangerous bumps. Whistle Shipping will have to pick it up. Tell your shipping company to come to Tito Boulevard. I'll meet Whistle's courier in the *one place that he'd never be caught dead in*—as soon as tonight's curfew is lifted—to discuss nirvana and the other rewards of friendship."

"Is Martin—"

Ingrid hung up.

George knocked on Frank's door and found a gun barrel in his face. "Someone has Martin, Frank!" Frank ushered George into the hallway where the listening devices were less likely to be planted. George related the call verbatim and a minute later repeated the scenario to Gil and Debbie. He spread his street map. "Where are we supposed to meet her? There is no Tito Boulevard."

Frank grinned widely and sniffed, "You've heard of de-Stalinization where all the statues of Stalin were pulled down? Well, the same happened in the post-Tito years. Street names were changed. *This* is the old Tito Boulevard," Frank pointed to a red line on the map.

"The ex-Tito Boulevard is a long, long street," George frowned.

"What do you make of it, Frank?" Gil demanded. "Is it a setup?"

"No, no, no. Ing Carlsen has the kids. They couldn't be in better hands," Frank added, the relief ringing in his voice.

"Who's Ing?" Debbie asked.

"Ingrid is my close friend—a TV journalist from Stockholm. Smart as the devil and with a face like an angel. I spent the most erotic month of my life with her. If I'm the globe's greatest gifted lover—a fact that I was unable to demonstrate to you—I owe it all to Ing."

"Stick to business," Gil stated firmly.

"This *is* relevant," Frank groused. "Ing wants more than just handing over the kids. She mentioned nirvana and rewards."

"Rewards I understand," George said. "But *nirvana?*"

Frank sighed. "For her thirty-first birthday I gave her thirty-one long-stemmed roses. Scandinavians love flowers, 'cause their summers are so short. I also promised her thirty-one consecutive nirvanas."

"Really?" Debbie blushed.

"He's making this up." Gil scowled.

"Not the promise," Frank protested. "Before we ever reached thirty-one consecutive heavens, a couple of wars broke out. She was assigned to one battlefield, and I was assigned to the other. That's the last time I saw Ing, but I heard she was reporting on the Croatian elections."

George tapped Frank's shoulder impatiently with the folds of his map. "So the nirvana thing means *thirty-one*. Thirty-first Street and the former Tito Boulevard."

"Right, but I don't get her place-that-I'd-never-be-caught-dead-in bit," Frank puzzled.

Debbie nodded knowingly. "Let's get dressed. I know where she wants to meet you, Frank."

"Where?"

"In a church."

*   *   *

Several churches lined the former Tito Boulevard, but only one sat on Thirty-first Street. The church was relatively large and set close to the street. The building dated from the 1890s and showed a century of neglect with darkened limestone walls and crumbling statuary. The single onion domed steeple provided the church with interest if not beauty.

Across from the church, a small, unkempt park gave the ex-trampers a sense of shelter.

Frank advised, "Ing kinda stands out, making her easy to follow. So in case this is a trap, stay back, and watch my back."

"I'm going with you," Debbie insisted.

"No way," Gil stated.

Debbie pointed to the church entrance. "Have you seen even one man enter the church? No. Only a few old ladies in shawls. I go with Frank so *he* doesn't stand out so much." Debbie moved forward, and Frank followed.

Frank and Debbie adjusted their eyes to the dark of the church. Boards covered windows that once held beautiful stained glass windows. A smaller open window and the flicker of votive candlelight provided the only illumination.

Frank directed Debbie to a pew at the front.

"Now what?" she asked.

They didn't wait long.

A figure with a scarf on her head sat in the pew behind them.

"Who's *she?*" Ingrid asked suspiciously, pointing to Debbie.

"A friend," Frank explained. "We thought a man walking into a church with a woman would attract less attention.

"I'm Amy's future stepmother," Debbie snapped. "Where are the kids?"

Ingrid smiled, "The kids are unhurt. They were a bit dehydrated and anxious to get back to their parents—which will happen as soon as it's safe to move them."

"Thank God." Debbie sighed tearfully.

"I want to talk to talk to Frank alone," Ingrid insisted.

"Fat chance," Debbie stated.

Ingrid forced a smile. "Frank dar-ling, I have two choices. Or rather *you* . . . have one of two choices. You obviously have put a lot of time and money into this operation, and I'd hate to see you lose it. But *choice one* is for me to call the UN or police and have the kids point out the home of their kidnapper."

Frank shook his head vigorously. "Don't do that! They need to be back with their parents immediately. We can nail the kidnapper without them."

"Perhaps," she mused. "The children seem afraid of the police."

Ingrid weighed her next question carefully. "It was ridiculous of the Butcher to think he could return as his brother and not be detected."

Frank shrugged. "Once Klav's elected president, everyone'll figure he's the Butcher or worse. But by then, he'll be so insulated that no one will ever be able to prove it or do anything about it. Just like Saddam. Once in power, you can't get the bastard out, short of an all-out war."

Ingrid grinned. *The savvy Frank Ferret has just been tricked into confirming my bizarre theory. But now's not the time to grind it in. I'll save it for when he does something stinky.*

"So we have to act now," Ingrid said.

Debbie moved to Ingrid's pew, and Frank followed. Debbie growled, "The only thing we have to do is to turn over the kids, *right now!* Or you'll be picking up hands full of blonde hair off the marble floor, thank you very much!"

Ingrid slid behind Frank. "I like her. She's almost as tough as her stepdaughter. We'll go for the children now, but there's no hurry. They're sleeping and quite safe."

"What's the second choice?" Frank asked.

"You could elect sharing my reward."

"*Your* reward!" Frank fumed.

"Calm down," Ingrid said sweetly. *This part is delicious.* "I said *I'm* willing to share. I didn't hear you say that *you* were willing to share."

"I already have two partners."

"Well, they can take their cut out of your half. And once we're married, you won't be able to tell the difference."

"Ing, the guy is supposed to do the proposing," Frank said softly but with distress in his voice. His thoughts raced. *Damn, I want to take her in my arms. But if I do, she'll end up as another dead lover.*

Ingrid sniffed, "I've waited and waited and waited—pampering your quaint American ways. So I have to speak up."

Debbie smirked. "I like this girl,"

Frank squirmed. "Ingrid, you know I love you too much to marry you."

"Ugh, what a line! How many times have you used that?"

Frank set his jaw angrily. "Women around me get killed!"

Ingrid realized she had crossed the line. Amy's story of Rose's murder fit. "I'm sorry about Rose O'Hara. But I knew the risks when I chose this lifestyle. I suspect your friend Rose did too."

"It's worse than you think. If it's not just the cross fire between these idiot Yugos. There's a bunch of furious fruitcakes who think I'm a CIA master spy who needs pay back."

"Are you?"

"You know better than that! But I impersonated one once or twice, so every terrorist, neo-Nazi, drug domo, and bad guy who's had a buddy burned by secret agent Insect One, thinks that I'm to blame."

"Are you?"

"Only partly."

Frank continued. "It's more than the reward. Yeah, maybe the money was to make me feel more deservin' of that rich ambassador's daughter I've been courtin'."

Ing rolled her eyes. "Darling, you'll *never* be deserving of her or any of your other lovers, including me. But the difference with me is that *I—don't—care.* I love you, Frank, for your undeserving, unrespectable self."

"But it's the respectability I need to save my life. I need to be *so big* that the people who'd like to put contracts out to put my head on a spike can't afford the price—so big that they'll feel thankful I'm not hurtin' 'em anymore."

"Very well, Frank. You keep the fame, respectability—and the byline. I'll keep the money. You'll quit while you're on top, and I'll just quit. My family has disowned me for living on the edge, and I need the money."

"I get the story, and you get the money?" Frank asked for confirmation.

"That's choice one."

"Ah, I can't do that. My friends are counting on the reward money."

"Damn, right we are," Debbie inserted.

Ingrid grinned devilishly. "Well, there's always choice two, Frank. If you want half the reward, you can always marry me. If I'm a citizen of the U.S., the taxes on the reward will be half of what I'd have to pay in Sweden."

"You sure know how to manage household finances," Frank groused.

Ingrid put her soft hands on Frank's newly shaved face. "Frank darlin', if I didn't know you better, I'd be embarrassed at your lack of enthusiasm. I know you're afraid of settling down. And I believe you have a sincere concern for the safety of the women around you. My conditions are simple. Two children raised in clean, beautiful Stockholm where there is no crime. I'll expect a modicum of fidelity and total abstinence from wars. After that, if you get bored with nirvana, you're free to find yourself another battle ground, and I won't try to stop you."

Debbie pushed Frank into Ingrid's arms. "Kiss her damn it, and seal the agreement. I want the kids *now!*"

As the trio slipped out of the church in a tight formation, the sound of the rifle shot startled Frank. "Hit the ground," Frank shouted. Another shot, from a closer rifle answered. When Frank turned around, he saw Debbie and Ing laying on their backs with Debbie sprawled over Ing. Frank threw his body over both of them and became aware of a rapidly expanding pool of blood.

CHAPTER 18

Taking the Bait

Amy awoke from the dank chill air. Martin had his jacket on under a quilt pulled over his head, so his fight was with the light coming in from the curtainless hotel window. The hotel's cramped hotel room held a double bed and a couch suitable for sleeping. A cracked mirror covered part of the ceiling. Ing had left bottled water, four hard rolls, a tiny jar of jam, and her Swiss Army knife for spreading the jam. A box of granola bars suggested lunch. The night before, while they were moving to a different hotel, Ingrid had told Amy and Martin that she was going to get their daddies, and that if she was not back when they awoke, they were not to worry. She also told them not to look out the second-story window and not to open the door. There was no phone. "Bad guys can force people to say things. They can even imitate your parents' voices."

Ing thought for a minute. "I could be followed back, so I'll send Frank Ferret, the man you know as Dr. Whistle, here. Pick a password."

* * *

Clutch's return rifle fire quieted the gunman in the car.

Gil ran to Debbie's limp body.

A wild pistol shot from the driver of the car ricocheted off the pavement. Clutch's second volley of rifle fire answered. The car holding the dead or wounded sniper roared away.

Debbie clutched her side in pain as Gil cradled her. "Ooh, I hurt, but the bullet didn't go in. I might have a bruised or broken rib."

Ingrid's eyes were closed, and blood covered her side.

Frank pulled away Ingrid's coat. He had to find the wound and stop the bleeding.

The rest of the team gathered. Each held a gun, except Clutch, who gripped a rifle with a folding stock. Clutch's face was red. "I killed 'im. I killed 'im," he cried.

With streaming tears, Frank said, "Ing's not dead."

Eve pushed Frank away and applied her silk scarf as a compress. "The bullet passed through her arm."

Debbie opened her blouse to reveal Pip's bulletproof vest. "The bullet must've deflected off my vest into Ing."

Willie was frantic. "Leave her. We have to get outta here."

Frank's coughing voice, said, "Don't get near me, Willie. Don't say another word."

Virginia shoved Willie out of Frank's punching range.

George said, "Clutch shot the sniper, but his driver got away. They could come back—with reinforcements. If we can't move her, we have to prepare for another attack."

Gil cradled Debbie in his arms. She pushed up and scrambled to her feet. She felt wobbly, but more important things demanded her attention than a bruised rib. "Ing didn't tell us where she hid the kids," Debbie cried. "She was going to take us there."

George slapped his forehead. "Geez, Frank! What the hell were you talking about all that time?"

The whooping of a distant shrill police siren startled the trampers. Eve said, "Pick her up, gently. I don't think she has anything broken. Ing could be unconscious from the fall or the pain."

Their van pulled away seconds before the police arrived. Virginia held Clutch, who was trembling. "I killed 'im," Clutch kept repeating.

Willie looked over his shoulder and grumbled, "We're all going to end up incarcerated in a Yugoslavian concentration camp."

Frank snapped, "Don't worry, Willie. They'll just shoot us. Saves on bread and water."

Eve shouted, "Be quiet! All of you! Now listen. Head back to the hotel. I'd rather take care of her than explain to a hospital how she got this bullet wound. I'll need some medical supplies."

Frank said, "I'll get you an operating suite if you want. All you need around here is a checkbook."

"We need something for her pain," Eve countered. "Even a small wound like this can cause shock."

"Will she be okay?"

Eve didn't answer, but injected two tranquilizer shots that she had brought along for the children. "Your Ing won't bleed to death. She shouldn't even lose the use of her arm. The problem is whatever I give her for her pain might delay her regaining consciousness—keep her from speaking. And I'd feel a hell of a lot better if she would wake up if only for a minute."

"So would I," Gil agreed soberly.

*   *   *

Ingrid awoke when they wrapped her in a slicker to hide the bloody clothes. "Oh! This hurts," she said in Swedish. She rambled in Swedish, to the dismay of the trampers. Ingrid stiffened with a spasm of pain and dropped back into unconsciousness.

The trampers looked at Frank.

"I didn't understand every word. She wants me to get the lizards who shot her, or she won't let me make love to her."

"The kids, man!" Gil demanded.

"Ing named a small hotel. Said something about a password knock. I'm the one who has to go."

Eve glared. "Do it! I'll take care of your woman, but so help me God, you better bring back my boy unhurt, or you won't have anything left to make love with!"

Gil surveyed Clutch's muffled hysteria at having killed someone, and Willie's plain fear. He took the gun out of Willie's hand and handed it to Debbie. Willie protested, but Gil said, "We need a cool finger on the trigger. I don't need you to go shooting holes in a maid."

*　　*　　*

The small three-story hotel that housed the children stood at the corner of two narrow cobblestone streets, a block from a busy commercial boulevard. The hotel took up a small block. A row of small, undistinguished businesses faced the hotel. All were closed except for a video store, which the rescuers felt too dangerous to enter. "Better not to be seen," Frank explained.

From the boulevard, Frank held small, unobtrusive binoculars to his eyes and handed them to Gil for confirmation. "Whaddya see?"

"Yeah, it's a trap," Gil reported. "The hotel entrance is surrounded by three cars with two to four men each. Their even spacing suggests military types. There might be another car around the side. Exhaust is coming from the closest car."

Frank nodded in agreement and motioned George and Virginia to keep a safe distance away from the line of sight to the hotel. Frank put his slim binoculars in his pocket. "The serpents are using the kids for bait."

"Are you sure?" George asked.

Frank pointed to the closest car. "No one runs his car to keep warm in Croatia. Fuel is too scarce; unless you're the biggest snake in the pit, then you can afford it. But if you can afford it, you won't be coiled up in front of a fleabag brothel of a hotel."

Frank squeezed his hand into a fist. "We can walk in, but can we walk out again?"

"How many bad guys?" George asked.

"At least ten soldiers spread among three, maybe four, cars," Gil answered, fingering his rifle with the folding stock.

"You can be sure they know they lost a fellow sniper this morning," Gil guessed. "So they'll have plenty of firepower, and they'll be quick to use it."

Frank gave Virginia Slater a sheepish smile. "Ginnie, I'm glad you came along. You're gonna trade your Rodeo Drive duds with the first hooker uniform we can find."

Virginia nodded dolefully. "I've been contemplating a career change. The world's first profession isn't exactly what I had in mind, but then again, I might have more self-respect."

Frank took a torturously long half hour to place a black market order and find a hooker. The evening was too early for most of them to be out and about. Frank also purchased an oversized overcoat to hide his other purchases.

Virginia changed clothes in an alley, while the men stood guard and snickered.

"It's cold on the legs," Virginia complained about her red leather micromini. Frank's normal response would be an offering to massage

Ginnie's chilly thighs, but Ing's shooting left him in no mood for flirting with his sexy partner.

Frank stopped walking toward the hotel and spun Virginia around in the opposite direction. "This is a mistake," Frank frowned.

"I'm not a convincing hooker?" Virginia replied, teasing her hair.

"I just don't want to see another lady I'm fond of getting shot or killed," Frank answered.

"So now you're fond of *me*?" Virginia laughed sarcastically. "Why did you wait until after you're engaged to that Swedish sexpot to tell me you were *fond* of me. I might've been fond back."

"Get outta here, Slater. Go back. It was a bad idea."

Virginia grabbed Frank by the collar. "Damn you, Frank. I'm a mother of a little boy with potential medical problems. That's why I put up with Willie. He bought me three million dollars of paid-up life insurance to take care of my boy if anything happens to me. I want to watch him grow up healthy. But if I don't do what I have to do to rescue those two kids, I could never live with myself. Now let's get going."

Frank sighed. Frank prayed that he would get the first bullet so he wouldn't have to hold another wounded or dying woman in his arms. He splashed whiskey on them both from an outrageously priced miniature bourbon bottle purchased at their hotel's minibar. The couple practiced a stagger and laughed a real laugh as they fell in toward each other.

Virginia shivered. "I don't care what part of me you touch as long as it's uncovered and has goose bumps. Touch anything else, and I'll punch your lights out."

Frank and Virginia began the short walk toward the hotel. They walked down the middle of the cobblestone street, now empty of traffic.

Gil and George hid in the shadows behind a truck. They could watch Frank and Virginia and easily see the three death squad cars with occupants watching the hotel and studying the loudly laughing couple.

"The cars are out of pistol range, but with this rifle, I have the advantage," Gil whispered.

George snorted, "You've been away from law enforcement too long. Nowadays, bad guys have automatic pistols. They can't aim at anything with 'em, but they spray an awful lot of lead in your direction."

As Frank and Virginia raucously giggled their way toward the hotel's entrance, a man exited the nearest car. He strode in front of the couple and held up his hand in the manner of a person who was used to stopping people in their tracks. He looked at the couple and pulled a picture out of his pocket. He looked at the bearded man in the photograph and up to Frank's clean shaven face, barely visible in the red light from the hotel's window. The man tipped his hat and blew a kiss at the pretty prostitute.

Virginia blew it back then nuzzled her face in Frank's neck until they were in the hotel. She whispered, "If we get through this, I'll never be frightened of anything again. After this, life's on cruise control."

"We're not on the on-ramp yet." Frank checked in, using as few Croatian words as possible. The pair hurried up the stairs and to the room where the children were supposed to be hidden.

"Good, there's a guard in front of the door. That means the kids are still there. Do your thing, Slater."

Frank taught Virginia the Croatian word for snake. She shouted *Zmija* at Frank and slapped his face. She strode to the guard as if shifting customers. Virginia put her arms around him. The guard grabbed her, kissed her with a bristly face, and pawed her with heavy hands. Virginia heard the thud and felt the guard's heavy body slip to the floor, almost dragging her down with him.

Virginia spat on the fallen guard who had groped her. "You owe me big time, Ferret."

"Can't, Ginnie. I'm engaged."

Frank gave Virginia the unconscious man's pistol, patted his pocket, and scooped out a key. "Pass key?"

"Hurry, Frank!" Virginia urged. "Those hoods could come up here at any minute."

Frank turned the key and heard the lock release. He stepped back in case someone decided to shoot through the door. He tried to open the door, but a manual bolt kept it from opening. Frank did a shave-and-a-haircut knock. No answer. He said, "Kids, it's your pal, Dr. Whistle. Your folks are waiting downstairs. Let me in." No sound.

Virginia said, "Break down the door."

Frank rolled his eyes. "I'm just a skinny reporter, not a three-hundred-pound NFL tackle. And this old door is two and one half inches of solid oak. Nor, for obvious reasons, can I shoot around hopin' to hit the bolt. Let them hear your voice, Slater. Maybe you should try knockin'."

Inside the room, Amy and Martin hid under the bed. "No password," Martin whispered. "That's not Dr. Whistle."

*　　*　　*

The desk clerk stepped out, flapping his arms around himself to keep warm. He headed to the car full of men. They rolled down a window releasing a cloud of cigarette smoke. The clerk jabbered, pointing upward. The doors opened, and the men scrambled out as the cue for Gil to fire his first shot into the car. Gil's second shot hit the gas tank, and the car exploded, sending glass flying and knocking the occupants of the car down.

Men in the furthest car scattered into the street to avoid the same fate. George's rapid fire brought down two of the men, and the third man reentered his car and sped away.

Ratac's men watching the other side of the hotel heard the gunfire and entered the hotel through a side door. One began firing from the front door, and gunshots came from a front window.

"Damnit, four of them went in!" George shouted. "Only two of them are shooting at us. That means the other two are going after the kids."

* * *

The explosion startled the would-be rescuers. But Frank and Virginia didn't panic until they heard the commotion at the bottom of the stairs.

"Knocks!" Virginia exclaimed. "That's it! Hurry! They're coming."

"Knock, knock!" Frank shouted.

No answer. Then a small voice said, "Who's there?"

"The interrupting cow."

"The in-ter-rup-ting—"

"Moo!" Frank hollered.

After a pause, the giggling started, and Martin pushed against the bolt. It didn't move easily, but finally slide back.

Virginia hugged the children and pulled them to the dust-covered window.

Frank waited at the door, and when he saw the first gunman round the corner to his hallway, he discharged his Glock frantically. The gunman's yelp surprised Frank. *I actually hit someone!* The gunmen took cover behind the corner and fired back without aiming. The body of the guard who Frank had knocked out lurched as an uncontrolled bullet smashed into him. Frank shut the door, locked it, bolted it, and jammed a chair under the doorknob.

Virginia already had a harness attached to Amy, and Martin was attaching his own harness. Only three harnesses could be hid under Frank's newly purchased overcoat. Frank said, "Take your time kids, but not too much time."

"You remember how to rappel?" Virginia asked anxiously.

"Of course," Amy said with a huff. "Debbie taught me."

Watching the children creep down the wall seemed like an eternity. Martin hit the ground first and helped Amy out of her harness.

Bullets pierced the door as Virginia stepped out of the window. Frank fired low through the door, and the shooting stopped. He didn't wait to attach the harness. Taking his black, silk scarf to protect his hands, Frank slid, almost uncontrolled down the rope. Landing hard, he took the three harness ends and tied them to a lamp post. The pursuers would still be able to climb down the ropes, but not as fast. They would have to go hand over hand, and that would make them easy targets. They would realize it and take the stairs.

Frank picked up a protesting Amy and began to run.

Gil emptied his rifle at the last source of gunfire, discarded the weapon, and scooped Amy out of Frank's arms. George squeezed Martin, and the group ran toward their van. If the explosion and gunshots attracted attention from the locals, they were smart enough to stay out of sight. As they passed the vacated gunmen's car, Frank noticed the exhaust still running, and said, "Take *this* car! Give me the keys to the other van, and I'll run decoy."

"Good idea!" Gil said, and stuffed Amy into the car while she wailed empathetically about the car that was on fire.

"I'll drive," George insisted. "I drove hammer down blood runs from the airport to L.A. hospitals for a year." In an aside to Martin, he said, "If you ever drive this fast, you won't get a license till you're forty."

Frank found Virginia running with him step for step. "Isn't it hard to run with heels?"

"If that's not a setup for a punch line, I don't know what is. And if you don't slow down, I'll show you how much shoes can hurt."

Frank slowed on the main street. The glow and smoke of the burning car could still be seen on the edges of the orange tile rooftops. Virginia took off her high heels and renewed the pace.

Frank opened the van door. "Get down in the backseat. I'm going to do a drive-by to let the serpents think we're headed in the opposite direction."

"No, thank you! I'll ride up front so I can take the wheel if you're shot. And how do the snakes know it's us if they don't *see* us?"

Frank gunned the van past the hotel where the confused gunmen were deciding whether to give chase or tend to their wounded comrades. Frank fired his last round in their direction and sped off. The drive-by shot inspired a wild return volley.

Five kilometers away, Frank pulled the van into a narrow, unlit side street and turned off the lights. "I have to reorient myself and figure out the safest way back to the hotel."

"Oh, what a letdown," a euphoric Virginia chuckled. "I thought we were parked in Lover's Lane."

Frank laughed and gave Virginia an affectionate peck. "You are some package, Slater."

"And you're about the most exciting rogue I've ever met. And I've known a few scoundrels. God help the woman that marries you!"

"God helped my first wife. She dumped me on our honeymoon just 'cause I stepped out to cover the war games in Granada, or was it Panama? Too many wars, too few wives."

"Do you want to try it, Ferret?"

"Try what?"

"Living together. A war game. No real losers. We might even merge forces."

"You just got done telling me that my wives need divine intervention."

They laughed, and there was a long, awkward silence. Virginia broke the impasse. "I know you're engaged to the most beautiful blonde on the face of the planet, but from what Debbie told me, Ing had to twist your arm. Debbie said that the only thing you two have in common is sex."

Frank chucked. "Ing *did* twist my arm. And as for sex, with Ing, sex would be enough. If Ing has a fault, it's that she's too perfect. Except for putting the locks on my war coverage, she doesn't want to change me. Can you believe that! A woman who doesn't want to change me? She wants me just the way I am. *I* don't even like me just the way I am."

"She's putting on an act." Virginia sighed. "Once Ing gets you housebroken, you won't be able to recognize yourself."

"I sure hope so," Frank said.

"Sounds like you want to go through with it. With Ing."

Ferret grimaced. "The idea's growing on me."

"Just because she was shot?" Virginia speculated. "A relationship based on sex and sympathy? Don't I get something for a near miss? Back in the bordello, the bullet missed me by only—"

Frank kissed her on the lips.

"You're holding back, Ferret."

"Sorry, I promised Ing a modicum of fidelity. I didn't think a modicum could be so hard."

CHAPTER 19

The Only Solution

In the Rocklin hotel suite, Amy chattered like a happy chipmunk. Martin went through the motions of clobbering Tinsley, until George picked Martin up and held him over his head. No one totally believed Martin until Amy took ten minutes to retell the story. Halfway through her story, Frank and Virginia came in the door.

Debbie gave Frank a soft thank-you hug so that she could whisper in his ear, "Better wipe the hooker lipstick off before you look in on Ingrid, you creep. She's sleeping comfortably, just in case you're still interested." Debbie glared at Virginia.

Debbie shook her head, and muttered, "From Frank, I expect it. But I thought you had more class."

Virginia winced. "Don't lecture me, Debbie. My feet ache. I've a stubble rash from kissing a porcupine. I'm half naked and both halves are cold. I'm dressed like a whore, but I still can't drum up any business—even with a rake like Ferret. I'm so depressed that I don't think my self-esteem will ever recover."

Gil bounded over to embrace Virginia. "Thanks for getting the kids back, Ginnie."

Virginia smiled, and when Gil turned his back, she wrinkled her nose at Debbie. "I think I'll dress this way all the time."

Amy resumed her story. Stopping for a breath, Amy handed the Breakneck Download diskette to her father. "Eliz-a-beth said this was im-por-tant."

"Oh, will Willie be pleased," Virginia gushed.

George snorted, "What the hell's so important that Willie would chase it halfway around the world? Where is the little weasel?"

"Down in the bar establishing an alibi," Debbie replied. "He doesn't want to be seen in the company of 'murdering cowboys.'"

"And where's Clutch?" Virginia asked.

Eve snickered. "I left our sharp shooting cowboy in a fetal position, supposedly guarding Ing."

Debbie scowled. "Don't laugh! Clutch came through. If he wasn't the marksman that he is, Ingrid and I would be dead."

Virginia caressed the software diskette. "What would you pay for a plug-in that would increase the speed of downloading Web sites by 11 percent?"

"Nothing!" Eve answered for George. She was on a high. Her Martin was back. Her brave husband was safe, and Ing was healthily swearing in Swedish. Eve was tearfully happy, and she could care less about software.

Clutch entered the room, saw the children, and smiled. He left and came back with a raincoat, which he placed over Virginia's bare skin.

Virginia gave Clutch an affectionate pat and continued, "Let me ask the question another way. If two large software operating systems each cost about the same, but one does something faster than the other, which would you buy?"

George grunted. "I see your point. It's an advertising plum. Every system has to have it."

"Right!" Virginia beamed. "Less than pennies to make, pennies to sell, but every new system in the world has to have it until something better comes along, which, in the computer industry, is yesterday."

Virginia slipped the diskette into Gil's laptop. She soon made a copy of it, which she handed to Gil. "In case, I lose it."

Gil held the diskette like it smelled bad. "You didn't give me this for safekeeping."

Virginia grinned. "Willie's trying desperately to figure out what makes it work."

Gil shrugged. "Since it's not a hardware or wiring solution, it must have something to do with the cache."

George joked, "Cache is something you spend."

Amy rose up to a school teacher's posture. "Not this cache, Mr. King. Cache is where you store your Internet addresses."

Gil chuckled. "Among other things."

Virginia nodded. "That much Willie knows. But that's *all* he knows. Breakneck was written by an unorthodox programmer who sent it to us wrapped in brown butcher paper. Willie can't figure out the language. This programmer is using a hybrid language that's all his own. Either he's an idiot who mucked up standard computer language and got lucky . . . or he has an intuitive gift to think in four dimensions."

"Willie's doing reverse engineering?" Gil accused more than asked.

George said, "I've heard of reverse engineering. But what is it?"

Gil shook his head. "That's when a competitor figures out what your program does and then works backward to get at the same solution. It's like a generic drug. Different formula, but same result."

"Why bother?" Debbie asked.

Gil looked intently at Virginia. "Because he's trying to cut the developer out of a fortune in royalties? It's legalized stealing."

"It wouldn't be the first time," Virginia confirmed. "That's how Willie got started in the business."

"And you want me to help Willie rob some poor soul of his idea?"

Virginia snapped back quickly. "I know you won't let him. That's why I gave you the disk. If you can decipher what's happening in this program, Willie might give you a piece of the action. Enough to keep your creditors away. He might even rescind his virus rumor."

Debbie jerked to attention.

Virginia missed Debbie's reaction and continued, "And honest to God, Gil, I didn't have anything to do with that. I only found out about it when his secretary sent me an e-mail asking how to void the Rocklin Software purchase order. Purchase orders are something Willie never gets involved in, unless he's trying to hide something. He hates you so much, Gil, and yet he's afraid of you. Willie wanted to ruin you so that you'd get out of the picture and give him a chance at Debbie."

"What are you talking about?" Debbie asked.

"Knowing you, Debbie, I'm surprised you didn't strand Willie on that glacier."

Gil intervened. "Debbie doesn't know that Willie's responsible for my financial troubles. One thing I learned in law enforcement was that you don't judge without facts. I wasn't absolutely sure beyond a reasonable doubt until you confirmed it, just now."

George growled, "Ya gonna kill 'im, man?"

"No, I'll do what Virginia suggests. If anything, Willie inadvertently brought Debbie and me closer together. Sooner or later, his dirty tricks will catch up with him."

Debbie glowered. "Gil's too nice. *I'm* going to kill him."

255

*   *   *

Willie wiped the canned tomato juice off his face. "Don't you think you're overreacting?" The tramper's brunch club couldn't help but laugh at Willie's shock, except for the children, who couldn't believe Debbie's anger.

Gil put a hand on Debbie's shoulder to keep her from jumping on Willie. "Dern, maybe to you it's the loss of one little resale product. But I have a garage stuffed full of computer disks and CDs, all wrapped and ready to be shipped—Amy's smiling face on each one—but with no buyers in sight. I borrowed mightily to have enough inventory to meet your demand. But then you renege on our deal. The great people that work with me may delay cashing their checks for a while, but eventually they have to feel secure. I'll lose them. I can lose my house. Fortunately, I have a great gal in Debbie. She'll tough it out with me. But how do I pay the banks and get rid of the virus stigma?"

Willie shrugged. "Declare bankruptcy. Screw your creditors. Change your name. No one will know."

"Sure! I'll tape over Rocklin Software on thousands of diskettes. I'll stick a "Don't Look Under This Label Software" over my name.

Willie looked at his tomato-juice-stained, favorite T-shirt. "I don't know what to say, Rocklin. I'm sorry for both of you, truly sorry. I wouldn't have done it if I hadn't loved Debbie so much. I was going to send you the bill for the private plane I chartered to take us out of New Zealand. I'll tear up the bill for a wedding present."

The breakfast club got up and left, leaving Willie alone with Virginia and his Breakneck Download disk.

He looked at his stone-faced assistant and asked, "Was it something I said?"

*   *   *

Tinsley and Marcus Turner parked their bullet-pocked car in front of the Bymarovitch villa. They looked suspiciously at each other. Two missions to kill the trampers failed. Seven of Bymarovitch's loyal soldiers were wounded, one seriously shot by his associates. The amateurs' firepower and deceptiveness were underestimated. Worst of all, the two children hostages were found, only to be lost again. The Butcher would blame one or both of them. Each mercenary was anxious to point blame at the other.

They didn't get the chance. The Butcher had spent the day campaigning, and he was tired. His body slumped to one side in the large hand-carved wooden chair in his library. He quietly listened to his soldiers' stories. "You took the wounded to our private hospital?" he asked for confirmation. Ratac tempered his anger at this unforgivable act because his rage simmered elsewhere. "Wounds in war I can tolerate for loyal troops. We send these warriors back into battle. On these covert missions, I might even abide one wounded hero." His calm voice began to rage, "But to allow seven failed soldiers to heal while our movement festers is intolerable! That many weak soldiers are vulnerable to capture. It would only take one of them to say the wrong thing to the wrong person, and it would hurt our movement."

"Sir, do you want me to increase the guards at the hospital?" Turner asked.

"No! Evacuate the doctors and torch the hospital to the ground." Ratac didn't add "with the wounded in it." He didn't have to.

"Sir, I'll personally put a bullet in the head of each soldier," Tinsley inserted.

"Don't bother," Ratac said. "Maybe this lesson in failure will smolder into their memories for their next lives."

Ratac stood and stalked toward his reporting mercenaries. "The most magnificent event in the history of the Balkans is within my grasp. I'm about to launch the most important action since the assassination of Archduke Ferdinand in Sarajevo that started World War I.

"However, two small children escaped—*twice*. As long as they were my hostages, I didn't have to concern myself with their inconsequential parents who knew my secret. Was this lapse caused by me?" Ratac looked directly at Turner.

"No, sir," Turner said, hiding his nervousness. "I heard you tell your daughter about the notorious CIA assassin Ferret. Obviously, he has the weapons and will to challenge us, but we will destroy him and his friends."

Even though Ratac warned Elizabeth about her dangerous friends, he really had nothing but condescension for the trampers: "A mere journalist with a reputation for impersonations, a failed FBI man, and a minor police officer. How dare they think they can walk on the same battlefield as me!"

Ratac paused to recall the memory of his greatest battlefield triumph. The Butcher had captured a UN company. Ratac had taken their uniforms, then posing as a UN contingent, he managed to talk a large band of the enemy to lay down their arms. The Butcher then marched the enemy into the woods where they were executed. *How could a genius such as mine be stymied by a small group of civilians? This must not happen!*

The tic in Ratac's cheek pulsated, even worse since his plastic surgery. "I recruited the best soldiers of fortune that existed. Both of you performed admirably in New Zealand. But when it came to real fighting, *you failed!*" he screamed.

Ratac sprang from his chair, lunging at Tinsley. The Butcher hit him with a single blow to the neck. The muscular Australian mercenary dropped to the carpet, his neck broken, his mouth open where he had bitten his tongue, his eyes bulging from side to side—a cry for help from the only part of his body that could still move.

Turner swallowed and thought feverishly of how to fend off Ratac's probable attack. *Diversion?* "Sir, he's not dead, yet. Shall we watch him here, or would you like me to drag him somewhere else?"

"What would you do?" Ratac answered, his nostrils flaring.

"Since Tinsley's not making any noise that would interfere with your phone calls, we could just leave him on the floor and watch him suffer."

The Butcher smiled. "I hesitated to tell you this earlier because I know you'd become attached to your New Zealand mission wife."

"Yes, I was hoping Paula would join us by now," Turner said, relieved that the subject was changed.

"Unfortunately, Frank Ferret killed her before she could carry out her mission. You might want to think of an appropriately painful death for the American assassin."

Turner clenched his fists. "You can be sure I will."

"When I'm elected, I'll have an inspired job for you, Commandant Turner. Learn Croatian," he ordered. "Study all you can about tanks and"—he paused with a wider smirk as a solution firmed in his mind—"but that can wait. First, find the best sniper among our soldiers. I'll need him soon—very soon."

* * *

Willie was invited back for a team conference that Debbie called in the UN parking lot. Leaning against an armored car, Debbie's eyes twinkled that same way they did when she was coaxing trampers to do a bungee jump. "With all this collective IQ power, we should be able to outsmart the Butcher's brains."

Clutch said, "Huh? You want something, Debbie? Anything. Just name it."

Debbie looked at the ground and muttered, "Thanks for not asking that question a year ago."

Debbie went from person to person placing her hand on shoulders and gripping hands. "Elizabeth!" she said to each tramper.

"So?" Willie responded.

"So what are we going to do to save her?"

"Save her from what?" Willie asked with exasperation. "She's probably never looked so appealing in her life. She has jewels and furs. She's a screwy girl speaking her screwy language to millions of screwy people who treat her like a rock star. Lizzie will be at the right hand of power. You and I may despise Bymarovitch, but you have your kids, and I have my disk. We don't even know if this Bymarovitch is the tramper who was on our trip or his brother. His brother Klav may be just as evil.

"So let's extricate ourselves from this disgusting situation while we're ahead. If Lizzie can tolerate being the Nazi cheerleader for a murderer, it's her dilemma. If she can't, she should log off. That's what I'm doing. I don't know what the rest of you cowboys are going to do, but I'm making vapor trails to the good ol' United States of America."

Eve felt Willie deserved a reply. "Mr. Dern, if you had heard the children's entire story instead of getting smashed in the bar, you would know that Elizabeth is fearful for her life. She's afraid of being *permanently* logged off. The Butcher needs her in his election bid, but as soon as she stops verifying his identity, the Butcher has no further use for her."

George inserted, "The Butcher will kill her in an instant, and if Rose's murder is any example of his MO, he'll blame it on his election opponent."

A collective silence followed. George's MO observation made perfect sense.

Eve nodded first. "Elizabeth is in big trouble, and I wish we knew how to help her, but we have to take Martin back home before something else happens."

Gil said, "My sister, Phyllis, is—was—in Rome for a medical conference. She's on her way here to take Amy home. She can take Martin too. Um, there's another reason I want her. She's a pediatric psychiatrist. The kids are acting like their kidnapping was just another adventure, like sailing in the hot air balloon, ocean kayaking, or rappelling down the cliff."

"Maybe there's a message in that"—Debbie clucked—"but we don't want to take any chances. Sounds like Martin would be in good hands."

Eve and George's eyes met. "Oh well, Elizabeth risked her life to save our son." Eve sighed. "I guess we can spend a few more days to help her, but how?"

"We have to get Liz out of the Bymarovitch mansion," Debbie stated.

"I'll bet it's an armed camp," George guessed, and no one challenged his logic.

Frank tapped on a Croatian newspaper and noted, "Bymarovitch is giving a preelection eve speech in the main town square tomorrow night. Elizabeth is on the agenda."

Clutch coughed for attention, "When you're huntin' skunks, you don't crawl in their den. You wait till they come out for water. This Butcher fellow has to get to the town square. So we stop their car on the way in. There won't be as many critters guarding her, and maybe Liz can get away."

Virginia shook her head. "And maybe she could be accidentally shot. I say it's too risky."

The group stood in silence. *How could they possibly get Elizabeth safely away without increasing the probability of her death?*

Finally Frank spoke. "The Butcher's gonna kill her."

"We know that," Clutch said.

"I mean tomorrow night at the election rally. What better place? Just like George says his MO is to make it look like someone else did it."

"How, Frank?" Virginia asked.

"A sniper's bullet. A bomb's too unpredictable, too messy. The Butcher could blow himself up."

Gil leaned forward. "When do you think he'll do it?"

Frank thought for a few seconds. He had suffered through hundreds of election speeches. "The Butcher will have Liz shot while she's on the podium where she'll be a clean shot for a sniper. Better early than later when bored listeners turn off their televisions. The best time would be during the introductions when they hold each other's hands in the air. Everyone's payin' attention. Liz'll be up front and visible. The shock value of a man's daughter being blown away as she's holding her father's hand would be tremendous. Even in a place like this, which has been swimming in blood for so long they're practically immune to it, the Butcher will get sympathy, and judging from his act in the hotel lobby, he knows how to milk it."

"We have to warn Liz," Clutch advised.

"Hard to do," Frank replied. "If the Butcher finds out Elizabeth's been warned, he'll kill her right away."

Virginia shuddered. "We have to do *something*."

Frank nodded soberly. "I guessing Liz will be wearing a bulletproof vest like the one that saved Debbie's life. They're heavy, bulky Russian-made models, and from her bulky look on television, Elizabeth has one on when she appears in public. That's not uncommon for public appearances round here."

"But she is bulky," Willie reminded.

"Not that bulky," Debbie disagreed.

"That could save her," Eve said.

Clutch shook his head. "A high-powered rifle might be able to cut right through a vest—if there *is* a vest."

George added, "Vest or no vest, they can do things to a bullet's tip to pierce through a vest."

Virginia summed up, "Elizabeth will be shot when she's being introduced. She'll *might* be wearing a Ruskie bulletproof vest that might, or might not, stop a bullet from going through, or . . . the sniper could use a head shot. Warning her, if we could, will only speed up her death. We're stuck. Maybe the UN?"

If anyone thought getting help from the UN security force was a good idea, no one said so.

Willie stomped away. "I've heard enough. The UN will never believe you, and even if they did, you can't use them because Lizzie could be killed in a cross fire. It's the same reason you couldn't tell the UN to rescue the kids. You have a hopeless situation. I'm going to pack."

Willie turned to say, "Please pretend you don't know me. You never heard of me. I never flew you here. Lizzie's made her bed, so there's nothing more to say, and especially nothing more any of us can do."

Debbie closed her eyes, visualizing an event she'd rather not see. "I know what we have to do," she muttered. "We have to shoot her—*first.*"

* * *

With the drapes tightly drawn in the suite, Clutch cleaned the rifle like a conservator caring for the crown jewels. He handed the weapon to Gil who put it to his shoulder. Gil inspected the rifle and said, "There must be another way."

"What if we could get the real Klav to expose his brother?" Clutch offered.

"That wouldn't put Liz in any less danger," Virginia said, and Frank nodded agreement.

Willie had packed and returned to the group. His curiosity was too great to be left out, and he hoped that the others wouldn't do anything rash that could rub off on him. "Maybe Klav is too afraid of his brother to come forward."

No one accepted Willie's idea. Fathers fight for their daughters.

"I called my family to tell them the kids were safe, and how to get in touch with us," Debbie said. "When we talked, they said they haven't found a trace of Klav. Elizabeth might have made up the name on the postal box. Stevens is a common name. Dad thinks Klav may have never existed—at least not in New Zealand."

Frank wrinkled his nose. "What if my inspector pal is tapping your folks' telephone?"

"We Kiwis don't do that sort of thing," Debbie shot back, even though she didn't know for sure.

Frank pressed on. "Your mum and dad know the kids are safe, so let's cut the contact. I'll bet the New Zealand police would love to extradite me if they knew where I was."

"You're being paranoid, Frank," Gil said. "Croatia is too young a country to have set up extradition treaties."

"You're probably right." Frank sighed. "But I'll have to live out the rest of my life here 'cause I won't be able to go anywhere else."

Willie smirked. "With your lifestyle, Mr. Ferret, it will be a short stay."

"What if Klav followed Ratac to Croatia?" George offered to refocus the group. "What if they're working in cahoots?"

"That would explain a lot," Eve admitted.

The group pondered George's premise. "Then the man who met us in the hotel lobby, really could've been Klav," Willie said.

* * *

THREE CORNERS, NEW ZEALAND

Brian McWard watched the village post office from opening time to closing. The workers in the merchandise-filled, patron-empty post office became suspicious of Brian after the first half hour, so he pretended interest in one of the pretty young clerks. The friendly clerk had just started a summer internship for college, and Brian found himself enjoying his role of spy.

Finally, a humorless postal supervisor said, "Enough!"

Brian took refuge on a hard, sometimes shady, wooden bench overlooking the post office entrance. Brian's new friend, Shari, joined him during her breaks, and that night they took in an old movie.

By the fourth day, Brian was intrigued with Shari, but discouraged with his lookout duty. He would have preferred to follow Debbie to Yugoslavia and personally teach those murderous kidnappers a lesson. Splitting his concentration between Shari and the post office gave him little time to notice the dark-haired person watching him.

Near the end of the workday, Shari left her post early. Brian and Shari ate ice cream cones and shared war stories on their most colorful professors. Brian was in the middle of such a story, complete with musical sound effects, when a middle-aged man rounded the corner and entered the closed post office. "Hold my cone," Brian ordered. "If I'm not back, I want you to know I think you're awesome, and I want to keep seeing you." Brian shot across the street, causing a speeding car to brake to a screeching stop. Brian entered the post office in time to see the man close the gray door of his postal box. *First box, third row! And he looks a little bit like Lafate. No, a lot like Lafate. It's him!*

Brian headed for his motorbike and driving one-handed, called the "Klav alert" to Ian. Ian had aerial maps of the area, a privilege accorded to a citizen on the agricultural planning commission. "Only one station in that direction," Ian noted. "No need to follow close."

Ian joined Brian on a narrow rough dirt road on a plain of arid, volcanic ash and short scrub brush. Brian loaded his motorbike in the back of his father's truck, and they continued their long, slow drive across the plain and into an isolated valley. The target destination to Klav Bymarovitch's station was even more remote than their farm. The McWard farm had opened up a valley. Ian had cleared a road and other farmers followed. This ranch, however, surrounded by inhospitable land, had stood alone for nearly thirty years. A small flock of ordinary looking sheep announced that they were nearing what could be Klav Bymarovitch's home.

"Those ewes are old. Not well-cared for," Brian noted.

Ian nodded, "He must hav' been doin' it all himself. This Klav mon is either lazy or not well. Now his station's dying too."

Ian parked his truck a walking distance from the house. The sun had dropped behind the mountains, but under the glow of the turquoise sky, they could still be seen. He didn't want to startle the exiled brother of Ratac. Ian's strategy didn't work. A shotgun blast sent both men diving into the gritty ground.

"You're trespassing!" the man with the shotgun yelled.

"Don't shoot, mon! We're friends of your daughter."

"Where's my daughter's tattoo?"

"On her right shoulder," Brian called. "It's a blue dove." He had admired the tattoo on one of Elizabeth's visits to their farm. When he had suggested getting a tattoo also, his mother went volcanic. Brian also knew the location of Liz's tulip tattoos, but that wasn't something you mentioned to a father with a shotgun.

Klav lowered his gun. "Stay together so I can shoot you both with one shot. Now take ten steps forward, and state your piece."

"I'm Ian McWard. My daughter, Debbie, works with yer daughter. Liz is in danger—from yer brother."

Klav nodded gravely. "Come in. Tell me what you know."

They followed him into the darkness of his small wooden house. An oil light glowed in a plain room with a carefully laid stone fireplace and a wall of books. Klav could have explained that the electric generator was broken, but he wasn't the type to give explanations.

Klav looked almost like a double for the Ratac Bymarovitch who had visited Ian's home as Lafate. Klav had longer hair. He was a few pounds heavier, and his face was tanned, but his eyes were weary. He was a defeated man, and his body posture showed it. Klav dropped into a chair near the window. "Forgive me if I sit, but my blood pressure is out of control, and I don't dare go to the hospital again. They ask too many questions."

Ian took the last statement as an order to answer, not ask, questions. Ian told Klav what they knew and suspected about Elizabeth and Ratac. Klav said nothing, but Ian noticed the man's neck muscles tightening and his breaths coming deeper.

A dog barked. Klav asked, "You brought company?"

Ian frowned. "No!"

Klav turned off the oil lamp. "Get on the floor," he ordered.

Bullets exploded through the window. The automatic weapon sprayed a magazine of bullets throughout the room. The gunfire paused. Then another volley raked the room.

Brian hugged the floor while wood splintered around him. Ian found shelter in the stone fireplace.

The door, shredded by bullets flew open from a kick. A silhouette appeared at the door. Klav's shotgun erupted. The figure lurched backward. A second figure aimed his pistol in the direction of Klav's muzzle flash. Klav's shotgun fired first, and the man toppled.

Klav reloaded before stepping outside.

"Damn, I killed a woman."

"That's Mme. Lafate," Brian coughed from the gunpowder and the gory sight of Lafate's fatal wound. "She tried to kill us before. I think the man is a tramper called Stanley, but his hair color is different. I recognize the jacket as the same as someone's I saw hanging around the village."

Klav covered his face. He had lived for years with the fear of this moment. The danger finally had come, and he had survived—for now.

Ian didn't like the way Klav was breathing. "Lie down, mon." Ian ushered Klav to the only chair not shattered by bullets.

"We hav' to plan, mon. We'd best bury the bodies and avoid the police. Yer brother is pretending ta be ye. Yer daughter is helping him get elected ta head yer old country. We think he intends to kill your daughter. Ye need ta go to Croatia and threaten ta expose him. It's the only way ye can save Elizabeth. Klav? *The only way.* Do ye hear what I'm saying?"

Klav Bymarovitch clutched his chest and slumped off his chair.

CHAPTER 20

How to Shoot a Friend

Willie reluctantly agreed to nursemaid Ing, while the trampers left to find a place to practice shooting. The parents didn't want their children separated from them for even a minute, so they were dragged along. A few miles out of Zagreb, the trampers collectively agreed, "This is a beautiful country." Indeed, the hillsides with dense pines, pointed cypress, and the snowcapped Dinaric Alps in the distance were postcard perfect.

"How about here?" Clutch recommended, pointing to a treeless field.

Frank laughed loudly, and Gil snickered.

"Why ya laughing?" Clutch asked.

"See those fence posts with the little red skulls on them?" Gil replied.

"Yeah."

Frank explained, "Those pretty little red skulls are to mark land minefields that haven't been cleared."

The group laughed briefly, but the seriousness of war quickly intruded into their thoughts.

At a crossroad, a UN armored patrol car stopped the tramper's van. The only advice Frank had time to give was, "Children, pretend you have cheeks full of chocolate cement.

"Adults, make sure our rifles don't stick out from under the seats."

Normally, a glance in a civilian van by the checkpoint guards would suffice. The soldiers would see six attractive, neatly-dressed Americans with two children on laps, flashing their passports. The soldiers would wonder about the sanity of parents taking children into a recent war zone and even question how they were permitted to enter the country in the first place, but they would be waved on. Instead, the soldiers circled the car, pointing their guns. One went to the armored vehicle and returned with an officer.

"Good afternoon, Frank," the British officer in charge said cordially. "Sorry to delay you, but a car fitting this description matches one of the vehicles that sped away following a shoot-out in the red-light district last night and at a church before that." The captain smiled at the beautiful women that made up Frank's party and the two smiling kids with puffy cheeks. No one in their right mind would take kids along if they planned trouble. The captain sniffed the women's perfume and thought briefly of his wife who claimed he could smell gunpowder a half mile away.

Virginia nuzzled Clutch. "Captain, do you think I'd let my man go anywhere near a red-light district?"

"No ma'am, but just the same, I have to ask. We're trying to get things to quiet down in this hellhole. And it's working. We sure hate to see people getting killed again. I'm afraid we'd have to stomp hard on anyone who breaks the truce, for any reason."

"Was anyone killed?" Clutch asked.

The group held their breath. Clutch wasn't known for subtlety. They knew he was upset at the possibility of having killed someone and feared his reaction to the answer.

"Not that we know of," the officer said. "Bloodstains everywhere though." He looked accusingly at Frank. The captain liked Frank. His articles and broadcasts often slammed the UN and British high commands, the Pentagon, and the foreign policy wonks. Ferret's entrapping interviews had tarnished the careers of more than one of the highest top brass.

Enlisted men and junior officers, however, looked forward to Frank's journalistic support. Ferret was a friend of the grunts who risked their lives. *But this gunpowder-smelling car matched the description of the drive-by shooter, and even had a bullet hole in the back of it. Still . . . bullet holes weren't all that unusual, and in a world with few friends . . . .* The captain said, "Have a nice holiday, folks. And I'd suggest you stay in your hotel after dark. Don't wait for curfew. You're being watched."

"By whom?" Frank asked indignantly.

"By their side and our side. Not that you'd do anything wrong, but for your own protection."

Frank started to protest.

The captain cut him off. "Make that suggestion an *order*. If you have time to debate it, then I have time to search your van."

They drove away, with Frank chortling because the other car that the UN patrols were seeking was parked across the street from their headquarters. Leaving a fair amount of distance between themselves and the checkpoint, they selected an isolated farm. Frank asked the owner if they could do some target practice in a frozen field for a modest fee. The farmer accepted the generous offer of money and was not anxious to argue with a carload of armed foreigners, no matter how friendly they seemed.

Out on the field, Clutch paced off three alternative distances. They weren't sure where their sniper could be hidden, but it wouldn't be close to Bymarovitch's stage. Empty wine bottles provided the targets.

"Can't you get a bigger target?" George said.

Gil answered. "If Clutch is an inch off either way, it shouldn't matter. But the target is small. Clutch has to hit Elizabeth in the right shoulder before she turns on the steps to the platform."

"Why the right shoulder?" Clutch asked. "Why not dead center?"

"The bullet will knock Elizabeth down in either case. On the shoulder, there should be some swiveling action. Dead center would hit her hard. There'd be no give."

Eve added, "Our hearts are in the middle of our chests, but there's more of it on the left side than the right. A shattered rib could do more damage there than on the shoulder. The stomach area would be second choice, but we're getting near the edge of the vest.

"And an arm in front of the stomach could be lost or cause Elizabeth to bleed to death," Eve said. "Ing's bullet left her with a minor arm wound, but it could have been life-threatening if she hadn't gotten prompt medical care."

Clutch looked worried, a stark contrast to his boyish grin. Virginia rubbed his back. She said, "You can do it."

"I've never shot rubber bullets before," Clutch said. "I doubt if they spin the same or have the same trajectory. Particularly at this range."

Frank said, "Shoot high. I guess. Oh hell, what do I know? I don't do guns."

"Put your fingers in your ears, kids." Clutch peered through the sniper scope, saw the red dot reflecting off the bottles, fired at the closest bottles, and hit each one. "You're right, Frank, ya need to reckon high."

Three middle-range wine bottles shattered with three shots. At long range, Clutch's arm began to tremble. The movement was not noticeable enough to see, but the spasm was scary enough for Clutch to say, "I don't think I can do this. I keep thinkin' of the varmint I shot and probably killed. He was a no good skunk tryin' to shoot up Debbie and Frank and Ing. I didn't have time to think about it. It's like pinch-hittin' against right-handers. Before you know it, you're up and swinging. No time to think about it. No time to worry." Clutch took a deep breath as Virginia patted him again. "I'll try. Everyone's counting on me. But I better have backup, just in case I start shakin'."

Gil said, "I'd better do it, then. I was a sharpshooter—once upon a time. The only problem is that I haven't shot anything between my days in the FBI Academy and last night. Last night it took me two shots to hit a gas tank. I'll need practice. How many rubber bullets can we spare?"

"Not enough," Frank said.

George said, "Same problem here. I'm an expert with a police revolver, but hardly ever fire a rifle. If I can get in close enough, I can do it with a pistol."

Frank grunted disapproval. "I don't have any rubber bullets for pistols, and if you did shoot Elizabeth at pistol range, I wouldn't have the foggiest idea of how to get you away from the angry mob."

Debbie took Clutch's rifle. A flock of crows flew overhead, scolding the team for shattering their silent feast with gunfire. Debbie trailed the crows for a second, and with two quick shots brought two crows tumbling out of the sky. "I can see that none of you've had your crops and food on your table threatened by bloomin' creatures that move. Wine bottles don't move. Elizabeth moves. To hell with trying to see these little red laser lights. Shooting is an instinct where I come from." Debbie shot a more distant crow to prove the point. "Elizabeth's my friend, and she can't afford a near miss. It's my crazy idea. I'll shoot her."

After a few more practice shots, the team headed away to pick up their newly painted ambulance.

Only Gil noticed Debbie grab her side with a grimace of pain when the van hit a bump.

*　　*　　*

Frank threw dirt on the shiny surface of the ambulance. "It'll have to do. At night, the newness won't show."

273

Eve said, "I watched an ambulance pull up a few days ago. The attendants don't wear surgical masks. It may not be customary here. It may arouse suspicion. That could be a problem."

Frank said, "Just get me a list of everything you need to make it look authentic. Stretchers. Oxygen tanks. White shoes. Name it, before I totally run out of Captain Cook's money."

Gil said, "I'd feel better with *us* pulling up the ambulance. But without masks, we'd be recognized. Is there any chance you could recruit some locals?"

Frank scowled. He didn't want to admit that Gil was right. "With enough money, I can pay someone to pay someone to have the emperor's crown jewels here in twelve hours, but there's not enough money to get a local to do something against the Butcher. I could recruit a million willin' Serbs, but that could restart the war. It has to be his countrymen, or at least a neutral country, and people whom I can trust."

Virginia scowled back. "Surely, the Butcher's not universally loved."

* * *

The old man who was Elizabeth's maternal grandfather eyed Frank suspiciously. "How did you find me?"

"It wasn't easy."

"Were you followed?"

"Lost 'em. They're following my friends."

"I'm a brokenhearted man, Mr. Ferret. You promised me that you would bring me my beautiful granddaughter. But you brought me a traitor."

"Do you think the man running for election is Klav or Ratac?" Frank asked.

"From his looks, he could be either one. It's been such a long time. You're suggesting that the man running for president isn't Klav?"

"I'm not suggestin'; I'm tellin' ya."

"It makes sense. Klav was more soft-spoken."

"Elizabeth, your granddaughter, is going along with Ratac until she gets a chance to escape. She thinks he'll kill her. We know he will—tomorrow night."

"Escaping Ratac will be difficult."

"That's why I need your help."

Elizabeth's grandfather listened to Frank's plan and shuddered. "I've heard of people killed by rubber bullets."

"Do ya have a better idea?" Frank pressed.

"No. I think you're right about Ratac planning to shoot her. It's the only way he and his former communists and militarists could win. We Croatians are not crazy, war-happy fools that you Westerners imagine. We have good sense. The Bymarovitch name is well-known, but certainly not respected. On the other hand, we would rally around any father whose daughter was killed by the Serbs or an opposition candidate."

The grandfather stopped and shook his head. "But you wish to shoot her first? I just don't know."

"Our sniper is the best shot I've ever seen," Frank lied. Gil had told him about Debbie's pain spasm, and Frank's concern was mounting.

"Then the ambulance picks her up?"

"Yes."

"And takes her where?"

"We haven't decided, yet."

"All right, I will help you. I have friends who are not afraid of the Butcher. Or rather, I should say, they *are* afraid of the Butcher, but aren't afraid to lose their lives to avenge things he has done to their family members."

"Super!" Frank exclaimed, elated that he finally had a local ally.

"You'll need a safe house to hold Elizabeth," the grandfather stated. "This, I can provide her."

"Now we're cookin'!"

"You also want me to furnish young men to act as ambulance attendants."

"Yes," Frank said. "Attendants don't wear masks, so we need people who won't be recognized."

"Then I can't help you. My local people are sure to be photographed and identified. Another problem is that the people I can gather to help are older—much older. Ambulance attendants are young and athletic. They move quickly, and in this case, they must move with exceptional speed."

Other details were discussed, but Frank left the meeting with only half a victory. Who could he get to pull off the rescue?

*   *   *

Frank rejoined his friends at the hotel trying not to show his dejection.

"Do you have change for one hundred kuna?" George asked. "I need something smaller for tips."

"Right," Frank replied, with his mind on more life threatening problems. Frank noticed a small piece of folded paper stuck in the corner of his wallet. He pondered the phone number on the paper for a minute before its context was remembered.

Frank stepped into the hall for privacy and moved toward a window for better transmission of his phone call.

"Hello, sweet cakes, I promised you I'd call you."

"You did? Why bother?" snapped the pretty Slovenian graduate student on the other end of the call. "And for you're information, I was drunk as a lamppost that night when I offered to go to your hotel. I don't sleep with strangers."

Frank squirmed because he couldn't think of the young lady's name. All he could think of was sweet young thing two.

The woman continued. "Why didn't you say you were a famous journalist? Gregory is working on the EU application. He says your help was invaluable. He'll want to thank you. In fact, we'll all want to thank you."

"That's why I called. I'd like you to gather all your drinkin' pals together for a conference call."

"Why?"

"Well, sweetie, I'm recruiting volunteers for a secret project."

"For what?"

"Just tell 'em, I need help in stopping World War III."

* * *

PLESO AIRPORT, ZAGREB

About to board his plane to the States, Willie felt entitled to a good-bye kiss from Debbie, but she declined. Willie sighed. "I said I was sorry."

Willie turned to Virginia, "Let's go, girl."

Virginia shook her head. "If you'd tried to carry my bags, you'd see I didn't bring any. Debbie's too polite to say it in front of all these people, but you're a slimy shithead, Willie. I'm not going back with you. You're not smart enough to know the difference between right and wrong. I can't work for an idiot. I hate myself for ever having loved such an egocentric numbskull."

Willie looked puzzled. "You're upset. These people are planning something that could be gravely dangerous. Don't let them talk you into doing something foolish. Come away from here now—before they get you imprisoned or even killed."

"I'm staying."

"Come back to your old job when you calm down. I'll give you a raise."

"Cement brain! How many ways do I have to say *no*?"

Willie's puzzled brow furrowed with concern. "What will you do?"

"Well, since my contract prevents me for working for your enemies—which is about everyone in the computer industry—I may take a try at raising my son. Gil did it from his home. I'll give it a try."

"You'll starve."

"I'll figure something out. Maybe I'll sell my memoirs to a tabloid."

Willie snorted. He knew that Virginia was too proud to do anything that crass. Willie glanced at his twenty-dollar watch. He couldn't wait any longer to board the plane. He looked back incredulously. *What the hell happened? What'll I do without Virginia?* Willie panicked. "I'll marry you, Virginia. As soon as we land."

"Go marry yourself, Willie—the only person you'll ever love!" she called back in her most dignified voice. "I'm marrying Clutch."

Clutch, who was pretending to read a newspaper and not intruding on the discussion, said, "Huh?"

Virginia nodded, her confidence growing. She caressed Clutch's cheek with the tips of her fingers. "Clutch dear, tell Willie where you want to take me on our honeymoon."

"Huh?" Clutch remembered the endless barrage of insults that Willie had heaped on his intellect. Now Willie had a fearful "Say it isn't so" look on his face. *To lose a prize like Virginia to a "dumb dolt" like me—whatever a dolt is—has to crack Willie's marbles.* Clutch put his muscular arm around Virginia. "Oh, we're going to Disney World!"

* * *

Pediatric psychiatrist, Dr. Phyllis Rocklin, arrived in the same airport a few minutes after Willie left, but going through customs and arranging an instant visa took time. When she finally exited to the open area where her brother, niece, and a variety of other people circled, she was tired, angry, and a bit fearful.

She crouched so that she could embrace her brother and Amy at the same time. "Are you okay?"

"We're both fine, Phyl," Gil said. "No one's hurt."

"Oh! You make me so mad! I was just about to get it on with this Freudian stud at my Rome conference when I got your message. 'Come immediately. Urgent.' And why this godforsaken country? I thought you were going to New Zealand. And is that Clutch Cooper over there? Introduce me for heaven's sake."

"Later. You're taking the next plane home with two kids. Extend your vacation. I need you to take Amy and Martin to the States." He gestured to Martin, who looked suspiciously at the attractive woman who was supposed to take him home.

"You look great, Amy!" Phyllis gushed.

"So do you, Aunt Phyllis." Aunt Phyllis did look great, and Clutch made a mental note to find out if she lived in an American League franchised town.

Phyllis gave Gil a limp gesture of her hands and an expectant expression as a request for an explanation.

Gil sent Amy with Clutch to get her aunt some bottled water, and shrugged. "Amy seems okay. Martin seems okay. Both have had some scary experiences. They should be frightened out of their sneakers, but they're not. I'm out of my element on this. What do I know about posttraumatic stress syndrome and all that stuff? I get crazy mad right from the start, so I don't know how it works with other people. Amy will explain what happened, in detail, on your trip home. Believe every word she says. Watch for any signs of trouble, and do whatever you have to do. A man named Sid will meet you in New York and take Amy to Denver, and—"

"*I'll* take Amy to Denver!" Phyllis insisted.

"I was hoping you would. Expect to bring them back here to testify—"

"Stop, right now!" Phyllis ordered. "If the children were harmed or threatened, the last thing you want to do is to have them testify. This awful place has probably never heard of victim's rights. *Absolutely no testifying!*" Phyllis cocked her head. "I think Daddy could use a few pills to settle himself down."

"Not me!" Gil protested. "I have Debbie to settle me down, and I don't believe in screwing with brain chemistry." He reached a hand toward Debbie. "Although . . . I could have used a handful of that trash a couple of days ago."

Debbie moved in. "Hi! I'm Debbie McWard. Plan on being my maid of honor as soon as we follow you back."

Phyllis made a happy squeal and embraced Debbie. "Thank God, my brother's finally come out of his monastery! Oh, you're so pretty! I'll be delighted to be your maid of honor. When did you meet?" The question was *when* not *where*, and both Gil and Debbie noticed.

"A few weeks ago," Gil answered, waiting for a nonverbal cue of disapproval.

Phyllis couldn't ignore the previous discussions with her brother on not rushing into marriage. "Not much time to experience difficult times together, but I'm sure there's plenty of years for difficult times. I couldn't be happier for you both."

"We're not planning on any more difficult times," Debbie said. "We've had our quota for a couple of decades."

* * *

Amy's story, along with illustrations from her journal, didn't finish until the plane was well over the Atlantic. Then Martin, usually quiet around adults, filled in the gaps in gruesome detail.

When Aunt Phyllis heard about the plan to shoot Elizabeth, she took a pill.

CHAPTER 21

The Accusation

THE REGENT ESPLANADE HOTEL, ZAGREB

The trampers started to feel a twinge of optimism when Frank reported back on his meeting with Elizabeth's grandfather. The optimism was short-lived. An American lieutenant knocked on the doors of each of their hotel suites. When they didn't answer, the room clerk opened the door for him.

The lieutenant peered at the startled trampers. "Mr. Frank Ferret?"

"How can I help you?" Frank replied cordially. Frank found that acting cooperatively was generally more productive—especially when you didn't have a choice.

"General Bream wants to speak to you, sir. All of you." The "all of you" didn't include Clutch and Virginia, who were getting body massages as a way to relax, and Ingrid, who was recovering in a separate room, reading Chaucer.

"Let's go team!" Frank said brightly. He wanted everyone out of the suite before Clutch and Virginia returned.

"What does this mean, Frank?" Debbie whispered. "Clutch and Ginnie can't pull this off by themselves."

"It means we're gonna be watched so closely that it's doubtful that any of us can pull off our plan. And that's only if we're not arrested." Frank's worry was that Clutch and Virginia would try to do exactly that. They would return to their room and conclude the shooting was up to them. Virginia was doing a great job of keeping Clutch from flipping out, but what if he started shaking as he pulled the trigger? The thought made Frank shudder. He'd have to punt.

"What's your default plan, Frank?" Gil asked.

"It doesn't happen often, but when all else fails, try the truth."

A convoy of three jeeps drove the trampers across the street where the military headquarters was billeted. Frank had picked their hotel for its proximity to the UN forces and the safety the nearby soldiers provided. A bomber or assassin who went after the trampers would have a hard time getting away. Now Frank and the trampers had no chance of getting away.

The lieutenant escorted Frank, Gil, Debbie, George, and Eve into General Bream's office, a converted hotel room stacked with cardboard file cabinets, but with only one ominous file folder on the general's desk. The trampers took positions around a long foldout card table. "Good to see you again, General," Frank said with his friendliest of smiles, a snappy salute, and an extended handshake. "It was really nice of you to see us, General. We really need your help, sir."

"Sit down, sit down," Bream said cordially. Bream leaned back and laughed—not a friendly laugh. The graying general had come to his position from a lieutenant in military police, decorated for heroic work in dangerous places. Bream had added several degrees—including a degree in international law—on his way up to being the leading expert on running an occupation force. Despite all his knowledge, he would privately admit that he was in over his head when it came to understanding the Balkans.

He rapped his pen as if playing taps. With penetrating eye contact, he said, "Ferret you have more chutzpah than a life insurance salesman at a funeral. One minute you're blasting my military policy as if you actually knew what you were talking about, trying to torpedo my career, and the next, you want to bring a whole party in here." The general paused to smile at Debbie and Eve. "They're welcome, anytime. But you, Ferret, are a piece of work. I bring you in here for a castration, and you start by asking *me* to pucker up. When we were looking for Bymarovitch, did you share your information? I think not."

"Rose is dead," Frank blurted. "Murdered by Ratac Bymarovitch."

The general's demeanor changed like a piece of charcoal turning into an ember. He picked up his phone. "Get me the latest on Major Rose O'Hara. ASAP."

A slender lieutenant scurried in and saluted. "This just came in. Major O'Hara was murdered in New Zealand." She looked at Frank. "The chief suspect is a Mr. Frank Whistle, a.k.a. Frank Ferret. He was released without bond because of what the Kiwis called some heavy-handed pressure from the White House. Ferret is missing and believed to have skipped the islands illegally. He's also wanted for questioning in the murder of two airport security guards."

"That will be all, Lieutenant."

The general pivoted his swivel chair to the wall. Reading the statistics of dead servicemen always hit him in the gut, but Rose reminded him of his daughter. His whole body hurt.

"Ferret, I'll say this just once. If you had anything to do with Rose's death, I'll volunteer to be a one-man firing squad."

Frank nodded gravely. "Rose and I were working together—sharing information, trying to figure out who the Butcher was. We got too close." Frank took a deep breath. "I loved Rose," he heard himself saying.

Bream rubbed his eyes. The tremor in Frank's voice was convincing. "Where's Bymarovitch now?"

"He's posing as his brother, Klav. And if we're not careful, he could become the next prime minister of this powder keg."

"You're not telling me anything I didn't suspect," Bream informed. "This Klav fellow starts a political campaign, but he's nowhere to be found. Then he suddenly shows up—returning from New Zealand. Odd, yes? But can you prove he's an imposter? I doubt it."

"Yes, I can prove it," Frank pushed. "His daughter, Elizabeth Stevens, is stringing him along."

"You mean Elizabeth Bymarovitch?" the general interrupted.

"Yes, but Elizabeth's afraid for her life, and she was protecting the kids of my friends here."

"Protecting kids?"

"Yes, the Butcher kidnapped them to keep us from blowing the whistle on him. Liz helped the kids escape, so now her life is in danger. Give her protection, and she'll turn on Ratac in a second."

"Can you guarantee that?"

"I think so," Frank answered.

"I'm sure of it," Debbie said. She hesitated. "She may also be protecting her other father: Klav, the man that raised her. If you could ask my government to find and protect him, I would guarantee her cooperation."

Gil added, "My daughter spoke to Elizabeth Stevens Bymarovitch during the time she was kidnapped. Elizabeth described the man claiming to be Klav Bymarovitch as a bad man who Liz was afraid of."

The general scowled. "Who's to say that *Klav* isn't the bad man who Elizabeth was afraid of? Did Elizabeth live with her father?"

Debbie pondered the question before answering, "Yes, and she never spoke poorly of him. She never spoke of him at all, even when I asked her."

"So Klav could be the bad man of whom she was speaking?"

"I suppose, but I doubt it."

Bream leaned forward. "Did Liz actually say Ratac was posing as Klav?"

"No," Debbie said.

"Isn't the kidnapping enough?" Gil snapped.

"Can you bring in these children for a deposition?"

Gil answered. "My sister just took them back to the United States."

"You didn't answer my question."

Gil sighed in frustration. "So far my daughter and George's son haven't shown any posttraumatic stress reactions to being kidnapped. My sister is a pediatric psychiatrist. She tells me in no uncertain, blistering terms that Amy and Martin are to have no more association with this affair, or they could be permanently scarred."

"I'm not hearing the right answer, Dr. Rocklin," the general fumed.

"My God, man," George snapped. "My son's only nine. Gil's daughter is seven."

The general flipped the pen he was holding, and let it fall with a clatter. "Jesus! *Seven!* You expect to bring down the world's most wanted murderer with the testimony of a seven-year-old?"

"You didn't hear *me*, general," Gil stated. "I have no intention of allowing my daughter to testify. Would you let one of your children go through that ordeal?"

Bream scowled. "In other words, you don't have lint—except for Bymarovitch's terrified daughter." The general sagged. "But then, neither do we. Yet I feel in my bones that the Butcher pulled a switch on us. As soon as Klav started his radio campaign ads, I asked the New Zealand government to give us background on him."

"And?" George asked.

Bream leaned forward. "There *is* no Klav Bymarovitch in New Zealand. Never was a Klav in New Zealand. At least, he has no address or phone, never served in the military. Never was arrested. He never voted. Never paid taxes."

"That's *something*," George commented. "He claims to be from New Zealand, but there's no sign that he ever lived there. That sounds like a phony to me."

"I wouldn't charge the hill with that as my only weapon," the general grumbled. "How did you get your children out of the country if they were never granted a visa to get in? In fact, I don't see how any of you got into Croatia, except Ferret."

Ferret squirmed with an innocent grin. "Phony IDs are a growth industry here, and everywhere. You just have to know who takes the most flattering snapshots." Then as a quick diversion, Frank reminded, "Elizabeth's last name was *Stevens*. Will that help? Try *Stevens*. Not *Bymarovitch*."

"Might as well be *Smith*," the general grumbled. "Our cooperation from the Kiwis was reluctant to begin with, and since you skipped out on them, I suspect we Yanks may have run out of favors."

"You're not giving up?" George growled.

"I'm afraid I don't have much choice," Bream said. "If I was smart, I'd ship you back to New Zealand to face trial. Then the Kiwis might be more willing to cooperate on the Klav Bymarovitch matter. But don't worry. I'm not going to let the Kiwis extradite you back. I don't have the time for it, and who knows what dirt you have on the White House. No, I don't have any choice in the matter. The Bymarovitch Affair has been taken out of my hands. The State Department has taken over everything to do with Bymarovitch."

"Whaddya mean?" Frank asked, standing up. "We've been wasting our time here?"

"I hope not," the general replied. "My hands are tied, but I'll have my people stay out of your way—for Rose's sake. In other words, you and your detail have to carry the flag on this one. Good luck. But if I catch any of you with as much as a BB gun, Ferret will be able to write about the unreasonable harshness of military justice from his stockade."

Frank slumped. The general had sent them mixed messages, but essentially left them toothless. "So now we have to go through the same thing with those State Department wonks?"

The general nodded. "It shouldn't take too long. Allison's down the hall. She'll throw you out after a minute."

*　　*　　*

Assistant Secretary of State Allison Quill gave Frank and his "detail" more than a minute, but without comment. Quill was a handsome petite woman whose hair follicles wouldn't dare deviate from their pinned-down place. Her temporary office had the clean order of a surgical suite. Frank remembered her pretty smile, but today she didn't even offer a diplomatic façade. She peered stone-faced over her Ben Franklin glasses. Finally, she requested to speak to Frank alone. While the others stepped out reluctantly, Frank knew that an off-the-record briefing was coming. Two witnesses can corroborate one another. Quill would only share that which could be effectively denied.

"First of all, Frank. You don't have any real proof. Nothing that can stand up. Do I believe your story? You have to concede it's fairly far fetched, Frank," she said in a deliberate mockery of Frank's alliterative, on-air style. "Even if I believed parts of your grand conspiracy—can I do anything about it? Not really."

"I'm listening, Allison," Frank encouraged with his notepad closed.

"Here's the scenario, Frank. Klav, or Ratac, if your theory is true, was a late entry in the election, so his Justice Party is a distant third in the polls with no chance of winning. The man we'd settle on to win should get 40 percent of the seats and be declared prime minister. Bymarovitch and the number two candidate split the rest of the hard line vote, assuming that our man wins. The number two candidate—I have trouble pronouncing all the consonants in her name, Dbrogrb—is every bit as bad as the butcher Bymarovitch."

"Does she kill people?"

"No, but Dbrogrb's rhetoric will set the peace process back. If she's elected, we can expect the Serbs to use it as an excuse to cause trouble. War could start up, again. Dbrogrb wants nothing to do with reconciliation with their neighbors or reestablishing relations with the West."

"In other words, she can't be bribed," Frank surmised.

"At least not by us. I didn't say that. She's cozy with the Russians. Our offer of foreign aide was summarily rejected."

"So you think Dbrogrb will put Croatia in someone else's camp?" Frank knew the Russians were more ethnically sympathetic to the Serbs than the Croats, and that such an allegiance was a stretch, but he wasn't going to start a new argument with Quill. Then again, maybe Quill knew something. Massive Russian aid to Croatia would be worth every ruble if could drive a wedge between NATO's forces in the west and Greek and Turkish forces in the east.

Quill smiled for the first time. "No, because Dbrogrb won't have a chance of winning. Why? Because Bymarovitch is splitting the hard-line, lets-get-even vote."

"Okay, Allison. But can we go after Ratac, after the election?"

Quill shuffled the few papers on her desk, stacked them, and sat them down again. "Have you listened to Klav or Ratac—listened to his radio commercials? The peace rhetoric is downright inspiring."

"Ah, Ratac doesn't have to spout war. His name is associated with hate, revenge, ethnic cleansing. The man's a great manipulator. By spouting peace, he appeals to both camps."

Quill shrugged. "Even if he was Ratac, he sounds like someone with whom we could do business. He would've been our preferred candidate. We'd have slipped him campaign money if he had any chance of winning."

"Thank God for that," Frank growled.

"Frank dear, listen. I know you'd like to collect the reward on Ratac, but it was a mistake for us to have put it out. I'm trying to get our allies to rescind it. When Klav loses the election, I'm suspecting he'll fade away—maybe to another country for his own safety. On the other hand, if Klav *is* Ratac—something I seriously doubt—and he goes before the International Criminal Tribunal for the former Yugoslavia, the Croats will expect us to arrest certain Serb leaders."

"A rat for Ratac," Frank muttered. "That's only fair. If you arrest a murdering Croat, you arrest a murdering Serb."

"That's unlikely to happen without considerable bloodshed." Quill removed her glasses and rubbed the bridge of her nose. "The 1995 Dayton Peace Accords are working, except in Kosovo, where things are ugly and could get uglier. We're down to eight thousand troops in Bosnia. The tensions up here are starting to calm down. Let's leave it that way, Frank."

Frank tried hard to suppress his anger. "Dropping the reward would look like you're going soft on war criminals. We wouldn't want the American electorate to get the idea that the administration is soft on war criminals, would we?"

"Your warning will be taken on advisement, Mr. Ferret. But I wouldn't spend your reward money, just yet."

* * *

"Well, Frank, is the State Department going to help us?" Gil asked, as the military police escorted them back to the hotel.

"No. They *like* Bymarovitch. They'd fund his campaign if he had a chance of winning."

"What do you suggest we do?" Eve asked.

Frank forced a sheepish grin. "Debbie, warm up your trigger finger."

*   *   *

Clutch and Virginia were glad to see the other trampers return. Ingrid was sitting up and alert. "Don't you *dare* get yourself arrested, Frank," Ingrid warned. "Conjugal visits are not enough."

Debbie muttered, "On the other hand, jail might keep Frank faithful."

Clutch was euphoric that Debbie was back. "I was afraid I'd make the shot and not know how to escape."

"We didn't expect *you* to escape," Frank said with a straight face.

While Clutch looked dismayed, the others exchanged glances in hope that one of them had the answer on the problem they had avoided. Gil voiced it first. "How do we pull off Debbie's escape after she makes her shot?"

Frank stroked Debbie's trigger finger. "Debbie has the advantage of being a woman. The authorities are less likely to stop her," Frank speculated. "All she has to do is make it to the street."

"Debbie's not exactly the kind of person who blends in," Gil argued. He was feeling increasingly uncomfortable with Debbie's role as a sniper, but talking Debbie out of saving her friend was out of the question.

Frank took six water bottles and arranged them on the dresser. "The speaker's platform is here. Liz will enter from the left. The best line of sight is from the conveniently flat roof of an apartment building, four stories high. To get to the top, Debbie can take the stairs or climb up the outside from a fairly wide alley.

"I think I'd be more conspicuous climbing up the outside," Debbie said. "I'll take the stairs."

Ingrid said, "I have a black wig back at my hotel. A disguise might help."

"Thanks," Debbie said.

Frank smiled at Ingrid's wig suggestion. Even in her drugged state, she was contributing.

"Debbie could wear the garb of a Moslem woman, all covered up," Clutch offered. She could carry the rifle under her robe."

"We haven't seen many Moslems in Zagreb," Frank replied patiently. "A Moslem might even attract more attention. A raincoat with a hood should be good enough."

Gil picked up the water bottle standing for the apartment building. "Debbie and I will be strangers in an apartment where everyone knows everyone. Going up the stairs shouldn't be a problem. We can wait for a clear stairwell. When we leave, it's another matter. We can't wait for the halls to clear. We're more likely to be seen and reported."

Frank scowled. "Good point."

Gil asked, "What if there's someone else on the roof watching the speech?"

Frank replied, "I don't think so. The roof is far away, and it's cold. Yesterday, the front-runner gave a speech in the square, and there was no one on that roof. There were a few guards on the close-in roofs."

Gil persisted, "If we make it to the street, how are we supposed to make our get away?"

"I'm workin' on it," Frank said. Frank knew, but he didn't want Gil to get upset. What had started as a risky, bad idea now seemed like a riskier, worse idea. The shooting of Elizabeth would have to be perfect. *What if it rains? Will Debbie be able to see the target? What if Liz isn't wearing a bulletproof vest? Everyone takes my word for it. But do I know for sure?* Finding a way for Debbie to escape unseen was unlikely. What had started as an almost good idea was generating problems faster than solutions. Frank needed another front to attack.

* * *

A Rented Croatian TV Studio

Curt Campbell prepared to go on camera. As a producer, he seldom went in front of a camera. The last time was when an anchorwoman retched on her dress, thirty seconds before airtime. Curt preferred to be behind the cameras. Good-looking word readers came and went. The brains that actually wrote, directed, and made things happen had much more staying power.

But the Ferret situation was different. Curt needed the wiggle room. If Ferret was right, Curt could write himself a one-way ticket to anywhere., *Here I come,* 60 Minutes*!* Curt had teased himself when Ferret first proposed the spot. Then reality set in. *If Ferret is smoking rope, kiss both our careers good-bye.* In Ferret's case, it wouldn't matter; Curt would kill Frank before he could be blacklisted again.

The stage director's hand went down, and Curt began his introduction.

"At times journalistic ethics teeter on what could be a terrific story and a true one, and what could be a terrific story—but not true. If anyone else but Pulitzer Prize winning reporter, Frank Ferret, had come to me with his bizarre accusations, I'm afraid I'd throw him out. But this is the same Frank Ferret, who brought us the freedom movement in China. He wrote of the courage of Gulf War soldiers, and he's the same man who exposed neo-Nazi terrorists in London.

"If Frank is right, a notorious war criminal may be brought to justice. However, if Frank *is* right, war could resume in Yugoslavia. And if he is wrong, a statesman who could bring peace to the Balkans could be forever smeared with suspicion.

"Which is it, Frank?"

"I'm right on this one, Curt," Frank stated firmly. His speech was rapid and crisp. "My accusation is that the man who is running for the prime minister of Croatia is not Klav Bymarovitch, but rather his brother Ratac, one of the butchers of the Balkans. Ratac is an indicted war criminal who dropped out of sight several months ago. Ratac underwent plastic surgery and took the place of Klav as a way to return to power—in an even more powerful position than before."

"And you can prove this, Frank?"

"Alone, it would be difficult to prove. But if we had the combined resources of the U.S. CID—that's the Army's Criminal Investigation Division—Britain's MI6, and the UN's other investigating bodies, we could bring this mass murderer to trial."

"You're saying these agencies aren't cooperating now?"

"Not as much as they could. The great powers need to pool their information. It shouldn't take much to get the goods on this pig. He's systematically directed the rape, mutilation, and murder of thousands of innocent women and children in the name of ethnic cleansing and demagoguery."

Curt held his ear. "Hold everything, Frank. The control room just informed me that a phone call has just been received from Klav Bymarovitch, the candidate for the prime ministry of Croatia, and the man Frank Ferret accuses of being a fraud.

"Patch him in here, please."

"You're on the air, Professor Bymarovitch."

"Thank you, Mr. Campbell. I am, indeed, Klav Bymarovitch, and I am appalled at Mr. Ferret's insane charges. I would like to dismiss Mr. Ferret as a lunatic, but the electorate deserves a reply. So I make you this solemn pledge. Immediately after the election—only two days away and *before* I'm sworn into office—I will meet with the UN Election Commission in front of the world press and anyone else who thinks I'm not whom I am. I'll answer any and all questions."

The voice on the phone hardly paused. "I can understand why Mr. Ferret might jump to this false conclusion. My brother was supposedly looking for me in New Zealand a few weeks ago. The last time I saw him, however, was over twenty years ago. We resembled each other then. People thought us twins, when really, we were a year apart. Ratac and I had a disagreement, and I haven't heard from him since. While Ratac was searching for me in New Zealand, I had already planned to return and serve my beloved homeland."

"Well Frank," Curt cut in. "Are you willing to meet with Mr. Bymarovitch?" The edge in Curt Campbell's voice told Frank that his credibility had just blown away.

"If he wins or *loses*, I'll be there," Frank promised. He smiled to the camera. Bymarovitch's call had wiped out Frank's presentation. Crowds at Ratac's speeches would now bloat the Town Square and give him maximum television exposure to the curious electorate. Ratac's preemptive call kept him a step ahead of Frank and the trampers, and for the first time, Frank began to appreciate the bold genius of this murderer. Instead of marshalling an indignant public opinion to bring Ratac down, Frank had boosted Ratac's visibility, popularity, and power. There was no other way of saving Liz except to have Debbie shoot her.

CHAPTER 22

A Bullet is Not Enough

Frank drove from the television studio despondent and silent. George, who was riding shotgun—literally—asked, "Howdit go?"

"Don't ask," Frank answered sullenly.

A large black car pulled sharply in front of them. George cursed and Frank braked to a lurching stop.

Two men quickly exited the car with guns drawn.

George grasped the shotgun. "I can get one 'em if you get your head down."

Ferret murmured, "Hide the gun. These people want to talk. If they wanted us dead we'd be dead."

A third man in a trench coat left the black car. He walked slowly.

"Who are they?" George whispered.

"Old KGB has-beens who tried to kill me on bridge a few weeks ago. This won't be easy. That sewer rat won't believe a small lie, so I'll have to go for a whopper."

Frank stepped out of the car slowly. He opened his palms casually. "So we meet again. Have a nice swim?"

The man in the trench coat punched Frank in the stomach. "If it wasn't for CPR, I would have drowned."

Frank doubled-up and groaned, "Damnit, you ungrateful rat, you should be thanking me—not hitting me."

The man hit him again, and Frank rolled with the punch, feigning more hurt than he felt, but hurting nonetheless. The man drew his gun and clicked the safety off. "And why should I be thanking you?"

A car passed them, but there was no way to signal for help, and it was unlikely anyone would see Frank being shot, let alone help. The pause for the car to pass gave Frank's racing mind a few precious seconds.

"I brought Klav's gold back from New Zealand, didn't I?" Frank growled belligerently.

"Really?"

"You saw my interview tonight?"

The man laughed affirmatively.

"So you saw it and figured out where to find me. Well, I asked the identity question that all the smart people are asking, and Klav phoned in on cue. As a result, Klav is the focus of attention, while I, and any other accuser, appear foolish."

The man in the trench coat shook his head incredulously. "You! Working with Klav?"

"No, not Klav. Use you head! Do you think I would cast my fortunes with a dead brother? Do you think I would sell my soul for less than a half million in tax-free dollars? You and I may end up chattin' 'bout old times in the same circle of hell, but until then, I'll be one rich sinner. So before you play *get even*, ask yourself if you want to snuff *Ratac* Bymarovitch's speechwriter."

The mention of Ratac's name weighed the gun lower. The rumors were right. Ratac was posing as his brother.

"The gold?"

"Ratac brought the gold back to fund a private army. If you want in, send him your résumé."

The spinning blue lights of a police car startled the adversaries.

Frank pointed at his attacker and shouted in Croatian, "Thieves! Robbers! They have guns!"

The man in the trench coat and his gun were caught in the beam of the police car's spotlight.

Frank dived to the ground a second before the police fired a volley from an automatic weapon. The three KGB men crumpled and lay motionless.

"They tried to steal my Swiss watch," Frank said from the ground, pointing to his thirty-five-dollar Hong Kong knockoff. He'd use the watch to bribe the police, skipping the questions, police reports, and search of his shotgun-laden car.

Frank didn't need to employ the bribe.

"Go back to your hotel, Mr. Ferret," the closest of the policemen said. "The curfew will start soon." He slipped back into the police car without examining the dead bodies.

Frank called, "Tell Ratac, thanks. I owe him one."

The police car burned rubber leaving.

Frank returned to the car, backed it up, and headed toward his hotel.

George said, "Before I have a heart attack, do you suppose you can tell me what in the hell just happened?"

"I pulled a stall on this KGB fellow." Frank grimaced, rubbing his stomach.

"KGB?" George exclaimed. "Geez, now we have Russians against us."

"Not exactly," Frank explained. "The KGB was dissolved in 1991. These guys are—or were—the local Yugo's version of an alumni chapter. They were after Klav's gold, so I knew they wouldn't kill me right away."

Frank sighed. "So I stalled. Fortunately, it worked. Did you notice those police? Martin said Elizabeth told him to avoid the police, kinda implying some of them were on more than one payroll. The cops were just waiting for the traffic to clear to protect me. Then they killed three people, left them like litter in the road, and went out for doughnuts."

"Why protect you?" George exclaimed.

"Why? Because Bymarovitch can't afford to have me splattered over the obituaries so soon after the TV interview. My killin' would look like Klav's retaliation for my accusation."

George laughed. "Who would've thought your guardian angel is a mass murderer? I guess that makes you bulletproof."

"Yep, for a few days," Frank agreed, then sighed. "But only up to Inauguration Day. But as a credible journalist, I'm as good as dead already."

* * *

ZAGREB'S NOISIEST PUB

Rod Brickle rapped his beer mug to get the attention of his fellow journalists. "It's time to bury the Ferret, again."

"Amen," the chorus responded from their positions around the bar.

"Ferret's really gone over the top this time," Brickle said.

"He's giving us slime peddlers a bad name," a newspaper reporter inserted.

"He'll be lucky to get a job reporting weather on Radio Antarctica," a German television producer quipped.

"I feel sorry for him," a young photographer ventured. "He gave us newbies a lot of advice when we were starting off."

Others nodded, but no one was willing to admit how much their rival had helped them.

"I heard that Ing moved in with him. Ferret sent someone to clear out her hotel stuff."

"Why didn't she do it herself?" Brickle probed. Her disappearance at the same time that Sergei vanished had made the journalists nervous. Now they were glad she was alive, but the men in the group, all of whom had fantasies about sleeping with Ing, had another reason to resent Frank.

"My source says that he almost got Ingrid killed while he was nosing around," another said.

"Maybe he *is* on to something," Brickle puzzled.

"Naw!" the crowd protested.

*   *   *

Darkness arrived early in the Town Square. Flaming torches behind the speaker's stand reminded Frank of film clips of Hitler's hypnotic use of backlighting in his speeches. As predicted, a curious crowd filled the square to overflowing. Campaign workers passed lighted candles to the spectators, giving the gathering a religious flavor. The crowd was a mixture of a few revenge-minded victims holding a placard saying, *Klav! Justice to All Serbs*, and a larger contingent of war victims' signs reading, *Klav for Peace at Last*.

Local police, some with explosive-sniffing dogs, kept a wide circle around the speaker's platform. Bymarovitch's private army scattered throughout the crowd and on the nearby rooftops. The press corps had its own sizeable mob and filled a roped-off area between the crowd and the speaker's stand. If someone threw a hand grenade at Bymarovitch, it would fly over the heads of the press—a fact not lost on Frank as he positioned himself near the edge of his fellow journalists. Normally, in such a potentially hazardous position, Frank would take his photo and retreat from the front lines, but Frank knew his absence at this event would arouse more suspicion—especially once Debbie started shooting.

Frank also worried about people noticing him whispering into his radio, so he sang softly to himself. A sudden moving of his lips wouldn't attract attention.

On one of the furthest rooftops, Debbie and Gil waited in the shadows of a wide chimney. Booted footsteps startled the couple. Gil motioned Debbie to back away. A uniformed soldier exited from the stairwell door. *Only one.*

With two large strides, Gil slid behind the soldier. Gil made one slashing hit to the back of the soldier's neck. The soldier fell forward, face first. His weapon was a high-powered rifle.

"The assassin?" Debbie mouthed.

Gil shook his head, "Too young, but then again, these kids start killing when they're in diapers."

He examined the soldier's rifle. "No sniper scope. This guy's just a lookout. The sniper's still out there. You have to get your shot off before he does."

Gil wrapped duct tape across the man's mouth and eyes. Then he secured the man's hands behind his back with handcuffs that Frank said he had brought from New Zealand.

"Is he alive?" Debbie mouthed the words.

Gil nodded, but put his fingers to his lips in the event the unconscious man awoke to hear a woman's voice. He pointed to the man's radio. It was the same type that Frank had provided the team. Gil gave a gleeful smile.

Debbie returned a puzzled look.

"With these walkie-talkies, each side can intercept the other's communications, except we good guys know what channel they're broadcasting on, and the bad guys don't know ours," Gil whispered.

Gil spoke to Ferret in French. "We just sang one of the roof rodent's private guards to sleep. What would a roofer say when checking in? Their channel is *One*. The badge on my roofer's fatigues says Romnov."

Frank waited a long minute before answering. "*Romnov* won't do you any good. They're checking in by number. As soon as you hear someone repeat a question twice, answer . . . . Frank slowly repeated a Croatian phrase.

"What does that mean?" Gil asked.

"Damned if I know," Frank grumbled, "but they're all saying it."

Gil switched back to Channel One. Gil wished that he had heard the soldier's voice. Was it high or deep? The soldier looked about sixteen. Not too deep. The question came quickly. The reception crackled. Gil welcomed the chance to hide behind the static. Then the question came again with the tone of irritation. Gil answered. A short acknowledgement followed. Gil relaxed, but only for a minute. Now it was up to Debbie.

Debbie crouched as she moved to the edge of the roof. The building stood two stories higher than the other buildings around the square, but farthest from the speaker's stand. Even with the distance, part of the crowd backed into the front of their building. Debbie could smell the sausages from the street vendors below—a sign that normalcy was creeping back into the city.

Debbie assembled her rifle and tested the sights on the ramp leading to the left of the speaker's stand. The air was misty, but if the rain held off, Debbie would still be able to see her friend clearly. Debbie's heart raced. Her bruised rib began a hurtful spasm.

Gil squeezed her arm. "Let me take the shot."

Debbie shook her head. "I'm fine. I've done crazier things without losing my cool."

"Such as?"

"I can't think of any, just now," she replied with a half laugh.

Gil handed her the soldier's cap. "In case you're seen from a distance.

"I can see soldiers on the rooftops below," Debbie noted. "One of those could be Ratac's sniper." Debbie wondered if she could kill or wound the sniper before he shot Elizabeth, but that was not the plan, for which she was grateful. Stopping the assassination wasn't enough to free Liz. Frank predicted the sniper would shoot from the cover of a window, so she couldn't help scanning the dark windows of the closer buildings.

"Frank says they're coming." Gil announced. "Ratac's leading the way. Lizzie's three steps behind. Frank says to watch out for the strobe lights."

Debbie firmed the rifle butt to her shoulder. The strobe lights, music, and other possible distractions had all been carefully rehearsed. Even the roof guard was not totally unexpected. A Taser and duct tape were only a few of the things stuffed in Gil's grocery bag. Hopefully, little else would be used.

After all the waiting, things seemed to be happening too fast. Bymarovitch strode up the ramp, his arms outstretched over his head and his hands in fists. Elizabeth followed two yards behind Ratac, but closing. She was dressed in a full-length ermine coat that added an inch to the height of her shoulder. The band played its patriotic march even louder. The crowd cheers echoed off the buildings.

Debbie tracked her laser beam to Lizzie's shoulder, aimed to the left, and squeezed. Debbie didn't feel the recoil. She saw her friend topple from the ramp, out of sight.

Frank shouted "Go!" into his walkie-talkie and raced to the speaker's stand. The guard who would normally have stood in his way had turned around to observe the commotion behind him. The press corps ran from the direction of the speaker's stand. The wail of the ambulance scattered others in the candidate's entourage who crouched on the ground to avoid another shot. Others just stood, looking confused.

The ambulance emptied of the false paramedics. They slipped a stretcher under Elizabeth's body. Her head was covered with blood. Lizzie wasn't supposed to fall from the ramp. The fake ambulance crew had prepared to dump blood, but the blood was already there.

Frank turned around. A few brave journalists followed Frank to photograph the victim or to take cover behind the speaker's stand. Frank held up his hands for them to stop. "She's dead!" he hollered. "A sniper has killed Bymarovitch's daughter." He repeated shouting statements in Croatian.

Frank looked back as Lizzie's stretcher rolled into the ambulance. He had planned to say that Elizabeth was dead. Now he wondered if what he said was true.

On the speaker's stand, Bymarovitch's voice boomed. While the rest of the would-be president's cabinet cowered and jumped from the speaker's stand, Bymarovitch stood defiantly to the side of the bulletproof plastic that shielded his podium. If the timing of the sniper's shot was different from what Ratac expected, he didn't show it. Debbie's shot had preempted the sniper's intended shot by only five seconds Ratac pointed at a nearby building. "The shot came from that window. Catch the assassin. Bring him to me!"

Gil had to pull Debbie from the building's edge. Debbie seemed in shock. "Liz fell off the ramp! She wasn't supposed to fall. What if I killed her?"

"The sooner we get out of here, the sooner we'll find out," Gil urged. "Your shot looked true to me," he lied. He couldn't tell from this distance. "Now the fast way down."

Debbie fumbled with the bungee cord. The repelling equipment had been abandoned rescuing the children, and the bungee cords were a distant second choice for escape. Debbie's hands were shaking. Gil fastened the cord for her. "Don't hit the side of the walls," he cautioned.

"You're the one I'm worried about," she said. Gil had declined bungee jumping on the tour.

"Don't. I did some dumb things in my impetuous youth, and bungee jumping was among them."

Debbie jumped, trying to stay clear of the walls. As she bounced up, she kicked off one wall. When the cord came to a rest, a black truck pulled under

Debbie. Debbie undid her cord and dropped into Clutch's waiting arms in the truck bed. George backed up the truck, and Gil sailed down. He had mathematically estimated the stretch of the cord, and a minute later he held Debbie in his arms on the truck bed as the assassins crouched under a tarp.

Candidate Bymarovitch didn't break his tirade until guards dragged the limp figure of his Bosnian archenemy Sadad before him. Ratac had put the enemy he had shot at the plastic surgeon's garden in captivity for a moment like this. Sadad sat propped up on his knees—his eyes glazed with drugs. Bymarovitch towered over him. "I'm told that the assassin who killed my daughter is a wanted Bosnian war criminal who vowed revenge on my family. How I want to strangle him with my bare hands! That is what the critics in the press want me to do. But unlike our enemies, I am not a murderer. Justice must prevail. *Justice will prevail!* And it will be a swift justice—*a hard, final justice!* No more will the Bosnians and Serbs terrorize my people! Let none of you listening who have been scarred by our enemies believe that the rapists and killers of our women can get away with these atrocities. I swear on my dead daughter's soul that when I am prime minister, I will heal your wounds—*one way or another!*"

At first, the speech drew stunned silence then the frightened and angry crowd began its roar of approval.

Frank tried to blend with the departing crowd—candle and all. A block from the square he spotted three men following him. Frank elected not to escape in the getaway truck so as not to slow them down or arouse suspicion to the others. But now Frank had to repeat what he had been doing for his entire time in Yugoslavia—trying to shake a tail.

The tails aren't tailing, Frank concluded. *They're chasin'.* When Frank increased his pace, the tails broke into a jog. *Not UN tails. Locals. Bymarovitch's boys.*

Frank rejoined a crowd-congested street where he asked for and received an election placard from a pretty lady member of the crowd. He held it high so the tails could see it. Then he lowered it and traded the placard with a short teenager for a different sign. The ploy worked. When Frank looked back, there were only two tails. One uncertain follower had split off to chase the first sign.

Frank rounded the corner into a four-foot wide alley. The crowd in the street would not protect him once the tails got close. When the tails turned into the dark alley, Frank's press camera startled them with a blinding strobe light. Frank's placard came crashing down on the forehead of the closest follower. With a graceful lunge learned in Fencing 101, Frank thrust the long candle like a sword. His taper went straight at the Adam's apple of the second pursuer. The man struggled on the ground, gasping for air.

Frank moved briskly away from the crowd and toward the hotel. His breathing returned to normal, and he felt satisfied by the way he had attacked the Butcher's tails. *Still, someday, I'm gonna have to learn how to fight.*

*   *   *

Eve boarded the ambulance a kilometer from the shooting site. The volunteer ambulance crew of young Slovenian graduate students had little medical knowledge, but the expression on their faces told the story. Elizabeth had a serious head injury—a *very* serious head injury. Gregory had put a compress on the abrasion.

Eve pushed aside the blood-soaked ermine coat. Head wounds bleed. Eve wished she had more than one rotation in emergency treatment. Eve's specialty of genetic counseling didn't help much with the patients she had advised lately.

She examined bruises on Elizabeth's shoulders. Debbie's shot had been perfect. The rubber bullet had broken Elizabeth's right clavicle, but the break was a simple fracture. The bulletproof vest had protected Elizabeth's body from the fall, but the left elbow was swelling. *Probably a bone chip,* Eve guessed. *No paralysis. But . . . . this head injury could be fatal.*

Regain consciousness, Lizzie. Wake up, damn it!

Elizabeth's eyes didn't flutter until her grandfather's associates transferred her to a truck and took her to the safe house, a private home in the countryside. Elizabeth tried to focus on Eve's distraught face. "Where am I? Who are you?"

*   *   *

Ingrid's Hotel Room

Ingrid put down the morning paper. "Bymarovitch's party received 60 percent of the seats in the Sabor. Frank should have been Ratac's campaign manager."

"Don't rub it in, darlin', Frank groused. "Ratac's not sworn in, yet. We have one more crack at him."

The rest of the trampers circling Ingrid's bed exchanged dubious glances.

"Who's gonna testify?" Virginia asked. "Lizzie?"

George sighed. "Eve says Lizzie has temporary amnesia."

"How does she define temporary again?" Gil asked.

George shrugged. "Short-term memory loss is not uncommon with head injuries and morphine. It gets better after a few days."

"And if it doesn't get better?" Debbie asked with pleading in her red eyes.

George squirmed. "Then it's not amnesia. It's brain damage."

Frank put a comforting hand on Debbie's shoulder. "Lizzie's not in Yugoslavia any more. I had her driven out this morning. She'll get the best care possible."

Gil raised an eyebrow. "She's well enough to move, but not well enough to remember?"

"What are you saying, Gil?" Debbie asked.

"I'm probably wrong, but what if Liz is playing possum? She's afraid for her life. She's afraid for her adoptive father's life. And she could be trying to protect us too."

"I hope you're right," Debbie said. "If she is sandbagging, I bet I could talk her into testifying."

"It's too late for that," Gil replied. "I don't know medicine, but I know a little law. A person who's been diagnosed as having amnesia doesn't have much credibility as a witness. A sharp defense lawyer will say we planted the memories on a blank slate."

Clutch broke his silence. "Then Ratac gets an intentional pass, and there's nothin' we can do about it?"

Everyone else answered together, "No!"

CHAPTER 23

The Gator's First Bite

The UN delegation arrived in three limousines proceeded by two police cars and four policemen on motorcycles. A recent snowfall gleamed crystal clean under the sun and seemed a more appropriate surrounding for a Christmas pageant than for an inquiry to establish the identity of the Croatian prime minister-elect. A select group of reporters and translators followed in a caravan of six vans, three with satellite dishes. Two cameramen would feed images to the pool. The group parked in the circular drive around the Bymarovitch villa. A single unarmed guard beckoned them to enter.

On the second floor of the villa, the traditional grand room showcased a round table furnished with crystal carafes of ice water and decorated with low sprays of red hothouse flowers. The warmth from the fireplace welcomed the chilled visitors. Sunlight streamed in from the curtainless windows of two French doors, yet the television team quickly set their lights in place. They could never be sure if, or when, the clouds might roll in.

Frank, Gil, Debbie, and George seated themselves on one quadrant of the mahogany table. Virginia sat against a wall of floor-to-ceiling oil paintings in carved, gilded frames. The accusers held an empty high back chair for Eve, who waited for a lab report at the hotel. Clutch also remained at the hotel, since his celebrity status would distract attention from Frank's accusations. Clutch expressed no enthusiasm in sharing Frank's hot seat in the spotlight, anyway. Twelve UN officials, some in military uniform, took the other half circle of the table.

Frank pointed out two assistant U.S. secretaries of state and a British minister of justice, who were not part of the joint election commission. They took nearby seats against the wall. "The heavy hitters are here, but I don't know whose side they're on."

"What's the agenda?" the business-savvy Virginia asked.

"Hit 'im hard, and hit 'im fast," Frank answered. "Never let a gator have the first bite."

Bymarovitch made his grand entrance, a black armband contrasting against his gray suit. He circled the room, bowing graciously, and shaking hands with each official and most of the press. He took his seat at the head of the table, and as the suspense built for his reaction, he took off his clear glasses, rubbed his temples, and paused before speaking. He waited until the photographers aimed their bright lights, and the red lights on the television camera came to life.

"Gentlemen and ladies, I'll speak in English, since those who conspire against me and those who would judge me are English-speaking, not Croatian. For over two decades of my life, I've lived in English-speaking New Zealand, hiding from the wrath of the vengeful KGB. I learned the ways of democracy. I reveled in the free air of freedom and fairness of

Western justice. And now the same Western justice that I learned to love demands that I prove who I am.

"I'll tell you who I am! I'm a man who loves his country. I want to give the gift of democracy to my country. Although I was duly elected largely because of the popularity of my brother, Ratac, I want to undo the hurt on humanity that this overzealous patriot inflicted on our land in the search for lasting peace. I seek only to take the reins of my brave country and begin a new era of cooperation with the countries of the West and East, and even the Bosnians and Serbians, who committed such horrible atrocities against my people—and me personally. It is the time to heal the festering wounds, while my own open wound—the assassination of my daughter—rips my heavy heart. But instead of being able to mourn in peace and prepare to govern my country, I must defend myself against the same people who I would hope could be my allies."

Bymarovitch's voice shook with emotion. "Tell me, what man has to prove who he is?"

Frank snorted. "You've never tried to cash a check? Let's see your New Zealand driver's license."

Ratac glared at Frank. "Yes, Mr. Ferret, I believe? I would like to humor your mischief-making, but I do not drive. I have never driven."

The press corps laughed at their friend. Ferret had scooped them on this story, and if it turned out to be a hoax, it would quiet several of their irate editors who wondered what they were getting for their money. Ingrid's shooting also angered the press corps. Ingrid was popular with the media contingent, and rumors were spreading that Ferret was responsible for her disappearance.

Gil put a flat hand on the table next to Frank's closed fist. "Slow down, pal. Ratac just won the first two rounds; don't go swinging wildly."

Frank nodded. "The bastard's good," he whispered. "Ratac makes it sound like he's speaking off the cuff, but it's a memorized speech."

"Too many adjectives?" Debbie speculated.

"Right," Frank replied. If anyone knew superfluous adjectives, it was Frank.

George leaned into the whispered conversation. "I've heard enough innocent pleas to spot canned bullshit, but so what?"

The laughter having subsided, Frank wrote on his notepad,

> *Ratac is rehearsed. Probably ready for everything we have to throw at him—which isn't much. Have to surprise him. Throw him off his game plan. Make him lose his cool.*

"Easier said than done," Gil muttered.

The U.S. Assistant Secretary of State, Allison Quill, stood up. "My country wants to apologize for this humiliation. Nevertheless, we want to thank you for meeting with us to put these ugly accusations to rest."

"There goes round three," George groused.

Bymarovitch smiled graciously at Quill. His smiles were short, as they drooped back into the somber expression of a man numbed by mourning. "Thank you, madam secretary. I have one request, however. A hallmark of democratic justice is to be able to face your accuser—to defend yourself. Since the persons who perpetrate these lies against me seem accountable to no one, I would like to have an associate question them regarding their motives."

"That sounds reasonable," Quill responded.

"How say you to that request, Mr. Ferret?" she asked.

"Suits me fine," Frank said, knowing he had been talked into a trap that he couldn't decline.

Bymarovitch smiled again. "Since I am not schooled in legal proceedings . . . ."

"This is not a legal proceeding, Prime Minister-elect Bymarovitch," Quill interrupted. "Only a quasi-public hearing."

Bymarovitch gave another sick smile and glanced to the television cameras broadcasting around the world. *How much more public could it be?* Even Frank was beginning to feel sorry for the Butcher. Bymarovitch said, "Nonetheless, I was offered assistance by an American barrister. He seems to think the credibility and motivation of my accusers is in question. Who am I to judge others? But he would like to ask a few questions.

"Could one of the guards please escort Mr. Hancock to this table."

Frank dropped his pen.

Debbie asked, "What's wrong?"

George answered grimly, "Ron Hancock is the most flamboyant lawyer in the U.S. He's put more killers back on the street than all the prison breaks in history."

"On technicalities and confusion," Gil added.

"He gives a bad name to sharks," Frank said, "but the press loves 'im."

Ron Hancock walked forward from a shadowy corner in the back of the room. He slapped a few backs and greeted some of the American press by name. Hancock sported a double-breasted, bright blue blazer and a scarlet Gucci tie. Hancock's mane of thick white, designer-permed hair flowed with his broad effusive movements.

The camera persons became alert. This was turning into a cameraman's dream: handsome accusers versus the charismatic godfather of criminal law.

Hancock set his briefcase down as if to open it then set it on the floor. "Won't need this. We're all friends here."

He fiddled with his water glass like a movie prop and smiled at Frank. "What a pleasure to see you again, Spider. I'm sorry about your troubles in New Zealand. Do you mind telling these nice people what you were arrested for?"

Frank squirmed. "I was released."

"For?"

"My roommate was murdered by Ratac Bymarovitch or one of his associates."

"That's not how I heard it. Who was the major suspect?"

"The Kiwi police held me for a few days. But then they realized I didn't do it, so they released me."

"Under heavy pressure from someone in the United States, I believe. Would you care to tell these folks who that was?"

A no win answer, Frank told himself. "No, I can't." Hancock was politically connected to the Palmer opposition. Revealing Mary Beth Palmer's role in his release would not only betray Mary Beth, but provide Hancock with a trove of ruinous headlines he would use to attack the administration.

"Can't?"

"Won't."

"You posted a bond?"

"No, it wasn't required."

"So you don't have to forfeit it since you skipped that country."

"I had to help with the safe return of Dr. Rocklin's and Dr. and Sergeant King's children who were—"

"Then you're not interested in the two-million-dollar bounty on the head of Professor Bymarovitch's brother?" Hamilton interrupted.

"That's secondary," Frank said, and the press corps laughed.

"It's not a *bounty*," Debbie inserted. "It's a *reward*, and it wasn't Frank's idea. The UN put out the reward because this man, Ratac Bymarovitch, is an indicted war criminal."

"Really?" Hancock smirked.

"You must be the cute Debbie McWard everyone's whispering about. You're traveling with Gilbert Rocklin?"

"Yes. I'm his fiancée."

"Lucky man. Of course, we understand these things. You're a pretty little lady, Ms. McWard. I understand you model bathing suits."

"Yes, but I also—"

Hancock interrupted again, "Let's not take the time of these busy people to go over your adventurous resume. I'm sure it's an impressive one." He grinned and double arched his bushy eyebrows. "I know I'm impressed."

While the press corps chuckled, Debbie fumed. "The bastard just dismissed me as an immoral bimbo," she muttered.

"You got off easy," Ferret whispered back.

Hancock turned to George. "Mr. King—or should I call you Sergeant King? You're a policeman?"

"Correct, sir."

"Not a detective?"

"With downsizing, I'm better off keeping my seniority as a desk sergeant."

"So you're not an investigator?"

"I was. Not anymore."

Hancock scratched his forehead. "That's too bad. Maybe with a little experience, none of these accusations would have ever been made."

In an attempt to deflect Hancock's attack on George, Gil cut in, "*I* have experience. I was an assistant director of data security for the FBI."

Hancock's deep nods took the eyes from Gil. "Yes, yes. And after your orientation, how long were you actually doing field work? Catching bad guys and that sort of thing."

"Six months."

"Only six months? With a prestigious position like that, why would you ever leave? Could it have anything to do with your arrest for manslaughter?"

"I was never arrested, never charged," Gil snapped back. "A corporate president that I had brought down in an undercover operation shot up my house, killing my wife, and then came looking for me. I struck him."

"And killed him," Hancock stated, more than asked. "One blow to the head?"

"Yes," Gil replied.

"Now why would police arrest someone for defending himself?"

Gil took a breath. He wouldn't lie. "There were two issues. One was that my wife's killer wasn't in my house at the time. I had rushed him—knocked him off my porch. The other was that they didn't believe I could break a man's neck with one punch. Multiple punches wouldn't have been an issue with a private citizen. But for a law enforcement officer, it implies possible police brutality."

"That must have been psychologically devastating. Do you have bitter feelings about law enforcement and justice, Gil? May I call you *Gil*?" Hancock wasn't going to acknowledge Gil's doctorate.

"Well Ronnie, let's say that I've elected to find another line of work."

Hancock slapped the table. "Don't blame you, Gil. It would be better for all concerned if you stuck to making software for little children."

Hancock made his first mistake. He mentioned *children.*

Ferret jumped in. "The children of Dr. Rocklin and Sergeant and Dr. King were kidnapped by Ratac Bymarovitch. This fact seems to be overlooked."

Quill cocked her head like a scolding teacher. "In fairness to us all, we cannot address *all* the crimes that Ratac was alleged to have committed. Our task here today is to clear Prime Minister-elect *Klav* Bymarovitch's name so that he can move on with his prime ministry—"

"Or . . . ," Frank cued.

Quill scowled and interrupted. "*Or* determine if there is some merit to your allegations. Is that what you wanted to hear, Mr. Ferret?"

"Yes, ma'am. I was startin' to think we were the ones on trial. Two children were kidnapped, so we wouldn't blow the whistle on this man. This didn't happen months ago. It *just* happened."

Hancock leaned forward. He had been quiet too long. "That is terrible. Where are the children now?"

"Safe, in an undisclosed place," Gil answered.

"Good. Good. And how did that happen? Did you pay ransom?"

Gil answered. "No, the children escaped."

Hancock's eyebrows elevated. "Two little children escaped from the Butcher of the Balkans? Really, Gil! That's another tale that's hard to believe."

Gil explained, "Their escape was aided by Elizabeth Bymarovitch."

Hancock blew a stream of air. "How sadly inconvenient. A story that can only be verified by the dead daughter of a grieving man. Shame, Gil. I would have hoped you had more sensitivity."

Bymarovitch couldn't accept his hired hand doing all the dirty work. He inserted, "Perhaps, these children of whom you speak will come forward and identify the boogie man who carried them away."

Gil answered, "The King family and I and my fiancée decided that for the continued safety and mental health of the children, we wouldn't allow them to testify."

A thin groan of disdain came from Rod Brickle and the rest of the press corps. Part of the room darkened as the sunlight dulled. A light snowfall returned. The hilly roads would become slippery when wet, and the print reporters wondered if they would be get back to the city to file their stories. The television press, led by Curt Campbell, had no such worries. They had their satellite dishes. Both media were becoming impatient with Ferret. If the only stories they could file were the ridiculous accusations of a maverick reporter, who would care? Another example of irresponsible journalism would smear the profession.

While Quill admonished the press to be less reactive, George growled under his breath, "The Butcher *knew* we won't use the kids! Quill must have told him."

Ferret wrote on his pad, *Her office could have been bugged, but more likely Ratac guessed. Be thankful. Ratac is less likely to go after the kids.*

Ratac continued. "Did your children see anyone who looks like me?"

"Not exactly," Frank said, "but a member of our New Zealand tour group—a Mr. Joseph Tinsley from Perth, Australia—kidnapped and tried to attack the children, right in this building. I have this picture of Tinsley that I took on the New Zealand tour."

A British officer, Colonel Jameison, who had remained silent, stood up and picked up the photograph. "May I have this? We found an unidentified man this morning. This photo looks exactly like him."

Hoping that the colonel would place the man near one of Bymarovitch's villas, George asked, "Where did you pick him up, sir?"

"In the dumpster behind the hotel you're staying at."

The colonel glared at Gil and chose his words deliberatively. "The murder victim appears to have been killed with a *single blow to the head*."

Even the jaded press people gasped. They had done their homework and weren't surprised by Gil's earlier admission of killing his wife's murderer with one blow to the head. But now the similarity of the way Tinsley was killed— If Gil believed Tinsley had kidnapped his child, it gave him a motive to kill Tinsley.

The panel speculated the same thoughts, and Hancock now made sure the watching world knew. The similarity of the killing made Gil look like the guilty party.

Hancock's momentum increased in the speed of his comments and the strength of his deep voice, "Even if the murdered Mr. Tinsley had something to do with your children, he had no association with President Bymarovitch other than having visited New Zealand."

"I don't know what game you five people have cooked up," Hancock roared. "Is this an attempt at extortion? Is this a political dirty trick? Or a deflection of your own wrongdoing? I don't know. I don't care. But I think all of you owe Professor Bymarovitch an apology, so he can get on with the governing of this great country."

Virginia tugged on Frank's sleeve. "Your gators are killing us. Do something before there's nothing left for them to bite!"

CHAPTER 24

Even Higher Ratings

During the break, producer Curt Campbell went on air to apologize to his viewers for allowing Frank Ferret airtime to rant his theory. Privately, Curt and his bosses weren't the least apologetic. The shooting of Klav's daughter brought them high ratings for a violent event that might have been otherwise ignored if not for Ferret. Curt's network smelled Ferret's blood and sent Curt to Zagreb for the follow-up. The world's sympathy for the grieving father, promoter of peace, and victim of journalistic lies, deserved an outraged defense. Curt launched an impassioned attack on Ferret. "Frank Ferret has relinquished his role as an advocate of the underdog and tilter of bureaucratic windmills for that of a desperate chaser of sensationalistic rumors. Now he claims to have DNA evidence to refute Klav Bymarovitch's identity, but the new prime minister-elect never submitted samples for such testing."

Curt shook his head in dismissal. "Stay tuned. We'll resume as soon as the session reconvenes. One hero will emerge; another will go down in flames. Sorry, Frank Ferret, but I smell smoke."

*　　*　　*

THE HOTEL

Eve fidgeted in the empty hotel lobby waiting for the courier carrying the needed DNA slides for her presentation. She would compare the DNA from Ratac's drain hair and Elizabeth's maroon hair sample that Frank had routinely collected from most, but not all, of the trampers. "Process of elimination," Frank had said.

Clutch stood at the doorway to the noisy bar, watching the election hearing on the bar television with most everyone else in the hotel, and casting frequent looks in Eve's direction.

Ing had strongly insisted on accompanying Eve to her presentation, but Eve insisted that the recovering woman rest until the last minute. The last minute had already passed.

The courier's car pulled into the driveway, and Eve rushed out to sign for the package. She darted back into the hotel lobby, tearing at the wrapper. The slides were neatly packed with a cover letter in English. Eve read the cover letter and slumped into a sofa. "Damn that Ferret!"

"That's what I say," the familiar voice of Amelia Stanley came from behind the chair. "Don't turn around. I have a bloody gun with a silencer under my scarf.

"You have your car parked in front, ready to go to the villa, correct, Doctor?

"Yes," Eve said.

"We'll go for a little ride then," the woman said. "Pardon me if you don't make it the Bymarovitch villa on time for your presentation."

"I can pay you more than Ratac can," Eve offered.

"I doubt it. But even if you could, working for the General is a one-way hole. I'd be content to go back to my old profession of flying drugs to feed the American habit. But there is no returning once you follow Bymarovitch. The penalty for failure is a painful death. The penalty for betrayal is too horrible to think about." Her pistol nudged Eve to a standing position.

From his position in the bar, Clutch waited for Mrs. Stanley's hand to tilt downward before throwing the ashtray. The round chunk of glass rifled threw the air like a baseball thrown from right field to third base. The ashtray glanced off the woman's head, and she sank out of sight behind the sofa.

Her pistol slid across the carpet, and Eve scooped it up. Eve ran into Clutch's arms.

"That was scary," was all Clutch could think to say.

"It happened too fast for me to be scared," Eve said. "I'll probably start shaking when I give the DNA presentation."

Clutch looked about. The thud of the ashtray on skull hadn't attracted attention. The desk clerk was doubling as a bartender, and the blare from the television loudly masked the brief confrontation.

"Now go!" Clutch advised. "Take your stuff to the hearing, Eve. Take Ing too. I'll call the police on Mrs. Stanley," he said, although he couldn't think what the charge would be without Eve to testify.

Eve shook her head. "We have to take Amelia with us. Stanley can expose Ratac. My slides can't. They're no damn good."

Amelia Stanley lurched from behind the sofa and ran unevenly out the door into the street. She began to stagger, with Clutch three strides behind.

The screech of the taxi's braking and the thump of metal against bone ended any chance of Mrs. Stanley exposing Ratac.

* * *

THE HEARING ROOM

Eve walked in with Ing on her arm, and both took seats against the wall. The entrance of the attractive women broke Hancock's rhythm. Eve looked prim, stone-faced, and businesslike in a designer suit. Eve felt like trembling but remembered the first night interning in an inner city hospital ER when the gunshot victims filled the waiting room. *If I can do that, I can do anything.* Eve had decided not to say anything about Amelia Stanley's attempt to kidnap and kill her. It would only upset George. She wouldn't mention the woman's death either.

Ing appeared pale, but her neatly combed blonde hair never looked better, and her bandaged arm raised curiosity. The males became more alert, and the press corps waved greetings. She smiled at Frank. As weak as Ing felt from her bullet wound, she wasn't about to miss this story. The faint return smiles from Frank and the team told her that they were on the ropes.

Frank slipped Eve a wide-eyed questioning look, which she answered with a back-and-forth rotation of her hand that could only be interpreted as *maybe.*

Eve noticed curious eyes looking at her, so she scribbled a note, folded it, and passed it to Frank. Eve smiled hard, as she had a triumphant secret, but her stomach felt like she was diving off a high board into a waterless swimming pool.

Debbie whispered, "We're dying, Frank. Call for a time-out."

Frank shook his head, "It's just like in lacrosse. You can't call time until you've got the ball."

"Agreed," Gil acknowledged, "but the Butcher has the ball, and he's not giving it up without a good reason—like a steal."

"Madame Secretary," Gil called. "I'd like to call a brief recess so that we can set up to show some slides."

"Certainly," Quill replied, "but may I ask the nature of the slides?"

"Certainly," Gil answered back. "We're going to do an electronic analysis to show that the voice on Klav's radio commercials is the same as that of Ratac. And to top it off, Dr. Eve King, who is a board certified geneticist, has some DNA slides to prove that the man calling himself Klav Bymarovitch is actually Ratac Bymarovitch."

A buzz went up.

Bymarovitch paled. "I did *not* donate blood for such testing."

"Nor should you have to, Prime Minister-elect Bymarovitch," Quill said sharply.

Frank pulled conspicuously on his black hair and motioned for his team to leave their chairs. The team huddled in the cold of the adjacent rooftop balcony, away from the questioning press.

Frank chortled. "Good timing, Gil. That's the way to ice him. Now the momentum's on our side."

"Did you see the look on Ratac's puss when you touched your hair?" George exclaimed. "Red as a stoplight!"

"I noticed a tic," Ingrid added.

Gil turned to Eve. "You're up, Doctor."

Eve shuddered, more from fear than from the cold. "You don't need a geneticist to pull this off. You need a poker player."

"Did you get the results of Ratac's hair from the Australian lab?" Gil asked. "The hair Frank found in the pipes of his apartment?"

"Should I tell them?" Eve said solemnly.

Frank mumbled something.

"I beg your pardon?" Gil pressed.

"Cat hair," Frank murmured. "A frickin' fur ball, but I'm not sure we could have used it as evidence anyway."

Quill approached the group, brushing the snowflakes off her glasses. "People, you haven't shown us much. Unless your DNA results can raise some serious doubts, I'm sending everyone home. And as for you, Frank. You might want to polish your Pulitzer, pal. You'll need it to find work."

Frank smiled weakly. "You'll see."

Quill said, "Take your time on the slide show. Hancock wants to bring in a doctor from the city. Wander around the villa. We'll reconvene in two hours."

*   *   *

In the privacy of his office, Bymarovitch raged, "She claims to be an expert doctor? A woman? A black woman? How *dare* she try to match my DNA?"

Hancock poured himself a port and growled back, "You tell me! Your research has been on target up to now. So you tell me."

"I've never submitted blood or hair samples," Bymarovitch screamed. "How can that doctor claim to match my DNA?" He clutched his cheeks to stop a nervous spasm.

Hancock snorted, "Your barber. Ferret must have collected your hair that fell to the ground."

"Not possible! I've been burning my hair for years—ever since I started dying it."

Bymarovitch began to curse. "Of course! He invaded an apartment that I used to rent. He entered disguised as a plumber."

Hancock's white eyebrows raised again—not in surprise, but in admiration of Frank Ferret. Unlike Bymarovitch, Hancock never underestimated an opponent. "That would do it. Hair outta the drain."

Bymarovitch picked up a two-inch thick book and angrily tore it in half. "I may have to implement my contingency plan."

Hancock poured another port. He didn't like his client's plans. They were too precise, and he didn't want to hear about them. *The difference between an engineer and an artist*, Hancock told himself. Hancock considered himself an artist of the bar. Yet the Croat politician's plans had worked well, until this.

"And what about the electronic voice analysis?" Hancock baited.

Bymarovitch laughed, his face still red. "You'll soon see that you're in the presence of a genius, Mr. Hancock. Accept it!"

*   *   *

George reminded Frank, "You said 'never let a gator take the first bite.'"

Frank grunted.

George grumbled back in frustration. "The gator's already munched our best parts."

George looked hopefully to his attractive wife. "I take that back. Eve, baby, you're one best part he ain't munched. Your turn to chew 'im up and spit 'im out."

Eve smiled at her husband's encouragement and squeezed his hand. The advice seemed futile.

Bymarovitch entered the room last, his head cocked high. If he looked rattled at the beginning of the break, he showed no flushing, no tics—only a tight-lipped determination.

Hancock whispered in Quill's ear, and she announced, "The Prime Minister-elect wants to make a statement."

Bymarovitch took off his glasses and rubbed his eyes. "Yes, my friends. I have a statement—a confession, if you will." He paused to make sure all the cameras were aimed in his direction. "I am probably increasing my risk of assassination by revealing this at this time. But I am a truthful man and cannot remain silent any longer.

"I, Klav Bymarovitch, may be partly responsible for the death of my brother, Ratac."

Stunned silence.

"Ratac came to me at my home in New Zealand. We went out on a boat on a river near my home. Ratac thought no one would hear us out on the water. He had this ridiculous idea of using my name to return to power. I, in turn, berated him about the atrocities of which he was accused, perhaps falsely, but perhaps not. We argued. As you may have heard, Ratac was known for his explosive temper. He lunged at me and fell overboard. In fact, we both fell overboard. The current was swift. I looked for Ratac, but couldn't find him. I managed to crawl back on the boat and searched until dark for him. I believe his body was swept out into the Tasman Sea."

Bymarovitch's voice boomed. "It was then that I decided to return to my homeland to undo the damage that Ratac did. My late daughter, Elizabeth, supported me in this effort."

"Do you need a moment to compose yourself?" Quill asked sympathetically.

Bymarovitch waved her off. "When I arrived here, Ratac's radio commercials were already airing. So it was *his* voice your electronic analysis matched. His campaign was well underway. I added to it. I used some of Ratac's old staff and dismissed most of the others.

"I also heard Ratac had kidnapped two children and sent them to Croatia, but I could hardly believe it. Apparently, Elizabeth did. She asked me to find this brute she called Tinsley. I helped her locate him. I discovered that he was an Australian mercenary under Ratac's employ. Tinsley was unaware that Ratac was dead, so he trusted my daughter. She bravely went to the children and freed them. I offer apologies to the families of the children for the actions set into motion by my dead brother."

Quill called a two-minute time-out for everyone to digest this bombshell.

Eve looked sick.

"What if this man *is* Klav?" Ing murmured then shook her head vigorously to shake away the effective tale.

Frank motioned for his electronic voice expert to go home and to send Willie the bill. Frank looked at each of the others on his team. "The Butcher has given us an out. We can all go home and say it was a justifiable misreading of the facts. Win-win. No one loses."

Ing said, "Klav, or Ratac, does it matter? Someone tried to kill me, and he's the only one around here who's powerful enough to have ordered it."

Debbie spoke first. "I trust Amy and Martin, and I know what the kids said: 'Elizabeth was afraid of Lafate.' Amy said Liz thinks 'Lafate is a bad man.'"

Debbie's eyes blazed. "Lafate is Ratac. Ratac is our phony Klav. I don't want Amy growing up in a world where butchers like Ratac run free."

"Let's finish what we started," George said.

Everyone looked at Eve.

Eve sighed in frustration. "I had slides prepared, but I haven't had time to study them. They're too small to read without a microscope. I don't know if they'll prove anything."

"You'll be able to read them when I flash them on the screen?" Virginia asked. She had produced many a computer-projected show for Willie.

"Yes, if they're clear."

Frank brushed Eve's concerns away like he was fanning himself. "Make up somethin', darlin'. I do it all the time."

George gave her a hug. "You can pull it off. Go for it!"

"Easy for you to say! Make up somethin'! The medical profession will want my diploma back," Eve grumbled.

Quill reopened the meeting. "In view of what Prime Minister-elect Bymarovitch has just said, I will entertain a motion that we call this case closed. What we have is a legitimate misinterpretation of events. I believe a simple apology from Mr. Ferret should suffice."

She turned to Bymarovitch. Would you agree to that, Prime Minister Bymarovitch?"

"I forgive them," Bymarovitch said, but let us not call any more attention to this slander than what already has been rendered."

"Mr. Ferret?" Quill quizzed, the impatience in her voice showing.

"Madame Secretary, we will not rest until we see the murdering bastard, Ratac Bymarovitch, behind bars and danglin' from the rope of world condemnation! We aim to prove that this fast-talkin' fraud *is* that murderin' muther, and we aim to do it now!"

"Be careful, Mr. Ferret! You're going over the line," Quill warned.

The television crew shook their heads and grinned. Their old drinking buddy and rival was losing it. The "muther" would be bleeped out in the satellite truck, thanks to the five-second transmission delay, and Ferret's anger would sound even worse.

Frank spoke fast to keep the momentum. "I introduce our expert geneticist, Dr. Eve King, a board certified genetic counselor who has been used as an expert in forensic cases throughout the United States."

Hancock replied, "Our medical expert is a graduate of Warsaw University. Meet Dr. Wysocki."

Eve noted that Wysocki wasn't introduced as a geneticist. Hancock had to find an English-speaking doctor to bluff a rebuttal to anything she said.

Dr. Wysocki was a youngish-looking man with a tan brush cut and a nervous smile. "It's nice to meet you, Dr. King. I refer to your textbook often, and I follow your research in Lancet and the New England Journal of Medicine."

"Then you'll know that the DNA of a father and daughter can always be matched."

"Not nec-es-sarily," the young doctor hesitated. He'd been paid well to disagree with everything, but his coaching was brief and Eve sensed he was uncomfortable in his role. Eve's textbook that he claimed to have read was on obstetrics, not genetics. This would not be a battle of knowledge but of will power.

Eve overtalked him. "If a genetic defect is found in only one in twenty thousand persons and is passed on from a dominant paternal gene, we can reasonably assume that the same gene found in an assumed daughter will confirm a parental relationship. Correct?"

"Yes," said Wysocki, "on a confirmatory basis that would be true. The daughter would always have that defective gene, but—"

"And working backward, the father would have it too," Eve clucked.

Virginia turned on the projector, and the first slide appeared. "In Elizabeth's specimen, I found the gene for an almost certain disposition to a specific type of acute paranoid schizophrenia—usually associated with violently insane sociopaths, such as the Butcher." Wysocki leaned forward, about to question the statement.

Knowing that physicians seldom have time to keep up with their professional reading, Eve quickly added. "See my lead article in this month's *JAMA*." She had the lead article in *JAMA*, about inherited allergies, not schizophrenia.

"I skimmed it," Wysocki lied.

Frank inserted, "For the record, *JAMA*'s the *Journal of the American Medical Association.*

Quill scowled and whirled her hand in confusion. "Wait a minute, Doctor. You're saying that Ratac Bymarovitch is a paranoid schizophrenic due to a genetic anomaly?"

Eve nodded. "That's pretty obvious from a hair sample Mr. Ferret obtained from his former apartment."

Bymarovitch's cheek twitched.

Quill wouldn't let it go. "Ratac was alleged to be a genius with a ferocious temper."

Eve looked Quill in the eye and then focused on Bymarovitch. "Oh, the Butcher is a genius, all right, and a certifiable lunatic. It's a compatible combination and a dangerous one. Look at the Unabomber, Theodore Kasinski."

Colonel Jamieson stepped into the conversation. "Then how do you explain Elizabeth Bymarovitch, who from all reports, is neither a genius nor genetically insane?"

Eve answered without hesitation. "Women carry that gene, but do not exhibit its effects. Hemophilia is the same way. If Elizabeth had lived, more than half her male children would be psychotic before they reached adolescence." Eve continued with a stronger voice. "That's if she carries the gene set. I haven't had the opportunity to view these slides, but they should show that Elizabeth is the daughter of Ratac Bymarovitch, not Klav Bymarovitch."

Ratac squirmed. *This woman dares to say I'm insane. She would take away the daughter I sacrificed to win the election and make the world think I'm a cuckold! Elizabeth is not my daughter! I have nothing to fear. But if Elizabeth is really my daughter, then I killed her.* His head swam with confusion, and his ears buzzed from out-of-control blood pressure. His carefully memorized speeches evaporated.

"Well, I'll be—" Eve whistled. She flashed a third slide on the screen too fast for the young doctor to study it, then a fourth slide. She paused to get her thoughts together as much as for dramatic effect. "Elizabeth is not Ratac's daughter after all. Her DNA has no matches with the Butcher. You're right after all. The rumors of Ratac's syphilitic impotence and unfaithful wife must be true. Elizabeth must be someone else's daughter."

"STOP THIS!" Ratac shouted. His chessboard brain had been turned upside down. His head flushed hot with anger at the insult.

Ratac leaped toward Eve.

George pushed him away, knocking him off balance.

George couched to meet Ratac's next rush, but Ratac drew a gun. George backed up, shielding his wife.

Ratac swiveled to Colonel Jamison. "Your sidearm, sir."

The colonel reluctantly slid the pistol toward Ratac.

The guns seemed to calm Ratac. He regained his composure, but it was too late. Ratac called to his lone unarmed guard. "NOW!"

Ratac snarled at the camera crew. "Get off the floor and take your pictures of the new prime minister. *Bymarovitch!* I did not use a first name on the ballot. I was elected in a fair election, and my party won a majority. I have diplomatic immunity! And I have power! At this moment, six tanks and two armored personnel carriers from my personal army are surrounding this seat of power—*my* seat of power. And all of you are guests until the Croatian minister of justice comes to swear me in. Then, and only then, will I consider releasing you. But you Americans and British have my permission to remove your occupation forces from my country if you want to see your diplomats again."

*   *   *

NATO HEADQUARTERS, ZAGREB

General Bream bellowed from in front of the television set. "Get some assets up there! I want our drivers on the horn.

"Ferret *was* right!" Bream growled. "That fake politician finally blew! Bymarovitch *is* the Butcher! And he's holding a room full of VIPs as hostages with his rebel tanks on the way."

Bream had worked hard at destroying the heavy weapons of the Yugoslavian combatants, but he knew the balance sheet didn't add up. Compliance was hard to achieve among those whose trust had been a casualty of war. Tanks, artillery, and rocket-mounted truck beds were out there—somewhere in a country honeycombed with caves. If Ratac Bymarovitch said tanks were coming, the general believed it. "A lot of things could come unraveled today."

A usually unruffled captain stammered, "Two of our choppers are down for repairs—"

"How many can we put in the air?" the general interrupted.

"Uh, one, sir, but there's whiteout visibility here."

"Put it up!" the general roared and waved his arm upward, but then froze. "No, we can't afford to lose our strongest asset. The odds are bad. Even if we take out six tanks, the chopper could still take a hit. Put it up, but tell the whirly to stay low and out of range."

The captain nodded. "The Butcher could tank the hostages outta there, and with the snow covering their tracks, we wouldn't have the slightest idea where he took 'em."

The captain hesitated. "Since the election, most of our heavy assets are heading for Kosovo. Even if we got some firepower up there on time, we'd be outgunned."

A corporal shouted from his phone, "General, sir, there's a report that the Serbs are going ballistic over Ratac being alive and leading the country. They've already moved twenty heavy artillery pieces out of hiding. Maybe more. The same chatter is coming outta Bosnia."

A sergeant rushed a phone to the general, talking as he moved. "Sir, our drivers don't have a clue as to what's going on. They have side arms. Should they attempt a rescue?"

"Of course!" the general shouted then said, "As you were! No engagement! If this Butcher's as crazy as they say, there could be a blood bath of diplomats. No, tell the drivers to move out. Back to the city. Away from the tanks. The last thing we need is a firefight we can't win. It would embolden the hot heads on all sides to start shooting again."

The general dropped back to his chair, his eyes transfixed to the chaos on the television screen. "It's up to the people in that room. God help 'em."

* * *

THE HEARING ROOM

"Relax, my guests," Bymarovitch said calmly. "I'm sorry you had to see my burst of anger. But fact be known, I've wearied of my charade. The Klav I created for you was a weakling who would succumb to anything for peace. The Ratac I give you will do anything for peace, even if it means removing all who would stand in his way—my way.

"You're about to see history being made. When I'm prime minister, you'll see only one Yugoslavia, a much enlarged Yugoslavia. As Tito ruled with an iron hand, I will rule with—"

Colonel Jamison cut in, "Guests hell! You lunatic! You can't get—"

Bymarovitch's arm shot out and caught the colonel on the side of head. The colonel went down in heap. "If you don't want to be a guest, then you can be a prisoner of war!" Ratac screamed.

An aide went to the colonel's side, but the Butcher pointed his gun and snarled, "Leave him! He's not dead. If I had wanted him dead, his head would be rolling out the door."

Ratac turned back to George, the man who had dared to surprise him with a push. The American policeman would have to pay, but Frank had positioned himself in front of George. George stood against the wall in front of Eve.

Frank was not a physical challenge like George or Gil, but Frank Ferret had been the chess player on the opposite side of the board right from the beginning. Ferret had to be destroyed on their mutual

334

battlefield of wits and words. Still, the temptation to intimidate his adversary by aiming the muzzle of his pistol at Frank's nose was too much for Ratac to resist.

Frank had a chair between himself and Ratac. Frank's mind raced for a weapon. *The chair is too heavy to use as a club and too short to tip over on Ratac's gun hand.* Frank leaned closer to the gun muzzle in a surprise bravado. He told himself that if he saw Ratac's trigger finger twitch, he'd try to slap the gun. *One chance in a hundred of not gettin' my ear blown off.* And that was Frank's best expectation.

Frank noted that the television cameras were still glowing live with their red lights even though their cameramen were cowering against the wall. *At least my death will be evidence against this bastard—documented for history and played forever for journalism students that won't know where Croatia is on a map,* Frank thought.

Frank readied to stall his way out of impending death. Frank had stalled, conned, and deceived all his life, but seldom had the adversary been so smart, and the muzzle of the gun so close. "You outfoxed me, Mr. Prime Minister. I thought I had ya by the drain hairs, but you totally outsmarted me. But why in the hell did you have someone shoot Elizabeth? You probably would have won the election without her murder."

"Ha, you wouldn't believe me, but I didn't have Elizabeth shot. Someone tried to shoot me and hit Elizabeth instead."

"I know." Frank laughed. "I've known all along. Ya could say that I too have a confession to make, Mr. Prime Minister. I screwed up, big time! It was *my* sniper that brought down Elizabeth. You were never the target. You should be grateful to me. I gave you a winnin' ticket. You never would've won without me givin' you the sympathy vote."

"You fools, all of you," Ratac snarled. "It was *my* idea to shoot that daughter of a whore. Elizabeth didn't deserve to live. You just beat me to it."

"You don't know how relieved it makes us to know that *you* were also plannin' to pop your daughter," Frank crooned. "We figured that if we didn't shoot her, *you* would. And you *would have*! You just told us and the world that you'd have blown the head off the woman you thought was your daughter! Just to win a damn election?"

Ratac stiffened his arms as he prepared to shoot.

Ferret laughed. "Want to hear a great story, Rat? Lizzie's still alive! She's in bad shape 'cause of the fall, but we had Lizzie's best friend, Debbie, do a sharpshooter number on her with a rubber bullet. Knocked her off the stairs. We were ready. A bunch of concerned students dressed up as ambulance attendants, and they picked her up before you knew what was goin' on or cared what was goin' on. Her granddad provided a safe house for us until we could sneak her out of the country. You were too busy deliverin' your winnin' leader-of-the-land lies to insist on opening the closed casket at the funeral home. Yep, we unintentionally handed you the election . . . but we *didn't* give you diplomatic immunity. Elizabeth will be at your trial—on our side."

Hancock edged toward Ratac and said, "You've been talkin' way too much, Mr. Bymarovitch. Put away the gun. Don't worry about a trial. I'll get you off. Just stop talking! There are voters watching you, and they are gonna think you're crazy."

Ratac slapped Hancock with his gun barrel, and the white-haired lawyer fell hard to his knees.

Debbie made her move. With an overhand throw, she threw a floral center piece down on Ratac's gun hand. The gun discharged—the bullet grazing Hancock's thigh. Ratac held on to the gun, but just barely. He struggled to resume his grip.

Gil vaulted the table—knocking the gun out of Ratac's hand with a sweeping roundhouse kick.

Jamison's aide charged Bymarovitch, only to meet an explosive fist to the chest. The aide fell, gasping for air.

Gil grabbed Ratac from behind. From the corner of his eye, Gil saw Ratac's two door guards rushing forward, one with a large knife, and the other 'unarmed' guard with a miniature single-shot handgun. Pushing off Ratac, Gil's legs elevated and kicked the knife wielding guard in the face, knocking him unconscious.

The gun carrying guard took aim, but George tackled him, pushing his arm up, and discharging the bullet into the ceiling. The shot sent the crouching diplomats squirming to the floor. They were already deafened from the first gun shot and gagging from the smell of gunpowder and fear of certain death.

The distraction of George's tackle caused Gill to loosen his grip, and Ratac flipped Gil over his head. Gil landed hard, but managed to stay on his feet. Ratac leaped forward with a jump kick. Gil grabbed the thrusting leg. Gil accelerated Ratac's momentum, tossing him toward the French doors. The window door gave way to the hurtling weight of the man. Crashing glass shards scattered over the balcony. Ratac bounded up from blood-spattered snow. If he was in pain from crashing through the glass doors, he showed no sign of it. Emboldened cameramen trampled over the broken glass to keep the combatants in focus.

The two adversaries circled each other. Both men discarded their jackets. Gil looked calm. "It's over, Ratac! One of your guards is out cold, and George King is sitting on the other. You don't have a weapon or anyone to help you." Gil wasn't sure that Ratac was weaponless, and he wasn't sure the powerful man could be subdued. The slippery crust of snow made karate kicks less of an option. Gil's superior speed and flexibility were no longer an advantage. A toe-to-toe punching match was most likely, and both men had powerful arms capable of instant death.

"Give it up, Butcher. You can't make it down the stairs without fighting through a room full of angry diplomats who will beat you to death with their obsolete We Love Klav signs."

The Butcher looked over his shoulder. The only safe way to escape the roof balcony was a tall trellis, covered with a thick, dormant Wisteria vine. Ratac could easily climb down if sufficiently outnumbered, which he was. Ratac had a snarl on his lip and blood trickling from his knee. He laughed viciously. "Thank you for showing me the way out, Rocklin."

Gil heard the low growl of approaching tanks. The Croatian tanks would provide Bymarovitch protection and escape if he could reach them. If Ratac didn't escape, his soldiers would surely attempt an attack on the villa to free him. The persons in the villa couldn't possibly defend or escape such an attack.

Gil stopped circling to plant himself between Ratac and the trellis. "The easy way would be to let you escape, but I think we're safer here with you as our prisoner. So you'll have to get through me first, Butcher."

Frank and George moved in to help Gil. Frank held a photographer's light on a long metal pole, hoping to smack the cornered murderer.

"Stay back," Gil warned. "He could take that pole away from you, and that would put me at a disadvantage." Frank and George stopped. Both men had seen what the Butcher could do with one punch and decided to stay back. If Gil could get Ratac down, they would rush him.

There was no doubt that Gil and Ratac were two evenly matched foes. One carefully placed blow could end the fight and end a life.

Gil felt confident that he could outfight Ratac, but he knew a lucky blow from the Butcher could leave his friends defenseless and vulnerable. *Would Ratac have his tanks fire into his own house?* Gil asked himself. Debbie and the rest of Gil's friends could be killed.

"I'll make you a deal, Butcher. Move all the tanks except one, and I'll let you go." Gil planned to have everyone scatter into the wooded area.

Ratac's tank might track down a few of the people from the house, but most would be able to escape.

"*Never!* I'm going to kill you, Rocklin, then my tanks will level the house with all of you in it. But you die first."

"So be it," Gil said, "but when you see my hit coming, I want you to think of all the innocent people you've killed. Think of the children you've frightened and know the meaning of fear."

"You foolish boy," Ratac snapped. "I'll punch your ribs through your heart." Ratac delivered three powerful blows in rapid succession that Gil deflected. Gil dodged another Ratac punch that shattered a flowerless clay pot.

Gil countered with straight punches to Ratac's left shoulder and chest. Ratac had padding under his clothes as part of his disguise. The padding slowed Ratac's movements, but only slightly, and it absorbed some, but not all, of Gil's punches. Ratac winced and coughed blood, but stood his ground. Ratac edged toward the broken pottery, grabbed a handful of frozen dirt, and threw it at Gil. Gil moved quickly to avoid dirt in his eyes, but he slipped.

"You die!" Ratac screamed. As he started to pounce on Gil, Frank slipped a large loop of extension cord over the Butcher and pulled. Ratac fell to one knee cursing, but quickly slipped under the cord. Both men rose to resume fighting. Gil landed two hard punches that knocked Ratac across the balcony. Ratac's left arm appeared limp with pain. The Butcher sensed he would lose to the younger man and concentrated on one last effort. With a large glass shard held like a knife, Ratac charged.

A shot boomed.

Ratac somersaulted, clutching his foot.

Debbie stood with Jamison's gun.

Gil scowled. "Whaddja do that for? I had him."

Debbie smiled sweetly. "Yes, dear. I'll tell all your friends how you had him. But humor me, will you? We Rocklins don't take chances."

The diplomats' cheers masked the growl of the closely approaching tanks. From the veil of snow the shadows of the tanks appeared. Eight rebel tanks circled the house—two tanks on each side. The personnel carriers stayed further back under the falling shroud of snow. One tank could easily destroy the house and everyone in it. The occupants of the TV satellite trucks had left their trucks abandoned, but still running. They had fled with the limousine drivers.

* * *

100 YARDS FROM THE VILLA

Commandant Marcus Turner was not a tank commander. He had been a British commando until he was dishonorably discharged for his neo-fascist activities. Ratac provided Turner and his assigned ex-IRA terrorist wife a new chance at wealth, power, and random revenge. Now Turner was getting a chance to earn his keep. Turner knew his troops disliked his Britishness and lack of their language. He suspected that Ratac would dump him when the madman didn't need him anymore. If Turner was to survive, he needed to make a bold move. He hollered to his translator, and tanks stopped in their full circle of the house. Turner pointed to the second floor windows, and the gunman tilted the huge artillery barrel in that direction. Turner popped his head from the turret. He hated the claustrophobic and oily tank interior. He hoped he didn't have to blow up the villa; Turner liked to see whom he killed. On his bullhorn, he ordered, "Give us our prime minister!"

The last sounds of celebration in the Bymarovitch mansion came to an abrupt halt.

CHAPTER 25

The Seige

Chip Shumaker hollered for his mother to turn on the television. "Mom, the man that called me from Croatia—the man with my Breakneck Download. He's about to get killed."

Around the world and on prime time in the United States, television producers rushed to cut into regular broadcasts and run tapes of the fight. Editors silently, and not so silently, cursed their on-the-ground reporters who had missed this deception. Those who had dismissed Ferret as an out-of-control wild man to their bosses now feared for their jobs.

From the villa, Curt Campbell reminded his listeners that he was the only one who gave airtime to his "lifelong friend" Frank. His delivery lacked conviction as his voice shook with fear, and he rued his decision to go in front of the camera. When the rattling roar of the tanks came through the broken window, Curt was one of the first to desert his spot in front of the camera. Like the other journalists, he didn't take time to sign off.

The press and diplomats scrambled to the wine cellar, where they found automatic weapons outnumbering the dusty wine bottles. The contingent could not fight off an attack from the tanks without at least a rocket launcher. The six-member tramper team and Ingrid remained on the second floor. They quickly decided that safety from the menacing tanks depended on holding Ratac.

Gil carried Ratac into the library where he couldn't shout commands to his army. Ratac whimpered over his wounds. Gil's blows had cracked a rib, dislocated a shoulder, and had broken a forearm on the Butcher. His bullet wound in his foot was loosely wrapped with a blood-soaked chair cover. He saw Eve bandaging his lawyer and said, "Dr. King, give me something for the pain."

Eve stared at him blankly.

"Please," he moaned.

Eve turned her back. "Fuck you, Butcher!" George gave her a kiss.

Three military men returned from the wine cellar, each with two AK-47s. Gil met them, and one handed him a weapon. "And what do you expect to do with the muskets?" Gil asked.

"Help us barricade the doors, sir."

Gil shook his head in disgust. "Are you going to barricade the walls too? 'Cause if you fire one shot, here's what they'll do. The tank will crawl up the walls and knock 'em down. Sure, this is Ratac's villa, but do you think he cares about real estate values?"

Frank joined in. "Those are Ruskie T-72 Dolly Partons out there—reinforced armor up front. There's nothin' in our pantry that will scratch their paint. Plus, they're mounted with smoke grenade launchers."

The military men, more accustomed to shmoozing at diplomatic cocktail parties than to handling weapons, suddenly lost their bravado. Gil seized on their uncertainty. "Back to the wine cellar!" he ordered. "If you stay up here, all you'll do is draw these fanatics' fire. Your big shots are wetting their diplomatic sashes down there. Go hold their hands before one of them has a heart attack. Once the Butcher's mercenaries retrieve their hero, they might not take the time to hunt you down. *Move it!*"

As the men hurried down the stairs, George followed them to get more rifles and lock the VIPs in the large wine cellar. Perhaps the tank soldiers wouldn't look for them, but the chance was remote. The steps to the wine cellar were steep, but sturdy. Only two light bulbs illuminated the cold, tomb-like cellar. One wall held aged wine barrels, some empty. Five floor-to-ceiling, wooden wine racks filled the room. The center of the room held two crates with SPLIT stenciled on their sides. One crate contained pistols, and the other held automatic rifles and magazine clips. The George snatched three more automatic rifles from the open crate.

With his traffic cop voice George ordered the military men into position behind wine barrels. "Don't shoot if someone comes down the stairs. Wait till several of them are down here, and you can catch the bastards by surprise. That way you won't shoot me if I come back down for more ammo.

"Press people and diplomats, don't touch the weapons. You're more likely to shoot each other. I want you in the back row and crouched on the floor. Automatic weapons tend to leap and shoot high."

George led the unarmed persons to the rack furthest from the door. The barricade would help reduce panic and give some of the less knowledgeable a false sense of security. The bullets would easily penetrate the wooden shelves, but the panicky diplomats didn't need to know that. George spotted a rack of wine bottles against the wall that wasn't dusty. *Recent additions,* he assumed, pulling one out with his free hand, hoping to find the needed rocket launcher. Hidden behind the bottles were canvas bags piled in a pyramid shape. He grabbed the smallest of the bags and was surprised that he could barely lift it. *If only the bag contained hand grenades,* he wished, but knew they didn't. Back on the first floor, George cut open the heavy bag and peeked at its contents. He whistled at the shiny coins. "A hell of a lot of good you are," he said to the bag.

Back in the grand room, Gil called to the women. "I want you ladies down in the wine cellar with the others."

Debbie shook her head. "You think Ratac will kill all the men and forget about us? There's no chance. I shot him. Eve humiliated him. He's not going away until he rolls a grenade down the cellar steps."

If you're lucky, Frank thought.

"Hide in the upstairs closets then," George suggested. He knew the cellar would attract attention first.

"And let the people in the wine cellar be decoys? I won't do that," Debbie said.

"Nor would I," Eve snapped.

Frank shrugged. "It's an even chance. The VIPs act as decoys for you. You act as decoys for them. But if you must know, it won't make any difference. Even if we make sure Ratac is unconscious, his troops probably already have their orders. If they don't find the same people they saw on television, they'll scour every inch of this place for us."

Gil said, "Maybe. But what if they *didn't* see us on television? Tanks don't exactly have CNN on cable. Maybe the women can hide."

Frank brushed aside Gil's attempt at finding hope. Wherever the tanks had come from, they were sure to have been monitoring the events at the hearing. "The only way our heads are gonna get outta this scalpin' is for the cavalry to ride over the hill. We need some friendly fire, fast."

Virginia said, "We have cell phones, but whom do we call?"

Frank saw red lights on one television camera tilted at the floor. "The power's still on." He found the sound switch. "Aim the camera, Gil."

Frank pulled Ing in front of the camera. "Give me a hug, Ing! You always have higher viewer ratings than I do."

Frank held Ingrid with one arm and spoke into the live television camera. "If there are any UN divisions in the neighborhood, we sure all would appreciate you folks stopping by. There'll be wine for everyone—on Ratac Bymarovitch, "the Butcher." The wanted war criminal who would've duped the world—who impersonated his brother to avoid imprisonment—who would have shot his own daughter to win an election—who would've held the UN's election commission as hostages. Well, if any one in the eight tanks that are surrounding this death trap are listening, Ratac is our hostage. If you want him, you have to deal. If—"

The red lights on the cameras suddenly blinked off. George pointed to the monitor. "Look, it's Turner! With a helmet, camouflage duds, and the works."

Turner spoke from the satellite van, now sheltered behind a tank. He was about to get his fifteen minutes of fame, and he was charged with importance. While a renegade soldier held a small television camera, Turner spoke. "This is Commandant Marcus Turner. I have come to rescue our party's prime minister from the interference of a world conspiracy. You have two minutes to bring our leader out here, or we begin shelling. If we have to enter the house, no one survives. Give me your answer now!"

Debbie whispered from the window, "They won't shell us."

"How do you know that?" Virginia gasped.

"'Cause their soldiers are sneaking up in the bushes," Debbie finished.

Gil added, "They can't shell us without the chance of killing Ratac."

"The SOP for rushing a hostage situation is tear gas and lots of firepower," George said. "Don't underestimate tear gas. It's hard to shoot at anything when your eyes are burning out of your head."

The camera came back to life, and Ferret spoke firmly into the lens, "Turner, do yourself a favor and slither back under your rock. You're through! The Butcher's political base has just vanished. He was elected because of sympathy for his dead daughter. Ratac *planned* to have her shot for that sympathy vote. *His own daughter!* So where are his advocates now? Maybe the UN would've cut him some slack if Ratac had overwhelming support, but the fine folks of Croatia have been betrayed. Do you think they'll give you and the other Butcher's soldiers swill and shelter? They'll turn your tails into the UN in a tenth of a second."

Debbie appeared on camera long enough to say, "The rebel soldiers are at the back door."

She looked at the camera, "Mom, Dad, all my bothers, and Amy. I want you to know we went down fighting."

Watching the monitor snap to gray, George said, "Turner pulled our plug. He doesn't want tape of his killing us."

* * *

In Atlanta, the news announcer cut in. "We seem to have lost our live transmission from Croatia. To review: reporters Frank Ferret; Ingrid Carlsen, from Reuters; and a group of their friends proved to the UN's Election Oversight Commission that Klav Bymarovitch, the recently elected prime minister of Croatia, is an imposter. The man elected is really his look-alike brother, Ratac Bymarovitch, one of the butchers of the Balkans, an indicted war criminal, accused of involvement in Operation Storm—which, according to Amnesty International, displaced three hundred thousand Croatian Serbs—and of committing other murderous atrocities against thousands of civilians.

"Those of you watching our live transmission saw several persons injured by the Butcher as he took the entire Commission hostage. Then Dr. Gil Rocklin, the president of a children's software company near Denver, Colorado, engaged the Butcher in hand-to-hand combat, until New Zealand tour director, Debra McWard, Dr. Rocklin's fiancée, shot the Butcher in the foot. All this right here, *live!*

"Rocklin disarmed the Butcher, but unfortunately, the Butcher has already called in eight tanks. The Butcher's troops are now storming the house where the Commission and U.S. Assistant Secretary of State, Allison Quail, are holding out. I repeat: we have lost live transmission. We will return if anything more develops. But as of now, it looks like some fine American, British, and French diplomats, world press, UN soldiers, and innocent citizens are being attacked at this moment. We can only pray for their survival."

The studio switched to a background tape on the election and Elizabeth's apparent assassination. Nothing else would be broadcast on the news channels but the *crisis in Croatia*.

A slender woman producer who had once dated Frank rushed out of the control booth for someone to embrace. Tears ran down her face.

The announcer gave her a comforting shoulder. "I didn't know you still cared so much about Ferret."

The woman caught her breath between sobs. "That son of a bitch will be remembered as the man who won his third Pulitzer—posthumously. And I'll be remembered as the flake who fired him!"

* * *

George looked through Frank's small, but powerful, binoculars. "Turner's in the lead tank! He's stopped. No one's moving. Is that good or bad?"

Frank murmured, "Maybe the troops are confused."

"But they're not going anywhere," Virginia noted.

They waited for the attack.

Gil and Debbie held each other. Gil said, "We almost had it, Deb. A perfect life. The reward money would've allowed me to avoid bankruptcy and would've given us a fresh start."

Frank held his rifle gingerly. "You would have still gone bankrupt, Gil. It would've taken six months for the bureaucrats to process the check."

"Now you tell me," Gil swallowed. There was no point in being angry at Frank's deception.

George cleared his throat for attention. "When I was down in the cellar, the VIPs were trying to figure which end of the rifle the bullet comes out. They were too busy to notice this. He reached into the bag and pulled out a handful of gold coins.

Eve laughed. "Gee, we'll be the richest corpses in the graveyard. Still think money is important?"

"Not likely we can use it for a bribe," Frank said. "And if they know we have the chips, they'll come after the rest of them no matter what happens to the Butcher."

Virginia shouted, "*Movement!* Frank's pep talk must have swayed Turner. The mercenary's splitting! But the other tanks aren't budging. Too bad Frank doesn't speak better Croatian."

Ingrid nodded. "I was thinking the same thing. All of this was in English. So the troops probably have no idea what went on here." She hesitated. "I speak a little Croatian." Ing looked at the three other women in the room. Of all the full chests, Virginia had a cup size advantage. "Virginia, come with me, and start taking off your blouse."

"You expect me to screw the invading army? I'm good, but not that good."

Ingrid's skirt hit the floor. "Help me off with my blouse, Frank, these bandages are awkward. Then go hide."

"I hope you know what you're doin', darlin'," he said soberly.

"What's she doing?" Debbie asked.

Frank answered. "Ing once told me that the secret to her survival on the battlefield was that soldiers never shoot a naked lady."

"Will it work?"

Frank hesitated then nodded. "You, don't know Ing. It'll work. She'll give my same speech in Croatian and say that the UN attack choppers are whirlin' round waitin' for the weather to clear. The solders will spend a few minutes droolin' over her body then they'll hightail it back to wherever they had their tanks stashed."

"You really believe Ing and Virginia can pull it off?"

"Yeah." Frank sighed.

"If you think we're going to come out of this," Debbie asked, "why do you look so glum?"

Frank banged his head against a dead television camera. "'Cause I won't get in on tape, damnit!"

*   *   *

Turner urged his driver to move faster—back to the hulking caves where the tank and other ordinance would be hidden. A volley of smoke grenades fired in front of the tank's path mixed with the whiteout snow and made perfect cloud under which to hide. But first, they had to reach the smoke cloud.

The other armed vehicles could fend for themselves. The tank occupants waited in confusion in the proper military manner, but whether they attacked the villa or were attacked, they would provide cover for his escape.

Turner cursed. This assignment had turned out badly. Time to return the tank to its hiding place, flee the country, and spend his up-front money.

The gunman at his 12.7 mm. antiaircraft machine gun heard the flapping of the chopper's rotors before he saw the Apache attack helicopter. The turret man jabbered in Croatian and pointed upward.

Turner saw the turret man aim the antiaircraft machine gun. "No! Don't shoot!" Turner screamed at the Croatian gunner as the tank entered the smoke cloud.

The gunner fired a noisy burst in the direction of the chopper.

The Apache answered with a heat-seeking missile. The tank's explosion left a hole in the ground that burned for twelve hours.

Norm Aspen

*   *   *

As soon as the second tank turned tail, the other mercenaries followed. Whether Ing's nude speech swayed them to the side of good and righteousness or whether the loss of their commander spurred the retreat, no one would know for sure. But to the Frank and the trampers, Ing and Virginia were their saviors.

It was hug time in the villa. Frank waited for the chilled ladies to dress and comb their hair before resetting the televisions and purposely waiting to tell the frightened group in the wine cellar that the "coast is all clear." "Icing the adversaries makes them more appreciative," Frank said.

Allison Quill left the cellar first. Her smile conveyed she was glad to be alive, but—

She murmured something about dodging one firing squad only to face another one from President Palmer.

But a diplomat is always a diplomat, so Allison gave Frank an on camera kiss. Nearing sixty, Quill was still a spicy lady, and Ingrid kept a possessive grip on one of Frank's arms. "How did you miracle workers do it?"

"You don't want to know," Ingrid said. "You'll have to read Frank's book and watch *our* TV special to find out."

Frank grinned at the dismayed diplomat then looked into the hot camera and said, "Assistant Secretary of State, Allison Quill, was the lynch pin behind bringing Bymarovitch down. She knew that a heavy-handed arrest of the Butcher would cause civic and military unrest. She advised us to let Bymarovitch bring himself down. Ratac's crazy enough that sooner or later, we knew we'd hit his hot button and he'd blow. He blew! Thanks, Allison. You're one brave diplomat."

Ingrid took over the spotlight while Frank walked an astonished Allison out of camera range. Allison gulped, "I didn't expect that, Frank. Thank you. You saved my life twice, today. If you want my body, you can have it."

"Gee, thanks," Frank said, rakishly running his fingers through his hair, "but Ing might not like it." His grin was mischievous. "I'll settle for a few phone calls."

"Name it."

"You used to work for the Justice Department?"

"You want some New Zealand parking tickets torn up?" Quill concluded with a sarcastic laugh.

"Uh, I'll send you a list," Frank said with a smile.

On the other side of the room, Ingrid turned the television cameras back to their confused owners. Ing had a better sense of overexposure than Frank. Rod Brickle, Curt Campbell, and the other reporters still seemed rattled from hiding in the cellar, and the contrast between their fumbled questions and the cool answers of the Ferret team made the team look even more heroic. Each network began by interviewing Eve and George.

Ingrid rejoined Frank, who was giving Quill a bye-for-now kiss. Frank was grinning widely. "It'll be nice to visit New Zealand, again . . . and Mexico . . . and California . . . ."

His happiness waned as he saw his excited rivals in the press switch their interviews from George to photogenic Virginia. "We're not gettin' a dime out of this."

Ingrid replaced her cell phone and cocked her head like a dime didn't matter. "We don't need it, Frank. My father is so ecstatic that I'm alive and not going to cover any more wars, he told me he'll restore my allowance."

"Geez, Ing. An allowance? At your age? Damnit, I don't want to interfere with your family, but you're making a good living. So am I, although the bullion comes in bursts. Your papa's trying to control you with loose change."

"You think so?"

"I know so! My stepfather's a corrupt, millionaire televangelist. You don't see me juggling his collection plates so I can catch a few fallin' dollars."

Ingrid frowned. *Even with a frown, Ing looks beautiful,* Frank thought.

"It's not just a *few* dollars, Frank." Ingrid sighed. "You know that my father owns half of downtown Stockholm, don't you? Then there's the Jorg Carlsen cruise ship line. I usually don't mention it."

Frank bit air, but he was never accused of being speechless for long. "Of course I knew that," Frank coughed. "Like I said, things like that don't matter to me. And I don't want to interfere with your side of the family. So if it makes Papa smile to stuff our cookie jar with krona, whom am I to fool with his fun? Do you think he might pop for three hundred thou to shore up a psychiatric hospital in Sarajevo?"

"I think I know the one you have in mind, Frank. It's an excellent idea. I'm sure Papa can even do better than that."

Frank's grin grew wider. "That's supersensational, Ing." He kissed her and walked back into the range of the television cameras. He elbowed Gil and Debbie off center stage. "Everyone's asking me what I intend to do with the two-million-dollar reward. I'm only interested in journalistic truth and justice. I didn't capture the Butcher because of a reward. That would be crass bounty hunting. I never wanted the reward. Neither does Dr. Rocklin, lovely Debra McWard, the brave King family, heroic Virginia Slater, or my wife-to-be, Ingrid Carlson. But I *am* going to file a claim for the reward."

In an aside to a technician, Frank ordered, "Roll the tape I gave you, earlier."

Frank smiled as Amy and Martin mugged for Rose's video. "I'm recommending that the reward go to these two young people who proved to us, beyond a shade of doubt, that the man calling himself Klav was really the Butcher. The darlin' little kids were kidnapped by the Butcher so that we wouldn't blow a whistle on 'im. But these resourceful young Americans escaped."

Curt Campbell felt it was time his voice was heard. "With the assistance of Elizabeth Bymarovitch," the announcer recalled.

"Right. Elizabeth pretended to go along with the Butcher to protect the children. But it also helped that Amy Rocklin was taught self-defense techniques by her father and that Martin King, a nine-year-old, smacked his kidnapper with a chair. The kids tobogganed down to Zagreb in a cardboard box, but once there, no one would help them. They avoided the security police who were on the Butcher's payroll. They were cold. They were hungry. And no one in sight spoke English."

"Did they have any idea where they were?" Rod Brickle read questions from the back of a business card that Frank had given him.

"A rip-roarin' question, Rod! The Butcher was passing himself off as a Frenchman, so the kids logically thought they were in France. Little Amy Rocklin knew French from the French language software that her father designs for school kids. Amy took the tip money she made from playing Chopin in a hotel lobby and asked for a chocolate crepe—in French. *Crepe du chocolat, s'il vous plait.* Ingrid Carlsen heard of the French-speaking children, heard their story, and realized their danger. Ingrid completed their escape. Ingrid was shot in the process. Debbie McWard was also shot, but not seriously. Virginia Slater and George and Eve King helped with the rescue. All these folks who helped me are heroes and heroines, but the two kids deserve a world's thanks, praise . . . *and the reward.*"

"Frank, that's very generous of you," Campbell said, not believing what he was hearing. "But going back to Gil Rocklin's software company. Isn't that the one that had a virus?"

"No virus. Never was a virus. Dr. Rocklin was a top computer security honcho for the FBI. If anyone knows how to disinfect viruses, it's Gil.

"I don't know what rattlesnake started that rash rumor, but some unnamed sources say it's the way for a large, hungry serpent of a software company to swallow up a sparrow for next to nothin'."

*　　*　　*

THE CROATIAN PARLIAMENT BUILDING—TWO DAYS LATER

Allison Quill reluctantly entered the Parliament Building for the Sabor's, the Croatian congress, swearing in of Mrs. Dbrogrb as the new prime minister. The winning Justice Party was in shambles and couldn't agree on a substitute candidate. Ratac Bymarovitch, their imposter leader and candidate, was now universally discredited and in jail. The individual future of party representatives looked bleak. All they could hope for was some key posts in the cabinet, and Mrs. Dbrogrb provided the over- and under-the-table incentives and hard-line leadership they craved, now that their leader was gone.

Allison sat in a row reserved for foreign VIPs and looked around to see if Frank was among the journalists. *Oh, to be ten or twenty years younger! Could I drive that man crazy! But he's such a bastard!*

By bringing down Ratac, Frank had stuck Allison with Mrs. Dbrogrb as the new prime minister. The vitriolic, runner-up candidate had increased her venom lest she look weak compared to Ratac. *Damned, Ferret! He left me with a mess.*

As the dignitaries and press took their chairs, a bustling from the rear caught her attention. Frank's laugh could be heard. Frank and Ingrid moved to the front of the hall. They had their own independent, his-and-her crew of four television cameras and . . . Ratac Bymarovitch! No, it wasn't Ratac. This man had a sun-weathered face. He looked heavier, and his smile seemed sincere. A young man pushed Klav Bymarovitch in a wheelchair.

354

Ferret held up his arms and shouted, "Let me introduce the *real* Klav Bymarovitch.

"Prime Minister-elect of Croatia," Ingrid added.

While the meager press crew tried to gather around Klav, the determined man left his wheelchair and pushed his way to the front of the room.

Klav addressed the officials at the front dais. "I am Klav Bymarovitch. If my party will have me, I am here to be sworn in as prime minister."

The buzz from the onlookers became a roar. Prime Minister-in-waiting, Dbrogrb, stood, and shook her fist—a most unfeminine and unpresidential act.

The temporary chairperson gaveled the crowd and spoke for the stunned officials. "I'm afraid there's much we don't understand."

"Then let me explain," Klav began. "When I heard my daughter was shot, I flew here as quickly as I could. To my joy, I find that Elizabeth, my beloved adopted daughter, is recovering in Austria. She was forced to cooperate with my brother to protect two kidnapped children. She apologizes for the deception. And she has no permanent injuries or memory loss from being shot. I will go to her again immediately after this meeting.

"But first, I claim the leadership of the Justice Party and my prime ministry to which I was elected."

The officials jabbered in confusion.

Klav continued. "My brother has done great damage to our great country and to the human race. He has disgraced our nation and my family name. I intend to act as interim president—without pay—for no more than one year or until another election, with true candidates, can be held. During that time, I will devote my energies to healing the wounds among those who used to be our neighbors."

Klav looked at Frank and Ingrid. "While you deliberate over what I have said and before I repeat it in Croatian, Serbian, and Dalmatian, I wish to thank my friends Frank Ferret, Ingrid Carlson, and their friends for saving my daughter and bringing me here to fulfill my duties."

The Sabor's members filled the hall with shouts of triumph and protest, while the press threw up their hands in defeat. Frank and Ing had scooped their colleagues again by creating chaos and making the news.

Bymarovitch's party members no longer needed bribes from Dbrogrb's party to cooperate. The hard-liners could no longer call the shots, and if the articulate outsider, Klav, was speaking a peace agenda, so what? At least they'd have a job come next election.

Allison Quill smiled at Frank and called him over to whisper, "When I run for the Oval Office, would you like to be my campaign manager, Frank? And my press spinning secretary when I'm elected? I'll need a veteran liar with a straight face."

Frank grinned. "Why thank ya, darlin', but I was thinkin' 'bout a more challenging job like Chief of Frickin' Protocol."

*   *   *

PLESO AIRPORT, ZAGREB

The ex-trampers waited for the plane to take them to New York and from there to their homes. Frank and Ingrid were headed to Stockholm "to meet the family." Gathering at the gate, the euphoric friends felt sad at parting.

Warnings from the UN officials that Bymarovitch would send his friends to retaliate against them were dismissed by Frank with a casual "Don't fret the assassins, I've been workin' on it."

"I guess this is good-bye," Debbie said to Frank. She gave him a more than friendly kiss. "Wow, if I'd had known you were such a good kisser . . . ," she whispered.

"I tried to tell ya," Frank grinned.

"And you'll probably tell me that the two of us were meant for each other. Two kindred souls living on the edge."

Frank scratched his forehead, "You wait 'til now to tell me you're interested. Damnit, Debbie, I'm an engaged man."

"Pooh, the only thing that holds you and Ing together is sex," Debbie scoffed.

"That's not true, darlin'. There are other things. I just can't concentrate on 'em when you mention that first stuff.

"You got yourself a great man, Deb. Stick with him." Frank hurried away from Debbie, muttering, "'Tis a far, far better thing I do."

Debbie turned to Virginia and handed her a wad of Croatian money. "Did you hear all that, Ginnie? You win the bet—about ten dollars. I thought for sure I could show you what a scum ball Frank is."

Virginia smiled. "You did better than that. If Frank turned *you* down, then I don't feel like such a loser. Eventually, my tattered self-concept may start to mend."

Virginia watched Frank pulling Ingrid off Gil with Clutch looking left out. "Oh, I'm nuts about that man!"

"Which one?" Eve laughed.

"Any one of them," Virginia replied.

Gil shook hands with Frank, and they whispered concerns that the women couldn't hear.

Gil knew the threats of Bymarovitch's retaliation could not be taken lightly, but there wasn't much he could do about it. No sense in worrying Debbie. Certainly the danger would be less in the States, and if not, there was always the Federal Witness Protection Program. Losing one's identity, career, friends, and relatives would be a small price to pay to keep Debbie and Amy safe.

Until that unwelcome time came, Gil would try to save his company. Debbie deserved a comfortable life. He checked his watch to calculate the time in Illinois, recited a memorized phone number, and looked for a telephone.

*   *   *

STOCKHOLM, SWEDEN

Ingrid dropped her head on the pillow in exhaustion. Frank knew Ing's arm hurt. "You never complain."

"Why should I?" she said. "I'm so deliriously happy. I'm only sorry I don't have the strength to give you a warmer welcome back."

Frank's brow furrowed. "Ing, it's almost dawn. If I get any warmer of a welcomin', I won't be able to walk."

"Oh! You're just fishing for a compliment—which you justly deserve. And speaking of warm welcomes, my parents actually like you."

"Don't sound so surprised." Frank chuckled.

"In fact, they are so ecstatic that I'm finally getting married that they're doubling my allowance and giving us their cottage by the sea as a wedding present."

"I like cottages." Frank sighed. "A nice small place that's low maintenance."

"Twenty-one rooms," Ingrid clucked.

Frank waited a few seconds before asking, "Why do we need twenty-one rooms?"

"In the summer our relatives and friends come to visit and visit and visit. Do you like parties?"

"I've crashed enough of 'em."

"Well, in the spring, Mama gives parties at the cottage. I suppose I'll be expected to keep up the tradition."

"What kind of parties?" Frank asked with apprehension.

"Mostly fund-raisers for the opera. Do you like opera?"

"Does a poor runaway boy from the jazzy streets of N'walins dig opera? Surprisingly, yes. I usually watch from the wings while I aspire for the aspiring divas. Or, I might bluff my way on to the stage as a spear carrier. In short, I love to watch opera, but *not* the fashion show snorin' in the first ten rows."

"First thirty rows," Ingrid corrected. "Our family always has third row center."

"Ugh! Doesn't matter." Frank shrugged. "If you want me to smooze with your mama's cronies, I'll oblige."

"We don't have to stay in Stockholm long," Ingrid offered. "We don't have to stay in Stockholm at all. I thought you'd need a month or two to finish your book."

"*The Killer and the Kiwi* will be done in a week or two," Frank stated flatly. "I was writing it as it was happening. I got caught up while I was in jail."

"How did you get a computer in jail?"

How do you tell your fiancée that you cheat at cards? Frank thought. "I told the jailers that it was the only way I could write a confession."

Ingrid didn't believe him, but it didn't bother her. And as for a book in two weeks—Frank was always the first to file his dispatches. He was fast. "Then you don't need a few months sitting by the keyboard?"

"Nope, we leave a week from Monday. I rented a three-room hut on Tahiti for our honeymoon. No computers, no cameras, no interruptions."

"No big wedding, either. You could have asked me," Ing said.

"I wanted to surprise you." Frank kissed Ing between her breasts. "Darn ol' Debbie said the only substance to our relationship is sex."

"Isn't it wonderful!" Ing giggled. Then she turned serious. "Debbie accused me of the same thing. I suppose she thought she was being helpful, but I resented it. It's none of her business how we spend all our waking hours."

"Yeah!"

Ingrid let out a deep breath. "I read where there's a new war breaking out in West Africa."

"Buried on page forty-two, no doubt."

"Yes, *right* on page forty-two. Only two column inches. It's the same old story. People don't want to hear about it."

"Same ol' corrupt government, ethnic hate hustlers, ruthless revolutionaries, greedy arms pushers, and Western policies written in colonial days," Frank snapped knowingly.

"Some young cubs are down there trying to tell the story," Ing clucked. "Hungry do-gooders from Oz."

"The mates will get their bloody arses shot off," Frank clucked.

"True."

"Then maybe the big powers will pay attention."

"Doubt it. And it's a hundred ten degrees down there," Ing snorted.

"A hundred twenty with a malaria fever chaser," Frank added. "They'll wither."

Frank stroked Ing's good arm. "When do you get your bandages off?"

"Ten days."

"Oh. Just as well. I thought we might hop down on our way to our honeymoon hut."

"Africa's not on the way to Tahiti," Ingrid growled.

"Just as well."

Ing ran her tongue over Frank's ear. "I found your Tahiti tickets in your jacket."

"So much for my surprise," Frank groused.

"And the clipping from page 42," she added.

"Oh," Frank said awkwardly.

"We leave for Africa next Wednesday," Ingrid announced.

Frank grinned so hard it hurt. Frank carefully slid his body over Ing— careful not to touch her arm. "Let's see if we can find an air-conditioned hotel down there."

CHAPTER 26

Hard and Soft Landings

Ratac smirked with glee when Pervich, his former aide, sat across the wooden table in the windowless visitors' room.

The cautious prison guard took Ratac's crutch away. He had been warned that the infamous prisoner could use it as a weapon. The entire prison staff wanted their controversial prisoner transferred to The Hague as soon as possible. No inmate in his memory demanded this level of security. But even a man charged with crimes against humanity was entitled to a lawyer.

Pervich waited for the guard to leave before he started talking. "How are you, General?"

"I'm in great pain, but eventually I'll be acquitted, and the pain will be nothing but a distant memory."

"I don't think so, Pervich stated. "The American journalist has forwarded hundreds of interview tapes to the judges—interviews with the people you tortured and with the relatives of the people you killed.

361

There are too many witnesses to discredit—too many victims to pull on the sympathy of the judges."

"Damn that Ferret!"

Pervich nodded agreement. "I used my lawyer's credentials to see you, but I cannot represent you. I haven't the slightest idea of how to defend you."

Ratac twisted in his chair like a caged animal. "Maybe I'll never get out of jail, but you can give me comfort."

"How?" Pervich asked.

"The people who put me here must die," Ratac whispered.

"Yes, they probably should, Ratac."

"You'll do it, then?"

"Tracking them down would cost a great deal of money."

"I *have* a great deal of money. Hire as many assassins as you want."

Pervich hesitated. *People who bring this much bad news to Ratac have to watch their heads*, Pervich thought. "Comrade, you have no money."

"How could that be?"

"Your brother has claimed his half of your inheritance. He's taken over your homes and intends to turn one of them into an orphanage for Serbian children. The papers are calling it a gesture worthy of Gandhi."

Ratac slammed the table top so hard that the guard looked through the barred window. "Damn that fool!"

The Butcher's cheeks twitched, "I have gold hidden in my villa."

"Not anymore. The American policeman turned it over to the Croatian government. It might be returned to the families of dissidents from whom it was taken."

Ratac's nostrils flared. "I have money in a German bank account."

Pervich shook his head. "The American lawyer you injured has put a freeze on your accounts. He's suing your estate for millions of dollars."

"Suing? My estate? I'm not dead! Add that bloodsucking lawyer to our hit list."

Pervich shrugged. "No one will do it, Ratac."

"I must have some loyal supporters."

Pervich shook his head. "I don't know who. We were all afraid of you. Now no one is afraid of you."

"I won the election. My people love me. Surely, there is one among them who can afford a plane ticket and a gun."

"Your people feel betrayed. They are ashamed of you and ashamed of themselves for believing in you. They are disgusted with you. The people feel you are as bad as our worst enemies. 'Any man who would plan to shoot his own daughter to win an election does not deserve to live,' or so they say. Is it true?"

Ratac shouted, "Why did you come here, you disloyal bastard! Of course, it's true. That girl was not my—"

Pervich stood up with a noisy scrape of the chair against the cement floor. "I had to hear it for myself. The people are right. You disgust me. You don't deserve to live. But, unfortunately, they have no death penalty. You'll get life imprisonment."

"Desert me then. I'll find a way. I'll find a way to avenge all my enemies and disloyal followers, starting with their children."

*   *   *

JAMAICA, NEW YORK

In New York's John F. Kennedy International Airport, Amy and Martin knew that they had to go their separate ways. Amy was with her nervous aunt and a tough-looking older man named Sid, who insisted the children wear sunglasses indoors and, if you looked carefully, carried a gun. He used to work for Amy's dad, he said. Martin's Uncle Ike was there for him. Uncle Ike was a cop, like most of the males on George

King's side of the family. Amy would fly on to Denver, and Martin would fly to Los Angeles.

Gil and Debbie stayed in Croatia to help Dr. Whistle, and George and Eve stayed with them to "teach that so-and-so that you don't mess with the Kings and get away with it." Neither family expected trouble from Bymarovitch in the States, but "just to be on the safe side," both families called in "favors owed" to have experienced law enforcement officers "ride shotgun" for the kids.

Martin looked at Amy's tennis shoes. "I gotta go. I get a window seat." He paused. "For a girl, you're pretty cool."

Amy said, "You're a pretty cool friend, Martin." She gave Martin her prized Kiwi hat.

He blushed. "Gee, thanks." He gave Amy her original Denver Broncos cap back. "Would you like some baseball cards?"

"Just the new players like Clutch. Dad has an autographed Babe Ruth card, but I've never seen Babe Ruth on television."

"I think he's retired, actually."

As Martin walked away heading toward his gate, Amy called, "Dad said I can post my journal on my Web site. And I'll send you an e-mail."

Martin smiled. "*Brilliant!* So will I."

* * *

THE PRISON

"You have another visitor, Ratac—your sister," the prison guard announced.

Ratac felt a surge of adrenaline. *I have no sister!* Whoever would risk posing as his sister had to be a supporter intent on aiding his escape. Ratac could easily overpower the guard, but getting out of the small jail presented another, far greater, problem.

If this woman's plans didn't include his escape then maybe she could order the assassinations that Pervich was unwilling to carry out. An unpleasant thought occurred to Ratac. *What if the woman is a journalist sneaking in to get an interview?*

The guard ushered a thin sickly-looking woman with wild hair into the visitor's room. She couldn't be a journalist. She looked unkempt—even for a reporter. Barely able to walk, she was hardly the type to aid his escape.

"Do you remember me?" she asked.

Ratac's near perfect memory recalled the voice, perhaps her face, but no name and no context. "Vaguely," he answered. "Remind me."

"Sophia," she reminded.

"Why are you here, Sophia?" The woman still didn't register.

"It will come to you," the woman smiled weakly.

"Can you help me escape?"

"Perhaps," she said.

Ratac doubted her words. "Can you deliver orders to have my enemies punished?"

Sophia shook her head negatively.

Ratac slouched back in his chair. *The woman is a crank.* Her insipid smile and glazed eyes wouldn't even offer intelligent conversation. *But Sophia can be useful.* Ratac motioned for the guard. *Timing is everything.* When the guard handed Ratac his crutch, Ratac turned his head abruptly—a subtle, yet effective, distraction.

Ratac watched as the guard's eyes shifted. *Only a second to act.* Ratac plunged the edge of the crutch into the guard's stomach. The guard bounced off the wall and fell forward. As he fell, Ratac delivered a savage blow to the back of the guard's neck.

Sophia gasped, "You killed him!"

"Not quite. But I'll kill you if you don't do what I say."

Ratac took the guard's night stick. He limped around the table and pulled Sophia from her bench. Placing the night stick in front of her neck, he said, "I don't need this stick to break your neck but it adds to the visual effect."

"They'll catch you," Sophia warned coldly.

"They already have me. I have nothing to lose. I'll make it across the street to the church and claim the tradition of sanctuary. It'll take the Pope himself to pry me out of there. I only need minutes to call my friends. Only minutes to order my revenge."

Still limping, Ratac pulled the woman to the hall. Within seconds, four revolvers were aimed at him.

"Don't shoot!" a ranking policeman ordered.

"Wise." Ratac smirked. "I can break her neck in half a second. I have killed one guard already. So place your revolvers on the floor."

The policemen reluctantly complied.

Ratac scooped up a gun and placed it in the woman's back. He didn't want the revolver visible. His enemies wouldn't shoot him while he held a nightstick, but a gun was different. A policeman afraid of his own life would shoot. Ratac would hide the gun until he had to use it.

"Walk ahead of me," Ratac ordered the unarmed police. "Tell your comrades to lay down their arms, and the woman won't get hurt."

Sophia began to laugh.

"Shut up, you crazy bitch!"

"Yes, I *am* crazy. The law won't do anything to me. Do you know why I came here?"

"Quiet!" Ratac pushed past the lobby filled with helpless police.

"I was curious," she continued, "curious to see fear on a monster's face."

"I am not afraid! If I can make it to the streets, my supporters will shelter me." Ratac stepped outside the door of his prison. A lunchtime crowd of workers filled the street, reducing the chance that a policeman would chance a shot in his back. A miss would likely kill someone.

Sophia continued to laugh, "Frank Ferret said you've learned the meaning of fear."

"Ferret sent you?"

"No, but he left me money and told me where you were."

"He's a fool. Ferret and his friends are the ones who will know fear—not me."

Sophia snapped, "You should be afraid because you're about to die."

Ratac squeezed the nightstick on Sophia's neck as a warning to be silent.

Her choking returned to laughter. "I was afraid. Afraid I wouldn't be able to get close to you. So I could do this. The woman plunged her thin plastic dagger into Ratac's stomach. The second stab hit the jugular vein in his neck.

Ratac staggered.

"Yes! I see the face of fear!" the mad woman screamed with glee.

*   *   *

CHERRY CREEK, COLORADO

Margaretta patted Eiffel's head and opened the breezeway door to the Rocklin home. In the garage office, she looked at the stacks of cassettes, diskettes, and CDs and sighed. *Too bad. And Gil is such a nice young man.* Gil was an international hero, but a bankrupt one—or close to it. She felt proud having worked with him. Margaretta would donate her time to help Gil close the business, at least until she could find another job.

While she logged on to the computer, Margaretta noticed that the fax machine was out of paper. She logged into the Internet and checked the Rocklin Software web page for "hits," the number of visitors who had sought out the site. Margaretta's jaw dropped. "Must be a mistake." She checked the orders page and picked up the phone.

"Bring your bridge club to the Rocklin garage, quick. And all of their friends. Jobs for everyone!"

* * *

Mrs. Fish marched Amy to the principal's office. Amy wasn't worried. Amy liked the principal, and she hadn't done anything wrong.

In the principal's office, all eyes turned their eyes from the television to Amy.

Amy smiled infectiously.

"Dr. Kile," Mrs. Fish began. "I need to have a parent-teacher conference with Dr. Rocklin. It seems that Amy Jean Rocklin is making up stories and getting her classmates all stirred up."

Dr. Kile tried his best to look stern. "You haven't watched television lately or read the newspapers, Mrs. Fish?"

Mrs. Fish wanted to tell Kile that she was too busy grading papers to watch television, let alone read newspapers.

The principal didn't wait for an answer. "What kind of stories is Amy Jean telling? Anything about being kidnapped? Escaping in a box? Playing a piano for food? Speaking French? Jumping out of windows?"

"Why . . . yes," Mrs. Fish stammered.

Dr. Kile smiled. "I saved a tape for the staff meeting. And you'll want to look at Amy's Web site—over two hundred thousand hits so far. You never saw drawings so cute, and her story's all true, including the million-dollar reward."

Mrs. Fish blushed. She wasn't thinking about Amy's Web site.

Dr. Kile said, "I'd better get a PO for some of Amy's French CDs before they sell out."

* * *

Whittier, California

Martin's classmates liked him. They didn't understand why he didn't act goofy and hip like some of the black kids they saw on television sitcoms, but that was okay.

"How you gonna spend your million dollars?" they all wanted to know as soon as they hit the playground.

"I'm gonna have a big party for all my friends."

"Wow!"

"But you gotta wait till I'm twenty-one. Something called a trust won't let me spend it."

"Twenty-one! Geez, Martin, you'll be an old man," his best friend lamented.

Martin shrugged.

"Hey Marty, did ya really knock out your kidnapper with a chair?" a classmate asked.

Martin straightened his Kiwi baseball cap. "I tried to reason with him first."

*　*　*

San Jose, California

As Willie whisked by his receptionist, she said "Good morning, Mr. Dern," but she looked the other way. Willie didn't notice. She wasn't that pretty, so he seldom looked at her. His office door was open. His office was one of the envied plums of the highest floor—a corner windowed office. The wall-to-wall computers shut out half the sunlight, and that was the way Willie liked it. Inside, the chief executive officer of the company and chairperson of the board sat sober-faced in his black swivel chairs.

Willie dropped his notebook computer on his desk with a thud. He gave a brief smile to his business associates, whom he called empty suits behind their backs. "Morning, guys. I've had a bad couple of weeks. My vacation ended up dodging bullets in Croatia. I was marooned on an island. I was robbed. It cost me a small fortune in private airplanes, one of which broke down during a layover in Newfoundland.

"And worst of all, Ginnie decided to quit so she can take care of her kid. One lousy vacation!"

"Have you been reading the papers?" the CEO said gravely.

"No, I came straight from the airport. Massive jet lag. Haven't slept for two days. My eyes only look open."

"Well, then I'll read it to you."

"Show him the recording instead," the board chairman said. The board chairman looked older than his sixties—an age rare in the software industry. His wrinkled brow was a battle scar from running a dozen companies throughout his career.

The DVD fluttered to life. The CNBC logo appeared in the corner of the screen. A square-jawed man read from a page. "The Antitrust Division wants to categorically *deny* that we're presently investigating any large software company for unfair competitive practices."

A young reporter, armed with Frank's fax, asked, "What about the virus rumor, started to ruin Rocklin Software?"

"No comment."

"Did Willie Dern give the order?"

"I don't know . . . who Willie Dern is."

"And this is the Antitrust Division?" Another reporter laughed.

The square-jawed spokesman winced. "Look, all I was asked to do is to make a true statement in order to dispel unfounded rumors that could adversely affect the cost of an innocent company's stock. When there's evidence of wrongdoing, then that's another matter. You can be sure we'd look into deliberately set libelous rumors."

The VCR screen turned to slate gray. The dapperly dressed CEO tapped his gold, Cross pencil on the edge of the desk and pointed to a poster on Willie's wall. "You have a motto, Willie. 'I don't believe in that which I can't count.' Count *this*: Our shares on the London market are down 10 percent as a result of that interview. When the NASDAQ opens, we could lose another 10 percent."

The chairman of the board closed his eyes as if in pain and added, "How much do I love money? Let me *count* the ways. I love my inflated stock prices. I love the money I don't have to give to political hacks to stifle silly investigations. I love the money I don't have to pay lawyers to defend giga-dollar lawsuits we can't win."

The CEO waved an invoice. "I *don't* love paying a detective agency for what is undoubtedly an illegal wiretap."

Willie started to say the invoice should have been directed to him personally, but his boss waved him silent. *If only Virginia had been on the job to intercept the billing*, he thought.

The chairman rubbed his eyebrows. "Then there's the little stuff. A cute little kid brings down a bad man 'cause she learned French on an insignificant piece of educational software with minuscule market potential. And guess what? Now every little kid on the planet with access to a television knows her story by heart. And what do they want for Christmas? *Crepe du chocolat, s'll vous plait.* The cute little, millionaire girl is on the jacket cover. Even the French kids will buy it. I'll have to find one for my grandkids. Should have been no problem. We were going to distribute this crepe crap. But will I be able to snitch a copy from our warehouse? No, I'll have to sign up on the waiting list that will be wallpapering Gil Rocklin's garage.

"Then the little cutie face sells *Sushi Please, Karate for Kiddies,* and who knows what else? Video games, like *Dodge the Butcher?* Rocklin is no fool. He'll figure out things we'd wish we thought of, and he'll have the money—our money—from punitive damages, plus access to capital markets to finance them. What if he brings out security firewalls? That's his specialty, I believe. Suddenly, we have another damn competitor.

"Willie, your job has been to make us money, and up to now, you've been a damned good rainmaker. But you killed way too many fluffy clouds in the process."

Willie couldn't believe he was being lectured by a tag team of empty suits. "And I'll kill more! I'll squeeze every drop of rain outta those clouds before they know what's happening."

Willie could feel the pulse of anger. "How in the hell do you think you got to where I got you to? You and the whole executive staff haven't had a creative idea in years. *I* had to find the ideas, hire the talent, and squash the competition before they could hurt us."

"Well, Willie," the CEO said sadly, "I just got my first creative idea."

*   *   *

Minus his company car and stock options, Willie ordered the cab driver to stop on a quiet side street so he could make a phone call from his cellular phone before the company turned it off. Willie had always intended to start his own company before he was promised the CEO job—now gone forever. The Breakneck Download software would be his ticket back. But Willie couldn't afford a copyright scandal following his current troubles. He'd get the developer's sign-off.

"Hello, is this Chip Shumaker?"

"Yeah?"

"This is Willie Dern. You sent some software to me to review."

"Yeah?" Chip replied.

"I'm starting my own company, and I'm looking for new talent to be vice president for Internet development software. I'd like to fly you to San Jose tomorrow to talk about my new business. You can help me pick out an office building."

"Cool!"

"You'll come then."

The muffled voice called, "Ma, Willie Dern wants to fly me to San Jose tomorrow. Can I go?"

A woman's voice said, "Who's Willie Darn—some pervert you chatted with on the Internet? Of course, you can't go."

"Ah, Mr. Dern, I'll have to work on my mom."

Willie's fears were realized. *A teenager!*

"Forget her, Chip. You don't need her anymore. Geniuses like us don't need anyone. You're an adult. Act like one."

"Ah, I'm fifteen, but I'll be sixteen next March. And Mom needs *me*."

Willie stifled a groan. *Worse than I thought. Fifteen years old!* "That's good, Chip! Loyalty. That's what I like about you. And as for fifteen—that's when I started. Genius knows no age bounds."

"Yeah? I heard Mozart was making CDs when he was only four years old!"

Willie wanted to cry. "Come to San Jose, and you'll make more money than you and your mother have ever imagined."

"Really? Maybe later, after I come back from Denver. I don't want to miss too much school. Our chess club's in the finals again."

"Denver?" Willie's stomach tightened.

"Yeah, my new friend, Gil Rocklin, has found a way to double the speed on my Breakneck Download. The guy's a super geek!" Chip said it as a term of affection.

"You haven't sold it to him?" Willie asked, his eyes closed and not wanting to hear the answer. "After all, we had an implied contract when you sent your disk to me. An agreement! You and me, Chip. Whatever Gil Rocklin knows about Breakneck, he stole from me."

"Oh. Gil wouldn't steal. He's an ex-FBI agent. But I wouldn't want Gil to get into trouble, so you can buy Breakneck if you still want it. But you won't want it. It's not worth much anymore. Gil and I came up with a better one: Hop, Skip, and a Download." We kinda reverse engineered it over the telephone. Like I said. It should be twice as fast."

"You didn't sign anything with Rocklin, did you?"

"Ah, I'm fifteen. I can't sign a contract. Only my mom can. But Gil and I are still kinda partners on it. That's the way Gil works. If you do it, you get the royalties, and he's getting me an autographed mitt and personal batting lessons from Clutch Cooper. When I graduate, I'll be working with Gil part-time as team leader for R and D, and he says I can go to work for anyone else whenever I think I can do better. So how can it be better?"

Willie suddenly felt a migraine developing, and he didn't get migraines.

Chip sounded ecstatic. "I'll have enough money to go to the prom and put in a new hard drive. I get to play around reprogramming anything I want to. Gil teaches me what he knows, which is more than I can get from any book or class. But I want to go to a good, tough university, so he's pulling strings to get me into his alma mater, MIT, with room, board, and tuition, and I'll be getting spending money from Gil until the royalties kick in. Plus, I get an even hotter geek job when I graduate—if I want it."

"And my mom loves him. Couldn't get her off the phone with 'im. I faxed him the signed papers a half hour ago."

Willie's stomach hardened to concrete.

Chip continued, "Did you see his pretty fiancée and little girl on television?"

Willie's throat felt permanently dry. "No, I missed the boat on that one too."

*   *   *

Approaching the USA

Virginia rested her head on Clutch's shoulder during the last hours of the flight to New York. He enjoyed the silky feel of her hair and her faint perfume. When she awoke, Clutch said, "How about I call on you whenever I'm in your town. Just where is your town, anyway?"

Virginia squeezed his hand. "It was San Jose. Now it's anywhere I can get a job. My contract forbids me from working in the computer industry for two years. So I have to find something else to do."

"Instead of quitting, you should've asked to be traded," Clutch said solemnly.

Virginia's eyes rolled at the statement, until Clutch said, "Just kidding."

She shook her head and smiled at being taken in. *How much of Clutch's dumb ballplayer act is real and how much is it for fun. Does it matter?*

Virginia squinted thoughtfully at one remote possibility. "With all the media experience we received, Frank arranged an interview for me as a business reporter for a New York television station, but I doubt if they'll consider me. The job wouldn't have paid as much money as I was making with Willie, but I would've had predictable hours to spend with my little boy."

Clutch let it soak in. "Then we share the same town. Your town is my town. We could do a lotta datin' when I play the Yankees."

"I don't think so, Clutch. I'm not interested in datin'. It's not because I don't like you, Clutch, because I do. I'd like nothing more than to wrap my body over yours until we can't stand it anymore."

Clutch loosened his already loose collar.

Virginia stifled a laugh and continued in her businesslike, matter-of-fact manner. "But I don't want to go through what Debbie went through with you. You treated her like just another roll in the hay, and as a result, you dropped a great catch."

Clutch winced and looked at Debbie and Gil, eyes closed and snuggling in the seats behind them—pretending not to listen. "I sure did," Clutch admitted.

The plane landed with a bump and a roll, and on cue, the passengers rushed to empty their bins of carry-on suitcases, only to wait as the plane retaxied to a special gate. A flight attendant pushed his way toward Clutch and Virginia. "Excuse me, but I thought I'd better warn you. There's nearly a hundred reporters gathered at this gate."

Clutch began to fidget. "Why me? Gil, I'd understand. But a hundred reporters? Oh cow chips! I said I was bringing back a bride. I don't have a wife. I'll tell them that when I got there the pool was plumb fished out."

Virginia raised her narrow eyebrows into a skeptical arch.

"It won't float, will it?" Clutch groaned. "I'm a loser. There go my endorsements! The guys will all say I can't get up for the game. I should've hung on to Debbie when I had the chance."

They walked through the tunnel to the gate where the reporters and television cameras stood ready. Clutch said, "I'll run by 'em."

Virginia laughed. "Ginnie to the rescue. You helped me get the last jab at Willie, so it's the least I can do." She inserted her arm under the back of Clutch's shirt and around his waist. She pressed her cheek against his shoulder. "You can introduce *me* as you fiancée, if you want."

"Wouldja? That's awfully nice of you, Ginnie. But it won't work. They'll expect a big wedding with all my family and—"

"And a thousand reporters," Virginia added. "Tuxedo endorsements. Honeymoon destination endorsements. Baby food endorsements. You need a new business manager as well as a wife. I'll only agree to marry you if the wedding's in San Jose where *my* family lives. If I can't spend every hour of the day keeping you sexually inspired with me, then walk away. Just like Frank and Ingrid."

Clutch suddenly felt his neck warm. "Well, I guess I can afford to fly my kin in. Okay, California it is." As the reporters circled the tunnel exit, Clutch said, "Ginnie, I love you! I've had the tingles for you ever since we first shared that rental car from the airport." He fumbled for the engagement ring that he had bought for Debbie and slipped it on Virginia's outstretched ring finger.

Virginia dropped her carry-on and kissed Clutch, "I'm really fond of you, Clutch."

Walking behind them, Gil and Debbie exchanged smirks and fell back.

Debbie whispered, "Ginnie's determined to provide for her little son, no matter what."

"And wait till Ginnie's mother moves in with them," Gil added.

Gil pulled his wide-brimmed Kiwi hat over his face. He was tired of dealing with reporters. He whispered back to Debbie, "I wonder if somebody should warn Clutch about California's community property laws. The honeymoon won't be over before she cleans him out of half of everything he has."

Debbie thought, *Ginnie's in for a shock if she thinks she can cuddle Clutch and walk away. After a honeymoon with Clutch, Ginnie might have to rethink such plans.*

Debbie smiled to herself. She was too pleased with her own prehoneymoon to broach her experienced observations on the matter.

Debbie jabbed Gil with a free finger. "Did that vixen try to manipulate you that way?"

Gil flushed, remembering how he accepted Ginnie's address and phone number, with his sincere pledge to contact her *after* the vacation, so as not to embarrass Debbie. Gil shook his head sadly. "If anything, she was more seductive with me. But I was faithful to the core."

As the trampers exited the tunnel, a roar went up. Jaded reporters led the applause.

The first reporter heard over the din of questions asked, "Virginia Slater, how does it feel to give up working with a journalistic legend like Frank Ferret to join the news desk for a national network?"

"Me? News desk? That's not the job I'm interviewing for."

"Well, I believe that's the job you got if you want, Ms. Slater," the reporter replied. "Credibility and honesty—bravery with beauty—are scarce and expensive commodities. Rumor has it the network was afraid someone else would get you."

"*Really!*" Virginia said. Her damaged self-concept started to stir. *Credibility? Honesty? Ha!* She remembered Frank mumbling something about priming the pump for a bidding war. *Another case where rumor becomes truth.*

While Virginia faced her dizzying options, a lone microphone wandered in front of Clutch. "Aren't you Clutch Cooper? How is it that you know Ginnie Slater?"

*   *   *

LOS ANGELES, CALIFORNIA

George picked up the pile of telegrams waiting at the front door. Telegrams made him nervous. They usually announced the death of a distant relative. They were probably congratulatory, but he couldn't just ignore them.

Eve took a letter opener to one with scalpel-like precision. "Wow! Get this! The governor offers both of us his gratitude for our bravery and that of our son."

"Frank and Ing must be getting a lot of airtime."

George held an opened telegram without speaking.

"Well?"

378

"Ah, one of the 'burbs saw me on CNN and wants me to interview for police commissioner."

Eve snatched the telegram. "This is close to where I work. We'd probably have to move there, but Martin wouldn't have to change schools. And with your master's in police administration, you'll be a shoe-in."

George sighed. "Fewer slugs to deal with—except for the politicians. And semidecent hours. More time to spend with Martin."

"And with me," Eve added. "I've decided to cut back on my hours. Maybe I'll deliver a few babies again."

"You liked that once. But the liability insurance for an active ob-gyn will wash away a lot of income."

"So what? We don't have to worry about the cost of sending Martin to med school anymore."

"True." George smiled. "We can coast."

"Not exactly," Eve grinned, as she gave her husband a kiss. "I was waiting for the perfect moment to tell you, but . . . . we may have another premed on the way."

*   *   *

CHERRY CREEK, COLORADO

Gil and Debbie walked past shrubs covered with yellow ribbons. They were glad their postmidnight arrival in Cherry Creek cleared the crowds of reporters and autograph seekers who had followed their journey. Gil lowered their suitcases, fumbled with his keys on the dark porch, and scooped Debbie in his arms to carry her over the threshold. "This is home."

Debbie beamed. "It's a beautiful house and beautiful neighborhood. Rolling hills, just like in New Zealand. And there are *people* here. I'll love it!"

"It's even nicer in the daylight. The neighbors are friendly. The schools are famous. Enjoy it while you can. Our next house could be a tent," he added lightly. Gil was more optimistic than before. Gil's sting operation with the FBI had cursed him with an untouchable whistleblower label. Even companies with nothing to hide were afraid to hire him. Now Gil's fame was that of the American hero who threw a bad guy through a window. Employers liked that. Gil might be able to work in the corporate world of computer security again. *So what if security work isn't as inspiring as running your own business?* Debbie and Amy deserved the security of a steady income.

Debbie said, "I don't want to hear anymore about living in a tent! That teenage genius is going to sign up with you."

"I sure hope so. Chip promised me his mother would fax a contract, but as soon as she talks to Willie, I doubt if we'll hear from her again. Willie can promise them the moon—and pay for it with his company's petty cash. All I have to bargain with are some old baseball cards worth about thirty thousand."

Debbie chattered brightly. "Even if Chip doesn't sign with you, we have your New Zealand travel CD. I'm going to write a Japanese language program for little kids. Maybe Colorado will honor my teaching credentials. I'd really like that—teaching kids music. Do you think the Denver Symphony might need another cellist? And if there's a wedding band I can sing with—"

Gil kissed Debbie on the lips to stop her prattling. There was no money to press New Zealand travel CDs. Debbie had no idea how thin the market is for Japanese language software in a country that regards foreign language instruction as a form of penitence—and symphony jobs are harder to land than making the cut in the NBA.

Hushing Debbie wasn't that easy. "Gil, maybe I should contact the American bloke who wanted me to pose for some kind of SI swimsuit issue."

Gil cocked his head. "Not the *Sports Illustrated* swimsuit issue?"

"Uh-huh, I think that's the one. He said it paid pretty well actually, but I would've missed my brother's graduation."

"Ah, Debbie, your bloke was probably a dirty ol' man trying to hand you a line."

"A line?" Debbie asked innocently.

"He was pulling your leg or trying to pull your leg," Gil chuckled. Despite all the dirty dealings she had recently experienced, Debbie still held on to her optimistic and trusting nature. "Your bloke is a phony whose line didn't travel all that well." Gil gazed at Debbie's curvy figure and clucked, "Then again, maybe not. Do all or none of the above, sweetheart, but only if you want to."

Gil turned on the lights. "I sent the bodyguard home. We won't need him anymore, now that Ratac is dead. My sister should be asleep. With Amy, however, it's hard to tell. She likes to read by flashlight."

Eiffel bounded excitingly around his master, sniffing Debbie.

"Oh my"—Debbie laughed nervously—"you said you had a dog, not a horse. He looks vicious."

"Eiffel is for show. Amy's goldfish are more aggressive."

Gil peeked in on Amy, who was sleeping soundly. He would let her sleep. "There's a kitten on her bed! Where did she get that kitten?"

"Oh, they're adorable together."

Gil puckered a silent kiss toward his sleeping daughter and closed Amy's door. *Life is good.*

Gil showed Debbie the spacious kitchen and headed for the breezeway to the garage. Margarita knew the balance sheet as well as her boss did and probably had left Gil a two-week notice so he wouldn't have to lay her off. The dream of his own business had been dissolved by Willie's virus rumors. And Willie could certainly outbid anything he could offer the Schumaker lad. Gil would have to move from the Denver area to Silicon Valley or Boston and hope to find work in their crowded labor markets.

"What the hell did Margarita do with our inventory?" he puzzled, looking at the empty shelves, and the empty in-tray on the fax machine. Gil decided not to mention his concerns to Debbie until he talked to Margarita.

"Can't business wait for tomorrow?" Debbie asked as she stroked Gil's cheek.

Gil took the hint and kissed her.

At the breezeway door, Gil noted a number on his personal answering machine and pushed Messages. "My sister likes to leave voice messages instead of writing notes."

"Hello, Mr. Rocklin, this is Mrs. Fish. Amy got into a little trouble today at recess. She followed a stranded kitten twenty feet up a tree, and I was afraid that we'd have to call the fire department to get the both of them down. But it worked out okay. Your little monkey brought the kitten down just fine."

Debbie elbowed Gil. "See! We can be as overprotective as can be, and Amy will still take risks. But she can handle it!"

Mrs. Fish continued. "But that's not why I called. I want to apologize for not believing Amy's show-and-tell when she said she was kidnapped and escaped. When I heard it was true, I was so embarrassed. I should have known that a fantastic father like you wouldn't allow his wonderful daughter to lie.

"But that's not why I called, either. Remember when Amy wanted to have me over for dinner? My husband and I separated last week, so I was wondering if *you'd* like to come over for dinner when you get back from Yugoslavia. Just the two of us. Umm, plan on spending the night."

With fire in their eyes, Gil and Debbie's heads swiveled sharply toward their daughter's bedroom. In unison they shouted, "AMY!"

*   *   *

Venus Klaus stirred in the sugar, sipped her tea, wrinkled her nose, and pushed it away. "Too sweet!"

The Victorian decorated living room filled with neighbors who leaned intently for Venus to tell them more about her trip.

"Weren't you scared to death?" one neighbor asked.

Venus looked at the ceiling, and milking the dramatic pause said, "I was afraid for those lovely children, who looked up to me like a grandmother—a *young* grandmother. Oh, it was harrowing, of course, with that horrible mass murderer killing my new friends, stranding us on a deserted island with bombs in our bungalow, and kidnapping those charming children.

"But all in all, I think it was my most enjoyable trip."